Praise for *Quicksand*

"A work of dark satire, [*Quicksand*] had critics comparing Toltz to writers such as Dave Eggers, David Foster Wallace and Joseph Heller.... Toltz is a talented writer and his use of various narrative techniques is thoughtful, creative and well worth examining for those who love literary fiction."

—*Fort Worth Star-Telegram*

"A darkly humorous portrait of friendship delivered in [Toltz's] particular staccato style, dispensing doses of clever wit and scorching social commentary."

—*Harper's Bazaar*

"The pleasure of *Quicksand* is in Toltz's energetic prose, rich with one-liners, Beckettesque dialogue driven by gallows humor and misunderstanding."

—*St Louis Post Dispatch*

"An ambitious, rowdy, and ultimately very moving portrait of an old friendship.... The narrative [is] memorable and distinctive, combining high seriousness . . . with comedic, high-spirited exuberance. . . . Toltz's talent is obvious from the first page, which, added to his signature mixture of humor, fearlessness, and barbed social commentary, makes one appreciate the comparisons he's received to writers such as Jonathan Franzen, Gary Shteyngart, and John Irving. . . . . An important young writer to watch."

—*Library Journal* (starred review)

"Toltz channels a poet's delight in crafting the perfect phrase on every highly quotable page. In his epic lack of employment and sincere lust for life, Aldo Benjamin is quite a memorable character. By turns hilarious and hopeless, Toltz's novel is a tender portrait of a charming and talented loser."

—*Publishers Weekly*

"*Quicksand* is a clever novel about failure and friendship, told with brilliant irony and black humor, peppered with exuberant wordplay and one-liners—"Love for God is just Stockholm syndrome," he comments—but it is ultimately a *cri de coeur* protesting the futility of suffering and celebrating the simple victory of being alive. An ambitious, energetic, darkly funny novel about the tragic futility of suffering and pain."

—*Shelf Awareness*

"Highly original, entertaining and almost impossible to summarize, this is a high-octane, adrenaline-fuelled, frenetic tour de force of sustained brilliance. There is wit, laugh-out-loud humour and linguistic fireworks and dexterity on almost every page."

—*Mail on Sunday* (UK)

"Brilliantly dark . . . The entire novel is buzzing with the power of human connection—the jokes, accommodations and shared mythologies of love and friendship. Even in a book overflowing with solipsists and monomaniacs, would-be artists and theories about art, it remains a creative force to be reckoned with."

—*The Guardian* (UK)

"A beguiling novel that confounds and astonishes in equal measure, often on the same page . . . Part Chuck Palahniuk, part David Foster Wallace . . . *Quicksand* has a thousand dazzling throwaway moments of brilliance. . . . A tour de force."

—*Australian Book Review*

"[A] narrative so brilliant, so fizzing with lucidity and comedy and horror and hard-nosed empathy . . . [Aldo Benjamin] is one of those rare characters who will live on in our collective literary imagination."

—*The Saturday Paper* (Australia)

"The energy, the hairpin turns, the narrative crashes, the stomach-churning ascents and trashed taboos: what a joy to surrender oneself to a writer of such prodigious talent."

—Peter Carey, Booker Prize–winning author of *Amnesia*

"Steve Toltz writes with a singular, propulsive energy, with sentences and characters that rise off the page with a force that leaves you almost breathless. There is more heart and joy and compassion and hard-earned wisdom in *Quicksand* than seems possible for a single novel; it is life, literature at its fullest."

—Dinaw Mengestu, award-winning author of *The Beautiful Things That Heaven Bears* and *All Our Names*

"What would happen if some genius were able to unite the high-wattage storytelling exuberance of Kurt Vonnegut, the combustive glee of Walt Whitman, and the reality-smashing despair of Franz Kafka? Impossibly, Steve Toltz has done just that, turning out a new masterpiece that is at once an old-fashioned page-turner, a tragicomic lament for the digital age, and an aching howl at the intractable existential dilemmas of our poor species. *Quicksand* is the sort of book that refuses to sleep between its covers on your nightstand; it is its own blazing, intricate, hysterically surreal universe, big and brilliant enough to swallow your own."

—Stefan Merrill Block, bestselling author of *The Story of Forgetting* and *The Storm at the Door*

"There are more lines of genius on one page of *Quicksand* than in the entirety of many very respectable novels."

—Elif Batuman, author of *The Possessed*

"Steve Toltz possesses an imagination that knows no limits. His work is mordant, prophetic, and very funny. He is a true original."

—Patrick McGrath, author of *Asylum*

Steve Toltz is a verbal magician and lunatic storyteller. Every page of this novel bursts with ideas and humor and pathos and incisive riffs that perfectly express the grand absurdities of the irrational universe, along with the smaller ones of a very particular friendship. *Quicksand* is the work of a writer in full command of his many outsized gifts, not least of which is his humanity."

—Teddy Wayne, Whiting Award–winning author of *The Love Song of Jonny Valentine*

"Steve Toltz's *Quicksand*—narrated by Aldo and Liam, two epic Aussie screw-ups and lifelong best friends—is one of the smartest, funniest, angriest novels I have ever read. But it's also a surprisingly touching meditation on friendship and family, on art and God, on law-breaking and law enforcement. . . . A brilliant piece of fiction from a novelist who so clearly sees the outsized pleasures and terrors of our troubled time."

—Brock Clarke, author of *An Arsonist's Guide to Writers' Homes in New England* and *The Happiest People in the World*

"*Quicksand* crackles with such intensity it made me turn the pages with a harder snap, lean closer, want to gnaw the words. This is a novel of sneak-attack seriousness, so funny it fools you into letting down your guard—then knocks you upside the head with intense intelligence, probing thought, raw pain. For all the wit and wisdom in this book, all the pleasures contained in its raucous, furious, fearless pursuit of truths, the greatest thrill comes when it strikes you that you've never read anything quite like it before, that you just might have stumbled—startlingly, unsettlingly—on something close to genius in the writing of Steve Toltz."

—Josh Weil, author of *The Great Glass Sea*

"The funniest novel of the past year . . . Genuinely moving."

—*The Saturday Times* (UK)

ALSO BY STEVE TOLTZ

A Fraction of the Whole

QUICKSAND

A Novel

Steve Toltz

SIMON & SCHUSTER PAPERBACKS

New York   London   Toronto   Sydney   New Delhi

For Marlowe

The author wishes to thank the Australia Council for the Arts and The MacDowell Colony.

Simon & Schuster Paperbacks
An Imprint of Simon & Schuster, Inc.
1230 Avenue of the Americas
New York, NY 10020

First Simon & Schuster trade paperback edition April 2016

SIMON & SCHUSTER PAPERBACKS and colophon are
registered trademarks of Simon & Schuster, Inc.

For information about special discounts for bulk purchases,
please contact Simon & Schuster Special Sales at 1-866-506-1949
or business@simonandschuster.com.

The Simon & Schuster Speakers Bureau can bring authors to your
live event. For more information or to book an event, contact the
Simon & Schuster Speakers Bureau at 1-866-248-3049 or visit our
website at www.simonspeakers.com.

Manufactured in the United States of America

10 9 8 7 6 5 4 3 2 1

The Library of Congress has cataloged the hardcover edition as follows:

Toltz, Steve, 1972–
  Quicksand : a novel / Steve Toltz.
    pages ; cm
  I. Title.
  PR9619.4.T65Q85 2015
  823'.92—dc23

                                                           2015010363

ISBN 978-1-4767-9782-3
ISBN 978-1-4767-9783-0 (pbk)
ISBN 978-1-4767-9784-7 (ebook)

I

Oh, plenty of hope, an infinite amount of hope—but not for us

—Franz Kafka

Two Friends, Two Agendas (one hidden)

DOWN AT THE FOAMY SHORELINE, where small tight waves explode against black rocks, a lifeguard with feet wedged in the wet and vaguely tangerine sand stands shirtless like a magnificent sea-Jesus. An ill-timed journey into a breaker knocks a boy on his little back. A bald man throws a tennis ball for his Labrador and a second, unrelated dog bounds in after it. Through a gauze of mist a brunette—tall, and from where we're sitting seemingly riddled with breasts—kicks water on the sunlit torso of her blond companion.

There are three other drinkers in the place, already tethered to the sun-bleached bar. It is eleven a.m. Slumped in his cumbersome mechanized wheelchair that squeaks somewhere down by the left back wheel when he's doing pressure lifts, Aldo squints out from sand-whipped windows into the tumor of searing light. He turns to me and says, "I'm nobody's muse."

I think: That's a great line *right there*. I take out my notebook and when he shoots me an outraged look I say, "That's right, motherfucker. I'm writing it down."

Aldo wipes the condensation off his beer glass and uses it to moisten his lips.

"I know you're tired of being fodder, but for me to finish this book," I confess, "I need at the most your blessing and at the least unrestricted access to your innermost thoughts and feelings—you know, fantasies secreted inside se-cret fantasies I already know about, that kind of thing."

"Jesus, Liam. You even take mocking yourself too seriously."

"I *am* serious."

We sort of leer mildly at each other in the mirrored bar.

"This book," I say, "will help you laugh at yourself again."

"I still laugh at myself."

"Not in proportion to how hilarious you are. Come on, Aldo. Where'd your sense of humor go?"

I know where it went, but on only his second morning out of prison I want to see if he will dare articulate it.

He doesn't—only dams a sudden gush of saliva with his sleeve—and when his face reddens in embarrassment I go rigid myself.

"You know," I murmur, "you could sue the state. Failing their duty of care."

He turns to me abruptly and pretends to startle—our old gag—and ex-plains how justice is either impersonal and indifferent or extremely personal and shamelessly vindictive, and how finding yourself in front of our volatile jury system means submitting your fate to a bunch of people whose omelets you wouldn't dream of eating for fear they hadn't washed their hands.

Aldo sets his mouth tight as I scribble that line, and add: *he says, with the eyes of a croupier doing back-to-back shifts*. Down the bar, a man with a long po-nytail who looks sunk in his own epic tale of woe gapes at us unapologetically.

Aldo says, "Have you ever had a woman say to you, Oh, you sad little man?"

"Not in those exact words."

He rotates his chair 180 degrees and shouts, "I recommend it to all women as a way to totally annihilate a person!"

The bartender says, "Can you two keep it down?"

I ask, "Who called you a sad little man?"

Aldo is chewing something, maybe a part of his own mouth. I ask, "Was it Mimi? Was it Stella? Was it Saffron?" He shakes his head. I ask, "Was it your physiotherapist? Was it your lawyer? Please tell me it wasn't that ear-candling woman."

Aldo's face is that of a child woken by lightning. He says, "Why should I let you write about me?"

"Because you'll inspire people. To count their blessings."

His smile, when it arrives, is already vanishing. "Hang on," he says, without inflection, and I know what's coming before it's uttered. "I've just had an idea—to take to market."

"Oh?"

I settle in and listen to the patter of seagulls' webbed feet on the skylight. Two patrons loud-slurp and emit full-bodied beer-ad "ahhhhs." Halfway out Aldo's mouth, soft bubbling sounds that don't mean anything. "The look on your face," he says, "reminds me of that waiting period between the guilty verdict and the sentencing."

"Just tell me your idea."

"You know how we are such optimists even our Armageddons aren't final?"

"What do you mean?"

"It's postapocalypse this, post-zombie-apocalypse that. People are honestly fretting about what to do after the end-times."

"Right. So?"

"So you know the slight embarrassment you feel for someone who says they never think about death?"

"Yeah."

"You know how it's weird that people will trust any old block of ice in their drinks?"

"Yeah."

"You know how people are worried their kid's going to turn to them and say, 'What did you do to the biosphere, Daddy?'"

I laugh. "True."

"You know how people used to want to be rock stars, but now they just want rock stars to play at their birthday parties?"

"Uh-huh."

"You know how we now think pornography is free speech?"

"Like, I don't agree with tentacle sex but I'll die for your right to produce it?"

"Right. And we always knew people hated their freedom, but now we know they're also contemptuous of privacy?"

"Sure."

"And you know how there's no replacement cycle too short for today's consumer?"

"Of course."

"And how now we have the internet you can't say, 'You ain't seen nothing yet' anymore since everyone's seen everything by the age of twelve?"

"Yep."

"And people are spooked that good and evil no longer struggle but just work different shifts?"

"Uh—maybe."

His eyes tour the room and return to me, renewed. "You know how the phrase 'At least you have your health' now refers to the state of your organs as commodities you can sell in a pinch?"

"Nobody thinks it means that."

"And how in our lifetimes we'll see the actual end of patience?"

His eyes probe my face for signs of impact.

"OK. Yep."

The ideas bloom and flare, bloom and flare. His fingers drumroll on the bar and end in a finger snap. "You know how people divide the world into white privilege and black oppression, and never mention Asians or Indians who're like, half the planet?"

"Uh-huh."

"You know how a surprisingly huge number of people like fake leather?"

"Yes."

"And how people actually believe the obstacle to happiness is that they don't love themselves enough?"

"Sure."

"And how when someone's coping mechanism fails, they just keep using it anyway?"

"Yeah."

"And how businesssapiens are always having power nightmares?"

"They're having what?"

"Bad dreams during power naps."

"If you say so."

Now he looks like a dog who has chewed through his leash and is waiting to pounce.

"You know how people still believe that happy couples don't have affairs?"

"Uh-huh."

"And modern relationships are more like, 'I'll be alone with your thoughts if you'll be alone with mine'?"

"Sure."

"You know how while we're enjoying reading dystopian fiction, for half our population this society *is* dystopia?"

"Aldo."

"Wait. You know how our fear of turning into our parents has become the fear of inheriting copies of their genetic mutations?"

"Aldo."

"Hold on. You know how nobody who complains about income inequality thinks they personally have too much money?"

"Aldo."

"Just wait. You know how when people talk of First World problems they forget to mention Alzheimer's and dementia?"

"Can you—"

"Wait!" A mouthful of beer spills onto his shirt. "You know how we're still stuck with this prehistoric flight-or-fight mechanism and now our bodies pointlessly secrete cortisol when we're just running for the bus?"

"And?"

"And how thanks to online comment boards, more people than ever before know what it feels like to be reviled?"

"What's—"

"You know how unrequited love has no real-world applications?"

"*What's your idea?!*"

"Disposable toilets."

A smile forms that seems surgically rendered. He clearly feels a vicarious thrill, *my* thrill, at hearing his own idea.

"What's that got to do with . . . How would that even work?"

"No, wait, hang on," he says with a frown, his hands clasped as in prayer, and I let him go on, about how "imposter syndromes are rife" and we are "spanked by the invisible hand of the market," how "venture capitalists are all trying to predict new trends in sexual orientation." And he just needs to find a way to appeal to "people who want their instant gratification *yesterday*," or to "the half of a couple who has to secretly vaccinate the kids." I think: Aldo's conspiratorial whisper is louder than most people's shouts.

A row of poker machines ding unmusically; two patrons have migrated over. The others at the bar are staring at Aldo with cocked heads. The old reflex in me stirs, readying to react at a moment's notice, and I note Aldo's fear of being recognized, then his relief that he isn't. I write: *He can't tie up all his loose ends because he has an odd number of them.* He lightly taps his temple with his forefinger. I write: *On second thoughts, he looks like a taxidermy fail.* He spitballs about "millisecond hands on watches," and an app in which you "type in someone's cutting putdown and a devastating comeback appears." It's like hearing someone incessantly switching TV channels from another room, yet only now do I realize how much I've missed this, how much I've missed him. I feel almost giddy. In an unhurried neutral tone reserved for placating irate creditors and arresting officers, he suggests "an Amazon-like marketplace with mandatory haggling," "attention-span restoration services," and "scheduled daydreaming slots for children." His voice feels good, like cold air, but now I am losing him, only managing to get down truncated phrases without their context: "husbands claiming backdated blow jobs" and: "withering emoticons of heteroflexible tweens." I scrawl: *Everything he says sounds like an echo of his marathon murder-trial testimony and everything he said before it now seems like a preview.* With one elbow leaning on his armrest, he gives me a slight nod of recognition, as if I had just sat down, and says, "Since it's inevitable designer babies will be as ubiquitous as Kalashnikovs . . . " His slow drift of ideas has begun to peter out, but they've worked to release the tension in his body. His legs, I notice, are momentarily tamed. The more he talks, the more he relaxes—until it looks as if he is sprawled in a lawn chair. This is his body on dreams.

I order another beer and consume it swiftly. At this time of day it's about getting the alcohol down.

Gradually, as each billion-dollar idea fizzles and vanishes, Aldo falls silent; he can do eerie stillness like nobody's business. Tufts of graying chest hair scale the V-neck of his too-small undershirt that's rising up to reveal his belly, shining like a large, newly washed potato. He has truck-stop arm-wrestling arms these days, on which his twenty-year-old tattoos—*Stella* and *Do Not Resuscitate, I Mean It*—have begun to fade and stretch. I remember when his biceps were wrist-sized. Now his veins are like blue ropes strapping him in. I write: *With his prison bulk—his strong upper body, his shoulders like rock implants—he is a heavy man in a heavy chair. I would not want to be alone with him in an elevator that isn't permitted to bear more than eight people.*

"What's the point of it?" he asks, gesturing to my notebook.

"For the reader, reading pleasure. For myself, financial reward. For you, catharsis. This will be easier than confession. I'll do it for you."

The man in the ponytail slides a stool closer. Aldo blots sweat from his cheeks with his sleeve. "So what'll you write about exactly? And I mean, *exactly.*"

"Your murder trial and astonishing testimony, of course. Your trillion failed businesses. Your dire luck. Your grim health." I could go on. So I do. "Your luminous desperation. Your impressive resilience. Your humiliating bankruptcies. Your dead child." I pause. I won't go further. Maybe just a little. "That tractor-beam personality of yours. How you're always womanizing, only with the same woman. Your thwarted suicide attempts—"

"I never really tried to kill myself."

"Get the fuck."

This is such an absurd lie—his suicide attempts were so numerous, so unambiguous, so well documented—I'm forced to try a different tack. "All right. What about those late-night prank calls you used to make?" I say. "First to old schoolteachers, then to people in the phone book with the same names as celebrities, and finally to the suicide hotline." On his face, a look of embarrassed surprise, like a janitor caught shouting lines of dialogue in an empty theater. I parrot, "Hello. What kind of noose knot would you suggest? A triple bowline? An angler's loop? A zeppelin bend? Which is better, suicide by cop or suicide by fatwa? Ideally, I'd like to liquefy in my sleep, or be taken by the hand and led to my coffin. I certainly don't want to go through the whole hire-a-hitman-to-kill-me-then-change-my-mind-when-it's-too-late *rigmarole*."

He almost smiles. "That was for laughs."

"Once I saw you draw a finger across your throat while looking at yourself in the bathroom mirror."

"I don't remember that!"

"Remember what Morrell told me?"

"Today of all days I don't want to think about that man."

Aldo bites his lower lip. I should probably pursue another topic altogether. "That nobody more snidely dismisses originality than the terminally unoriginal," I quote nevertheless, pulling up my stool. "He meant it as a put-down. And I hate to admit he's right about anything anymore, especially in light of, *you know*, but it still sounds right, and for the life of me I can't think of anything new either. That's why I've decided to write about not what I know, but who. If I could deploy you as my fictional attaché, so to speak . . ."

Aldo says nothing, his eyes trained on the window, at the slender cabbage-tree palms swaying in random gusts of wind. We both let out sighs and I think how over the years we've sat in bars long enough for them to gentrify around us. The bartender calls to someone in the back who I suspect is not actually in the building. Aldo reaches into his cup holder and pulls out a plastic bag crammed with medications and counts out two egg-shaped, five elliptical, three oblong, three six-sided, four barrel-shaped, and two diamond-shaped pills of every hue, and gulps them, three at a time, with his beer. More customers file in wearing same-colored walking shorts with socks pulled to the shin or old jeans I suspect never fitted even when they were new. Aldo greets each newcomer with a prison-haunted stare. They sit at the long bar, breathing like stampeding animals at a wallow, pretending to ignore Aldo's joggling foot, his alarming leg spasms, the incremental rocking back and forth. He has never been sedentary, although these days most of the motion and turmoil take place under the skin, at the level of his nerves: beads of sweat form irrespective of air-conditioning and without exertion; his hand perceptibly trembles when he holds something; he has constant goose bumps on his arms and legs, unrelated to external stimuli, and an overproduction of saliva that he slurps from his lip back into his mouth. He's stunted and subtracted, his central nervous system has gone feral, his bowels are on the back foot. He has a lifetime of sitting ovations, cloudy urine, and skullaches ahead of him. He's musculoskeletally fucked. I write: *Aldo's experience of time. His version of "past," "present," and "future" is "the memory of pain," "pain," or "the anticipation of pain."* Poor Aldo. The first half of his hair fell out in hospital, the rest fled his cranium in prison. Why couldn't God let him at least keep his hair?

I say, "I'm sick of looking at you and perceiving a smaller, meaner universe."

He laughs and says, "Tough," then starts telling me about the guys he met in hospital, a quadriplegic who risked breaking a rib if he sneezed and had to be on constant vigilance against pollen and pepper and sunshine, another with a malignant melanoma on his spinal cord, and yet another who'd dived into an unseen sandbar and whose fusion of broken vertebrae was now a centimeter off, and how it was both unbearable and heartbreaking to be stuck in the smoking area with these unfortunate bastards who were already doing one-handed wheelies by the time Aldo had only learned to transfer to a toilet seat. I turn my gaze downward, stifle a groan, and write: *I can't imagine a sadder thing in the whole world than putting socks and shoes on those useless feet.*

"What are you writing *now*?"

I show him. Anger is not one of Aldo's usual go-to emotions, so I am taken aback when he bangs his fist on his chair's tubular armrest and shouts, "I'll make your publisher pulp it while your daughter watches!"

The bartender leans forward and says, "I *said*, keep it down," then turns up Van Morrison disagreeably loud.

Aldo holds a stiffened finger in the air. I think: Here we go again. He says, "You know how if we had time travel people would use it to go back short temporal distances to make premonitions and look like big shots?"

"Yeah. And?"

"Never mind. Fuck it," he says and puts on his aviator sunglasses. "I'm going for a ciggie." He wheels himself out onto the balcony, to the sea-rusted railings where gulls are perched and where he goes through half a box of matches lighting his cigarette in the infuriating wind. From a distance, he has the worn yet sleazy handsomeness of a cruise-ship magician. He flicks the half-smoked cigarette at a seagull, narrowly missing it, and shouts back to me, "AS PATRICK'S DADDY ONCE TOLD HIM: IT AIN'T A PROJECTILE IF IT AIN'T AIRBORNE!"

I shout, "WHO'S PATRICK?"

He shouts, "MY CELLMATE!"

The bartender shouts, "SHUT THE FUCK UP!"

Aldo gives him the finger, then moves like a storm front inside, toward the handicapped toilets. He rattles the door handle.

The bartender yells, "That one's out of order. Use the downstairs one."

Aldo swivels his chair and gazes down the steep metal staircase.

"You're supposed to have a handicapped toilet."

"It's out of order."

"It's the law!"

"It's out of order."

Aldo takes a slow, deep breath and beckons me over. He turns around and rigidly faces the big window. I stand beside him, looking out at houses nestled in bushland with imbricated terra-cotta roofs and manicured lawns, at gnarled limestone cliffs, surfers carving up the lips of rising waves. He says, "With medical science improving at roughly the same rate as our environmental situation worsens, the most likely scenario is that the world will become uninhabitable at the precise moment the human race becomes immortal."

"So true!" I write that down and say, "This is going to sound gay . . ."

"Say it."

"You *are* my muse."

"Will you carry me to the toilet?"

"Of course."

He is not light in my arms. I carry him down the stairs and turn on my side to get him into the narrow cubicle. As I bend to gently lower him I can feel my back give out and—I have no choice, it's a split-second decision, pure reflex—I drop Aldo onto the seat. He hits his head on the stainless-steel toilet paper dispenser. In a small, hoarse voice: "My kingdom for an intrathecal morphine pump."

"You've outlived yourself."

"I never wanted anyone to say of me, 'He's breathing on his own now.'"

"Now do you understand why—"

"You do not have my permission!"

"Do I need it?"

Even back in high school he'd burden me with some unbelievable secret and beseech me to promise I wouldn't tell anyone, then when I betrayed his confidence to a mutual friend, I'd discover he'd already told them the exact same thing. In any case, the fact is I am not the only one intrigued enough about his existence to document it. I have copious rivals who've already depicted his protracted wince on canvas, daubed his dead-eyed, petulant expression in earthworm pink and Day-Glo yellow, drawn his convulsions like folds in fabric, sketched his legs to illustrate their significant loss of bone density, summoned his hunched form in glazed ceramic, in pastels and oils, in plaster and clay. I've viewed tidy little works in which can be seen the digitally animated collapse of his whole craniofacial complex, and murals of him face-planting into a quiver of arrows. My best friend has been cropped, doctored, photoshopped, bubble wrapped, and shipped. I've glimpsed his tired grimace on glossy variable contrast paper so many times I've felt sorry for my own naked eye.

"You going to stand there and watch?"

I go back upstairs to the bar and sit down. Clouds swim in a watery blue sky. It is loose, warm weather. I feel drowsy. The music is loud and I'm not sure I'll be able to hear Aldo calling me from inside the toilet. I look over my notes and think: I'll be annoyed if after writing a whole book, a photograph of his screaming face would have done just as well.

The bartender says, "You want something else?"

I sigh. "In 1929 Georges Simenon wrote forty-one novels."

"What?"

"A bourbon and Coke."

As the bartender pours, I light a cigarette.

"Go outside," he says.

I keep the cigarette going, sucking deeply.

"I'm calling the police."

I laugh and open my jacket just enough to show my gun.

The bartender leans forward. "So even writers carry guns these days?"

I go, "You have no idea."

The Long Gestation of an Idea

W E MAKE ART BECAUSE BEING alive is a hostage situation in which our abductors are silent and we cannot even intuit their demands," Morrell said in one of his bewildering conversational pivots, stabbing with his crooked finger the court documents I'd brought to school. This was my final year, a midwinter afternoon in the portable after all my classmates had left. On the muted yellow wall, Blake Carney's painting of a golliwog wearing a swastika had caught Morrell's eye and he froze in front of it and said something I'm almost positive was: "Unused talent exerts downward pressure on the spirit." My uncertainty was due to the grating transportation soundscape—the school being situated by a train station on the intersection of a busy highway underneath a flight path—which meant I had to use all my concentration just to hear him. And I wanted to hear him. While traditionally our Zetland High art teacher was depicted in toilet-stall graffiti as a talking anus, I liked the guy; other than the burst capillaries on his nose, and the creases ironed into his clothes at random angles, he was a relatively well-preserved and mostly calm man, keyed up only by absenteeism, pigeon feeding, obtrusive yawning, his own sinus infections, and the creative spirit. Morrell paced the classroom like he wanted to give me a guided tour of it. He said, "We create for the same reason we do anything: fear of the alternative," then pirouetted on the threadbare carpet and scooped from his desk his own book—*Artist Within, Artist Without* (that he'd snuck onto the syllabus to the chagrin of Mr. Hennelly, our weedy, terse headmaster)—and copied onto the blackboard, in perfect yet minuscule handwriting I had to squint to decipher, the following lengthy passage:

> *Shamefully, doctors neglect to tell new parents that an increasingly common postnatal complication is that a small percentage of babies will grow into anthropologists in their own homes, as if they'd been conceived in order to study and then record the dreadful failings of their mothers and fathers, who've no idea they've invited this cold-hearted observer into their lives. All these parents wanted was to produce cuter versions of themselves, poor bastards; instead they're saddled with an unsympathetic informer who won't hesitate to report them to the lowest authority—the general public. In other words, it is as the poet Czeslaw Milosz once said: When a writer is born into a family, that family is doomed! (Exclamation mark mine.)*

To give the paragraph time to sink in, he nudged a discarded Vicks inhaler with his boot and flipped on a single-setting exhaust fan that blew his own musty odor around the room. I sat impassively in the plastic orange chair, trying to remember how I act when genuinely fascinated. Amber dusklight fell across the ordered row of desks. Outside, the parking lot was emptying. Drafts were coming up through a rough join in the floor. Morrell stared out the window and yelled, "Don't feed the pigeons, Henderson!" then swiftly moved back to the blackboard and wrote: *It's important to always take sides. Both sides,* before he turned to check my face for rapt attention. "You OK?" he asked. I looked down at the kind of carpet you wouldn't want to bring into contact with exposed skin. He stepped closer, and for a second I thought he was going to reach for my hand or pat my shoulder. "I know what it is to lose someone," he said. My jaw tightened. I was close to tears, sniffling prematurely. There was nothing I could do, apparently, to hide the hairy goiter of loss and acute sadness emanating from my person.

The previous year, my big sister Molly had been crossing the street when she was struck and killed by a junior police officer during a high-speed chase on the Shortland Esplanade in Newcastle's East End. The judge asked if we wished to prepare a victim impact statement, but my mother had difficulties expressing herself without plagiarizing another mother's grief. Since we all wanted Probationary Constable John Green to suffer the way we had—or at least receive the harshest possible sentence—I agreed to try my hand at writing the statement. Over a long, queasy night I wrote how Molly's death constituted *an anti-miracle* and that we had become *axes and wood, chopping ourselves to death* and since the hit-and-run, we felt *ashen, hexed, skewed, exploded* and *downsized in heart and soul,* and feared *roads, cars, telephones, rain, birds* and had *full-blown panic attacks in the presence of sirens and police strobes and fading taillights* and dreaded the sight of *braids, orthodontics, low-set ears,* anything that reminded us of Molly: *halter tops, out-of-date perms, women,* and those *men she would never marry—that is to say, all men* . . . It occurs to me now that Probationary Constable John Green's eight months' minimum security sentence—my earliest taste of success—solidified me on the path of the artist (or, as Morrell often writes it, the *a*rtist, with a very small—8 point—lower case *a*). It was in a naked bid to prolong the limelight that I'd shown Morrell my statement with the proclamation that I was thinking of turning it into a short story for the *Sydney Morning Herald* Young Writer of the Year competition—that's what had excited him into this impromptu unsolicited after-class master class. (My statement also, incidentally, won me my parents' grudging approval. Prior to the constable's conviction, they had been less than encouraging of my early teenage creative efforts: short stories on my father's same-sex infidelities, then on Molly's body dysmorphia, and finally a one-act play in which I portrayed them as rapists and made them play themselves in the production.)

Morrell continued. He wrote: *Forget the pram in the hallway—the only enemy of art is unrelenting sexual thoughts.* And: *The first step is admitting all your novel-writing fantasies begin with you typing the words "The End."* And: *The good thing about being a beginner is you know precisely the value of your work (zero cents).* He suddenly lurched and fondled the louvered shutters that hung by a thread, in order to intercept Aldo, who was peering in through the smeared window, doing a masturbation pantomime. Morrell waved at him as if from a parade float, and wedged the window open slightly to allow his voice to carry outside. Aldo leaned his elbows on the sill and made a disdainful face I studiously ignored. In truth, I felt grateful and flattered to be the focus of Morrell's attention in the semester before he quit teaching to pursue his painting career, as he always threatened to do, even when I had to endure an advice spree taken verbatim from his own 211-page, single-paragraph hectoring screed, that Aldo thought impenetrable and hypnotically dull but I appreciated and not just because the word "masturbatory" occurred twenty-seven times, and that he now copied from onto the blackboard, writing to *not freak out when your one-trick pony dies,* and that a writer, if that's what I was to become, needs *a sniper's awareness of landscape + a sinister impulse to show reality its own face + a hunter's sense of hearing + a bedridden personality type + a consumptive's reading habits + an interior life like an iron lung + an open mind in regards to lumbar support + a visceral connection to the written word + a keen interest in capitalizing on the tragedies of your time + a capacity to live without exterior validation + an irresistible curiosity that gives you the moral right to eavesdrop or stalk almost anyone on the planet earth.* Each phrase he aggressively underlined until the blackboard made the classroom look like the situation room in a madman's HQ.

All this time I was inert, with an increasingly befuddled grin. From the window Aldo said loudly, "Jesus Christ Almighty," and walked away. Morrell now began to write aphorisms I didn't understand. *You can be wounded by applause but some standing ovations are lethal.* And: *There but for the grace of God goes God,* as well as explicit warnings that seemed to prod and twang my entire nervous system: *As soon as you've found yourself a fallback career, you will fall back on it. Whatever you do, don't gain an unrelated skill or gather specialized knowledge or master any kind of profession—once you're "qualified" you're on the hook for life.* His gluey eyes seemed to hold melancholy secrets when he said, "Most importantly, Liam, you have to find your natural subject." "What's that?" I asked. He smirked, slapped a nicotine patch on his arm, and said, "That's for God to know and you to find out." This was the last thing he said that afternoon. I remember Morrell stepping on his polarized sunglasses, which had tumbled from his top pocket when he'd bent down, and then doing what looked like calf stretches as he examined the blue bucket brimming with old rainwater that had leaked through the black mold in the cork ceiling, that the Parent Teacher Association was up in arms about. The most dominant aspect of this memory, however, was how strangely at ease I felt alone with Mr. Morrell that afternoon, so devoid of my usual acute paranoia of authority figures I didn't once hallucinate the sound of a zipper when my back was turned.

II

In the decade after high school, on the hunt for my elusive natural subject, I wrote copiously about my childhood fascination with spontaneous combustion, quicksand, piranhas, the bubonic plague, time capsules, the equator, stowaways, giant squid, narcolepsy, and a mission I undertook when I was seventeen to seek out our city's hunchbacks (we have two). I also wrote about my several love affairs with bisexuals of both genders, and how I wound up doing the kinds of jobs usually taken by illegal immigrants or prisoners on day release—that is, how I started at the bottom and worked my way sideways, from dishwasher in an Italian restaurant to dishwasher in a Japanese restaurant, from cashier in a sporting goods store to cashier in a pet store, and on and on, manning hotlines, donning fast-food uniforms, turning back people who'd wandered in to use the restroom, waiting for customers to ask directions to our competitors, barely tolerating my coworkers' we're-all-in-the-same-boat faces, and following the orders of bosses who seemed to have no stomach for nooses or razor blades so were trying to kill themselves by their general attitude. The problem was twofold: Nothing I wrote was any good, and living my own life vicariously had a cool, distancing effect. Instead of relationships I had exploits; instead of affairs I had escapades. I began to suspect that in my soul, something sinister and carnivorous had replaced curiosity, and I had purposely sought out an itinerant work life and found inappropriate men and women to fuck and nuzzle in cheaply decorated bedrooms just for the material. The unexpected exclamation point to this era came the morning after a one-night stand with a pale-skinned waitress with a barcode tattoo who called me a star fucker as I tried to sneak out the door. I turned and said, "What does *that* mean? Who's a star, you?" Apparently she'd been on a TV soap for a season and assumed my interest was based on her "celebrity." When she realized I didn't know who she was she cracked up laughing, which I thought was pretty irresistible. Her name was Tess, and eleven months later I found myself a married man in a delivery room tensely gripping her hand in a too-late-for-an-epidural situation as she was upstaged by the real star's grand, urgent entrance. As Tess wept, holding our brand-new raging red baby, Sonja, I remember detecting underneath my love, shock, and awe a well of pressure in my chest and the certainty that if I didn't succeed in my writing now, it would forever remain a hobby.

My signed copy of *Artist Within, Artist Without* had become my veritable bible and gave me plenty of conflicting advice, such as: *Muses inspire but also violate—innocently, like the kissing bandit; or horrifyingly, like the granny rapist,* and: *"Inspiration of the muses" is the "only following orders" of the creative act,* and: *When you're looking for Ideas just remember: People often die straining on the toilet.* It was in this confusion that I decided to take as my subject this three-pronged family of mine, that moved to an industrial suburb and into a small apartment with a rusting two-door Celica in the grassy yard and flying cockroaches in the living room and a Juliet balcony haunted by wet crows. Yet as the years passed and I wrote about the sour, stubborn screams of early childhood or the dripping tap of marriage or anything else for that matter—my nation's catastrophes and blood-orange sunsets; its old-timey genocides and Salvation Army bin fires; the New Australia, how there hadn't been a stoic among us for fifty years—I knew I still hadn't found the holy grail, my natural subject.

Moreover, whenever I was in mid-creation, a phrase from *Artist Within, Artist Without* would eviscerate me; I had repeatedly failed to structure an invented story in a convincing or original manner, and I could not, no matter how I tried, come up with engaging plots, write realistic dialogue or convincing characters, therefore when I decided that the traditional, conventional novel was a contrived and predictable anachronism and I should no longer waste my time with it, Morrell's work snidely castigated me: *An artist's theory of art is always founded on his shortcomings as an artist, his passion for that theory in direct proportion to the severity of his failures.* When I tried my hand at disrupting expectations of linear narrative and wrote one hundred pages of fragmentary scraps, random paragraphs that could be arranged in any order, I came across this quote: *Only when one is disappointed with the quality of one's content does one develop an exaggerated interest in form.* I had told myself I was being extraordinarily daring, but Morrell's book said: *Most times people talk of artistic risk, they are referring to commercial risk. Not "Will this succeed?" but "Will this be purchased?"* When out of pathetic desperation I attempted a pastiche of my favorite writings, often drifting into outright plagiarism, I found the putdown *Only those with no personal stamp do not believe in copyright.*

My future lay behind me. I was thirty years old and had been unspooling for more than a decade and was in the perpetual doldrums about my not-for-profit days and nights, envious of Tess's actor friends who had already abandoned their dreams and "grown" and "changed" while I watched myself metamorphose annually into the same thing I was the year before. To make matters worse, the relentlessness of parenthood—the unending string of sunrises, interminable housework, and separate schedules—seemed to be getting the better of us. Maybe that was why, when our paths did cross, and not just when I came home to find I'd been tried in absentia for some domestic crime or another, it was my impression that Tess had started luxuriating a smidgeon in my failures. Maybe I was just hypersensitively overinterpreting clues, but everything suddenly became deeply significant: the night she coerced me to plug my nostrils with Snore Less Nasal Cones; the day I asked her to scratch my back, and she left scars. And I'm pretty sure, though I can't prove it, that she stole my wedding ring in order to accuse me of losing it. At the same time, Tess's aura of self-sufficiency strengthened. Her Pilates classes, intended to rid herself of her pillowy post-baby body, turned her into a certified-organic fitness junkie; she weaned herself off shoplifting, made new friends, returned to university. It was like we'd boarded the same train but I'd wound up on an uncoupled carriage, stationary on the tracks. My grip on her was loosening and the more she slipped away, the more I realized I loved her; and the more I loved her, the more she seemed to lose interest in me. On the night of my thirty-first birthday I got so drunk I couldn't find my own mouth, and tiptoeing into a household of light sleepers, I slipped into the guest bathroom where I often went during dinner for a minute of mute howling. Through the window, a piebald moon cruised the sky. I fished *Artist Within, Artist Without* from the wastebasket where Tess had thrown it, accusing me of being unnaturally attached to this old teacher "with no pedagogical value" who lectured about art but had never produced a body of artistic work. I could see her point; Google told me that Morrell had still not followed up on his threat to quit teaching in order to paint, but I was reluctant to relinquish this textbook that I used as a kind of alternative I Ching. I desperately flicked through, looking for a lit path through the darkness. And on page 86 I found this: *When you begin a work, keep expectations low. Anticipate that you will be like the new groom who unexpectedly returns home from his honeymoon a widower.* That advice was a windfall; as always the book seemed to speak directly to my particular psychological impediments, this time my debilitating perfectionism. It inspired me to begin again. One last shot. But what would I write about?

Then, on page 99, this: *If stuck, descend to the floor of the abyss and exhume the idiosyncratic horror that made you.*

That was it. I would write about Molly's death—turn my victim impact statement not into a short story, but a novel! But rather than the point of view of the grieving brother, I would get into the head of the murderer, the young cop. And for that I would do research. I'd interview policemen. Or better: I'd fuck policemen. Or better still: I'd join the Police Academy!

And that's what I did, for six punishing months. After hours, I wrote about a recruit who underwent extensive fitness training and learned how to direct traffic, shoot firearms, and physically subdue multiple persons resisting arrest, and who, two months after the graduation ceremony, hit and killed a young girl with his car and had to live with the consequences. Yes, this idea was the right one, I was certain of it. And encouragingly, Tess thought so too. In a show of support she replaced the coffee table with a desk and turned our living room into a writer's retreat. She cooked or fetched takeout and though she may have delivered the meals to my desk with a puckered mouth and a caustic "I can't believe I'm serving you like this," on weekends she'd bundle Sonja out of the house to allow me to work, and when I wrote late into the night, the next morning she'd permit me to sleep in. I remember looking up from my desk one afternoon to catch sight of Tess in the doorway, watching me with the exact hopeful smile I'd been longing for.

As it turned out, my novel was another failure. For the next year, I accumulated rejections from every large and small press in Australia. Nobody wanted anything to do with it. Tess believed that my novel suffered from a lack of empathy and an almost autistic understanding of what makes people tick, which I took as a not-so-veiled criticism of my general life-problem. I felt, for the first time, actual despair. Not only had I let myself down, wasted another year, and done a disservice to Molly's memory, it was as if I had transcribed my genetic material onto the page and found it to be universally repellent. All I got out of *Artist Within, Artist Without* by way of consolation was: *Often one discovers too late that the chosen subject is wholly incompatible with one's talent, which is like a fatal illness only diagnosable after death.* This time, I wouldn't take his aphoristic text as an answer—I needed to hear from the man himself, and so

couriered a copy to Mr. Angus Morrell, c/o the Zetland High art department
that he singularly comprised. Two months later, he called me. I had not spoken
to the man in almost a decade and a half.

"Editing is performing one's own autopsy with forensic calm," Mr. Morrell's
caffeinated voice said in lieu of hello, "and if you're not a good editor, you're
like a battlefield surgeon reattaching the wrong arm. In any case, whatever happened here happened at conception. It's a real thalidomide baby of a book, tell
you the truth, and at the moment the tragic hero of the novel is the author, who
even the characters seem to feel sorry for. What you want—I thought I made
this clear—is for the reader to feel something akin to a hot teaspoon pressed
against a mouth ulcer . . ."

I hung up while he was still talking. There it was. It had all come to nothing. Well, almost nothing. Morrell was one hundred percent right about one
thing: Once you're qualified, you're on the hook for life. Rent day came around;
I was thirty-two years old, had a wife and child to support, and having literally
exhausted every unskilled minimum-wage position in the greater Sydney region, I realized, to my horror, that in researching and writing my novel I had
acquired the qualifications of a New South Wales police officer. That was it.
That was my fallback. And that, reader, is the stupid reason a passive and relatively lazy, fearful writer—neither a doer nor a fighter, nor a respecter of the
laws of man—perversely became a cop.

III

I was in a patrol car in the rain during a siege with three violent, glowering
adults—my fellow officers—in whose presence I felt almost ceaselessly unsafe,
positioned outside a weatherboard house in which a distressed and armed father in his forties had fatally disciplined his child and barricaded himself inside. Gridlocked cars honked in the distance and the house cast a single long
shadow across the empty trampoline and the summer brown of the unwatered
lawn. In my mind, this was the day it started, though it could have been others.

Apart from the weirdly high percentage of the female population who fe-
tishize men in uniforms, the joy of irresponsible driving, and the childlike thrill
of chasing people on foot (in real life, nobody ever stops to fight mano a mano,
and worst case you simply shrug and say, "He got away"), I hated the job. I

hated the chilling look on children's faces during domestic disputes; I hated the potluck of dragging a river; I hated the chore of finding bodies carbonized in clandestine meth labs; I hated Tasering and spraying and bludgeoning and cuffing and detaining and hauling and warning and fining and arresting and patrolling; I hated dying bikers who seemed mostly afraid of an effeminate death; I hated examining four-wheel drives with bits of infant skull on the tread; I hated interacting with sad people for whom only scratch-lottery tickets give them the will to live; I hated having a controlling interest in the short-term destinies of street prostitutes, hash dealers, and tipsy drivers; I hated serving apprehended violence orders to husbands and seeing the angry confusion of feared men who did not feel frightening; I hated how hard it was not to succumb to a bribe here, a confiscated gram of cocaine there, and the fact that despite a visibly displayed baton, canister of pepper spray, and loaded gun, I couldn't patrol the streets without some civilian asking me directions; and I *hated* how *at least* once a month a superior officer would look me dead in the eye and ask the same corny question. Like now, on the day of the siege. I had hoisted myself up in the seat with one eye on the jittery hand behind the curtain, when the old bearish sergeant, who always tried to imbue sexual tension when castigating female officers, turned to us and posed that familiar inquiry in a bladed voice: "SO FELLAS, WHY'D YOU JOIN THE FORCE?"

"My father was a cop," said Constable Brock.

"My favorite aunt was murdered, and I vowed to dedicate my life to making sure that the scumbags of this earth get the justice they deserve," said Constable Miller.

"What about you, Constable Wilder?"

What could I say? While most cops are the bullied in revenge mode, or pious bad eggs with dreams of deadly force, I'd come here by way of failure, by way of words rotting on the vine. I didn't want these men to know we were on competing wavelengths and they had every right to mistrust me, so I drew a blank and made no response. Policemen are excellent at staring unpleasantly, it has to be said. The lengthening silence was punctuated by the fleeing footsteps of more neighbors running for cover, and a voice over the radio asking, "Is Constable Wilder riding with you?"

"Unfortunately," the sergeant said.

"Constable, you know an Aldo Benjamin?"

I gritted my teeth. That question was usually a prelude to some onerous task I'd be called on to perform. "Old high school mate, Senior Sergeant."

"Swing by the station after your shift."

And I hated—I almost forgot—I *hated* how family and friends would inundate you with legal questions, such as my uncle Hamish who often probed me about drug trafficking—such as whether border patrols check hair extensions—and mates who demanded favors with speeding and traffic infringements, or expected special treatment when breaking the law or mired in legal jams, as my old friend Aldo Benjamin was prone to do. That afternoon, driving back to the station, I thought with increasing fatigue about how every few months, pretty much since the day I'd been sworn in, Aldo found himself in a dilemma that required my assistance: bar fight; bar fight with bartender; accused by neighbor of poisoning then running over beloved terrier; purchasing a gram of cocaine thirty seconds before a police raid; being a suspicious person, and then being a suspicious person in a vehicle; opening a car door into a bicyclist's face. Recently, he'd called early one morning to ask if I knew the age of consent. "Sixteen," I said. "Get dressed," Aldo said to someone else, and hung up. It's an open secret and practically an unwritten rule that every officer, regardless of rank, is allowed to step in and ask for special consideration for one fuckup: a father who needs around-the-clock surveillance; a cousin who requires a security detail; a wayward mate who needs backup or bailing out. It was with Aldo I more than used up this precious token. This was not your regular cheering up or sympathetic ear or shoulder to cry on, but a new definition of friendship, one that includes a little hocus-pocus with paperwork or actual armed reinforcements. Now I wanted to call ahead to the station to get a hint of what was waiting for me. It could be anything from possession to reckless endangerment, a gross misunderstanding or a bad judgment call. Some people defy the limits of your imagination and you just have to accept that.

I turned off the freeway. The majority of Aldo's sad imbroglios were related to his businesses going kaput. After we graduated, Aldo had grown into a serial entrepreneur and small-business owner with a knack for flooding the market with products that didn't sell, and starting ventures that actively repelled customers. For more than a decade he had demonstrated a special magic for attracting investors and losing their money, and because his repeated failures failed in multifarious ways, and because he always felt tremendous optimism for a project and then incredulity when it bombed—yet somehow managed to get back on his feet just when you'd counted him out—there were incalculable numbers of unhappy small investors out to get him, any of whom could be the cause of today's degrading emergency.

The chaos of those fifteen-odd years since high school had passed for Aldo in an entrepreneurial blur: his retrofitted 1963 Airstream Trailer food truck (it crashed), his warehouse dance parties (shut down by police), his vending machines stocked with health snacks like gluten-free flaxseed bars and qui-noa cakes (vandalized into disrepair), his prototype of a device that detected trace elements of peanuts in food (it simply didn't function), his tanning-salon taxi service (customers sued for melanomas and motion sickness), his *I'm Not Drunk, I Have Cerebral Palsy You Ignorant Fuck* T-shirts (three sales in total), his maternity clothes for goths (a demographic with an 85 percent abortion rate). Not to mention the failures of his midlife-crisis consultancy clinic, his Mexican taco stand, his foam eyewear, his recycled soap, and his doggie dental mints and pawprint art. His product launches were all teachable moments: He never knew his market, he foisted poor-quality merchandise on customers he ignored. Who were his lenders? Where did he find these foolhardy creditors with no radar? His mother, Leila, was always good for start-up funds. So was his girlfriend, Stella. Uncles. Friends (myself included). State government small-business loans. Angel investors, men with crushing handshakes—overcompensation for prior accusations of limpness, Aldo assumed—who'd take new shirts out of their thick plastic envelopes and change right in front of you. I suppose in his mind failure was unimaginable, despite its persistent recurrence. Otherwise, why would he have blown his mother's entire retirement fund, forty thousand dollars, to manufacture fashionable sandals in China? He didn't have excuses or explanations, he had anecdotes: how he bought inventory in bulk upfront; how he arrived at the factory to find they'd made the whole lot out of a synthetic flammable material that irritates human skin; how on the way to a key meeting he was stuck in a historic traffic jam that lasted from nine a.m. until five p.m. the following day; his realization that the replacement supplier's headquarters was in one of China's cancer villages he couldn't bring himself to enter. It went on like that. I remember when he came back from the debacle, he couldn't face Leila; he called her from a pay phone in Chinatown every lunchtime for six months, pretending he was still in Shanghai.

One afternoon Aldo and Stella were in the supermarket, and who does he run into in the frozen-food aisle? The look on his mother's face was his lowest moment, he said, and he vowed, "I will never again try to make it big in this world! I will merely subsist!"

So why didn't he listen to himself? Two reasons. First, because Aldo was a precocious sucker of the success industry. He'd always be listening to motivational talks, lining the pockets of a succession of tacky gurus, Tony Robbins types, and once, Tony Robbins himself. He read books with obnoxious titles like *See You at the Top* and *It's Yours—Take It*, and listened to audio-biographies of successful business leaders like Zig Ziglar and Warren Buffett and J. W. Marriott, Jr. He said things with an intonation that let you know he was speaking in quotation marks. He said: "Belief creates its verification in fact." He said: "I'm the only asset I'll ever have." He said: "The prepared mind takes advantage of chance." He said: "The secret to success is hard work." I thought: It's not much of a formula. The opposite is also true. Some failures work like bastards.

The second reason was Stella: While he provided emotional support and material for her music, found her rare records and allowed her to use his wilder pronouncements as lyrics, she in turn gave him strength to believe in his ideas even when they weren't inherently worth believing in. They were a genuine team, charmed by each other's blather; they regularly removed fear from one another's path and never let the other feel foolish, even when his businesses crashed and fizzled or she played some pretty bad songs in some pretty public places to raucous derision. They were an all-time great couple, one of those who even argued respectfully, like two nations stopping warfare to let the other bury their dead. After they divorced, I suspected it was the hope he might win her back that inspired him, each time he was ruined, to get back on his feet.

I always knew my insolvent friend was about to remount the entrepreneurial horse when he started talking about untapped markets. The aging population! Women over forty struggling to conceive! Couples with mismatched libidos! Honeymooners with creeping malaise! Insomniacs with global dread! Shoppers with ecoparalysis! Corporate bandits ashamed of their bodies! Upscale couples one set of genitals away from being totally interchangeable! Under-tens with overweening narcissism! Baby boomers in terminal decline! Rich space tourists! Face-transplant recipients! Speakers of all 6,909 living languages! That was Aldo, always trying to solve a dilemma. How does one delineate between hope and false hope? How can one tap into the nauseating pandemic of public marriage proposals? How do you sell a product to anticonsumerists? Where should one go to manufacture clothes for obese toddlers and newborns in the 97th weight percentile?

It was the answer to the last that took him to India. I drove him to the airport, and can still remember the thick veil of fear on his face as he disappeared through the departure gates. One month later he came back with a beard and mysterious scars and monkey bites and another series of rabies shots (his third!) and even further in debt, with only scraps of information about problems communicating with the tailor, about waists too high, crotches too low. I suggested he take a break. Just get a regular job like a regular person. Three months later he opened a steak restaurant on King Street called High Steaks, but Newtown, famous for its vegans, did not bite and High Steaks shut its doors. He stopped reading self-help and prosperity literature, wanting to go deeper into the psyche of his customers, and moved on to psychology texts, both popular and academic, and read people like Jaspers and Binswanger and Hoogendijk and Achenbach and Skinner and Piaget and Adler and Horney and Laing. Then he moved on to reference books: *The APA Dictionary of Psychology*; *Diagnostic and Statistical Manual of Mental Disorders*; *Journal of Consulting and Clinical Psychology*; *Clinician's Guide to Neuropsychological Assessment*. He said he needed a product that would appeal to people's solipsism, their unembarrassed love of self and abiding fondness for their own point of view. He seemed desperate to make *anything* on an industrial scale. Yet he had substandard luck and submental ideas: for instance, transdermal chocolates, patches that transmit after-dinner mints and dark almond whirls through the skin into the bloodstream, a product line that *Time Out Sydney* gave a devastating (if amusing) one-line review (*a confectionary Willy Wonka wouldn't touch with an Oompa Loompa's dick*). Aldo sold off the remaining merchandise for this last idea and came out even, which somehow, for him, was worse than complete failure. He said, "Often the thing that drives you crazy about failure is its proximity to success." Still, he bore his losses uncomplainingly. If only his investors would too.

The last time I was conscripted into action to assist him, he phoned me when I was at my desk gazing at a basket of pens, waiting for a transformation of the spirit. "I'm being chased!" Aldo hollered in a panicked tone, puffing theatrically as if to prove he was running. Agonizing quagmires and near-fatal setbacks were Aldo's specialty, so I had no reason to doubt the urgency of his situation. "Keep moving," I told him and he gave me his cross streets. I stuck my head in the senior sergeant's office and told him my best friend was yet again in mortal danger.

"Need backup?"

"Nah, I'm good."

A violet night sky was darkening with storm clouds. I schlepped out east to a fancy suburb full of up-market pubs with sophisticated bouncers and clothing boutiques so expensive they needed only one customer every seventy-two hours to stay afloat. I had to be careful; during a similar "situation" I'd phoned him only to give away his position to his pursuer, so this time I opted to scour the low-lit streets without fanfare. A white sedan was circling and when I approached, it U-turned and disappeared down a side street. I cut the lights, idled a moment outside a councilman's office, and stared at the poster of his bilious face, which I doubt had ever begotten a single sexual fantasy. A light rain fell soundlessly on the windscreen; on the streets, late joggers and contemplative men walked minuscule dogs. I moved off again, took a sharp turn down a residential street, and shined my spotlight on the discreetly lit sandstone houses. It was on my fourth tour of the block that I heard a shout; bright halogen house lights flicked on, and sprinting out from behind a flower bed was Aldo, moving like a projectile in the damp glow of orange streetlamps, a solid brick of a man charging after him.

I hit the siren. It startled me, as usual.

The assailant tackled Aldo and they rolled, looking like two men sharing a seizure. I hit the brakes and leaped out. Then they were on their feet and it happened fast: They were taking swings like old hillbillies settling their great-granddaddies' squabbles. Aldo went down while his attacker kept going, throwing wild punches in the rain. You could hear the thwacks of skull against pavement. I made straight for the aggressor and pulled him off.

"Taser him!" Aldo yelled.

I pinned the man facedown on the pavement and kept my knee pressed between his shoulderblades while I cuffed him.

"Taser him! Taser him!"

Residents staggered stiffly out of their houses, as if off their couches for the first time in a week. One of Aldo's eyes was beaten shut and there was gravel rash on his upper cheek; blood trickled down his neck over his older scars. He clutched a bruised or broken rib. He wasn't wearing shoes.

"Now," I said, assessing Aldo's attacker. Gelled hair. Thick, dark mustache. Colonel Mustard in his youth. "What seems to be the trouble?"

"Officer, this fucking cunt owes me fifty thousand dollars."

"What for?" I asked.

"I invested in his horror movie."

"I never said it would win awards!" Aldo said.

"It never even got finished!"

"I'm sorry, Kaplan. But you accepted the risk. Did I put a gun to your head?"

"You *said* I'd quadruple my investment!"

I let this fruitless discussion go on for a few minutes before sending the unhappy investor on his way, injustice clinging to him tightly as he trudged somberly down the street. Aldo made me stop at a McDonald's drive-thru for ice. The rain came down hard now and hit the dark streets. Aldo pulled out a pocket-sized first-aid kit he kept on his person at all times, and sprayed antiseptic on his face.

I said, "You're a fucking movie producer now?"

"Let me tell you something. The people who invest in films hate films. They wouldn't be caught dead at a cinema."

After reading about two young men who had produced a horror movie for $25,000 that went on to make over 248 million worldwide, Aldo had penned a screenplay, a period zombie movie called *Van Demon's Land,* set in 1788 and featuring four principal groups: colonialists, convicts, Aborigines, and a couple of French explorers. They'd spent six months trying to secure financing and distribution, had the thing cast, shot twenty minutes of raw footage (using Kaplan's investment), then attempted to use that footage to raise completion funds—to no avail.

"Seems that guy's got every right to beat you senseless. Fifty thousand dollars! Where does *that* fit on your Fair Price Index?"

"It was impossible," Aldo said, rubbing his jaw. "Every time I went into meetings with production companies, or with the government film-financing bodies, I hit a snag. The last meeting I went into they said there was too much dialogue. Film's a visual medium, they said. Well, that just got my nerves up. I said film *was* a visual medium, you're absolutely correct, but only until 1927 when it became a visual *and* sound medium, because that was the year Al Jolson did *The Jazz Singer*. Yes, but film is a visual medium, they repeated like robots. Unbelievable! So, I said, you haven't heard of this thing called the talkies? They said, 'But we don't understand why the convict William Henry Groom has all these long speeches.' Then I said, 'And I don't understand why all the film and literature of this country has to have as its main character a silent or laconic type. That's not like real life. My experience of people is they never shut up!'"

Aldo tapped his fingers on the window, maybe at the woman standing at the bus stop. "Anyway," he went on, "that was only one issue. Next they said, 'You can't have the zombies eating the Indigenous brains. It's OK if they eat the brains of the British soldiers, it's OK if they eat the brains of the British convicts, and we love when they eat the brains of the French explorers, but you can't have them eating the brains of the Aboriginals.' I asked why not, and you know what they said? *Cultural sensitivities*."

That was two months ago, and now, as I drove along the shadowed city streets in the convulsing afternoon traffic, it occurred to me that the only person genuinely pleased with the absurd non sequitur of my becoming a police officer was Aldo, who had perhaps foreseen how frequently he would require my assistance. This was without question the most inconvenient alliance of my life, yet at the same time there was nobody else with whom I felt the most real and relaxed version of myself. To be honest, my most relaxed version grated on Tess, and I had begun to fear there was potential for divorce in my future. And Sonja, my sweet little monster: She still worshipped me as little girls do their fathers, but that would draw to an end once puberty got its messy hands on her. And though I could always make friends, I could never again make an *old* friend—that time had passed for me forever.

And yet I didn't flash the light or put on the siren as guys on the force all sometimes did to slip through heavy traffic, because, I realized, I was reluctant to come to my old friend's rescue yet again, or put in a good word for him, or bail him out, or plead for special consideration. Instead of hurrying, I took alternative routes, slowed down at yellow lights, let civilians overtake, felt plain relief when a tunnel under construction forced all the cars into a single lane; and when at the lights I allowed a bare-chested methadone addict to clear my windshield with a quizzical pout, I finally understood how tired I was of being immured in a friendship that was taking such a personal and professional toll. If Aldo perceived himself to be a burden, or thought he had overshot the boundaries of our friendship, he had never given any indication. In fact, he had unwavering confidence that I'd always step up for him at a moment's notice and zero qualms about pestering me with the consequences of his unintentional yet frequent clusterfucks. Although it made me his enabler (Tess's words) I never hesitated or refused him, but even after saving his life or extricating him from whatever jam he was in, he'd only give me the bare minimum of thanks before trotting out incongruous snark, or lighthearted ribbing. Lately his troubles had increased in frequency and seriousness; I felt apprehension at seeing his name on my caller ID, and began to feel taken for granted. The cumulative effect of these favors was to tip the balance of our friendship—as failed writer and destitute entrepreneur we were in the same boat and I could laugh at his one mishap after another, but as a policeman I seemed to serve only one purpose for him and I was beginning to resent it.

At the station, I walked past the CAUTION WET FLOOR sign that had been there for months and into the restrained chaos of three men in wifebeaters, panting, with two sweaty constables standing over them. The men sat as if tight spaces had been drawn around them, afraid to interact. I'd clearly just missed a fight. The desk sergeant stared impassively at me.

"Your idiot mate's in there."

"What's the charge?"

"Wasting police time."

"That's not a crime."

"He doesn't know that."

He buzzed me through the side door. Aldo was standing beside the Wanted posters in the unpleasantly hot and glary sun-blasted corridor. He was wearing a bloodstained T-shirt underneath his old denim jacket, his slight frame bent into a posture of slothful defeat. He was quite a sight. Prematurely balding, prematurely graying, even though, if I remember correctly, he was excruciatingly late to puberty. What a sad and narrow prime he'd had.

"Here he is," he said. "Why do you still look like a bus driver in that uniform?" Aldo gave me something I can only describe as a knowing wink of despair. "How's things? How's Sonja?"

"She's starting to save her tantrums for the most public places with the fewest exits. Tess suspects she's using our mortification as her secret weapon."

Aldo laughed. "Everyone always says, until you have children you can't ever understand what it's like. That's just because they have no empathy, isn't it?"

"I suppose so," I said, stepping back. Aldo waved his hands when he talked; he was always knocking people in the side of the head and not apologizing. His existence needed room.

"Be honest, Liam, isn't fatherhood *exactly* what you thought it would be?"

"No, it's totally different."

"Liar!"

"Just take him home!" the sergeant barked.

The truth is, fatherhood was exactly what the culture had prepared me for: near-fatal fatigue, geysers of love, the cornered feeling that comes from being The Provider. But whenever Aldo asked about Sonja, I always detected substrates of old grief and even a smidgeon of unacknowledged jealousy that fatherhood had worked out for only one of us. There was also an imperative to change the subject before Aldo threw some awful fact in my face. (Last time, it was the epidemic of precocious puberty in seven-year-old girls.) By the time we stepped outside into an ambush of sunlight, Aldo already had a cigarette lit and was furiously inhaling, as if non-smoking laws were an inalienable human-rights violation. We leaned against my car and Aldo promised to email me a video of a blonde who had trained her pug to breastfeed. I noted with relief that in the ten minutes we had been together he had not mentioned Stella once. That was progress. I thought: Maybe his heart is finally out of quarantine.

"So you'll never fucking guess who's getting remarried," Aldo said.

"You're kidding." This was bad news, the worst. "To who?"

"Something called Craig, one of those sub-lawyer thingies."

"You mean like a legal secretary?"

"A paralegal something or other, yeah, one of those law careers where you're kitty litter for other lawyers."

"Remarried! What's he like?"

"I don't know much. I only met him once. He's lived in Italy and so went on and on about how lateness is culturally superior to being on time."

"What a cock."

He pinched the cigarette butt so tight it became a flat wedge he had to suck hard on to get any smoke through. The air grew heavy with the smell of impending thunderstorms and Aldo told me how, the week before, he'd followed them to Bronte, down to the beach where he saw Craig take his shirt off to reveal swimmer's abs lodged in a soldier's torso, and how Aldo had stood there behind some family's beach umbrella feeling a slow liquidation of his emotional assets. He let out a dry, glum laugh, bent down to pick up a fifty-cent coin and winced; I could see through the open shirt that his torso was wrapped in white gauze.

"And guess what else? She's asked me to be part of the wedding."

"No she didn't."

"She still considers me her best friend."

"Ex-husbands aren't best friends!"

"No shit."

We slid into the car. Aldo shifted the sideview mirror to steer clear of his reflection. We moved off into the three-lane highway and were quickly embroiled in heavy traffic.

"Part of the wedding," I said. "As what?"

"An usher."

"*An usher?*"

"That's how I said it. *An usher? An usher?* So I tear the tickets in half and with a flashlight show the patrons to their seats? Something like that, Stella said, laughing, thinking that my being lighthearted was proof of her good decision. But I begged her to reconsider. I mean, first of all, I almost *choked* when she told me the wedding is on a rooftop. I said, It's *outside?* Her whole life she's dreamed of getting married the traditional way that we never did, with the dress and the cake and the whole extended family, and then she goes and organizes an *outside* wedding? I mean, thirty-six years in the planning and *it can't rain?*"

He was breathing heavily and staring into the copper light that glinted off the skyscrapers from the setting sun.

"If I'm to be entirely honest," I said, just to stir the pot, "I never understood what you saw in her."

Aldo snapped to attention. "For one, she's naturally beautiful. I don't know if you realize this, but the whole time we were together, she never once wore makeup."

"That's like describing me by saying—He doesn't wear a hat. So fucking what?"

"So shut up and put on the siren."

"Grow up."

A long stretch of gridlocked traffic, and I had to actively resist the homicidal urge to plow through it or open the door as motorcycles weaved past. As usual, civilians who pulled up beside me looked straight ahead with fixed postures, or slouched down in order to hide their texting, or rolled up their windows gradually, or all of a sudden, to contain the smell of pot. Ten minutes later, we'd only moved two blocks. Aldo eased back into the seat and put his bare feet on the dashboard. I knocked them off.

If you wait long enough in life, your jealousies will eventually make no sense. Stella's devotion to Aldo had always nested a special envy in my heart. She *adored* him, beyond all bearable limits. She wrote *songs* about him, for Christ's sake, songs that she performed in public spaces in front of strangers. In that era, I had a few times made the tactical error of going out as a foursome; they behaved as if their love took place at a cellular level and whatever Tess and I had going on seemed—*was*—paltry in comparison. And now—poof!—that love was gone.

"How's your novel?" he asked.

"I'm taking a hiatus."

"You shouldn't let failure go to your head."

"You don't understand. When I write about a character, it's like getting a tattoo of them on my arm, and when it doesn't work out I carry the failure of the relationship around with me forever, like some celebrity—"

"Loser."

"The man just arrested for wasting police time is not calling me a loser."

"That's not how it went down."

"What happened?"

As we stuttered along in the peak-hour nightmare, Aldo told me the whole story.

Earlier in the day, he'd convinced Stella to return to Luna Park with him in the hope of rekindling their romance, a dud idea that misfired almost as soon as they got through the turnstiles. He had blurted out the whole spiel about them giving it one more shot. "She said, 'Face it, Aldo, the marriage was a failure.' I said, 'The relationship isn't a failure merely because one of us didn't die, and despite it being the gold standard for our whole stupid civilization, my death or your death is actually a ghoulish barometer for marital success.' Then we talked about the state of our union in those final months. She said it was rusted, leprous, and there was no wind left to harness. She said, 'A love drawn taut snaps eventually.' She said, 'Maybe our youths ended at different times, did you ever think of that?' I said, 'Let's lay all our cards on the table,' and I proceeded to tell her that somewhere affairs were had, by me, just two minor indiscretions that any competent marriage counselor would have *recommended* to couples staring down a commitment that stretches interminably into the future. Get it out of your system, I imagined the marriage counselor advising."

"The imagined marriage counselor?"

"Hey, my conscience is clean: I change it every week."

"That doesn't mean anything."

Aldo laughed loudly, then bit his lip as if he'd revealed something he had set out to conceal. "Anyway, I told her how deeply and permanently and profoundly hurt I was by the way she left me."

This I knew. One night Stella had pretended to talk in her sleep in order to confess to Aldo that she was in love with another man. "Aldo, Aldo, I've met someone," she murmured. She had hoped, he supposed, that he would feel as though she had left herself ajar and he could peek in when her mind was turned. She murmured, "Slept with him." And, "Leaving you."

At Luna Park Aldo ceremoniously forgave her, but it was irrelevant. Stella dropped the bombshell about her upcoming nuptials to Craig. This hit him hard. They stood like two mutes; he felt like a removed tumor that was trying to graft itself back on. He yelled into her eyes and nose—fuck you, you fucking fuck—and stormed off and wound up between the pavilion wall and the back of the Rotor, a narrow corridor that smelled of popcorn and urinary tract infections, where he stood sobbing, for just a couple of minutes, he said, when two lean, muscular teenagers, one in oversized sunglasses, or maybe safety goggles, put him in a headlock and escorted him at knifepoint to an ATM where they forced him to withdraw, in their words, "the maximum daily amount."

I laughed at the cold precision of that term. "What then?"

Stepping up to the bank machine, Aldo whispered to himself not to forget

his PIN, and promptly forgot his PIN. The teenagers' eyelids twitched erratically and their pupils were dilated; their brownish teeth and broken skin suggested methamphetamines, Aldo noted, and they looked to be no strangers
to violence, nor to fault-finding parents, low grades, truancy, nil self-esteem,
and a dissociative loss of control, and Aldo thought about how stabbing was
extremely high on his list of fears—to be *slashed*, while dangerous to muscle,
would be bearable, a wound he imagined to be hot and biting yet survivable—
but *stabbing*! That conjured up fatal thrust wounds and vascular organ damage
and unimaginably nightmarish punctured-lung/asphyxiation scenarios, even
less pleasant than a bullet in the stomach. ("How many movie villains have told
me how long it takes to die from a gut wound?" he asked me.) "Put in your
fucking PIN," the shorter teenager shouted, and in reaction to his mind's utter
blankness Aldo was now wearing a smile that may have been misconstrued as
sardonic or mocking. There was a tense silence, and other than stare into the
unappeasable drug-fucked faces of youth and say he had a low tolerance for
foreign metals, what else could he do? ("Besides, I think sluggishly on my feet,"
Aldo admitted.) At this point, he recalled, the teenager raised his knife hand in
a tight arc and brought it down at a diagonal rush, and Aldo thought: Slashed
it is! with actual relief as he went down on his knees and felt weirdly vindicated
that he had accurately deduced the (hot, biting) sensation before falling face-
first onto the hard concrete, which, on his cheek, was sun-warmed and gravelly.
A thirteen-year-old couple who had to take out retainers to kiss spotted him
and called for help, and he was tended to by the skeleton staff of Luna Park's
First Aid Station, interviewed by security personnel, and driven to the police
station where he was offered instant coffee and seated opposite a sketch artist,
a uniformed man so rigid and stony, Aldo said, he looked like "he would have
to be loved intravenously."

"That would be Constable Weir," I said.

It was then, Aldo continued, that it occurred to him, possibly out of an
overwhelming sense of the futility of the exercise, or the simple unlikelihood
of justice, how amusing it might be to describe his own face.

"You did what?"

There followed an intense marathon as Aldo recalled his precise features,
based on photographs and countless hours staring unhappily into mirrors,
and described himself with narcissistic intensity and an almost hallucinatory

level of concentrated precision (lightly copper complexion, slightly acned with multiple crosswise scars; clenched, rounded jaw; chestnut-brown hair thinning to a single vertical dagger; narrow facial shape with high forehead and horizontal wrinkles; bushy eyebrows and blue deep-set eyes with small irises; off-white teeth, medium-sized chiseled nose with pronounced nasal wings; low cheekbones; large earlobes; downturned lips, with tendency to lower-lip pout and a pouching of the skin below the lip corners, etc.). Constable Weir drew and Aldo examined and corrected and Constable Weir—despite the silently dawning realization of the farce—adjusted and redrew and grew weary of their collaboration but on the whole was patient, exact, determined not to fail him. After two and three-quarter industrious hours and now with barely restrained fury, Constable Weir printed and slid the image across the desk. Aldo looked at it impassively; he felt like the exact sum of his parts, no more, no less.

Is this him? Constable Weir asked.

Yes, Aldo said. That's the bastard.

An hour later we were in the Hollywood Hotel on Foster Street, talking about violent horror movies, the housing market, and our sex obsessions—torture porn, real estate porn, and porn porn—before Aldo began to ask me questions about Tess and our marital state; he was doing his amateur psychologist bit that he'd first developed to soften potential investors. I'd seen it a bazillion times. Using tactics gained from years of compulsively reading psychology, and wielding concepts that I'm not entirely certain he had a complete or even rudimentary grasp of, he would lean into someone's face and gently tug with his hypnotic, sibilant voice; he screwed up his eyes as if trying to see them through the fog of their complicated insecurities, which makes a person, I've noticed, strain to be clearer. Then he would lean back as if to give the subject space to knock down their own fortifications. He was pretty good at conferring the illusion of long-term friendship on a stranger, the way his gaze fixed on their pupils with such intensity. He even did this with me; I couldn't help feeling flattered by both his focus and what his focus illuminated: the subtle complexity of my own psyche.

"This isn't the life I planned for myself, but maybe that's what I like about it," I lied. But something about Aldo's single follow-up question, asked in a steady, uninflected voice ("How does Tess feel about your inability to complete a single work of writing?"), had me tearily confessing how her body used to be a standing invitation but now she had stopped allowing me to touch her breasts, which basically made them like fake pockets on a designer jacket, and how sometimes when she looked at me I felt I was being frowned upon by a tribe of elders, and how this marriage had become a bad trip I was going to have to ride out if I wanted to continue living with my daughter.

The problem perhaps was that Tess had undergone an unexpected blossoming of mind and spirit; the failed actress, ex-bartending punk, and occasional shoplifter that I married had now earned a social science degree and found a job with the office of the Public Guardian—essentially as a substitute decision-maker for people deemed to have insufficient cognitive capacity to make their own. All her clients had some kind of disability—acquired brain injury, drug- or alcohol-related memory impairment, intellectual dysfunction—and she made daily decisions about where they were to live, shifting dementia patients out of squalor into aged-care facilities, even deciding what medical treatment they should receive, most recently giving consent to an amputation for a retired bus driver who had refused it. Her passion for social work grew in direct proportion to my ambivalence for policing. In her presence I felt my deficiencies throb. Especially in the wake of that last, disastrous novel, my fizzled writing career was the elephant in every room of the house. Sure, I still had promise, but less of it, and more dribbled away each year. It seemed obvious that I should be doing the heavy lifting of Sonja rearing while Tess was allowed to flourish at her career, but I hadn't given in to her on that issue, and now we fought all the time, about whose parents were better grandparents to Sonja, about how best to discipline this fierce little wind of a girl, about who deserved the night out when babysitters were scarce, about anything. Tess was gnawing at the ties that bound us, and in terms of love, I felt like I was campaigning for my re-election, on the verge of being voted out by my single constituent, voted out of her heart by her head.

Aldo sipped his beer without taking his eyes off me. The lurking bartender took our empties and replaced them with fresh ones. I explained, almost sobbing now, that at first when I left for work, Tess would say, in a trembling voice, "Don't get shot," but as the years went by, that phrase had become imbued with its opposite meaning.

Aldo swished beer around his mouth before swallowing. He said, "Remembering the past is like watching a Hollywood movie, in that you never see the characters go to the toilet."

"What's that supposed to mean?"

He tore his coaster into little paper crumbs—and trotted out a few trenchant observations, "You're a frustrated artist in search of a consoling diagnosis, and it's interesting that the debilitating perfectionism that has torpedoed your professional writing career is completely absent in your relationship, which you expect to work entirely without your effort, as if a relationship has not only its own intelligence but its own will to live. Guess what, Liam? It doesn't." He then said that a person who won't abide reminiscence is someone who hates the present, and he also thought it was interesting I hadn't mentioned my fear that Tess had already found someone else (he was spot on—I suspected she had grown unreasonably close to the coworker in the fawn Windbreaker who dropped her home one time); he told me, in a tone I found uncharacteristically condescending, that "what you experience as emotional pain is only your *reaction* to the circumstance and you therefore bear a degree of responsibility for it." When I asked, "Has that comment ever actually helped anyone?" it was not clear by his shrug that it had.

Aldo, I could see, was in crisis mode himself; he was devastated by the shocking news of the wedding, and it was at long last dawning on him that he and Stella would never get back together, yet because his love had not diminished in any form, and was so thoroughly deflected by its intended recipient, it was in danger of growing into a kind of hate and he'd have no choice but to dissociate from his own heart, because loving her less "wasn't even a fucking option. And if you say, 'Don't worry you'll meet someone else,'" he warned quickly, "I'll fucking punch you in the throat." I said nothing. Slumped on our stools, taking in the beer-armpit-scented air, we were mutually inconsolable about our love situations. We were friends who now had one extra thing in common: We were both at the end of our rope. How did we get there so quickly? We'd not yet hit middle age. Why did we get such short ropes? Maybe fixating on our unachievable goals (Aldo's businesses, my writing) had somehow made us bystanders in our own love lives. Were we like hunter-gatherers returning to the cave each night empty-handed? Is that why our womenfolk had sought out better offers? While we were weeping about our unreturned love, the doors swung open and two young women in tight T-shirts and short shorts walked in flanking a breathtaking redhead, and though we both straightened our postures and endeavored to exude virility, it didn't lessen our losses. Aldo turned to me, and when he mimed a face contorted in lust he managed to pretty accurately express the oppressive helplessness of it; the last thing he wanted in this depressing moment was to be sexually aroused—it was a genuine nuisance.

The crowd thinned and the pub closed and we stood outside as a three-a.m. wind nearly took our heads off, like some curfew-enforcing act of God. Beside us, a handful of stragglers were trying to hail taxis that had just ended their shifts, the drivers refusing passengers who didn't live on their own exact street.

"OK then, I guess I'll see you later," Aldo said.

"OK then," I said.

We loved each other but good-byes were stubbornly awkward; I never really understood why; perhaps they were an expression of the disappointment of something left unsaid. No matter how open and honest we were, no matter how much we unburdened ourselves and admitted shameful secrets never before uttered aloud, we couldn't seem to depart fully satisfied with the transaction. We stood another long moment. I thought about Aldo's chronic fear of being alone. A frail half smile sat weirdly in his otherwise frowning face. He looked like he could break into laughter or tears.

"Do you remember when Stella couldn't go a full sixty seconds without touching me in some way?"

"It was annoying."

"She loved my smell."

"That makes one of us."

The wind abated and we shivered in the cold night's stillness, as Aldo launched into an unwelcome rambling monologue, which it was much too late in the evening for, about how Stella's kisses had felt one minute like she was violently cauterizing a wound, and the next like a feather-light brush of the lips that drove him crazy, and how she'd never once belittled him, except of course with her own merits and abilities, and now he had this horrible feeling that something bad was going to happen to him and he wouldn't be able to even get her on the phone. And did he mention that she was going to have a *Buddhist* wedding, though neither she nor Craig were strictly Buddhists? I smiled silently but it wasn't my real smile and he knew it.

"Anyway," he said, with a tinge of self-disgust, "I'm off!" We gave each other a sad hug and an extra squeeze as our mutual expression of regret. Aldo's keys jingled in his pocket, but I knew he never drunk-drove because of his fear of committing vehicular manslaughter. He set off at a dawdle and when he disappeared around the corner, leaving me in the empty street, I was struck with an overwhelming dread. Truth was, ever since high school, Stella had been the magnet that drew Aldo back to earth after he flew off onto dangerous tangents. In my case, when I'm feeling murderous and unhinged, it's anchoring to come home and see Tess and Sonja in a standoff or a cuddlefest or painting the toenails of our claw-footed bathtub. Aldo was going home every night as if he was a contaminated sample, to an apartment empty but for ferocious silences and his own potbellied shadow, with no one to refill the liquid soap dispenser or quiet his alarmist tendencies or take minutes or second motions or bounce ideas off or egg him on or talk him down—and until he was ready for bed he would often sit in his Poäng birch-veneer Ikea armchair for hours, feeling like an unaccompanied minor on a long-haul flight.

IV

Six months after that, my phone rang just as a young shoplifter, in an attempt to extricate himself from my handcuffs, had gotten in a tangle in my backseat while a proliferation of nosy citizens had risen in a unified spasm and were circling me with their phone cameras and mortal hatred. It was Stella on the line, her voice dripping with the old dislike, as if she were gazing ruefully at a photograph of me as she spoke. Aldo had assaulted her at the wedding, she said, before drinking himself into a coma.

I was speechless. It *was* entirely plausible that Aldo might try drinking himself to death at her ceremony simply to cast a black omen over her marriage, but would he have *physically* assaulted her? True, Aldo was already a well-known parasite and failure, had declared multiple bankruptcies, and was the kind of man you might come across sharing cigarettes in an alleyway with a masturbating hobo, but he certainly wasn't violent.

"Craig thinks I should take out an AVO," she said, as if Aldo were one of those acid-throwing jealous exes who seek to disfigure what they cannot have.

"You really think that's necessary?" I asked.

"Listen to me very carefully, Liam," she said, in a flat, unfocused voice—I suspected she was browsing the internet while talking to me—"*You're* his friend. *You* deal with him," and hung up. So what could I do but ride grudgingly to the rescue once more? I opened the car door and liberated the shoplifter from the handcuffs and took a stance that gave the crowd just the slightest hint of imminent arrests. In return, they gave me mock salutes and *heil* Hitlers. It was infuriating, but I couldn't give them the finger if I didn't want to see it on YouTube.

In the hospital room, Aldo lay flat on his back in perfect stillness, sheets firmly tucked to his chin as if the person who'd made the bed was unaware he was still in it. He looked full of oversized fears, like a ship in a bottle, in that you wondered how he squeezed them all in there. The room was suffused with a buttery light. Leaning against the window alcove, transfixed by his phone, was a short, middle-aged man with a boyish face, and on his head the answer to the age-old question of what happens to curly hair when it thins.

"This isn't it," Aldo said with fragility, as if the words were on a string he could pull back into his mouth at will.

"Good to hear," I said.

He meant this wasn't the thing he wouldn't recover from, the dividing, before-and-after event that transforms lives. I weathered the uncomfortable angle required to embrace him and noticed he was insufficiently bandaged around the neck, so that the edges of nasty lacerations were visible.

"I fell on a fork," he said.

"Cake fork nicked his jugular," the small man in the corner said, laughing, without looking up. "There was a lot of blood, which didn't make the wedding cake any more appetizing."

"Who has a carrot cake for their wedding anyway?" Aldo asked.

The image of blood-soaked carrot cake floated before my eyes. "Give me the highlights."

Aldo made a grunting show of sitting upright. "The *special* day," he said. "Let me tell you. Her celebrant looked tolerant. Too tolerant. In fact, he exuded an exasperating degree of tolerance, as if, in addition to Buddhist and Hindu weddings, he performed KKK and Taliban weddings." The man in the corner guffawed. Aldo described the whole event: rooftop ceremony amid a shitload of tropical plants, him wedged between burly female cousins as the passive-aggressive groom and kite-strung bride lit candles and incense at the foot of a shrine to Buddha and shat something out of their mouths about the fastidious discharging of marital responsibilities. A couple of incoherent blessings later, Craig got up to say that he was compelled by the inadequacy of language to understate his feelings, then Stella's uncle Howard made a speech that began as a nod to his hero L. Ron Hubbard but ended as a single long perverse sentence that made obscure references to a camping trip that had as its denouement an exploding toilet, while Aldo got progressively shitfaced and kissed an aunt with a face like aged pork, and at some point made an uninvited wedding toast.

"That was generous of you. Making a speech."

"Here."

Aldo handed me his phone. Someone had been kind enough to video it and send him a copy. On screen, the shaky image of Aldo stumbling up to the bridal table and snatching a champagne flute out of the groom's hand. "So, a Buddhist wedding! How unintentionally hilarious, considering the Buddha was a guy who abandoned his wife and child to do his own thing. Actually, don't tell anyone but *I* think *they* think the central tenet of Buddhist philosophy is that a lack of ambition is a shortcut to enlightenment. And *if*, according to the orthodoxy, the goal of life is nonexistence, then isn't it an act of mind-blowing hypocrisy and unnecessary cruelty, at the least, for Buddhists to have children? It seems Stella and Craig have misunderstood the idea of *the god within* to mean that they themselves are God-like. Not that they need draw on this inner power or expect miracles from their own core. It's just a nice feeling to be God, that's all. So let us all toast this infuriating couple by raising our glasses to this tired brand of cheap, self-aggrandizing pseudospiritualism! To Craig and Stella! If they ever live long enough to see their souls reborn into nonexistence, they'd shit themselves for never and never. Amen."

At which point, the obviously shattered Aldo tumbles off the podium. I handed him back his phone. "A mean-spirited, anti-Buddhist wedding toast, then."

"It was," the small man in the corner said, still without raising his eyes from his texting. "At the culmination of which, Aldo kissed several bare shoulders, accidentally hit the bride in the face, and collapsed under the drinks table, whereupon he drank his arse into a state so near death that he was rushed to hospital to have his stomach pumped."

"Doc Castle's my personal physician."

"The hell I am. I'm a doctor. Just not his. I'm more of a friend. Gary." Doc Castle extended his hand.

"Liam Wilder," I said.

"I've heard a lot about you, Officer," he said suggestively, as if he'd browsed a glossy catalog of my core life errors that very morning.

"Doc was my plus-one," Aldo said. "I would've asked you, but you were on the list of definitely-nots."

"Hell of an event," Doc Castle said. "She'll not forget that day too soon."

I looked hard at Aldo. "Did you try to kill yourself?"

"Why is he talking about suicide?" Doc Castle asked. "Just drank too much, didn't you?"

Aldo fell back into silence, thinking his memories into a fine dust, before he blithely threw off the bedcovers, exposing his pale body.

"What are you doing?"

"Getting the fuck out of here."

He climbed out of bed and wobbled on his feet and began to dress in his befouled wedding attire. While he looked under the bed for a shoe I had a premonition of déjà vu, not that we'd done this before, but that we'd do it again in the future.

"Should I go over and apologize to Stella?"

I had to break it to him. "She's taking out a restraining order against you."

Aldo bit his lip and sighed. "You can't ruin someone's wedding without paying for it the rest of your life. I get that."

"And this might not be the time to mention it, but she rang me about an hour ago," Doc Castle said. "You better pay her the thirty-five thousand dollars you owe her."

Aldo's body grew slightly hunched; he stood for almost an entire ghastly minute, during which I couldn't come up with a single consoling thought. Half in, half out of his clothes, he'd been drained of the will to dress.

I asked, "Aldo, want to stay with me a few days?"

"No. Just drop me home."

"Can I have a lift too?" Doc Castle asked, finally looking me in the face. His bored eyes were an arresting blue. "My wife took my car home."

"No problem."

Aldo wore a fogged expression as we moved down the silent corridor.

Passing the nurses' station, its desk strewn with files, Aldo suddenly seized my arm for leverage and jumped the counter. Oh crap, I thought. He flipped through the files until he came across his own. "Hey, don't go there!" An irate nurse at the end of the corridor was striding over. Doc Castle snickered. Aldo said, "Stall her," and I said, "Nothing doing." She yelled, "Officer! Officer!" as she barreled toward us, and when she reached Aldo he dummied right, a move she anticipated; she grabbed his shirt, he held the file beyond her reach. The bizarre choreography of their battle went on for another torturous minute.

"This is against hospital policy!"

"It's my file!"

Two men in gowns and slippers looked on. The nurse at last grabbed hold of the corner of the file, but Aldo wouldn't let go.

"You can have it," she said, struggling, "but you need to put in a request . . . in . . . writing."

"That . . . makes . . . no . . . sense."

The doctor and I watched on—it wasn't an unamusing spectacle—but the problem with being an officer of the law is that everyone expects you to intervene. A gathering crowd of onlookers now nudged me with their elbows.

"Aldo, cut it out," I said.

He let go all at once and the nurse tumbled back against the desk, file clutched to her colossal breasts. Condescension looked like it had been built into her face at conception.

"I'll get you that request," Aldo said calmly as we left, and the three of us slid into a mercifully awaiting elevator just before the doors shut.

In the car, Aldo asked Doc Castle a barrage of questions about his marital problems. Did his wife forgive him? Had he forgiven himself? How much had their daughter seen and did he think she would remember it? Aldo listened to the answers with his usual peculiar intensity. I tuned out. I didn't feel like hearing my friend's analysis of this doctor's creepy marital strife and I felt, in fact, a weak sort of outrage that grew in intensity until we arrived outside Aldo's apartment complex, Phoenix Court, a five-story redbrick horror with cement balconies that all had underpants drying on metal railings.

Aldo had moved into this building three years before, the year friends could not stop telling him he had reached the age of Christ's death. ('Fucking odd thing to say to someone," he said to me at the time. "What are they implying?")

His apartment was on the first floor, right above a butcher shop, and the knowledge that only floorboards and a couple of meters of putrid air lay between him and all those red-veined carcasses swinging on hooks made him fearful that he'd be visited by the ghosts of cows and lambs and chickens, and be woken intermittently in the night by an eerie moo. That, and the bad ventilation, and an undefeatable cockroach army, and surprise visits from the overbearing landlord, and the more or less constant sounds of wife beating drifting in from any number of adjacent apartments seemed to guarantee him, night after night, a steady stream of gruesome nightmares. One thing I knew about Aldo: He always despised dreams, even pleasant ones, for what he considered their tedious impenetrability and their shocking waste of creativity. He hated how every morning he had no option other than to open his eyes and remember. What was it this time? A faceless man? His dead sister, Veronica, scratching at an enormous red door? Regular dreams featured his cadaverous grandmother leaning against a tree with her oxygen tank, or his mother's island slipping into the sea, or else he was marching into a river with a broken piano on his back. "God, how the human brain goes on," he said once. "It's nearly impossible to not wake up embarrassed by the trite symbolism you've subjected yourself to during the night."

Aldo climbed out of the car and pushed his head through the open window and said, "Every time I return home I've forgotten how shit this area is. Do you think the people who live in this neighborhood have moved *up* in the world? I mean, Jesus, where were they *before*?"

"In hell," I said.

He laughed, and we watched him disappear into the building. What now? I could feel Doc Castle looking intently at me. "I don't suppose you're hungry, Constable?"

We drove to Woolloomooloo, to Harry's Café de Wheels, and sat on the wharf eating chunky beef pies with buttered mash and staring out at the impossibly blue sky and dark water, a doctor and a policeman, two urban professionals with apparently not a single thing to say to each other. Eventually we found the area where our working lives intersected: the overprescription of drugs that was hiking up the crime rate, with most break-and-enters being done specifically to ransack medicine cabinets—oxycodone, Vicodin, and Xanax were the most common prizes. And when that topic ran its course, the conversation turned quickly to where it was always destined to go.

"Quite a character, that Aldo," Doc Castle said.

His understatement was tinged with amazement; he genuinely didn't get exactly why he dropped everything to help our annoying, unfortunate mutual friend. "It's rare to get so attached to another human being in adulthood," the doctor mused. They'd met at a game of touch football about eight years ago, he explained, and they'd been friends ever since.

"Just don't lend him any money," I said.

"Too late for that, I'm afraid." It turned out the doctor had invested heavily in High Steaks, Aldo's defunct restaurant. "There is another level to our friendship, of course," Doc Castle said darkly. "At first he'd ask for advice or assistance, and then if I wouldn't mind scribbling a little prescription . . ."

Indeed, that confirmed my suspicions about their relationship; it was a mirror of my own. Just as often as Aldo needed my legal assistance, he called the doctor for medical assistance; when he required bailing out he called me; when he needed patching up he called Doc Castle. What I confirmed that day: I wasn't the only one on his speed dial, and Aldo's obsession with his body rivaled his fear of the law. He called Doc Castle for back spasms and sudden immobility, when he'd cut himself with a Stanley knife, for emergency tetanus shots, for burns, when he'd splashed boiling water on his hand or picked up metal pots by the handles, for concussions, for a deafness-inducing buildup of wax in the ear, when he was beaten up by disgruntled investors, to remove a piece of glass from his face (after a pub fight, or slamming the car brakes so that skis went through the front windshield, or falling drunkenly through a glass shower screen); he called him for a vast array of STD fears—warts, lumps, rashes, burning with urination—for fainting in other doctors' offices, for lacerations and broken bones and bruises and sprains after falling off ladders and down staircases, for cysts that needed to be removed, and for food poisoning and suspected food poisoning. Aldo called on Doc Castle to prove or disprove his own self-diagnoses, and to get emergency appointments with dermatologists, gastroenterologists, radiologists, podiatrists, and to book him in or bump him up on waiting lists for CT scans, MRIs, and the like. "Ever since he was a child," Doc Castle said, "he's been afraid of internal bleeding."

"I know!"

"He can't recall the exact TV show he saw it on, but from his childhood onward, whenever he's fallen, he's been convinced he has internal bleeding.

That's the first thing he asks. 'Doc, do I have internal bleeding? Do I? Am I bleeding internally?' Or else it's stitches. He always fears he needs stitches. 'Do I need stitches? Does it need stitches?' Doc Castle seemed particularly amused that we were *both* almost constantly on call, bailing out, rescuing, bandaging, advising, stitching, extricating, inoculating, disentangling. The tone of the conversation was jovial—we laughed about the absurdity of being conscripted as unwitting members of this fool's entourage—but still, my mood began to darken. This idea that there was something special about Aldo carried within it the implication that there was nothing special about us.

To break out of the conversation, I said I needed to make a quick call, and dialed my own number and heard my own voice asking me to leave a message. I whispered, "You're no good," and when I hung up and turned back Doc Castle was still laughing about Aldo. I laughed too, but I didn't feel it. I genuinely loved and pitied my old friend but there was no reason at all why his suffering should eclipse my own, I thought somewhat bitterly, or that, quite frankly, he was a special case in any way.

<h2 style="text-align:center">V</h2>

Not two weeks later, around five p.m., my mobile rang. It was one of those days: Every driver I random breath-tested exhibited suspicious behavior, smiling ferociously or flicking cigarette ash into their laps or making lewd eye contact as they wrapped their cracked lips on the tube and blew, or twitching with restrained violence or staring fixedly ahead or talking gibberish and acting disoriented, surprised to even find themselves driving, as if they were certain they'd left the house on foot.

"Constable Wilder?"

"Speaking."

"This is Detective Garnick, drug squad. We met at the trial of Norman Lester. I don't know if you remember."

"Of course. How's your eye?"

"I look like a fucking Chinaman."

"Can I do something for you, Detective?"

"This is just a courtesy call to let you know I've arrested a vet for selling Nembutal at the Montefiore, the Jewish retirement home down Gladesville way."

"Well done, you."

"It's a euthanasia drug. Also used to kill horses."

"And that's relevant to me because . . . ?"

"Aldo Benjamin's your mate, isn't he?"

My heart tightened, a palpable dread. What now?

"We got a list of clients. It seems your boy bought himself two bottles last week."

Nembutal?

Was Aldo finally going to do it? Ever obsessed with taking his own life, something that could be traced back to his father's suicide, had he succumbed to the cumulative effects of his long string of professional failures and the permanent loss of Stella? Was this his ultimate dramatic suspension of judgment? Had he decided to listen to the voices in his head, always with the bad advice?

I thanked the detective and hung up. The cars came in an endless stream, the whoosh and screech of traffic in my ears grew louder, and everyone was over the limit—everyone!—and for hours I booked citizen after citizen after citizen, feeling like the last sober man in a crazed nation that ran on booze. In every remorseful driver I saw Aldo's suicide, the agony of him second-guessing himself too late, and I was afraid I wouldn't catch him in time, that I'd walk in to see him flapping like a fish on the deck of a boat. These thoughts made me whimper, tear up, knowing Aldo's abject terror of physical pain. Yet for some reason I can't account for, I waited until nine p.m., after my shift, to drive over to Phoenix Court. There was a proliferation of abandoned mattresses on the rain-slicked footpath and every parked car seemed to have its own gang of youths perched on its hood.

Even from the elevator, thumping music could be heard that, as it turned out, was coming from Aldo's apartment. A party was in progress and I felt the vague sting of the uninvited as I made my way inside to see guests drinking, upper-torso dancing, and loud-talking over the music. Thin traces of cocaine were on the glass coffee table, next to bowls of guacamole brown at the edges. The heavy smell of hydroponic pot. There was something perfectly ordinary and yet unaccountably strange about this party, something I couldn't put my finger on. Aldo was standing by the flat-screen television with glitter on his face, chatting to a pale, scarfed woman with a theatrical voice that carried across the smoky room. "And I wasn't thinking," I heard her say, "so I accidentally signed my porn name." He hadn't seen me, so I started surreptitiously checking in cupboards for the Nembutal while reassuring guests either visibly spooked at the sight of my uniform or overly excited, mistaking me for a male stripper. As I mingled, it dawned on me, the source of the weirdness: about every third guest I encountered was sick in some way. I spoke to a double amputee, a woman with an incurable liver disease, a recent testicular cancer survivor, gaseous men and women who smelled like the slick coating on vitamins, people who had wasted legs or moony faces or who seemed to have been born into their dotage. Something implausible was going on. People who needed emergency molly-coddling skittered around the party discussing various treatments, the efficacy of this drug over that, superbacteria horror stories. They were all prototypes of a human being in God's workshop—strictly first drafts.

I marched over to Aldo, interrupting him mid conversation.

"Hey, I know this is going to sound fantastically insensitive," I said, "but seriously, Aldo, what kind of bullshit friends are these? They're all sick. How can they *all* be sick? I mean, two is a coincidence. Three's a pattern, but still within the realm of probability. But four? Five? Ten terminally ill pals? What gives?"

He didn't seem surprised to see me. "I run in different circles. You know that."

I did know that. Aldo lived in a way that often got me reevaluating my own modus operandi—lie low and keep out of people's way. Aldo had weed friends, binge-drinking friends, Spanish-class friends, indoor-soccer friends, science-geek friends, hipster friends, vaguely criminal friends, business friends, school friends, old friends, new friends—now sick friends—he was an indiscriminate friendmaker, often caught in a freak friendstorm. Aldo had a thousand confidants, a thousand allies who frequently, depending on their level of financial investment, became a thousand enemies.

"I need to talk to you."

"Come into my bedroom," he said, leading me into his monastic yet untidy room at the end of the hall. One lamp, broken. One double bed, unmade. One apple core on bedside table atop a stack of psychology textbooks. One chair covered in an avalanche of underpants and T-shirts. One couple dry-humping on the bed.

"Let's try the balcony."

Out there the air was brittle and cold. Over the Navy Yard, where three gargantuan vessels were anchored, storm clouds formed. To the south, fireworks and a shifting curtain of smoke.

"Where is it?" I asked, at the same time as he exclaimed, "Stella's pregnant!"

It took me a moment to register. "With her husband's baby?"

"Jesus. Why do you have to say it like that?"

Inside someone switched tracks from Radiohead to Stevie Wonder. Aldo tightened his frown and leaned into me.

"Where's what?" he asked.

"I heard you bought Nembutal from a vet."

He flashed a smile as if from inside a raincoat. "So?"

"Nembutal, Aldo. The suicide drug."

"So? So? So?"

I got annoyed now. "So why don't you just put a pistol in your mouth? Why are you sneaking around buying vet medicine? You do know that Nembutal is horse poison, right?"

Aldo stubbed his cigarette out on the frosted glass of the circular table and said, "Of course I know. You think I want human poison? You'd have to pour yourself *literally buckets* of human poison just so you can reach the point where you can say: This is enough to kill a horse. So why not go straight for the actual horse poison and consume less?"

All of a sudden I wished this were some artificial reality from which I would eventually be unplugged.

A throat cleared theatrically. Doc Castle came out onto the balcony lighting a spliff, followed by three other men who moved in a confident, guileless manner that suggested divorced fathers with new girlfriends, or content homeowners who had just paid off their mortgages that very morning. Aldo made the introductions. Jeremy Samuels, lawyer. Evan Pascall, dentist. Graeme Frost, accountant. I stood there letting my face go slack. Aldo Benjamin, snake! He'd built personal connections with the full suite of professional services for his stupid human life where emergencies came with bizarre regularity. He was at home on the edge of hysteria, where he lived his open secret: that he was a disaster waiting to happen, or a disaster that had just happened, or a disaster that was currently happening. This methodical gathering of human fire hoses was shameless. I felt used and was overwhelmed with disgust to find myself face-to-face with these friendships that were all ugly mirrors of my own. I thought:

Enough's enough. I would no longer offer myself as parachute, chaperone, or soft landing for this guy; I didn't care how far back our friendship went, how much history we shared. I was sick of being obliging. Aldo had now spent all his friendship tokens, and unless he had some ingenious scheme to get a fresh supply, we were fucking done.

I snatched the joint out of Doc Castle's hand and tossed it over the balcony. "You know what I've just realized, Aldo? I've had enough of you."

Aldo blinked, and Doc Castle and the rest of the professionals awkwardly edged backward as I went on a verbal rampage about how Aldo and I might have been genuine friends in the past but he had been using me for years. I even repeated Tess's fear that Aldo's most toxic, corrupting influence was not on my behavior, but on my destiny, and now I feared she was right; there was something contagious about his shit luck, and in his orbit one had a tendency to give oneself bad advice. It started to drizzle, affording the spectators the perfect excuse to return inside. Aldo hadn't moved; his head was cocked and he wore a strange sad smile, a practiced smile, as if he'd heard this speech before from others. Maybe he had.

"I know I'm a pain," he said. We stared silently at each other. A pulsing light from the nearby telecommunications tower went off. That seemed to be my cue. I stormed inside.

"Liam, wait," Aldo said as I tramped through the party into his bedroom, where I ejected the copulating couple and turned over magazines, tossed self-actualization tomes and dry psychology textbooks to the floor, methodically ransacked his cupboards, swung my arm in a loose arc underneath his bed, gathering socks and T-shirts and shoes I'll bet Aldo assumed he'd lost. His guests gathered at the doorway to make snarky asides and take photographs on their phones, but I doubted they could perceive the tendrils of Aldo's psyche twined around mine. They certainly couldn't have caught all the nuances of intimacy I felt while touching his things, nor seen the angry tears in my eyes. This was a friendship of nearly twenty years I was throwing away here. I rifled through his drawers, charged by the spasms of rage I'd ceded control to, and aware of the frightening effect an armed uniformed maniac must be having on spectators. It was in a white Nike sport sock that I found it: an opaque bottle with a stopper and an acrid odor rising out of it. I went into the kitchen, waved it in the air in prosecutorial triumph at Aldo, who didn't respond in any visible way. My plan was to pour it down the sink, but Aldo's non-reaction forced a melodramatic act; I smashed it on the kitchen tiles, and almost immediately the cat went to lick it up. I removed the cat, found a mop, and cleaned up the Nembutal before the animal could get to it and die violently in front of the whole party. Aldo watched all this with a compelling look of genuine, haunted sadness. I had robbed him of his last resort, seized his suicide from his actual hands. I thought: One man's tragedy averted is another man's fantasy deferred. I wrapped the broken glass in newspaper and stepped into the cold hallway without a word.

VI

For several months I took a well-deserved hiatus from my old friend, stopped returning his messages, resisted the temptation to call, slid the idea of him into a compartment with a hidden bottom. On Sonja's eighth birthday he sent a musical-ballerina jewelry box; that it was his first gift since her christening only exacerbated my annoyance and strengthened my resolve. At the same time I stopped writing. Outnumbered by bad ideas, I tossed it in, and this new commitment to personal and artistic failure somehow felt in concert with my sad abandonment of my hopeless friend. Once I almost weakened: his histrionic voice on my answering machine sounded like it came from the inside of a metal pipe, whispering harshly and cryptically about deep trouble. Sonja was playing on the floor next to me, a formidable punk princess sporting a pink tiara, her eyes smeared with her mother's mascara; she looked scared at the sound of Aldo's voice. It was a tough decision, but I deleted that message. Another afternoon, Stella telephoned to tell me she wanted to try to force Aldo to get an ordinary job to pay her back the money he owed, and couldn't I talk sense into him?

"Trying to make it rich after all these years is frankly stupid," she said.

It was an inoffensive request, but I didn't feel obliging. I said, "*You're* his ex-wife. *You* deal with him."

As the months of radio silence went by, I felt the gravitational pull of our friendship waning. The break started to feel irrevocable. Occasionally I'd wake with an ineffable sadness; there was no one in whom I could confide in the same way. I even missed Aldo's irritating habit of not understanding me on the phone ("Are you chewing?" he'd say. "What's that over your mouth, an oven mitt?"), and the times he'd call to ask my opinion on some random question (e.g., "Hey, do animals rape interspecies? I mean, a giraffe isn't going to try and fuck a swan, is he?"). Sometimes I'd be reminded of him by a simple object—guitar picks (he used to carry them for Stella) or black gloves (which reminded him of strangulation)—and of course I'd think of him whenever I drove by hospitals or medical centers or saw a GOING OUT OF BUSINESS sign, or when I had to fish an insolvent entrepreneur out of his own swimming pool. The strange thing was that in all that time we never even bumped into each other. As I drove past the Hollywood Hotel, or was arresting a hash dealer within a few blocks' radius of Phoenix Court, I'd keep one eye on the pedestrians in my periphery, but they were never him. Maybe he'd gone back to China or India or Dubai, to pursue some doomed idea to its dismal conclusion.

In any case, life without Aldo was OK. People shed friends all the time—why couldn't I? Besides, with his arduous existence excised, I could focus solely on my own demoralizing problems: I was under investigation for misplacing my gun; haunting my daymares were the mangled faces of an eight-year-old boy and his mother, crushed in the backseat in a car accident I had responded to; my marital discord had plateaued at a constant fever pitch; and Sonja had started displaying increasingly aggressive behavior. Always quick to hysterical anger, she'd sometimes sucker punch me when I kissed her; now, to our horror, she had started biting people, and other than muzzling her, we didn't know what to do. These were dark days that seemed meaningless and unending, and I could barely manage to get up in the morning.

Turned out, I was wrong about one thing: Tess and I hadn't plateaued at all. Our marriage evaporated almost instantaneously when I called home during a night shift to say good night to Sonja. She answered the phone with a delightful, high-pitched "Daddy!" and I told her a brief, sanitized version of my day's misadventures, after which she reciprocated with her own and then suddenly broke into a horrible adult laugh. *It was Tess, pretending.* "You can't even tell your wife from your eight-year-old daughter. Pathetic!" she laughed. This so humiliated and destabilized me, every ounce of love for her rushed out of me in one slick whoosh, and not until later that night, in the bleak surroundings of the Marco Polo Motor Inn on Parramatta Road, did a sort of bright side occur to me. That was a pretty juicy scene, I realized, and sat up writing until two in the morning. Unfortunately my brain made its usual pilgrimage to the mysteri-ous land where language dies. My imagination was impenetrably dark, boarded up. The ideas remained inexpressible, penumbral. I had linguistic thrombo-sis, my textual flow impeded by the narrowing of some creative vessel. I sat simpering at the desk, and thought: You fucker, you failed to cannibalize drug deals, corruption, murdered nurses, domestic disputes, drowned children, hit-and-runs, and now you can't even fashion a decent story out of your wife's sa-dism. You're done. I poured 330 milliliters of Heineken on the keyboard until the screen went green. I had been dodging success with drone-like precision for nearly two decades. That's it, I concluded. It's finished. Seems persistence wasn't the key after all.

Two months or so later, I had kept to my word. Although at times I felt a fraud, I had settled into a life I'd always feared yet secretly desired, a life unin-terpreted and unencumbered by art. To that end, I had got on with the job of being a competent officer of the law. I moved out of the motel and into a ware-house apartment on Kippax Street where Sonja stayed every second weekend. I read teenage vampire romances that would not inspire me to pick up a pen. I acted on sexual impulses with the kind of menopausal, unhappily married, horny strangers our pornography culture had turned me on to. In other words, I was doing OK.

Until the afternoon Senior Constable Ronnie Grant came over with a tired uncertainty and sat on my desk reeking of every disliked great-uncle from childhood. He picked up the picture of Sonja and contemplated it in a lurid fashion. I snatched the photograph back off him.

"You're wanted down at Surry Hills," he said.

"What for?"

"Your boy Benjamin."

I couldn't even muster a sigh. To my surprise, I experienced no deeper con-cern than the interruption of my workflow. I felt pleasantly anesthetized, or as if a wound had been expertly cauterized. Not even a feeling of déjà vu, nothing. Whatever Aldo had done didn't pertain to me in any way. "Leave me out of it."

"You sure?"

"Positive."

He gave me a bleary shrug and shuffled back to his desk. For ten minutes, I got on with finishing an evidence seizure report: *four knives, each with titanium*

4 centimeter blades; two transparent bags with traces of brown powder, possibly heroin; one mobile phone, Nokia. On the radio, the prime minister campaigned for re-election saying, "I'm just an ordinary bloke, and I want to do things for ordinary working-class families," and the opposition leader responded by saying he was just "an ordinary Australian who represented other ordinary Australians." I sighed, felt the cold snout of duty pushing the back of my neck. Five minutes later I was agitated beyond belief. What had Aldo done now? I fast-walked over to Senior Constable Ronnie Grant's desk, where he was the monosyllabic half of a telephone conversation; I stood for an agonizing twelve minutes until he finished his call.

"What's the charge?"

"Attempted murder."

A jet stream of ice entered my body.

"Was it Stella?"

"No," he said, glancing at the Post-it note on his desk. "Clive Gibson."

"Who the fuck is that?"

"Dunno. Clive Warren Gibson. Aged three days."

Three days? It couldn't be. "Stella's baby?"

"I don't know these people you're talking about."

I slunk furtively to the stairs, took two at a time until I reached the roof and almost leaped into the clear blue air. It was incomprehensible that he'd ever harm anyone, let alone a baby. I'd seen him knock the cigarette out of a pregnant woman's hand on the street. Unless.

From the rooftop I looked out with disdain at an exhausted city masking its exhaustion in a display of vitality: the backed-up traffic, businesssapiens (Aldo's word) hastening in the shadowed streets. On the building opposite, an Australian flag flapped in the wind. Why bother with flags? We know what country this is: It's the stupid place where twenty-plus million people boast about being ordinary.

On the way into Surry Hills station, a shirtless man with a bloodied face tried headbutting me. Everyone has potential for uncontrollable rages. I'd seen Aldo's customary impotent explosions against corporations, injustice, God, banks, government, greed, and ineptitude, but was I to believe that all his liberated demons had mobilized and marched on Stella's newborn? No, it was some absurd misunderstanding. Unless. Unless.

The desk sergeant eating a kebab nodded hello.

"I've come to see Aldo Benjamin," I announced.

Behind him, a senior detective with a harangued face and mirrored sunglasses pushed up on his head waved me over.

"Constable Liam Wilder?"

"Yes."

"Name's Doyle. Your mate's charged with attempted infanticide."

"It's a mistake."

Doyle made his eyes sigh—I'd never seen that before. "He had a note in his pocket."

"A confession?"

"Not exactly. Here."

He handed me a note in a plastic envelope. It read:

Dear Lord, when Fate jiggles her wet finger in my ear like a little sister, and I knock over jars of girlfriends' grandmothers' ashes and tip over scaffolding I am attempting to scale, when bicyclists clip me in passing and friends' pets die on my watch, what the fuck, you old Dog? I mean, it's hard not to take the spontaneous tumbling of shop displays the wrong way!

P.T.O.

On the other side was written:

Why, O Lord, is it my role in this life to be not just the falling clown, but the falling clown who other falling clowns fall on? In other words, how the fuck is an old lady grabbing onto my arm as she trips in a supermarket characteristic of ME?

(Amen)
Aldo Benjamin

I thought: Aldo, my poor, sad-lucked, kind-hearted fucked-up friend, this desperate and pitiful plea to a God he didn't believe in must really be the end of the line. I fought back angry tears and berated myself: What kind of friend had I been? I never helped him avert a single disaster. My desire to protect him had always come to nothing.

This train of thought was suddenly derailed by an unexpected event. That absurd prayer set it off: Nabokov's throb, Nietzsche's rapture of tremendous tension, Shelley's inconstant wind, Jarrell's lightning strike, Hazlitt's mighty ferment, Lorca's duende, Dickinson's soul at the white heat, Morrell's deadbeat dad (*who comes through when you least expect it, then disappears when you begin to count on him*), i.e., Inspiration. The idea that compels you to create with the urgency of flushing drugs down the toilet as the police are breaking down your door, or with the adrenaline that comes with stuffing a body into the boot of a car before the CCTV swivels back in your direction. I stood there immobile. The idea was spreading through my body like whiskey. A hodgepodge of passages from *Artist Within, Artist Without* swam in my head: . . . *you are in the business of immensities . . . precision is the next best thing to silence . . . only when you have lassoed multiplicity will there be nothing to add . . . write what knows you . . . to discover the point of your uselessness . . . above all, find your natural subject.*

And I had! The last cigarette shaken out of the soft pack of ideas: My sad old friend, who I'd met in 1990—a two-decade gestation period. Other people were mere vapor to me, but I knew *his* inadequacies by heart. No facile invention necessary; I'd give readers the realest person I knew. Of course, his life was anything other than "the way we live now." Nobody lives like him and lives to tell the tale. I'd tell his tale! I'd curate an exhibition of his foibles and follies. I felt luminous, intrepid, like a correspondent embedded in hell. I was going to make my report. Finally! My natural subject.

"You OK?"

I stood blinking at Aldo's note, trying to memorize it, eyeing the photocopier under the bulletin board in the adjoining alcove.

"Constable? What do you make of it?"

I'll tell you what I'll make of it! Insomuch as a friend is an exploitable resource, and since I can't, it seems, help him anyway, I'll mine Aldo for everything he is, and write about all the terrible things that have happened to him, a small, inoffensive human being who can't catch a break, and how he is somehow complicit in the worldly and supernatural crimes perpetrated against him.

Preliminary title: *Woe is He*. Or *Jokers of the Fall*. Or *Between the Water and the Clay*.

"Do you mind giving me a moment?"

I went to the men's room; the reflection of my rapacious face was jarring. My inner voice's faint excited whisper: *This is it. This is it.* Was this it? Was I sure? Morrell says: *Muses lay traps and conjure mirages.* On the other hand: *Some women you have to bed before you can reject them.* OK, I know Aldo told me untold things in absolute confidence but this was *minimal* compensation, the *least* I could recoup for my efforts. Besides, his life could *benefit* from close reading. The unexamined life is not worth living, as Socrates said, so I would examine it for him. Who else but a best friend could do that?

I opened my notebook and with hardly a moment's thought or hesitation, I wrote: *The weird truth is I've often become good friends with people I originally disliked, and the more I downright loathed the person, the better friends we eventually became. This is certainly true of Aldo Benjamin, who irritated me at first, then infuriated me, then made me sick, then bored me senseless, which led to his most unforgivable crime—occasionally, when in the process of boring me, he'd become self-aware and apologize for being boring.* "No no," I'd have to say, feigning shock at the suggestion, *"you're not boring me, please go on." I sometimes had to plead for Aldo to continue to bore me.*

I stared at that paragraph, and allowed myself a brief shiver of admiration for having expressed something true. The pen was still wriggling in my hand. I had more to say, much more. I closed my eyes and contemplated the daunting task ahead. To write this story would automatically throw me into a head-on collision with the meaning of fate, humanity's, sure, but Aldo's strange specific one too, for I could finally admit what I always knew to be true: He *is* unique, he who seems hell-bent on falling into the same river not twice but innumerable times.

And I could unravel, permeate, explain him.

Senior Detective Doyle gazed at me with a cool, suspicious eye when I came to his desk and asked to personally conduct the interview. Everything about me had become sinister, and he spotted that. "Your mate's having a manic episode," he drawled, as if being manic was evidence of his guilt.

"I will get him to speak," I said, and Doyle looked baffled and annoyed.

"You're not hearing me. He's *already* speaking, Constable." Doyle again made references to a manic episode; Aldo was either coked up or on methamphetamines or simply out of his mind. Yes, he *was* talking, he repeated, but not about the crime per se, this wasn't a confession, and he wasn't saying anything incriminating, though what he was saying was certainly very disturbing, and Doyle had left Sergeant Oakes in there to keep an eye on him. "In any case, Mr. Benjamin has been specifically asking for you to be present for the interview," he said with a light snarl.

"Thanks for mentioning it," I responded, then moved briskly to the interview room, as if all the nation's novelists were hurrying to beat me to it.

I entered to see Aldo, greyhound-thin, gripping the undersides of his chair as if he and the chair were hurtling through space. His hair was wet and combed back and looked like a kind of mold, and he was emitting an uneasy vigor and chattering like a small mob, explaining how he was ashamed of his long-held desire to see a mounted policeman thrown by his own horse. He turned away from Sergeant Oakes to give me a furtive hand gesture that looked like an aborted thumbs-up, but his eyes only lingered on my face long enough to convey vague disappointment, as if for a split second he thought I was coming in to tell him his bath was ready. Though the room was ice cold, and Aldo was in short sleeves, his face was sheened with sweat. Now he was saying he was tired of thoughts so self-pitying he believed he could hear God throw up in His mouth.

Sergeant Oakes busted out a nervous laugh. Talk about your captive audience; Aldo knew we *had* to listen to everything he said in case it could be held against him in a court of law. He was disgusted at all the horrible pretend laughing he'd done in his life, he said now, and was upset that he could derive pleasure only from the sight of the dogs of two introverts attacking each other in the street. Whether he *was* in the grip of a methamphetamine high still in its ascendance or having some kind of manic episode, he was shifting in the chair and shaking violently and picking at the skin on his forearm as if ants were strutting on it, seemingly set upon the herculean task of emptying his head, like in some mental stock-clearance sale where everything must go. He said he was depressed that if we ever advanced to a one-world government it would only mean that national wars became civil wars, and he was enraged how nobody admitted that the single most irritating thing in our whole society was being the captured person in a citizen's arrest.

He tilted his chair backward and said it was a further annoyance that a life strategy of minimizing regrets only winds up guaranteeing you suffer the maximum. I wanted to carry him out of there and put him to bed, and I wondered how far I'd get if I picked him up in my arms and made for the exit. Now, as he tilted back so far the chair looked like it would topple over, he said he was sick of watching so much porn it was affecting his genome. He brought the chair slamming down on the cement floor. He was revolted, he said, at how he was so impatient for the population to drop below replacement level he could barely contain himself. And he was grossed out that our only evidence of moral evolution was how we'd learned to forgive ourselves *during* the sins we committed, and not wait until after.

It was at this moment I noticed that he'd fixed his eye on some point in the room. What was he looking at? He was saying that it was very telling that the only time people looked serious was when they were counting money or watching their child vanish around a corner. Sergeant Oakes nodded at me morosely and I had the impression he'd developed a stoop since I'd first entered. I thought: It is us, not Aldo, who will crack under interrogation. Aldo swiped vaguely at his own face. I traced his focal point to either a tiny crack in the plaster on the wall or the fly beside it. He said there was a reason that "the kindness of nature" isn't a saying in any language. That people mistreat dogs because they can't handle that type of devotion. That we're not the worst civilization ever to blight the earth, but we're the most sensitive.

It struck me that every time he slammed the floor after titling backward, he edged the chair a few millimeters forward. He was saying that history isn't a litany of peoples and civilizations, it's a series of clinical trials. That the first sign of madness is inattention to Don't Walk signals. That the most significant impact of the digital world on our lives is we no longer wait for people to take their photographs when we want to pass in front of their cameras. "We just fucking go." Aldo rocked back and forth with metronomic rhythm and slammed the chair again, inching forward. Now I understood. He was in all probability aiming to lunge for the gun in Sergeant Oakes's holster in order to turn it on himself. Would he know how to take the safety off? If we intercepted him in time, would it be misinterpreted as an attempt on *our* lives? He said it was downright inscrutable that most people he met were as self-defeating as child pornographers who put their incriminating hard drives in for service.

Now he seemed about to make a move. He said we are always exaggerating when we praise someone's integrity, and that when you have poor intuition, *everything* is counterintuitive. Aldo's chair was less than a half-meter from Sergeant Oakes, who hadn't noticed, busy as he was kneading his own left shoulder. Aldo said he was sickened that he only fell into lockstep with his fellow man during earthquakes and when the Olympics were held in his home city, he was sad that a return to naiveté would require substantial damage to his prefrontal cortex, and thought it plainly weird that nobody but him realized that Islamophobia is merely repressed harem envy. His voice, I thought, was now communicating nausea and transmitting it directly to the listeners. He was sorry he couldn't articulate if pressed why he was so sure his life was superior to the life of a cow, and loathed the phrase "a serious, but stable condition," which implied a generally positive outcome while in reality meant someone's life was probably ruined, that they were to be a paraplegic, or a quadraplegic. "Take it from me. Serious but stable is nothing to cheer about."

Aldo's incremental inching had now put him in arm's reach of Oakes's holster, and when he made his move I intercepted him with a hand on his shoulder and shoved him back into his seat. Oakes wasn't sure what had just happened, and stood up at high alert with one hand balled into a fist and the other on his weapon, signaling me with urgent eyes his readiness to lend a hand in physically subduing this bona-fide danger to society.

I sat opposite Aldo and said I was going to conduct the interview, and that while the recording device was active he should remain still.

A long, distressing moment followed where his lips were sucked into his mouth and he trembled with intense concentration, as if he were trying to hold in his own odor. Aldo toasted me with his Styrofoam cup of water and spilled most of it down his chin, and in one long breath explained that what was worse than being treated like a statistic was being treated like a statistical anomaly. He insisted he had always felt, on any given day, that his worst fears would be realized, not the grave, but an automated bed or a cell. Not a shroud, but bandages or a uniform. Not death, but physical suffering or imprisonment. Nothingness was nothing to get excited about, but agony and incarceration were. That is to say, he had always felt extravulnerable to the whimsy of the microbe, or to damning circumstantial evidence, as in, he said, the results are in, the jury is back, the tests are positive, you've been found guilty, I recommend a course of chemotherapy, I sentence you to seven years' maximum security; because for him, he said, there had always been two totally separate and more or less autonomous civilizations existing parallel to regular society—the prison society and the hospital society—and he perceived regular society as a narrow bridge with the other two lying on either side, and he'd always been terrified of losing his footing and falling into one or the other, into a world of solitary confinement or of burn wards, of laundry-room rapes or skin grafts, and where he would finally fall—into the horror of the prison, or into the horror of the hospital—was his greatest fear.

"Wait," I said, "let me turn on the recorder."

An Unexpected Journey

ALDO'S MUFFLED VOICE HOLLERS FOR me through the bathroom door. The patrons in the beach club bar strike troubled smiles, their conversations silenced as they listen to his call of deep humiliation, or distress. I put down my bourbon and descend the stairs and rescue him from the narrow cubicle where he is perched upright with a feigned expression of boredom, as if a ride in my arms, to kill the time, might be just the thing. He drapes his arms around my neck and I ferry him, as if we are honeymooners, back up the steep staircase to his awaiting chariot. Once settled, he holds himself erect with perhaps his last remaining possession of value, his abdominal muscles, his face sharp and tightening in the sun's hard glare. "Let's go down there," he says, gesturing to the beach below. "I want to feel the sand."

"On your hands?"

"Why not?"

I can't think of a single reason.

It is a hot, blindingly bright morning near spring's end, the sky a luminous sea of pale blue swirls. Birds have made nests in the telephone poles. From the get-go, Aldo is angered by the broken footpath, its cracks and bumps. Brown leaves and sluggish lizards are crushed under his wheels as he rolls in and out of the thick shadows of overhanging trees. I walk beside him. When we reach the path that slopes down to the beach, Aldo keeps going.

"We're not stopping here," he says, without turning.

"Then where are we going?" I ask, catching up. His uneasy smile tells me nothing.

Through the sleepy green of the beachside suburb, we meander along the uneven footpath that lines the narrow road. Parakeets squawk unseen in the tops of large trees, and the air is thick with the damp odor of the sea. When the paved footpath ends, Aldo moves onto the road itself and keeps close to the guardrail that hugs the coastline, but his colossal chair forces cars to cross into the oncoming lane, lest they misjudge the overtake and knock him into the sea. En route, I'm thinking how he can never sneak up on a person again. Or trap any kind of animal.

"What's the title of your book?" he asks.

"*The King of Unforced Errors.*"

"Hate it."

"I'll change it."

"To what?"

"*Sour Grapes: A Memoir.*"

"No."

"*The Slowest Death on Record.*"

"Better, but not great."

"And the tagline is *He was afraid of life. And he was right to be afraid.*"

"Go suck a bag of dicks."

To our left, homes built on near-vertical inclines; on our right, between the pine-shaded houses, we glimpse a ribbon of blue, or sometimes through front windows and out back ones, a whole slab of sea. We say nothing as we pass steep staircases that wind out of sight, landscape gardeners on cigarette breaks, the sporadic estranged husband asleep in his car, mailboxes in the shape of whales, and bright blue houses with weather vanes swearing on rusted hinges. Without warning, he turns off the road into a trackless expanse of waist-high grass. Aldo, a man captaining his own vessel, is radiating fear and determination, and I follow into unexpectedly dense bushland where the sky is all but obscured by interlocking canopies. The chair hums ahead of me as I trudge along behind, watching twigs churned up in his wheels that, from time to time, falter on the

uneven ground. The sea air comes in strong wafts, and I feel a mishap is imminent; Aldo is sort of crouched now, tightly gripping the left armrest, and I catch
up to him on a sloping dirt pathway that forces his chair on a dangerous tilt to the
side. "Careful," I say, but then all at once we're on a forbiddingly steep descent; as
Aldo heads down he shouts for help, and I grab the back of his chair to prevent
it flipping over on top of him. "Don't let go!" he commands in a panic. With me
swearing and protesting, we teeter precariously on this scrubby path that twists
down onto a small cove. We make it to the bottom, to the shadowless edge where
the sand begins and the ocean roars and a breeze shifts the treetops and a raucous
cloud of birds burst into the soft light. The beach is walled in by steep limestone
cliffs on either side, and rising out of the sea is a rocky island, like an outpost.
Four-foot sets are rolling in from the horizon, and in the anarchy of waves surfers are ducking and weaving and dodging around the huge monolith of rock as if
they have impunity against bodily harm. It's spectacularly dangerous.

"A secret beach!" I say.

Over the crashing waves, Aldo explains that the ocean recedes far enough
to make it a beach only periodically, the last time being some years ago, when
he came here with the artists. "So not a secret beach," he says, "a *magic* beach."

Of course. Aldo had mentioned it during his toxic murder-trial testimony,
which had warped the courtroom furniture and the jurors' minds. Those of us
who heard it never stopped hearing it afterward, and despite an overload of
sympathy for Aldo, we kind of hated ourselves, as though it were our own ears
that had let us down.

"So *this* is Magic Beach."

I stare at the sand and the water and the small clusters of sunbathers and
think: People will label anything magical at the drop of a hat. Aldo pushes his
wheelchair forward until his wheels spin in the soft sand; he looks out, and for
a moment he appears to me as faceless as an old coin, as he gazes at the kami-
kaze water circus manuevering deftly around the island. It seems you could fall
from a wave and be thrashed to death on that big rock, or wipe out early and
be pinned against the sheer face of it. Or smash into the rounded boulders that
fringe its perimeter. Or tumble onto the smaller, wave-polished stones that line
the shore. Either way, these waves leave very little room for error, and there
seems to be plenty of opportunity to narrowly escape death or, alternatively,
not escape it at all.

"Look at these fuckers," Aldo says.

"The type of risk takers that smuggle heroin in their stomachs."

"People have to stop saying that adults have lost their sense of wonder. Maybe the fuzziness of a caterpillar's legs no longer impresses me like it used to, but people always do."

His face is bright for the first time that morning. A slip of fugitive cloud drifts by. The sun on its errand up the sky.

"What's the time?" he asks.

"I don't know. Midday?"

Aldo removes his T-shirt, and a silence forms around us. Here is his life-time of scars, his sickly pale skin a mess of them, and a small drainage bag half filled with urine strapped to his belly with a suprapubic catheter, a permanent silicone tube that goes into a stoma in his lower abdomen, doing nobody's eyes any favors. He catches me reeling and with a gaze locks our sad faces together. I am trapped in an old crate without a single airhole.

"People always talk about wanting to die with dignity," he says.

"They never shut up about it," I agree.

"And when they use the word dignity in that sense, nine times out of ten they're thinking of losing autonomy over urine and defecation, piss and shit, but for those of us who've already lost control of all that, what does dignity even mean?"

I genuinely have no idea. Our conversation cycles down to mere sighs. He spins his wheels once more but the chair doesn't move anywhere. "Liam," he says, "I want to go down by the water."

"Should I carry you?"

"No, I'll crawl."

Aldo shifts to the edge of the chair and performs a flustered though pains-takingly precise choreography: He gathers his legs, moves in front of the foot-plate, puts his fist on the ground, and with his chest on his knees and his weight on his fist, uses his arm as a pivot to land on the sand, where he drags himself onto his side so that the sack of urine doesn't catch and burst open.

"Sure I can't carry you?"

He shakes his head. This seems to be part of some outburst he's been incu-bating all year, but if he thinks me carrying him is a worse spectacle than him crawling on the sand, spoiling people's appetites, he is grossly mistaken.

I kick off my shoes and socks and realize the sand's too hot for bare skin, yet Aldo's crawling across it, oblivious—one of those dangers his deadened nerves keeps secret from his brain—so I rush down and scoop him up and he lets out a furious shriek that gets people's attention, people who don't mind gaping open-mouthed and scrunching their disgusted faces right at you. I get him to the water's edge and, carefully this time, lower him onto the wet sand where he's immediately ambushed by a wave; he spits and sullenly drags himself back a few meters, his legs looking like ramen noodles inside his sodden pants. He moves his lips silently, crunching sand between his teeth; his eyes hold a darkish glare.

I sit down beside him, light us both cigarettes, and say, "Share it with the rest of the class."

"Did I tell you about the guy I met in hospital?"

"Which one?"

"Nontraumatic myelopathy."

"Was he Greek?"

"He became paralyzed after a two-hour surfing lesson, not from an accident, but from overprolonged spine hyperextension, you know, while lying on the surfboard."

"I wish you would stop telling me these stories."

Aldo buries his cigarette in the sand, and with wounded eyes contemplates the healthy bodies carried in on green waves.

He says, "Did you hear that?"

"What?"

"Nothing."

He gives me an annoyed look, as if I should be able to hear the noises in his head too.

We continue to watch the surfers risking then saving their lives in a single gesture, but even daredevilry grows monotonous after a while. And maybe I'm wrong, but I catch a flash of disappointment in Aldo's face when one narrowly misses the rock—he is wearing his heart of darkness on his sleeve. He's even breathing aggressively.

Aldo consults my watch again.

I ask, "Somewhere you have to be?"

"It was Mimi who first brought me here."

"I know."

He turns his head to look at the incongruity of his cumbersome mechanized chair nestled at the base of the rugged cliffs that tower over this isolated cove. Getting his chair back up that steep pathway now seems unfeasible. My eyes survey the top of the cliff face, the incredible glassy houses with their endless vistas and wraparound balconies.

"They're not coming."

"Who's not?"

"I can't wait any longer," he says.

"For what?"

Aldo seems to be bursting out of himself. I am picking up frustration, sexual and existential, maybe at the idea of spending another couple of decades with the debris of himself, or maybe it's just the leggy, bikinied women sprawled in broad daylight ten meters from where we're sitting. In this twenty-first-century context, where we increasingly become, as McLuhan forecasted, the sex organs of the machine world, where does that put Aldo?

"See that fucknugget over there?"

Aldo is pointing to a dark-toned guy with bleached-blond dreads in Mambo board shorts walking out of the surf like he has left it for dead.

"Yes."

"Call him over."

"What for?"

"Just do it, will you?"

I feel an uneasy social transaction coming up. I wave at the surfer and he comes over warily, as if in fear we might remove the genetic stamp from his body.

He says, "What's up?"

Aldo says, "I'll pay you a hundred dollars if you'll lend me your surfboard for an hour."

"You serious?"

"Totally."

"Wait. Aren't you that guy —?"

"Yep."

The surfer's thinking face comes on; he tightens his mouth and flares his nostrils that, to me, seem larger than the diameter of his whole nose. He turns back to the surf as if to calculate the exact latitude and longitude where Aldo will perish.

"You gotta know what you're doing."

"I do."

The guy frowns, perhaps having noticed that Aldo is panting and sweating even though he's inert.

"There are only a billion safer places to surf. A mate of mine broke his hand here last month. Another guy I know cracked his skull. I've had a few stitches myself. And a punctured cheek. See?" He shows us a puffy pink scar underneath his right eye.

"I'll be right," Aldo says, and turns his face to the wind and scrutinizes the waves, then slides down a powerful wall of water—in his imagination—and is already toweled off and back among us.

It was 1990—we spent one hateful summer learning to surf in order to impress Suzanne Douglas and Kelly Stevens, but both of us quickly had enough of the indecision, fear, and impatience necessary to be truly bad surfers; we hated it equally, and soon wound up back on dry land attracting a whole other genre of girls with secondhand metal detectors.

The surfer is silent a moment. Then he says, "My cousin's got Parkinson's," as if that were some kind of synchronicity, and worth applauding. When we don't say anything, he says, "Well, shit. You can just borrow it for free."

"Deal!"

Aldo rolls onto his back and with lightning speed whips off his tracksuit pants to reveal tight black board shorts underneath. His eyes, cast in my direction, say, *Ta-da!* My uneasiness makes way for confusion. He had his swimmers on all this time?

"What about your thingy there," the surfer says, pointing brazenly to Aldo's suprapubic catheter inserted in the abdominal wall. The guy is now acting as if he's partaking in some long-scheduled Make-A-Wish event.

"I have to be careful the bag isn't torn from my body."

"Oh Jesus," I say.

"If this comes out, you'd be shocked how quick that hole closes over."

"Shock me," the surfer says, hand on his hip.

"Five minutes. Ten at the outside."

"Amazing!"

Aldo turns to me. "I'm giving you something to write about."

"I don't do obituaries."

Maybe, in a complicated spiral of human thought, Aldo figures dying is the ultimate act of self-protection. That is, once dead, nothing further can harm him.

He digs a small hole in the sand and opens the spout of his drainage bag and releases the foggy liquid into it and the air steams with the unique odor of sand and piss. I submerge a weary disgust and am reminded that it's possible for two things to be wrong in parallel—you can be paralyzed *and* have a psychotic breakdown. Aldo stares at me with a bemused smirk. He says, "Sick of revulsion yet?"

"Not yet."

"Tie my ankle to the board."

That has accomplice to murder written all over it. Don't I have a duty to stop him, if not as a friend, then as an officer of the law? Of course, as a writer, I am impelled to let him try.

"Aldo," I say, "think it over."

I want to impress upon him the obvious fact that things can always be worse, that even though he has been jailed and paralyzed, bankrupt and heartbroken, things can always spiral into an ever darker, ever bleaker hole. In this case, he could transition from paraplegic to quadriplegic. I wouldn't put it past him.

"Now carry me in."

"I'll get wet."

"Don't be a pussy."

It has been many years since anyone has called me that off-duty. The surfer helps lay him facedown on the board then we ferry him to the shore, like pallbearers transporting a coffin.

He says, "I feel like the Fussy Corpse."

"I can see that."

Our eyes meet and his reveal some inner explosion of pain he soundlessly bears. I realize he's crying.

"Are you OK?"

"I'm scared. I'm so scared."

"Don't do this," I say.

He doesn't say anything, but from his blanched and fractured face I know he is three-dimensionally projecting every possible negative and catastrophic outcome. The air sparkles around us. The surfer and I lower Aldo and the board flat onto the sea. The water is cardiac-arrest cold. The surfer says, "Good luck," and retreats back up the beach. I point out to Aldo that medical access will be difficult here, and if anything happens I don't know how I'll get him back up that cliff. He shrugs me off and starts paddling fearlessly to make it over the first wave and immediately slides off the board. I run in and lift him back on. Aldo hauls himself up and paddles out with a facial expression I would call arrogant distress, before sliding off again.

There's no way for him to do it. "Want to give up?"

Before he can answer, a four-footer crashes down and I hear him shout something that sounds like "Fuck me with a hadron collider!" as he vanishes into the sea. All I can see is the fin of the board poking out of a rush of white water. I sprint over literally fearing I will see viscera, and pull him up out of the surf. He is breathless and tripled over in pain. He looks like a drowning man whose one wish is to die in a fire.

When I get him back to shore I say, "At least you tried. You can still hold your head up high."

"No, it hurts in that position."

I laugh. He pats down his torso to confirm he is more or less unscathed. He sits up, catching his breath. Then says, "Push me back out."

"Do you think you're being brave or something?"

His face goes hard with bitterness. "Ever step on an ant and then lift your shoe to see that flattened ant crawling away? Would you call that ant brave?"

"Aldo. You can't do it!"

The surfer bounds over and nearly, but doesn't, high-five us both. He says, "Beautiful effort," and grabs his board and strides back into the surf, which rears up to greet him. We stare into the hazy glimmer and watch him ease past the breakers and out to the calm flat where he hooks his board 180 degrees and gives us a wave.

Aldo sighs, and asks, "What time is it now?"

"While we're waiting for whatever you're waiting for, can I interview you for the book?"

Aldo gives me his hardest stare. "Sell it to me."

"I know he's a force of darkness, but Morrell once said—"

"I'm not fucking kidding! Do not fucking talk to me about that man right now!"

"OK. Let me put it another way. You've let a lot of people down. Justly or not, you've been accused of some pretty horrific things. But you're a good person."

"A sleeper angel waiting to be activated."

"I wouldn't go that far, but you do have a strong ethical code, like when we were eating Chinese takeout in the park and you wouldn't let me feed leftover Peking duck to the ducks. Don't you want people to know about that?"

"I couldn't care less."

"Don't you want people to know how you were such a devoted groupie to your wife that you even became a character witness for a child murderer to advance her career?"

"Meh."

"Or back in high school, how you told me kids who become magicians to be popular only wind up exacerbating their unpopularity, and then you confiscated my wand and cape?"

"No one will give two shits."

"Remember what you told me you said at your sister's funeral?"

"Fucking terrorists."

"After that."

"Oh, I said it would annoy me to be killed by someone who doesn't especially hate me as an individual, or who I didn't personally betray."

"No, before that. You told us how, when Leila had organized the holiday in Bali for the three of you after your dad's death, you didn't go because you'd called the government's travel-warning number, learned that you needed a shot for Japanese encephalitis, and decided it would be a tedious if not fatal vacation. As you waved her off at the airport, you said to Veronica, 'It will be one of those holidays where you'll be jailed indefinitely for insulting the king, and I can move into your bedroom on a permanent basis. Enjoy eternity!'"

"So?"

"Enjoy eternity were your last words to your sister."

Aldo gave me a look that was a request for privacy.

"OK," I say, changing tack. "Remember when you borrowed money to get an exploration license in Queensland with Ron Franklin, to drill three holes in some prospect based on what, I can't remember."

"A ground magnetic anomaly."

"Right. And the three holes were drilled, and no significant mineralization was discovered."

"So?"

"And the next year, a UK company discovered uranium in that exact same location."

"That was bad luck, but I knew what I was getting into. To be born is to be forewarned."

I lunge for my notebook and write that down.

"Hey, stop that!"

"You know, despite your singular fate, to write about you is to troubleshoot the human spirit. I'm trying to appeal to your basic humanity here."

"Hmm." Aldo's mind is adrift now, his thoughts wheeling away. He's gazing sadly at the rolling blue ocean and the cloudy light like an old sea widow. He's determined not to help me.

Unless. Oh Jesus, yes. I don't know why I didn't think of it before.

"Stella's in it."

"She is?"

"Of course. I mean, she features quite significantly, as you might expect in a book about you. In fact," I say, "I've got the first chapter right here in my bag. It's preliminarily titled 'Aldo Benjamin, King of Unforced Errors: The Early Years.'"

"Aren't you even changing my name?"

"Don't you want to see your relationship from another perspective?"

"Give it here."

I fish the manuscript out of my bag and pass it to him. He rotates his bony arse until he has molded the perfect indent in the sand, wets his thumb, and plunges in.

Aldo Benjamin, King of Unforced Errors:
The Early Years

THE WEIRD TRUTH IS I'VE often become good friends with people I originally disliked, and the more I downright loathed the person, the better friends we eventually became. This is certainly true of Aldo Benjamin, who irritated me at first, then infuriated me, then made me sick, then bored me senseless, which led to his most unforgivable crime—occasionally, when in the process of boring me, he'd become self-aware and apologize for being boring. "No no," I'd have to say, feigning shock at the suggestion, "you're not boring me, please go on." I sometimes had to plead for Aldo to continue to bore me.

Aldo had transferred to our school in the middle of the penultimate year, and about a month into our friendship, after an all-nighter on pills, Aldo dragged me on a dawn tour of the shitty neighborhood he grew up in. We had to take two buses to get there, and as the sun rose over the city skyline, we ambled past forgettable stretches of warehouses running alongside a train station that "no unarmed woman should dream about walking from, even at dusk," past a greasy takeout shop where "one employee always kept a lookout for a health official," until we arrived at a narrow warren of residential streets where the people coming out of their houses were "uglier than in the beachside suburbs but not as ugly as in the mountains." The houses were all massive, all empty, and all had FOR SALE signs on their front lawns. The sight of his old

home territory was overexciting Aldo; as we moved through it, he bombarded
me with random facts about his family that he seemed to be reciting from a
census report: Only 35 percent of them were overweight, they had blue eyes,
his mother's side carried the degenerative diseases, his father's side had all the
madness. Mostly, he said, they were B negative. I thought: What the fuck is he
talking about?

Until I met him, almost all my male friendships were based on homoerotic
wrestling or the lighthearted undermining of each other's confidence, but
for Aldo and me, our connection was of like minds on pointless adventures,
whether that be taunting bouncers outside nightclubs, riding shopping trolleys
down suicidally steep declines, or attending first-home auctions to force up the
bids of nervous young couples. In those days, Aldo and I had such great conversations that every sunset seemed like the end of an era. We were young and
there were no unpleasant surprises waiting for us in bathroom mirrors. We did
things we wouldn't feel guilty about for literally years. Nobody was on a diet.

It was in the huffy silence of detention after the supervisor had left the room
that Aldo and I first spoke. His blue eyes and copper-shaded skin made his
ethnicity difficult to place. He was scrawling hairy penises on the desks; I was
vandalizing an overhead projector. The other students tracked our orbit around
the room as we emptied the fire extinguisher. Every now and then I'd catch him
staring at me as though out the window onto a fog-drenched paddock. I said
to him, "What are you looking at?" He said, "My sister Veronica was right. A
teenage mustache is pathetic. I'll shave if you do." I said, "Fuck you. What are
you writing there?" and tore the notebook from his hand. Aldo was working on
a project he called the Fair Price Index. Sandwiches (any kind): $3.50, haircuts:
$11.50, movie tickets: $8.00, soup: $6.00. I said, "What the fuck is this?" Aldo
said, "This is what I'm going to pay for goods and services in the future." I said,
"So no matter where you are, that's what you're going to pay?" He said, "That's
the plan." I said, "But that's ridiculous. You have to pay what they charge." He
said, "You can if you want. I'll pay what's right," and I said, "What a loser," yet
several weeks later, in religious studies, he offered me a sleeping pill to see who
could stay awake the longest and I accepted, and when we were sent out of
the room for snoring, he said, "Drink?" I said, "A park?" He said, "Toilet block
roof?" I said, "Lead on," and we stumbled drowsily to the nearby tennis courts,
on the way discovering the appalling miracle that we both had a dead sister.

We climbed the rusty drainpipe of the toilet block and sat on the hot concrete roof and spent the afternoon memorializing our big sisters, those lavender-candle-scented, introspective blabbermouths prone to selective catatonia. I told him about Molly's death by speeding cop, and he told me what happened to Veronica, how a few years earlier in Bali she was a passenger on a bus when a bomb onboard was accidentally activated; the terrorists were en route to their intended target in Kuta Beach, ironically Veronica's destination also. Aldo and I confessed in a delicious mania of grief how each of us had at one point wished his sister dead, and how this perverse magical thinking was driving us both quietly insane. We couldn't believe we had this in common too. While our grieving parents were hagiographers on the subject of their incandescent daughters, we often sat simpering in their silent bedrooms, bedrooms that were either packed away and stripped bare (Veronica's) or left unnervingly intact (Molly's). It was incredible that we had lost them at the same exact point on the relationship cycle, more or less at the same time, around their seventeenth birthdays, when they refused tickle fights and treated our smiles like swastikas, grew thorns, and mastered derision. We had both secretly idolized them and they treated us, their younger brothers, like plague carriers. Yes, it was amazing to us that we had both been abandoned and forsaken by our older sisters, both of whom wouldn't let us disturb them even as they watched the neighbors (Molly) or infomercials (Veronica)!

For months we poured out our secret grief every afternoon on the toilet block roof. We read their diaries, scoured their letters, obsessively compared and contrasted characteristics of these young women we'd lost, as if trying to decode some puzzle or classify a genus or species. In this way we kept the other's sister alive. While they had obvious differences—e.g., one had a voice like a glockenspiel (Veronica), the other a car alarm (Molly); one wept into pillows (Veronica), the other into stuffed bears (Molly); one viewed herself as a princess (Veronica), the other a high priestess (Molly)—there were so many disturbing similarities that the more we talked, the more they seemed like a two-headed creature with one narrow waist, twenty weird toes, and four double-jointed elbows; *an übersister*, made up of door slamming and mirror staring and the ability to make a bong out of anything (a Pringles can, a carrot, a golf ball) and fake tears and histrionic journal writing and shrooming breasts and crushing put-downs to parents and secret cigarette stashes and early periods and bathroom ruckuses and iron deficiencies and improbable boyfriends and acrobatic mood swings and excessive hair-dryer usage and lame henna tattoos. They stood in doorways unsure whether to enter or exit, and sleeplessly stared out rain-streaked windows. They often pretended to not see us (Veronica) or hear us (Molly). We consoled each other that their meanness was bravado, that the girls would have grown out of torture eventually. I recall how Aldo, as he spoke, would look at his left hand for evidence of his sister's incisor marks, sadly long faded, and reminisce how she would smoke her cigarettes in his room so he'd get the blame. I told him how I still felt phantom Chinese-burn pains on my arm, and how I hated when Molly held a mirror to me, literally. Aldo admitted he often sat in Veronica's bedroom running his finger over spilled nail polish that had dried on her bedside table, or trying on her hat collection—fake tiaras, chef hats, crowns, plastic halos, Indian feathers, Stetsons—or looking at her fake ID concealed in her annotated Anaïs Nin journals, or rereading dozens of Veronica's own poems; that was her main interest: poems about madwomen recently out of attics and those remaining in rooms of their own. It was in those unrhymed stanzas he learned things no brother wanted to: about periods and handsy uncles, how she hated blow jobs but wanted to be nationally ranked, how although she did not yet have a serious boyfriend, she wanted an open marriage. Mostly, as he sat on her bed, Aldo remembered her pitying gaze, as if she knew something bad was going to befall him and didn't want to be around to see it.

Together we said their names until their names lost power; we had seances every night and then suddenly we stopped, as though we'd grown out of them at precisely the same time. Our mind's eyes were sore and tired, we had exhausted them; there was nothing more to say, nothing left to interpret. We were two friends but also two brothers, not to each other, but to our dead sisters. And when those sisters receded into the ether, the brotherhood remained.

It should be noted, incidentally, that sometimes Aldo spoke like someone with hypothermia trying to keep himself alive. That's not to say he wasn't an acute listener—it was actually more common for him to ask a series of intrusive questions about your private thoughts and shameful secrets—but from time to time he'd burst into a furious monologue (a habit that was to become familiar to arresting officers and presiding judges in later years) or regale you with interlocking anecdotes in excremental detail, as if submitting to some maddening

impulse he himself seemed almost sorry for, and in the face of which there was
zero possibility of interrupting.

On that dawn tour, Aldo guided me to a street that had rows upon rows of
houses with houses stuck on top of them, clumsily added by affluent families
who had nowhere to go but up. It was his opinion, he said, that his pathological
fear of being alone came from the inability of his father, Henry, to stop reno-
vating their house. "Is that so?" I asked absently, as Aldo went on to psychoan-
alyze himself in his outside voice. In spite of periodic recessions, he said, these
renovations had been ongoing throughout his childhood and adolescence and
therefore, he said, sounding unexpectedly shrill, his phobia was not *just* a result
of growing up in what was for all intents and purposes an open construction
site, in a home that had containment areas and no-go zones and so many work-
place accidents the family always joked that they affected the national average;
nor was it simply due to his childhood being choked with dust, or one foot regularly plummeting down holes while the opposing leg bent to near-fracture angles, or because he slipped into cracks, tripped over exposed wires, was soaked
by leaky pipes, and threatened by half-demolished walls, and it wasn't *even*, if
that's what I was thinking (I wasn't), because he existed in a world in which
nothing was permanent and everything could be improved upon. I tried to
say something but Aldo had gained an unstoppable momentum. To rearrange
my facial expression or simply walk away were my only options. No, he said,
his actual psychological development was warped by the *construction workers
themselves*, the incredible team of unprofessionals he always felt cursed to remember clearly.

"Who are you talking about?"

We had stopped outside a beige three-story monstrosity replete with col-
umns, imposing doors, oversized chimneys, and church-like windows.

"This is it," he said.

Aldo knocked vigorously on the front door and encouraged me to press
my face against the bay windows. Through the tasseled drapes, we could make
out floral-patterned armchairs and a fake chandelier with plastic strawber-
ries. Growing up, any plan to slip downstairs and watch TV was often foiled
by the warm body of a stoned cousin sprawled on the couch, he explained,
and he couldn't get so much as a glass of milk without haggling with despotic
aunts with pyramids of hair and smudged eyeliner, or climb a staircase without

plodding behind slow-moving grandparents, or use the toilet without waiting until he got severe kidney pains, or go to bed without suffering twenty solid minutes of good-night kisses, or turn off his night light without listening to the incoherent bedtime stories of drunk uncles, stories so long and boring his pulse would slow to hear them. It was perhaps because, Aldo went on to speculate, at any hour of the day or night there were clusters of human beings three generations apart gabbing interminably in his living room that he'd felt gripped ever since by a terror of solitude. "And even at the time, I was *so* aware of this that often I'd wish they would all die at once," he said. "In their sleep, of course—I'm no monster."

We moved around into the backyard where the roots of an enormous tree had broken the terra-cotta tiles. From here the peak of the neighbor's turret was visible. Aldo stepped up onto the porch and rattled the French-door handles. Locked.

"We always put the key above the frame." He reached for the key, but thankfully there wasn't one.

"That was my bedroom," he said, pointing up. "I used to smoke out that window every night and pray to Zeus and Apollo to return Veronica from Hades or else to bring me celestial nymphs—I was really into Greek mythology back then." Aldo went on about how the sadistic ambushes and the use of enchantment and the monstrous libidos of these immortal gods rang true, at least to him. I lowered myself into a wooden chair covered in dried bird shit and contemplated how, from a certain angle, I could identify every personality defect in my best friend.

"You see," he said, "my parents bought this house two years after they were married, but it was Henry's brother, Brett, who started it all."

"Started what?" I asked.

Aldo's uncle Brett—who lived the better part of his later years in a swivel chair and then went camping by himself one New Year's Eve and died of a burst appendix—had always urged Aldo to accompany him down to the basement, which was spookier than most catacombs, where he'd swear himself to secrecy, then ask Aldo about his sexual awakening, and then, over dinner, repeat his answers to the rest of the family, to their sickening laughter. It was Brett and his wife, Cynthia, whose hatred of the saxophone was only equaled by Brett's proficiency in—what else?—the saxophone, who started the colonization of the neighborhood, or the Benjamin Sprawl, as they called it, when they bought the house next door. They were followed by paternal grandparents, a truckload of cousins, and copious uncles and aunts who, one by one, as the neighbors moved out, moved in. And *that* was why there were unsubstantiated complaints to the police that the family had intimidated the neighbors into selling—though while the Benjamins were one of those families where at least one person per generation gets himself into monumental debt and tries to fake his own death, they were not essentially criminals. Yet because Aldo's big-bellied, overtattooed cousins spent all day in the street teaching their underage children to drive cars, and because they were now well and truly entrenched in the neighbor-hood—sharing fences and tossing packets of sugar over them, waving to one another from opposite windows—the nightly family gatherings became mo-bile. They moved through the streets like a people on strike, hollering to each other, chairs under their arms or in wheelbarrows, eating dinner in one house, dessert in another. They renovated each other's abodes, and on birthdays and at christenings and recitals, on Friday afternoons and all through the week-ends, they were in one backyard or another with naked children everywhere and babies dangling from every breast, and there were out-of-control dogs and too many cats and driveways crammed with cars and someone was invariably blocking someone else in. You could always hear it: "You've blocked me in!" "Who's blocked me in?" "I'm blocked in!" All this could be misinterpreted by a certain sort of mind, Aldo supposed, as intimidation.

At this point, I had to restrain thoughts of my own childhood. Reminiscing is contagious.

"Anyway, the funny part of it was that the routine complaints that we'd intimidated the neighbors into selling inevitably gave way to the idea that we should intimidate the neighbors into selling. We did this a few times," Aldo said, in a slightly thrilled voice. "Let rats out in a backyard, made frighten-ing noises, played heavy metal, but our favorite was to gather at the door of a neighbor's house and stand there staring silently, even the children, twenty or thirty of us glaring wide-eyed with dreamy ferocity through the front windows, like some deranged inhabitants of a village of the damned."

I said, "You did what?"

"We very rarely descended into *actual* violence, the idea was simply to make the owners feel uneasy in their own homes."

"Oh, sure."

"Normally they'd call the police and we'd just retire into the garden next door and deny everything. Then the next day we'd be back again, a beast with a hundred fairly good-looking heads."

"I see."

"So in one of these intimidation sessions, we gathered outside number seventy-seven," he said, in a voice that flared up and died out like a cough in an empty cinema. "We had decided on standing in a semicircle and inching forward every ten minutes or so. We were aiming, if the owners looked out their windows sporadically, for a strange jump-cut effect. You get it?"

"Amusing."

"We thought so too. I remember asking my Dad how long we had to keep standing like that, and he said, 'Just another twenty minutes or so and we'll call it a day.' Then the door opened and out stepped a tall, gangly man with improbably long sideburns and maybe the smallest mouth I'd ever seen on an adult. He said, 'My name's Howard.' Uncle Brett asked if he had reconsidered our offer. He asked what we were offering. 'Market price,' we all said together. Howard laughed a laugh that I thought would cost him sexual partners. He said, 'Can you wait a few more minutes? My niece just put the kettle on,' and he kept peering inside as if waiting for something to happen. I started having the feeling that we were being set up, but nothing happened other than the near-medical impossibility that in all this time nobody in my whole gabby family said a word. Then a dark-haired woman came out who I thought was his wife, but I later learned she was his sister, and that the middle-aged siblings lived together in this, their childhood home."

I shuddered. Adult siblings who live together are a special case in our society. We are right to be afraid of them.

"The door opened wider and the niece came out and stood there in the evening sun exchanging multilayered glances with her uncle, and some cousin behind me was cracking his knuckles and I couldn't take my eyes off her, this creature with the dark eyebrows and nose ring and bleached dreads who looked like one of those girls who'd come out of a violent bout of acne scar free but with a permanent expression of hurt surprise and no concept of how beautiful she was. Her uncle was mouthing words under his breath, maybe doing a headcount, and the sun seemed to be setting inside the leaves and everyone was frozen in a stare-off, and finally the niece was staring right at me with an intensity that carried the promise of misconduct, when her uncle said, 'Stella, these are our neighbors,' and opened his front door fully, and Stella said, 'Won't you please come in.' Nobody did. They all turned and went home. Except me.

Under the stormwater blue of the night sky, dangling our feet off our favorite toilet block roof at the tennis courts, Aldo was eating a Chiko Roll with weird solemnity and talking about how I should have my sights set on a local beauty with one predominant physical flaw—an aspiring teen model with terrible skin, for instance—before getting totally worked up about his fear that if he ever got a girl pregnant he'd be the type of father who'd accidentally ash on his own baby.

"You seem stressed," I said.

"I'm eighteen this year."

"Mine's in two months. So?"

"So," he said, glumly, "soon we can be tried as adults."

I laughed. Aldo turned his red eyes mournfully on me, as if I'd failed the bid for mutual understanding. I looked up at the moon that spread a weak light over everything. He held up the fried thing he was eating. "There is no food group to which this belongs."

"Toss it."

He took another bite instead and went off on some tangent about how lame it was to be a guy sitting around waiting for girls to give us the thumbs-up, about how they got to be indoctrinated into womanhood by their own bodies whereas we had to reach manhood by performing some arcane task like going to war, or else had it forced upon us by violent and energetic sadists. I knew Aldo's horror of turning eighteen was twofold: the weirdness of approaching adulthood while his once older sister stayed ever young, but more pressingly—his persistent virginity; he had been such a late bloomer that Leila had dragged him to a pediatric endocrinologist who blithely insisted he take his constitutional delay on the chin. By the time he *was* developmentally ready, he was so besotted with Stella that it had to be her or nobody, and that was the real source of his anxiety, because he still had no firm opinion on whether she liked him *in that way*, even though she had held his hand at Henry's funeral, accompanied him and Leila to the airport to await Veronica's repatriated body from Indonesia, and afterward, with Henry and Veronica gone, when Leila and Aldo packed up everything and moved away from the Benjamin Sprawl into their fishbowl-like first-floor apartment on the other side of the city, on most afternoons either Aldo and Stella would make the hour-long journey to see the other, to smoke pot, sneak into concerts, hang out at Luna Park, break into neighbors' hot tubs on starry nights. Or Aldo would thread through the dense clot of tourists at Darling Harbour to watch Stella playing a "gig," which was really just her busking without a license outside the ferry terminal. Personally, I found her voice grating and her lyrics impossible to understand—the only one I'd caught was about her dream of fucking a toll-booth operator in his place of business—but when I articulated my critique Aldo snapped back, "Stella gives voice to the voiceless."

I said, "Only, she says things the voiceless would never say."

He said, "She said that meeting me was like finding money in an old pair of pants."

I said, "See, I don't know what that means."

It seemed to me that Stella was so dedicated to her vocation that if she and Aldo ever got together, her self-reliance would doom their relationship, as Aldo at that time was not dedicated to anything except Stella herself. There was also the unavoidable fact that while we were still wrestling our way out of childhood, Stella seemed fully adult. To accentuate this impression, she'd eccentrically give her friends a key to her house, since she kept losing hers—she said giving away copies was "easier than trying to change your personality"— she drove a dented Ford Falcon GT, wore corduroy and leather *and* denim, all together; and when she wasn't writing songs under a tarpaulin strung with fairy lights in the ferny backyard of her rambling house, she gave private guitar lessons to children and businessmen. *And* she had a high turnover of mentors she slept with: older, bearded guitarists who gave her hickeys that looked like attempts at strangulation. Aldo frantically insisted on "advising" her on these relationships; even while hauling around her amp and microphone stand like a Sherpa, he found ways to subtly run down or undermine her boyfriends. He was weirdly attuned to a person's insecurity and embarrassing habits and likely sources of shame. This is probably where he developed his rudimentary skill set in psychological manipulation—he found he could turn her opinion on a dude in one conversation.

So: Aldo and Stella locked arms when they walked; she would wipe her mouth with his sleeve after she ate; they played footsies; she'd often rest her hand on his knee when she talked. Now, he said in a declamatory manner on the toilet block roof, he needed "the matter settled." He itemized her finer points, including how she "enjoys scaring strangers with hiccups" and "yields to any suggestion whatsoever." His favorite thing on earth was "when she's sparking a cigarette at night, her face lit by matches in the dark." I couldn't take much more of this. "And the way she walks!" he shouted. OK, I knew what he meant—in those days we often fell in love with girls because of their postures; some girls have such straight backs it drives you crazy—but still.

"Soooo, I was thinking," he said, tossing me a cigarette I hadn't asked for. "*You* should have a party so I can invite her and, you know."

"Why my place?"

"Didn't you say your folks were away? *And* you have no neighbors."

It was true. We had just moved into an overlandscaped estate in a newly created suburb with identical streetscapes and pink concrete driveways and paved patios and brick-plinth letterboxes. Most houses had been sold off the plan but we were the first in, and there would be no further residents for four weeks. "What if nobody comes?" I said in a near whisper, and then, thinking of the epic party hurricanes that had legendarily decimated teenagers' homes, added, "Or too many?"

"Jesus, Liam, no one's asking you to go swimming with sharks during your menstrual cycle," Aldo said. "A little get-together. That's all."

The sight of my ruined house was compelling. The skylight smashed from below. The broken banister, suspended. Downstairs, every window shattered. A human-shaped hole in the plasterboard. The floor a minefield of glass and shredded Gyproc. My uncle's urn on its side, emptied of its contents. Graffitied walls. Tiled kitchen floor sticky with beer, red wine collected in the grout. Cat wearing my old McDonald's hairnet. Whatever carpet or curtains or couches remained carried the stench of cigarettes woven into the fabric. The front gate was all hinges and no gate, the pink driveway had been torn up, the Hills Hoist wrestled to the ground, the lemon tree set on fire, the letterbox kicked over, flower beds trampled flat. There was nothing left to protect. I remember promising my mother I would do the dishes.

It had started poorly enough. Aldo and Ben Stack were sitting on the bottom step of the veranda pretending not to notice that the street around us was abnormally quiet, as if even the cicadas had gone to a different party. "Who wants a cup of tea?" Aldo asked. "Your grandmother," I answered. He rose and moved toward the kitchen and I said, "Fuck, Aldo, if anyone comes in here and sees you making tea . . ."

Two hours later, the living room was too crowded to move in; chairs, coffee tables, and bookshelves had been repositioned and stacked carelessly to make room for dancing; people were stamping like horses trapped in a burning barn. Etiquette seemed to dictate putting cigarettes out directly on the coffee table rather than into the burgundy Persian rug. There were guys and girls piggyback jousting, kicking in sideboards, mowing the carpet, trampolining face first into the wrought-iron chandelier, pouring turpentine into the fish tank, pulling insulation out of the walls, and generally taking out their own puberties on the physical structures around them. Outside, teenagers jumping on cars, pulling the back door off its hinges, ripping up artificial turf, cannonballing off the pitched roof into our above-ground pool. It seemed that high-functioning sociopaths were flocking from all over Sydney. It got worse. Silhouettes of gangly marauders on the lopsided roofs of the neighbors' empty McMansions; plummeting rooftiles; the doors in the street piled up in flames; jeering boys launching beer bottles at the street lamps and porch lights; every last gravel stone in the driveway hurled through every window. I remember crossing our lawn where unconscious ladies were lit by the moon to sit weeping at the gutter's edge, and being worried about Aldo, who was lost in this somewhere, and furious that my best friend had deserted me in what was unmistakably my hour of need.

It was cold, sooty clouds in the sky. Students drifted in their early morning way, lightly dusted with a fine grimy car exhaust. Mr. Hanson, who looked like the historical Jesus, was getting out of his car. A plane flew overhead. I headed directly to the narrow space between the library wall and the canteen where I was greeted with an unwanted round of applause and unreturned high-fives and everyone fought over themselves to inform me that Natasha's brother and her friends were readying themselves to kill Aldo, to castrate Aldo, to knock Aldo's teeth out, all vying to posit the sick motives behind what my best friend had done—and what he did last night at my party, they said, was rape Natasha Hunt in one of the empty houses. "Tash *identified* him," Tina Carter said, sucking in her cheeks.

If the rumors were true, I'd have expected Aldo to look as if his conscience was eroding him like an excruciating illness, but when I found him amid blue clouds of smoke in the boys' toilets, he was deep in conversation with Jay Turnbull, discussing what I first thought was either the party or the plot of a movie, but I soon realized that Aldo was comparing Kristallnacht with the Cambodian Killing Fields—a senseless comparison if you ask me—in any case it was one of those conversations it does you no benefit to overhear. A kind of white noise roared in my head and I burst out with it: "You're being accused of rape!" He lifted a fearful face that looked like it had never known a smile. He was shaking, looking more afraid than he'd ever been in his life. Of course he knew, he said, why did I think he was hiding in the toilet stall?

This news had triggered in him an adult level of sweat. Aldo lowered his tone. "When they told you, did they say rape or sexual assault?"

"I'm pretty sure they said rape."

"Because sometimes they'll *say* sexual assault and you'll *assume* rape," he said, as if he couldn't catch his breath, "but when you read the details you see the assailant maybe only groped or at the most digitally penetrated his victim, which is horrible and equally uncalled for, granted, but a different ball of wax!"

"I don't think it really matters at this point. I mean, did you do either?"

"Of course not! Jesus!" Delirious tears began to fall. "I just want to be absolutely fucking clear about what I'm being wrongfully accused of!" Aldo said this rape accusation was the worst kind of prank, and that the police were most likely on their way to the school to arrest him, and he didn't know what to do. I said that to correct the error would be simple, surely, and he accused me of being "so fucking naive." Jay leaned against the wall and seemed to hang there, as if stuck on a coat hook. In the silence that followed, I recalled the time we were waiting with Ben Stack outside the Silverwater Women's Correctional

Centre in order to ask the next released prisoner if she would accompany one or all of us to the school formal. As we waited, Aldo and Ben argued over whether rape was about sex or power. Ben said it was about power. Aldo said sex. It was a heated argument even though neither seemed overly committed to his position. Aldo turned away from us as the electronic gates were sliding open to reveal the sinewy, cruciform figure of a woman with her arms outstretched. "Explain this, then: Everything *else* in the world is about sex," Aldo said. "Evolution. Reproduction. Cinema. Advertising. Nation building. Bridge building. Moon exploring. Art creating. *Everything* is about sex. Why not rape?"

Now Aldo stepped out of the cubicle and in a thin voice that echoed off the concrete walls said that around the time the party had almost hit its chaotic zenith, he had been sitting beside Stella on the divan making jokes about them sleeping together, jokes she unfortunately took as jokes. When he put his hand on her knee she laughed, and he thought: It's fucking galling that people take me as harmless even as I'm literally pawing at them, so he slid his hand higher, to her thigh. There was an excruciating pause as Stella leaned back and looked at his body as if she could use it to store paper clips, old currency, and bobby pins, then she took his hand and led him out of the house, onto the street, into the still, airless night and into one of the empty houses, to an apricot upstairs bedroom where the whole thing took place in near silence. She seemed to want clothed sex but he was determined to at least get her bra off, telling her, "If you think I'm going to lose my virginity without catching sight of a tit, you have another thing coming." Stella obliged; her breasts felt hard and cold, like packed snow, and his hands looked tiny and blue against her chilled white body in the moonlight. "Etcetera, etcetera, etcetera," he said, suddenly becoming shy. "But I can tell you one thing: It was one thousand percent consensual, that's for fucking sure, and we stayed in that bedroom talking until dawn."

"Will Stella corroborate that?"

"Why wouldn't she?"

Who knew anything about anybody? I trusted my friend, but it was beyond baffling why Natasha had identified him as her assailant.

Waiting for Aldo in the police station, seated on a sticky patch of dried Coke near the vending machines, I dug out of my bag *Artist Within, Artist Without* and turned to the section "Tribulations and Creativity." Morrell writes: *It is up to you to make every death of a parent a mixed blessing. Don't waste time rebuking God or cursing injustice. Rather, transmit your lived pain as solace or amusement . . . If they are also artists, the truly unfortunate have a wealth of material. If they are not artists, their transformative materials remain lodged in their souls . . . The neurotic civilian is an incredibly sad, tormented person while the neurotic artist can use his sadness and torment as a sculptor uses clay. Purpose, or the illusion of purpose, are both better than none.* I remember thinking, as I waited for my friend to emerge from his interrogation, that I was an artist and Aldo was not; I could write stories and poems, and Stella could write songs, while Aldo was not going to benefit from his problems in any way, was just going to suffer with no net gain.

Stella stood with her back arched, as if her breasts might take off if they weren't strapped in.

"I told them the truth. It's really unjust. We didn't even actually."

"What?"

"You know."

"What?"

"But he never even, which means he never has. So the question about whether he would is just so. You know."

"Stella, what are you saying?"

"What do you think I'm saying?"

"You didn't have sex?"

"We didn't fuck. We fooled around. We almost did. But he, you know. Ejaculated. Prior to. Oh God, I can't believe I'm about to say this word. Penetration. Then again, I also said ejaculated." She gave an awkward laugh.

"What?"

"Yeah. So that means, you know, technically he's still a . . . "

It was late; the setting sun reflected its reddish light in the street. Pedestrians seemed to move at the pace of gridlocked cars. I felt sick. Had Aldo neglected that detail of their rendezvous out of embarrassment? Poor Aldo! How sexually confusing can a single evening be? Rushed from a humiliating episode of premature ejaculation to a horrific accusation of sexual assault. Stella sat on the stone steps of the police station rolling a cigarette, her one bare shoulder emitting an odor of sunscreen. I thought: If this is true, a virgin accused of rape seemed the very definition of injustice.

Since moving away from the Benjamin compound, Aldo had lived with his mother, Leila, in their street-level apartment where all manner of pedestrians could see right inside the kitchen and watch them eating, sometimes in their underwear. They were more of an exhibit than a family, appearing to have no sense of being watched and always forgetting to draw the curtains at night.

Sometimes I'd swing by hoping to catch sight of Leila. She was an elegant, voluptuous woman, usually to be found smoking a cigarette and drinking from a bottle of beer, her skin silvered in the moonlight, and even from a distance I could feel her hot nakedness under that dress, this lady from the vanished Pacific island Aldo wouldn't name. My fascination was not entirely sexual. She valued my opinions, often told me I thought for myself, and was just as delighted that I hated the sound of Nina Simone's voice as she was by my pronouncement that *The Sun Also Rises* is a stupid name for a book.

Now, in the wake of the rape accusation, this exposed apartment was the worst possible place to live; car engines revved at late hours and misspelled death threats tied to stones were pelted through windows. When I arrived one afternoon they were sitting in the kitchen; his head was buried in his arms on the table and Leila sat leggily on a stool with a legal pad, pen poised. "What do you think, Liam? Should I speak to the girl's mother?"

What an idea.

"I don't think so."

"Poor girl. Still. We're in a tough spot; we must be careful not to be too aggressive." She put down the pen and said, "I'll ask Father Andrew. He knows some lawyers."

Aldo lifted his head. "I'll bet he does."

Leila ignored him and said, "Liam, did your parents ever tell you that part of being a grown-up is having the ability to assess risk?"

"Not that I recall." The idea of my parents saying anything remotely resembling that was laughable. Leila swiveled around to zap me with a disapproving gaze. "What made you throw a party like *that*?!"

Aldo hit his head on the table repeatedly. I looked away to the bunches of lilies by the sink, bulbs and dirt still attached, maybe pulled from a neighbor's flower bed, and to a pile of books we were force read in English class—*Catch-22, Pride and Prejudice, The Caretaker*—and a thick blue faux-leather edition of *Bulfinch's Mythology*, Aldo's old obsession.

"Darling," Leila said, stroking Aldo's hair, "this whole disaster makes me think of 'The Black Riders.' By César Vallejo."

"Mum, don't even start."

Leila cleared her throat. "*There are blows in life so violent—don't ask me! / Blows as if from the hatred of God; as if before them, / the deep waters of everything lived through / were backed up in the soul . . . Don't ask me!*"

"Nobody's asking you."

"Well, I'm asking you. How could they think you could do such a thing? Why did you have to leave the house that night at all?"

Aldo raised his head again. "Maybe we should move far away. Into the country."

"The country can be summed up in one image," Leila said. "A horse's eyes covered in flies. God has thoroughly let that animal down. It can't swat away shit." She reached across and tugged Aldo's earlobe, a gesture that had no evident purpose or effect. "No, I love this apartment," she said. "I fully intend to die here." She glanced at Aldo and added, "Don't look so excited. That won't be for a very, very long time."

"Don't be so sure. Matricide's making a comeback."

They both giggled.

I couldn't figure out what they meant by talking to each other like that. It used to stump me—my parents and I were painfully cordial and seemed to have based our relationship on a model that served families well in the Habsburg Empire, while Aldo and Leila layered theirs with a constant casual cruelty. A few months earlier he had given her a birthday card in which he'd drawn a picture of God in heaven sodomized by the hillbilly dead, with the words *I love you incrementally less each day*, and for *his* birthday she gave him one that said *Happy Birthday, you son of a bitch*. I might have envied their relationship, but I never understood it.

"I'm going to the loo, then let's go," Aldo said to me.

As soon as he left, she said, "You need to look out for him."

"I'll do my best, Leila."

Her eyes went to the window, where neighborhood girls hopscotched by. Maybe closed blinds made her feel claustrophobic (though I couldn't see how being hemmed in by foot traffic was any great improvement). Then Leila launched into a monologue about the inexplicable shambles Aldo's life had suddenly become, lamenting that this could be the ruination of her harmless, unimpeachable little boy. As she spoke, I was reminded of her voice-over work (her smoky tones narrated a commercial that pitted margarine against something called Buttersoft). Leila stubbed out her cigarette after four drags, and interrupted herself with questions to me—would you like cake or cheese? Do you want to stay in the kitchen or should we adjourn to the living room?—then snapped her fingers. "Find the real rapist—to prove his innocence we must unmask the real culprit. If this is not nipped in the bud . . ." This was fear talking, and fear can be verbose. She wanted constant reassurance while being totally resistant to any emotional comfort. "I thought the *something bad* that would happen to Aldo would be leukemia, but I was off, *way* off."

Clearing my throat was all I could think to do. An awkward silence descended. Leila had miraculously run out of things to say. My eyes explored the wall behind her head where, partially obscured by the long fronds of a spider plant, there was an old framed photograph of Henry, Veronica, Leila, and Aldo. They were standing in a yard with arms draped over each other's shoulders, tight little smiles and unbearably sad eyes—the kind of photo that rouses a memory even if you're not in it. Veronica's skin was marginally darker than Aldo's, more like her mother's, while Leila and Aldo, the last two surviving soldiers of a unit that had taken heavy artillery, looked vaguely restless, it seemed to me, as if they wanted to wander off into another photo altogether. Directly above that on the wall was a framed quote: *Blessed are they that mourn: for they shall be comforted.*

"What's your favorite biblical passage?" asked Leila, catching my interest in the quote.

Did she really think I would have one?

"The Ten Commandments?"

"Oh dear, Liam. Really? Moses did his best I'm sure," she said, "but at least Matthew didn't try to get the Sermon on the Mount down *in point form.*"

I wondered if she was a little drunk. "And this is certainly the right time to point it out to you—the Ten Commandments is a horrendous document made horrendous by the sin of omission. Where the fucking hell is Thou Shalt Not Rape?"

Her long fingers with their mauve nail polish seized my wrist. "Please keep an eye out."

"For what?"

"His father, Henry, didn't take well to stress, as you might know. They say these things are genetic, although I don't see how. How can a choice made in adulthood be genetic?" The silence grew broody. I understood now. She was talking about suicide. Every speechless second burned a hole right through me.

Aldo appeared in the doorway.

"Aldo!" she yelled at him. "I almost forgot. Listen to this."

She ran to the answering machine and played a message. "Leila, it's Hannah, we've just heard about Aldo and we're sick about it. Please call."

"How did *they* hear about it?" Aldo asked.

"Who the fuck knows?"

"Who's that?" I asked.

"Ech. The *Benjamins*," Leila said, darting glances at the window before turning to me. "They're a sort of tribe of monumentally rude shits, the kind of people who get kicked off ashrams. Well, some of them did. They're always mocking and urging each other to do something awful, and remember this one, Aldo?" She told a story about visiting Henry's cousin Miguel at his Umina beach house: he'd been arrested for assault and was forced to wear a home-detention cuff on his ankle; his range ran out three meters from the ocean, and they'd spent the summer taunting the poor bastard with ice-cold splashes of sea water.

Aldo wasn't listening; he was back sitting with his head on his arms. Leila made a childlike pout and at that moment a brick crashed through the window with another threat scrawled across it: *Your dead.*

The next day, I did my own feeble best to explain to Natasha's brother and his flinty mates that Aldo had an airtight alibi, but the more I defended him, the more it looked like they were going to tunnel bodily through my chest wall. For her part, Stella interrogated the girl in her place of residence; she threw pebbles at various windows until Natasha emerged, mellow eyed, and ushered her into a room with next to no furniture in it. Stella said that during the whole conversation the girl was holding what looked like a shoehorn and didn't make the slightest physical movement. "Aldo's a fucking virgin who doesn't know his way around the female body, whereas would you say your rapist seemed to know exactly what he was doing?" Stella asked. Natasha said nothing. A burning cigarette lay untouched in an ashtray next to them. Stella asked Natasha why, if it was pitch-black in the room, she was so certain it was Aldo. She said, in a voice that sounded like a finger was pressing on her vocal cords, "His silhouette." And: "His smell." And: "His energy," then described the same cold feeling she got whenever she was standing next to Aldo. Different strains of nausea grew inside both of them. Stella calmly demanded more details. Natasha said she had taken several bumps of the drug Special K and wanted to sit alone a moment. "He must have followed me in."

"Special K?!" Stella thought a moment, then in a stifled voice said, "Oh, you mean the horse tranquilizer and powerful dissociative anesthetic?"

Natasha smiled sarcastically. "It was him. I know it was him."

Stella spoke now with the ferocity of a mother fighting for primary custody. "It's not his word against yours, Tash, it's *mine* against yours."

"It was him it was him it was him!" she screamed, the sad spooky girl, as the room filled with moonbeams and shadows. "It was him it was him it was him," she repeated, her words seeming not just to hang in the air, but whirl like propellers.

After that, Aldo and Stella skedaddled together. Nobody could find either one. Feeling helpless, the only thing I could think to do was go around the school borrowing everyone's photographs from the party so I could scour them for clues. I saw nothing useful. Around dinnertime on the fourth day, my phone rang; it was Aldo asking if I could score some pot.

"Where are you guys?"

"Brighton-le-Sands Motor Inn."

When I arrived he hurried me inside. "Did anyone follow you?"

"Who do you think you are right now?" I asked.

Stella was demurely tucked in under the sheets but her breasts were visible and the room stank of latex and full body sweat. Aldo confided that Stella had definitely laid waste to his virginity and his penis now enjoyed full employment. "Great," I said, feeling crotch-level hunger pains and dropping into the red vinyl armchair against the window. As far as I could tell, they had watched movies, gotten drunk, eaten chicken-hero rolls they'd bought from the convenience store across the road and had to liquefy in the microwave on site, fucked on the stiff motel sheets like B-movie characters, and abused Leila's financial support by renting every $12.99 VHS porn movie in the motel's erotic video library. I felt an attack of my most chronic illness—the pain of missing out. The absurdity of these two high schoolers hiding in a motel room having the time of their lives just burned me. Aldo deflected my questions about how long they were planning to live like this.

"Until it's over," Stella said, with a melodramatic lilt to her voice. She had written three goopy love songs since they'd moved in, six pop songs and one power ballad; there was something about being on the run with Aldo, she said, that had inspired the hottest burst of productivity in her whole life.

Aldo offset my jealousy by assuring me it wasn't all fun and games; he was simultaneously living a high-adrenaline nightmare every time a car pulled into the parking lot or a child clomped in the next room or a housekeeper knocked unexpectedly or a neighboring guest kicked either of the broken vending machines, trying to retrieve a dangling Mars bar or a stuck can of Coke. He was on edge. And going crazy. He was stumped as to why Natasha had positively identified him and he flipped obsessively through the photos of that night that I'd brought with me, scouring the faces for anyone who looked like him. Aldo's own face was tense and he had fear-wrinkles in his forehead. He sat stewing and quivering with anger, trying to see Natasha's side of it. There was no doubt she was raped—she wasn't making it up—but why him? Why did she have to say it was *him*?

"I've written a song about Aldo's innocence," Stella piped up from under the sheets.

"Oh no," I said, and it occurred to me then that love is a decision, and the intensity of that love is more closely related to stubbornness than to genuine or spontaneous feeling. For whatever reason, Stella's heart was a nesting ground for desperate passion, and she had leaped into this union with her eyes open and her mind set on *adore*.

Walking into a nest of teachers in a staff room is like stumbling backstage at a theater: everyone half in makeup, half-costumed. Mr. Morrell was crouched down, staring into the bar fridge. He took a bite from a cold apple and returned it before sitting in an armchair with a notebook. After his wife died, I remembered, he was often called the Weird Widower, but that was years ago, and now he just seemed overly sad. He sat there like the heir to a throne in a country that had just overthrown its monarchy.

"Excuse me sir," I said from the doorway. I thought I saw him flinch, though I might've imagined it. "Come in, Liam!" he bellowed. The other educators fumbled with their soggy pink doughnuts as I approached. Mr. Morrell had been doodling on a student's essay: a picture of a face. He saw me looking and tilted it toward me and said, "What do you think?" the subtext of which I took as: Come on, Liam, universal acclaim has to start *somewhere*. I praised his artwork and then explained the situation: Aldo's girlfriend was a singer-songwriter from Beaumont Hills High who thought her protest song would win over the hearts and minds of the vengeful mob who might get to him before he could be cleared of any wrongdoing. Mr. Morrell thought it was an inspired idea. He'd fix it with the administration, put the whole scheme under his umbrella, as it were. Before I left, he asked, "Was it Valéry who called music a naked woman running mad in the pure night?" I said that I didn't know, that I didn't really run in those circles.

The students gathered to the flutter of pigeon wings and Mr. Morrell helped Stella hook up her amp and microphone to the school's PA system. "What did Hitler say? Without the loudspeaker we would never have conquered Germany? I play a little banjo myself," he said, then he took to the stage. "I have an announcement regarding an important interlude. An outside musician, someone who is not a student at this school—don't feed the pigeons, McKenzie!—has written a song about one of our students." He closed his eyes as if inhaling a pungent bouquet. "Her name is Stella Winter and without further ado"—he turned—"come on out, girl." The students erupted in jeers and boos as Stella strutted the stage triumphantly, as if the concert were already over and she had played a legendary set, like Janis at Monterey.

"Rapist's bitch!" someone yelled.

Stella throttled the microphone and bewilderedly glanced up at the biology-classroom window where Aldo cowered wearing an umpire's mask, before she shouted, "This is called 'The Aldo Benjamin Blues' and it is written in defense of an innocent boy," and as if deciding the treeless Zetland High quadrangle would be her musical birthplace, she did not sing so much as screech at the belligerent crowd, who leaned forward to discern the lyrics so they could hate them with more clarity and force—*He wouldn't harm a fly / Persecuted without knowing why / The girl she'd taken ketamine / And fingered Aldo Benjamin*—and aside from the bemusing miracle that the accuser had been blitzed on the only illicit substance that rhymed with the family name of the accused, the song seemed to be an ordeal for the singer as much as for the audience. It went from sounding like seagulls cawing inside a rainstorm to a muffled drawl, like when someone talking on the phone has let the receiver drop to their chin. For that reason, perhaps, the students were transfixed, and after it ended there was a deep silence that seemed to envelop the entire school, which now looked less like a crowd and more like a still photograph of a crowd scene. Then came the boos. Stella responded with a cover of Jefferson Airplane's "White Rabbit" that she dedicated, in something of a non sequitur, I thought, to "Palestinian women shackled during childbirth in Israeli prisons," a cantankerous finale that won her a vaguely fearful smattering of applause. After switching off the microphone and watching her pack away her guitar, Mr. Morrell congratulated her on her robust performance, the volume and intensity of which had canceled out any extraneous thoughts in his head; Stella said she had imagined she was in CBGB in '73 but "We live in an age where you can't be transgressive anymore. To make any kind of lasting impression I'd have to literally get up there and fuck a dog in the eye," and Morrell, seemingly unperturbed by the concept, said brightly, "You'd be surprised, Stella. Conservatism is like plaque; even once scraped away, it builds up again to problematic levels, so that what is now permissible can yet again become taboo—" He was cut off by the unexpected launching of missiles—pencils, textbooks, shoes, school diaries—and escorted Stella out of the line of fire. It was overall, I thought, a pointless debacle.

Two weeks later, the DNA tests came back from the lab exonerating Aldo. It was, coincidentally, the day Sydneysiders were protesting the government sending two frigates and a supply ship to the Gulf at the beginning of the first Iraq war. The news had not yet spread that he was forensically in the clear, so Aldo met me on George Street wrapped in bandages with dark sunglasses and a black hat. He'd come as the Invisible Man. I said, "Whoever told you an antiwar protest was fancy dress?" He seemed confused, to not entirely know where he was. He unraveled the bandages, and not a minute later let out a strangled gasp. I turned to see Natasha in the throng waving a SHAME placard in his direction and Natasha's brother running at us at full speed. Aldo shouted, "Wait!" as the brother lunged and Aldo fell down hard, face-first onto a broken beer bottle in the gutter that left a two-centimeter scar on his left cheek, still visible today.

The day after the DNA news made its way to her, with no leads to her actual attacker, Natasha wandered the school grounds with a haunted look that pressed into us—she was doubted, and doubted herself nonstop about who had come upon her drugged in the dark. The next day she dropped out of school, and later we heard she'd attempted suicide, and that seemed to deprive us all of the last slivers of childhood, as if her confusing and violent misfortune was a harbinger of uncertain and terrible futures for us all. We remembered back to when she had climbed out of the history-classroom window to chase the Mr. Whippy van, her perfect swan dive at the Year 10 swimming carnival, her rendition of "A Bushel and a Peck" from the year before's production of *Guys and Dolls*, yet we were powerless to restore her to that state, and because we had the idea that suicide was private and we shouldn't be talking about it, we didn't.

As for Aldo, even after the news circulated that he was officially cleared, neither Natasha's brother nor the police nor the vigilantes were especially apologetic about the ordeal he'd been through, and the police acted in tone and gesture like they might charge him anyway, as though by appearing incorrectly in the victim's memory he was guilty of tampering with evidence.

After this episode, Aldo still said everything with ziplock certainty, mooched around school barefoot, slipped easily between groups, boasted that he never ate breakfast (why hate breakfast? why boast about it?), was still careless with cigarette butts, silly when drunk, serious when stoned, hilarious on cocaine, jittery on coffee, and dizzy on glue, but he moved lizardly between classes, flinched at odd moments, stood at the edge of the quadrangle trying to look harmless, one hand half-raised in a permanent gesture of amiable hello or good-natured good-bye: the ongoing negotiation of a peace accord. He'd stand on his toes as if leaning against a stiff wind, his eyes on all the exits, now often talking to Mr. Morrell, who'd be wearing a white windbreaker or some other jacket with a vaguely nautical aspect. He spoke more intensely and something had woken up in his eyes: He was always wary, on alert, at complete attention, at DEFCON 1, and that's where he'd live his life from now on, as if a simple act of daydreaming were a perilous cognitive drift he couldn't afford. Always democratic in his alliances, now he became friends with *everybody*, even the most broken or strange or unfriendly or unwanted or violent kids, those with elongated foreheads and developmental disorders and those with criminal records and tattoos on the backs of their shaved heads. It was as if by surrounding himself with people, he was building airtight alibis for every minute he passed on earth. And maybe this all contributed to his bizarre behavior at the graduation ceremony months later, in the ugly quadrangle where our families were hopelessly locked in a crazy purgatorial session of never-ending applause, when our fellow graduates—those future real estate ingenues and up-and-coming heroin overdosers—filed up to collect their flimsy piece of kindling, and Aldo sat still as a stone. He was not afraid of being on stage in front of his prior accusers, as I suggested, but was actually contemplating, he later said, something jarring that Morrell had whispered to him in a conspiratorial voice just as he was leaving his classroom—"This is the last time you'll be able to sleep with sixteen-year-olds without everyone looking down their noses at you," he'd said—and so when the headmaster repeatedly bleated Aldo's name, and Leila nudged him with her elbow, and the unexpected stall in the proceedings resulted in an almost complete absence of sound, the silence amplified through the microphone and loudspeaker, Aldo didn't budge.

The following morning, it didn't matter how vigorously me and the guys who were traveling up to Surfer's Paradise for schoolies week rubbed the notion of unsheathed orgies in Aldo's face, and how much Stella begged him to accompany her to Melbourne for the Battle of the Bands, Aldo said that it was only in complete solitude and far from civilization that he could conceive of a life plan he wouldn't kick himself for six decades down the track. He packed a sleeping bag and a few provisions and took himself into the Ku-ring-gai Chase National Park, where he felt genuine envy for this or that bird, and aggressively bush-bashed through twisted paths all the way to a freshwater creek where he set up camp. A cold drizzle fell the whole long night, making his mission twofold: to keep his cigarettes dry and ascertain his destiny. *What was he going to do? What should he become?* Around eight p.m., he realized that having a boss, or some kind of superior, would be for him like being forced to wear clothes was for those people with extra-sensitive skin. Therefore, he must be self-employed. Other than that, and the certainty that he wanted to spend every waking second with Stella, he had no ideas. None. It was about this time that he bitterly lamented the decision not to join us up north, and feeling sorry for himself cried for hours into his inflatable pillow.

At three a.m., cranky and sodden and with some strange insect frothing in his inner ear, it hit him, the cardinal epiphany he'd been waiting for: that while money can't buy happiness, it *can* buy lawyers, it *can* allow you to litigate endlessly and buy off witnesses, and it *can* purchase expensive medications not covered by the pharmaceutical benefits scheme, and go to countries where experimental stem-cell treatments are better than nothing. If one needs to eschew authority, to hover even one inch above the law, to circumnavigate certain bureaucracies, to pay for detectives to investigate your case, to pay your own legal fees or, when ordered, to pay the legal fees of your opponents, not to mention bribes to keep yourself alive in prison, or to move you up on an organ-donation queue, the answer is always money. Tell the World Health Organization that money can't buy you actual years of life on earth and *they'll laugh in your fucking face!* So that was his big epiphany: He would knock the doors of prosperity off its hinges, provide himself and Leila and Stella with a gargantuan emergency fund, and with the excess—as a vague afterthought, a subfantasy—hack a philanthropic path through a jungle of poverty. That was the plan, and with no tangible skills or obvious enthusiasms, his only obstacle was how to achieve it.

II

I remember when Aldo stopped pretending to reach for the bill. It was the year his ringtone was the hum of crickets and he turned his sights on that vast potential field of golden poppies—the internet. His two big startups were a matchmaking service to hook up all the left-over single women in New York and London with all the one-child-policy single men in Shanghai and Beijing—he'd either overestimated the desperation of the women or underestimated their racism—and a porn website called Fruit 'n' Vag that specialized in links to repugnant and unthinkable niches like "Biblical" that *way* misjudged even sex-toy advertisers' willingness to be associated with videos of Mary Magdalene with the Good Samaritan's donkey. But no, he couldn't even make money in the oughts! Just like during the previous years of failed ventures, his crashed food truck, the shut-down warehouse dance parties, vandalized health-snacks vending machines, malfunctioning peanut-allergy divining wand, aborted tanning-salon taxi service, etc., he once again fell almost stealthily into arrears; he stopped even intending to pay bills, threw his mobile phone into the sea. As he had after all the other nosedives, he convinced himself he'd finally arrived at the terminus of entrepreneurial life, and his disconsolate figure could be seen trundling here and there, sitting in the sunshine smoking cigarettes, taking up a whole bench with his long body and overhanging feet, his head resting on corrosive bird shit, hardened gum, dried saliva. You would find him, in those days, in a crowded food court trying to saw through the burnt underside of a baked potato with a plastic knife, looking quasi-homeless, with shaggy hair and old jeans and moving with a strange lethargy, because, according to him, "Debt has its own pulse, central nervous system and physical weight." When Aldo heard his name hissed and bellowed from car windows and street corners, he'd give a discreet wave or shrug. When accosted in shops and pubs by various creditors who accused him of responsibility shirking or downright thievery, sometimes he ran, sometimes he accepted their insults, threats, and the occasional physical blow. Then there were those who came to his door, not just creditors, but their wives and daughters, pleading for money. He desperately wanted to repay them, but short of harvesting his organs, there was nothing he could do. To be ignominiously saddled with incalculable debts is to be permanently demeaned, and even though he borrowed from men who rubbed cocaine on their dicks and told relative strangers about it, he lived in a state of inferiority and constant mortification; he felt subordinate to everyone in any given room. In bathrooms he avoided his mirror image, from every angle a man in defeat. Even watching movies where the characters spent money on restaurants or clothes made him sick with jealousy. No wonder perpetual debt servitude is the most irrefutable factor in the male suicide rate, though just as often Aldo imagined an unlucky detective investigating his murder, sifting through photos of hundreds of enervated suspects.

And Leila! What he had done to his poor mother didn't bear thinking about. He'd broken every social contract when he borrowed from her and from his girlfriend. What exactly was it that made these women so blindly, so uncritically supportive?

One night Aldo was lying in bed praying to become a voiceless faceless thoughtless drifting eye cruising through space and time before disappearing in a violent white flash. This was not the first time he'd had a version of this fantasy. Stella was asleep in shrunken leather pants she'd worn in a sauna for a music video. He pushed himself gently off the mattress and went to the kitchen, poured himself a whiskey, and applied for a new credit card, then tore up the application and wrote the following letter: *Dear Sir/Madam, I'm honestly not sure about this alarming version of destitution whereby a veritable pauper is allowed to gad about like a respectable person and even apply for additional credit cards such as your bank sends me unsolicited in the mail. I try to reassure myself that "everyone's in debt nowadays" but the fact of it being an epidemic doesn't help one iota, any more than the knowledge of being swept up in a fatal plague would aid in any practical way the infected individual.* He tore up the letter, and dug out his mother's bills. That very afternoon, he had dropped by Leila's ground-floor apartment and stood on the busy street watching his mother at the sink, crushing her cigarette into the potted plant next to the wilted celery in a glass. Behind her, a man dressed in black entered and rested his hands on Leila's shoulders. He thought: Who's this motherfucker? The man in black smiled like a clown in a horror movie. His hair was white and his nose was so flat it looked to be embossed on a graven image of a face; he was a man with no profile whatsoever. Gah, another priest.

He went inside.

"Father Charlie, this is my son, Aldo."

The priest dropped his teaspoon into the cup he gripped with bony hands. "So this is the young man who couldn't be satisfied making a living instead of a fortune, who has impoverished his poor mother."

Aldo stiffened; he felt dirty just being in this priest's line of sight and thought, not for the first time, of what Henry would have made of Aldo dropping his mother in the lurch. He said nothing but thought: What's a man who clutches at straws for a living doing here anyway? Father Charlie stood there, one eyelid flickering. The kitchen was a mess. Leila could never close a drawer or cupboard door or replace a lid after using it. Stuck on the fridge door were overdue bills with red stamps and highlighted numbers from which Aldo averted his gaze and instead glared wildly at the priest, wondering if he was one of those men who came to God late in life, after he'd hit rock bottom and left a trail of sadness and illegitimate children. Father Charlie looked like he wanted to call on his higher power for backup. Finally he said, as if he had to unglue his mouth to speak, "I'll be off, Leila."

"Don't let the door hit you in the immortal soul on the way out," Aldo said. Leila betrayed her groan of disapproval with a slight smile.

With the priest gone, Aldo and his mother curled up on adjoining sofas in the living room, with its chintzy fake fireplace, glass purple grapes, and her framed self-portrait in needlepoint, and Leila debriefed Aldo on her status quo. She was being sued by her lawyer for unpaid legal fees; a breast cancer screening test was clear, but she had reason to fear false negatives; the local crime rate was up and she was *on the verge* of a home invasion; the students at her acting school had deserted her; and physically, her life was entering a new period, its worst one yet—varicose veins, osteoporosis. "And—I'm just going to say it. Block your ears if you don't want to hear it." Aldo blocked them, but not enough to stop the words *prolapsed uterus*. "Old age," Leila said, "it's like walking the plank." She buried her face in her hands and said, "Thank God my parents are dead and don't have to see their little girl in this situation." Aldo said, "That's a strange thing for an old woman to say." They talked on and on, they shushed each other and berated the other for shushing ("Don't shush me!" "You shushed me first!") and let the room darken around them. The night was full of eyewitnesses. Aldo stared out at the stuporous pedestrians: a man bone-white in the moonlight; a group of young people, one of whom grabbed his crotch and gyrated. She *had* curtains. Why didn't she close them? Some of the faces seemed close enough to touch. Only the barred windows kept the spectators from actually climbing inside. When it was time to go, the topic of conversation finally hit the target it had been ducking and weaving. Leila couldn't meet Aldo's eye when she confessed she had become so afraid of the bills she couldn't even bring herself to touch them. Aldo scooped up the pile stuck to the fridge.

"I'll take care of these."

"*How* will you? *How?*"

"I'll work it out. Don't worry so much."

Out on the road, Aldo stood under the yellow streetlights casting their little puddles of buttery light, and with shaking hands opened all the letters and bills and overdue notices. He was stunned; she hadn't paid her health insurance and it had expired, none of her medications were covered, and she wasn't paying the mortgage either. He drew in deep breaths and sat right down on the footpath and calculated: nine thousand dollars just to get back to one month behind. Taking care of the woman he had personally impoverished now seemed impossible.

In his own house at three in the morning, staring at those bills, he thought: I should have died in puberty. It was a cloudy night. Out the window, the blades of grass looked black. The tiniest sliver of moon was barely visible over the serrated treetops, and his eyes angled down to the garden he was contractually obligated to maintain, to the space between the brick barbecue and the dead tree, the designated location for the music studio he'd promised to build for Stella with the landlord's permission. Yet he couldn't afford the materials for a basic shed. This was something Stella had begun to mention, often and snidely. In truth, he had detected a subtle shift in his girlfriend's patience and attitude lately. She still paid uncomplainingly for their groceries with her meager earnings gigging at various pubs and her part-time sales job at Tentworld, and greeted him at the door with loving enthusiasm as if he'd just returned from World War I, but he felt demoted in her esteem and suspected she was getting through entire sexual episodes using muscle memory. At that moment, he remembered he'd impulse-bought a hospital-quality blood-pressure kit from a medical-supply company and for the rest of the week he'd have to skip meetings in order to be sure to intercept the postman. Aldo banged his head against the glass. How was he going to get out of this?

He shut his eyes, emptied his mind, savored the emptiness. He heard a voice, his own voice, say, "What about opening a B, B, & B—Brothel, Bed, and Breakfast?" Maybe. "Why not?" Because who wants to stay overnight in a brothel, that's why not. He gave himself a mental thumbs-down, and spent another minute moving his lips, waiting for sound to emerge. He said, "What about selling extra storage space to hoarders?" Now that had potential. Untapped customer base, unmet needs, plenty of room (heh-heh) for repeat business. Aldo slapped his hands together. His ambition was getting back up on its feet. He would not take dismal failure for an answer, and like always, his trampled spirit was set to regain its original shape. Or was it? There was something different this time; for once he didn't feel his irrepressible optimism skyrocketing, because now he realized the truth of his relationship—what he had long thought was symbiotic was actually parasitic, and he wasn't the host. He stood there in a sad daze, mourning every decent version of himself he'd ever imagined.

"Hey."

Stella was gliding toward him in her bathrobe like a weary traveler on an airport walkway. Aldo remembered she wanted to go to the cinema tonight but they couldn't even afford the tickets, and the dumb thing was she only went to the movies to eat popcorn. "Hey baby, you're awake," he said, putting his face through a sort of grinder to make a smile.

She leaned her hand on the fridge and loomed over him, oversized and fretful.

He asked, "Are you OK?"

"That depends on your idea of OK."

"Well, are you—"

"Pregnant?" she said. "If that was your question. Yes, I am. Thanks for asking."

Umm-ing and ahh-ing in the abortion clinic parking lot, they were horribly, almost comically indecisive, having peeked inside at the receptionist's bouffant, the unfortunate red carpet and jittery clientele, and were now sitting on the bonnet of their '94 Corolla arguing against each other's counterarguments as thoughts came in pairs with opposites attached. They used to have talks, now they had conferences. Stella's eyes were wide and steely, as if she'd evolved to a place beyond tears; she was saying how motherhood sets your career back five years, and in a world where five male years is equal to twenty female years, that just about fucks her. The sun was burning through the clouds and the puddles on the pavement had already grown hot. This baby in her belly wasn't the issue, she went on, because what you're betting on—or against—is a future child. If years later you can't fertilize an egg to save your life, then the one you threw back will be the one you regret.

"It would be an easier decision if I was established like Francesca, but I'm far from it."

Her frenemesis Francesca had released her debut album to acclaim and was now recording her second and touring the southern United States.

"On the other hand, we're about the right age to get going on this, biologically speaking," she said. "On the other hand—"

"The first hand?"

"As breadwinners, we're fucking losers."

Hot shame flooded his body. "We're so chronically in debt, I just honestly don't know how we'll manage," she said. Aldo felt blindsided by this obvious truth. Stella had come through for Leila, selling the Steinway grand left by her parents, allowing him to consolidate Leila's debts into one monthly payment, and while Stella had not given him a hard time about it, now he saw her nonchalance as all veneer. "I know you believe wholeheartedly in your high expectations and the yield they'll bring us, but what if they don't? I mean, sure, having a baby would give purpose to our lives," she conceded, "but bringing a child into a purposeless life to give it purpose is a strange sort of logic that ends nowhere, don't you think?" Aldo had never seen her so manic but knew she was worried that the integrity of her uterus had already been compromised by an earlier, half-regretted abortion, thanks to one of those mentors she'd slept with in high school (one of those older, bearded guitarists from her pre-Aldo days), and that this might be her last chance.

A woman pushing twin boys wrestling in a shopping cart passed by them and Stella slid urgently off the hood, as if late to an ambush. She startled the stout woman with her sudden approach and then had to bend down so they shared an eye line, their faces close enough, Aldo thought, to transmit conjunctivitis.

While she was occupied he reached through the car window and grabbed Stella's journal, wedged open on the backseat. Two lyrics on the dog-eared page caught his eye: *Hitler brought his A game / to the genocide*, a phrase taken verbatim from Aldo in conversation with her uncle Howard, the scientologist, and *I'm going to fuck you / back to the Stone Age*, which he'd expressed in a private moment of passion. He was, in all honesty, growing tired of being the source of inspiration for her songs—if he was parasitic financially, she was parasitic artistically, and what had at first felt flattering and mutual now felt weirdly draining.

Stella returned looking unsatisfied.

"What did you say to her?"

"I asked why she had children."

"What did she say?"

"She didn't know."

Stella put a cigarette in her mouth and lit it. Aldo imagined an ancient-looking newborn hacking like an old Vegas comedian.

"Should you be smoking?"

"Right now not smoking is like arranging deck chairs on the *Titanic*."

Aldo thought about sleeplessness, incessant laundry, and repurposed breasts. He alternated between a vision of a monstrous apparition of a deformed baby and one of a perfect baby, with negligent parents, falling down the stairs. He imagined the abortionist's backstory: a young man with a hook for a hand getting into medical school. He imagined Stella giving birth to a terra-cotta warrior, to an eel.

Stella crushed out the cigarette with self-disgust. "Drinking and smoking are part of my musical identity," she said, and added that on Sunday night she heard the smoke-torn bluesy voice of God tell her she should keep this child.

"Were you stoned?"

"So what?"

"Have we maneuvered ourselves into the position in which we can only do the negative act, the act of not-doing—in this case, not having the abortion? Because when your chief aim in every dilemma is to avoid excruciating regrets, once you've overthought something, doing the positive act—in this case, having the abortion—could haunt us forever."

"This! *This* is what I'm worried about."

"Meaning what?"

Since learning of her pregnancy, Aldo had voiced random facts: Statistically, human mothers are more likely than fathers to kill their own offspring. He had raised concerns about heart defects, cleft palates, spina bifida, clubfoot, Tay-Sachs disease, phenylketonuria, and meconium aspiration, where the baby ingests its own first shit and washes it down with amniotic fluid—every horror story he had ever been upset and haunted by in the Sunday papers. "Why not us? We're youngish, the odds are against anything terrible happening, but that's what makes them so frightening! We're one chromosome away from becoming nurses and carers!"

He thought how the older Stella got, the greater the risk of birth defects and age-related dangers and illnesses, and Aldo started to feel annoyed; he wanted to say the words he couldn't: This was her fault, always skipping her pill. She couldn't remember to take it, then would cram them in all at once to catch up; it was *she* who had said, "It's OK to come inside me." Stella turned up Jeff Buckley on the car stereo. It was inconceivable to have a major life moment without a soundtrack.

"OK. Let's be logical," Aldo said. "On the one hand, the problem with having children is that on your deathbed you're surrounded by people who'll profit handsomely from your death. On the other hand—"

"Hey look!"

The clinic was closing. It was already six o'clock. The stocky receptionist locked the doors and climbed into her white Holden and drove away. There was suddenly nobody around, as if a set had been cleared. Aldo imagined he heard the orange sun grunt with relief as it fell behind the buildings. Night was coming swiftly and the streetlights fired up.

"So I guess that's that," she said impassively.

"We can come back tomorrow."

"No."

It was all there in her eyes, a growing merriment, a decision. They stared with nervous excitement at each other, formulating the same future.

"It's going to be tough-going," Aldo said.

"Rule number one. We can't both have one foot out the door at the same time. When one person is feeling hateful the other isn't allowed. Second rule. We can both be depressed, but only on alternating days. You can take Mondays, Wednesdays, and Fridays, I'll take Tuesdays, Thursdays, and Saturdays."

"What happens on Sundays?"

"We'll be happy on Sundays."

"Deal," Aldo said.

"You sure?"

"Positive. You?"

"I'm in."

Aldo punched the air. "I can't *wait* for the next time some fucker says to

me, 'Unless you're a parent you can't understand.' I'll be able to wave my fucking baby in his face—"

"And you know what else I think we should do? Let's get married!"

"Hey now, one monumental decision at a time," he said. There was a long
silence in that cold spring twilight. How had she come to this absurd conclusion? What did one thing have to do with another, in the twenty-first century?
It was almost illicit! He was beset by a crazy moment of suspicion—had this
been her endgame all along? He said nothing, and said it for so long, Stella grew
sullen. He embraced her and whispered in her ear, "Listen, Stella. Whenever
I hear that someone has stayed monogamous for forty years it reminds me
of when you see in *The Guinness Book of Records* that someone has walked a
thousand kilometers with an egg on his head. I mean, I admire his endurance.
But what the fuck did he do that for?"

Three months later, despite Stella's dreams of an ambush of confetti and a rose-
petaled waltz up the aisle on the stiff arm of her uncle, they were married in a
blink-and-you'd-miss-it ceremony in the fluorescent-lit gloom of the registry
office with only six guests: Francesca, Leila, Uncle Howard, Tess, myself, and
Sonja. There was nothing time-honored about it. After the ceremony, at Stella's
insistence that their loved ones share in the total bliss of the occasion, the six of
us went with the happy couple to—their first ultrasound. Aldo was terrified the
baby would turn out to be missing a lung or already fossilized or Siamese twins
joined at the face. He was in a hyperactive mood, fidgeting in his chair. He turned
to the technician. "What did they use before ultrasounds—watercolors?"

"Aldo," Stella said, "let her do her job."

"There's its heartbeat," the technician said, and though we couldn't really make out anything human, everyone crowded around to praise the softly
throbbing center of this bewildering blur. I thought: For a puppet in a horror
film, you could do worse. Howard was looking at the technician's legs; Leila
squeezed my hand; Tess held Sonja up to the screen and whispered in her ear;
Francesca narrowed her eyes in obvious envy; Stella looked relieved and rap-
turous; Aldo was frozen solid and turning the air electric with his anxiety and
rotating nightmares. All the fears he'd ever had about himself metastasized to
that little aquatic creature. The specter of illness just got personal. Everything

that went wrong in his life from now on would have something to do with that baby, he thought.

He was wrong.

Leila's mortgage was unable to be refinanced, a writ had been issued by the bank to take possession of the property, and the sheriff was coming that very afternoon to forcibly remove his mother from her home, Aldo told me in a panic on the phone. I told him she could claim hardship, what with her loved ones dead, her island sunk, her culture decimated, her language extinct, her body failing, her money spent by her surviving child—

"We tried that. She got a stay of execution of the writ, but only for a period of seven days. That was six days ago." Aldo went on to tell me that the judge had had an annoying scolding tone, spelling things out in a condescending manner, and had said that not only did the lender have every right to take possession of Leila's property, but if the property was sold for less than the amount of the loan, she may be liable for the remaining balance.

"It's inevitable then. You should voluntarily surrender the property and avoid court costs."

"She won't. She won't go."

"So what do you want me to do?"

"Just be there when the sheriff comes."

I hung up and thought: Sons may suffer the sins of the father, but it is mothers who suffer the sins of the son.

Hurry up about it, we're already late! Aldo shouted to a heavily pregnant Stella in the Annandale Hotel. He knew she'd chosen this inopportune moment to swing by and pick up her last check because she dreaded the afternoon ahead even more than he did. While Stella spoke to the manager, Aldo pretended to use the toilet. He splashed himself repeatedly with cold water and had a quick tearless cry. He came back out just in time to see a pregnant woman toss a drink in Stella's face and storm away.

"What the fuck was that?"

"She asked me about my birth plan and I told her I don't have one, and she said it would be such a shame if you let them do a caesarean, and I said well, whatever it takes, right? And she said no, no, having a natural birth is the most primal experience a real woman can have, so whatever you do, don't let them give you a caesarean, so I said you've already failed the first test of motherhood, you know, by putting your own experience of being 'a woman' over the wellbeing of the child. You may be a woman, but you're no mother."

Aldo sniffed Stella's clothes. "Southern Comfort."

"I can't take it anymore."

"You're doing great."

"I feel like I'm three hundred weeks' pregnant."

"It's been hard."

"And my obstetrician keeps telling me I'm having a dream pregnancy."

"That son of a bitch."

"And I've got no more gigs booked! None!"

When they decided to keep the baby, Stella's goal had been to set down at least eight songs and then not take "We don't accept unsolicited demos" as an answer, give birth while the album was climbing up the charts, breastfeeding while on tour. Problem was, after the twenty-week mark, Stella had reptilian sweats and prenatal rage, was perpetually hungry and light-headed, beset with a hypersense of smell, extreme cramps, bleeding gums, the creepy feeling of heavy ovaries, and nipples so sore she couldn't wear certain fabrics. Everybody told her to get as much sleep as possible, as if sleep could be stored up in the body like water in a camel's hump, but due to her incessant discomfort, Stella had terrible insomnia. At thirty weeks she had to withstand the ubiquitous insensitivity of friends who told her she was abnormally small. When she popped, days were spent dodging citizens who believed it was socially acceptable to rub a stranger's belly. Although he was learning not to voice every neurotic forecast, Aldo got rid of their cat in fear of toxoplasmosis, refused Stella single sips of wine, and forced her to consume vitamins to prevent spina bifida. They had sex for the last time five months in, when a little pool of blood sent them rushing in a hateful panic to the emergency room. Without the home remedy of sex, things grew unbearably tense, exacerbated by Stella's inability to finish a single song; either it needed a bridge or had lyrical holes she couldn't fill, or she wrote out of her vocal range, or she kept vacillating between keys. "My career's going nowhere and it's about to be put on hold!" she fretted. Then there was the additional problem of live performance. On stage, Stella wore a maternity dress and held the guitar to the left of her belly, which made it hard to play. She sounded weird anyway; her diaphragm space was taken up by the baby so she had to bring everything down an octave; hormones thickened her vocal cords and her voice was hoarser than usual. Her feet were swelling and frequent bathroom trips interrupted the set. Aldo was unhelpful. "Loud prolonged sounds contribute to prematurity and low birth weight. Is that what you really want?"

Stella, already stressing about her future, chose now to stand in the street, dripping with Southern Comfort, and let out a torrent of abuse, accusing Aldo of only worrying about realizing *his* stupid ideas and working on *his* failed businesses and never being truly supportive of *her* music or doing anything serious to help *her*.

Inside Leila's apartment, the air bore a heavy odor of vintage colognes. Her friends—all members of the generation that took your arm with the force of a grappling hook—were there to lend moral support and face-stuff vegetable samosas and catch each other up on the progression of various ailments and upcoming funerals. It felt like, in other words, the premature wake of someone planning to die overseas.

I spent the best part of an hour trying not to inhale a yeasty stench and listening to what a son of a bitch that Aldo is. Every now and then I looked at the window to see the street procession peering in. A couple of schoolgirls with knee-high socks. Faces that resembled two a.m. mug shots. Why would anyone fight to stay here? That Leila was going to be removed from this overheated apartment with its permanent shadows and peeping eyes didn't seem like a tragedy.

Leila was standing by the bookshelf, holding a handbag in her own home. She wore heavy eyeliner and clownish red lipstick, and a burgundy dye stained her forehead like a watermark. She had gotten unbelievably old. Disconcerting folds of skin gloved her trembling bird-like hands. When she saw me she put her arms out and held them aloft. I weaved my way through a Hawaiian-shirted corridor of elderly guts and stepped into the embrace. Her dress seemed made from rough army-blanket material.

"Jesus Christ, this is so sad," I said.

I was still scratching from the hug when I turned to see a priest with white hair and rheumy eyes staring at me. She introduced him as Father Charlie. He gave me a crawly feeling that may or may not have been his personal fault.

"Where's that son of a bitch?"

"He'll be here," I said, wondering how long this bad-humored afternoon would last. It drizzled briefly and I could hear the cars on the wet streets. I had the strange idea that someone was going to suggest we all commit suicide together.

Around three there was a timorous knock on the door, and Aldo walked in with Stella waddling behind. He crossed the room to face his mother. "Where did you dig up these old fossils? Luckily I've brought my defibrillator. I'll start with this side of the room and work my way across."

Leila's laughter rang over the gray voices. She loved him. It was an airtight love. He felt forgiven. He hadn't meant to ruin her retirement.

Her friends gathered around and Aldo listened patiently to their wheezing admonishments and foamy critiques. Two plump women spun competing visions of Henry rolling over in his grave. An arthritic uncle misjudged the distance and finger-wagged him in the eye. I took a couple of steps backward, out of the blast radius. There was something gladiatorial about it. This was pure Aldo.

In his defense, he and Stella had made up a room in their house but Leila had refused it point-blank, not wanting to intrude. She wasn't comfortable staying with friends either and so she was going to a retirement home. Her packed bags, I now noticed, were in an unsteady melodramatic stack by the door. This was pure Leila.

There was a hard knock and forty guests made forty petrified smiles. The sheriff was rattling the door handle, calling Leila's name. "Mrs. Benjamin? Mrs. Benjamin. This is happening. This is happening today."

Aldo stood on one of the chairs. "Thank you, on behalf of my mother and me, for coming here today. There has been some unseasonable weather in my luck." He made a pointless gesture with his hands and laughed abruptly, like a serial killer trying not to sound diabolical to an indecisive hitchhiker. Two garbage men and the youths from the shelter next door joined the sheriff at the window and peered in, their shadows blocking the sun. Aldo said, "It's sad that Leila is losing her home. You all have homes; you know the value of a home. And in those homes, come to think of it, ladies and gentlemen, you probably have one room you never go into, just an empty space. Maybe it was a child's bedroom who moved out; maybe it's a den or study you don't really need anymore."

Oh no, I thought. He isn't.

"That space is worthless to you, but did you know that it may have value to others?"

Was Aldo going to pitch?

"There are people, obsessive-compulsive hoarders, who cannot help but accumulate possessions to the detriment of their very health and safety and who need, desperately *need* space, *your valuable space*. And all I ask of you, to help our lovely Leila in her hour of need, is the use of your spare rooms at absolutely no inconvenience to you, and with a small investment of a thousand dollars apiece, I can guarantee—"

"Get out of here," Leila said loudly. She stood hands on hips with an erect bearing that looked to be taking a physical toll.

Sad amazement grew on Aldo's face as he gauged the sincerity of her demand. He stepped down from the chair and bowed theatrically, slung his jacket over his shoulder, and went to the door. As he pushed passed the irritated sheriff, he glanced back around. I expected to see a sneaky smile but he looked so incredibly forlorn and serious, I wanted to press him like a dried flower between the pages of a book.

Two hours after Aldo had moved a terrified Leila into a neat brick retirement home nestled in bushland—he waved a teary good-bye to her at "medication cocktail hour"—he found himself at Paddington Markets contemplating a drifty-eyed clairvoyant at a tiny table, tarot cards fanned out in front of her. Aldo thought: Why not? Doctors tell us about our bodies, art about our souls, religion about our fears, but it's masseuses, prostitutes, psychologists, and fortune-tellers who join us at the extreme limits of our narcissism, and while we are desperate to be diagnosed yet don't want to be classified, and we don't want to feel bullied by hope, and while, sure, it makes no real sense to invest my mental well-being in a woman I recognize as having once worked for a short time making keys in the hardware store, I do need to know certain things: such as will I turn out to be like my neighbor, a ninety-eight-year-old misery of a human being still waiting for his formative years? I'm relatively young, and society admires that in a person, but how the hell am I going to break my mother out of that dreadful home and pay for a wife and child when I'm so irredeemably in debt? Aldo blurted out his fears and watched the clairvoyant stretch her plump fingers over the cards. "Your child will live to be a hundred," she said. Aldo found himself overwhelmed by an eagerness to change the subject. "*Only* a hundred? In this day and age?" he said, and then heard himself make a strange and totally random proposition, offering to pay the fortune-teller double to read her own palms while he watched.

She accepted, as if it were a classic, time-honored request.

A rosy future taken care of by her son. That was it. That was all she predicted for herself. "A good boy, always does right by his old mother," she said. It was physically irritating. Her whole future was predicated on the whim of her stupid son, who, it seemed to Aldo, was capriciously tormenting her. She said, "He's in there," gesturing to the inside of the shop. "You're the same age, you should meet him."

"Because we're the same age?"

"Jeremy!"

"Please don't call your son."

"Jeremy!"

That's when Aldo heard a voice shout, "Is that a fat version of Aldo Benjamin?" and a balding man who was indeed his own age strode over, adjusting his pants. Her son, it turned out, was an old sort-of enemy from high school. "Jeremy, there's only so much that deodorant can do for you on its own, you have to bathe eventually," Aldo said as they shook hands. They quickly began the old game of staring at each other's foreheads. Jeremy asked, "Are you going to the reunion?" Aldo said, "What reunion?" Jeremy said, "The twenty-year high school reunion." Aldo said, "That's in eleven years." Jeremy said, "Yeah, I'm not sure either, I'll see how I go." And Aldo said, "Isn't the ten-year one first?" And Jeremy smiled acidly and asked if Aldo had heard that Stan Maxwell had thrown his two-year-old daughter off a bridge in a murder-suicide that went wrong. "No way," Aldo said, horrified. He tried to square the villainous atrocity with the Stan he remembered, but he could only think of the poor little girl, and the abject terror she must have felt on the way down to her death. Oh, how awful! "But you said it went wrong. How? How did it go wrong?" Aldo asked in a panic. Jeremy was bright with the bad news. "Stan didn't kill himself," he announced. "Well, that's no surprise," Aldo said, "attempted suicides out-number attempted murders a thousand to one." Jeremy said, "It's always the quiet ones, eh?" "Actually," Aldo recalled, "he was quite chatty." That was one up for him. Then Jeremy grasped his shoulder and said, "Some of us are getting together to help him out. What about you? Would you be a character witness?"

"I'll pass."

"Stan would do it for you."

"Like fuck he would."

At that moment, a bus pulled up and a cluster of sixteen-year-old school-girls poured out and headed into the chocolate shop next door. Jeremy fell into a charged silence, and then in a quieter voice admitted that he had begun to find the sight of young girls' arms unbearable. "Unbearable!" he repeated. "Their thin, slender arms!" He sounded genuinely upset and Aldo was so terri-fied that he might say something further about their arms, he asked, "So what are you doing these days?" Jeremy said, "I organize Wave Rock, a music festival in the desert."

What happened next comes to Aldo as in an unpleasant dream—it comes with medical smells and desert winds and hairy faces floating out of darkness, and I will try to tell it like he lives it now, as a memory that waits in the street, engine idling, for whenever Aldo hates himself enough to take it for a spin.

It is two weeks later. Aldo and Stella are on a plane to Perth and then on a bus that barrels down a highway through bright-yellow canola fields and rolling hills of green wheat and salt plains and hours of straight road that stretches out like a long dirt tongue to nothing but nothingness and open sky and gas-station coffee and a flatness of land that is almost comic. Aldo, his head resting on Stel-la's shoulder, is thinking about his bargain, in which he agreed to be a charac-ter witness for the child-murderer Stan Maxwell if, in exchange, Jeremy would put Stella on the lineup for Wave Rock. He is thinking of the strange unruly silence of the courtroom and the character-witness testimonies amounting to nothing more than silly anecdotes about meaningless acts of banal friendship that seemed grotesque against the backdrop of a murdered daughter; there were genuine recollections of how the accused would grow introspective at story time, often lend lunch money, and—in Aldo's own contribution—later in high school, would go very far out of his way in the opposite direction to give you a ride home, though, Aldo added, we all did in those days. During his testimony, Stan Maxwell was looking at him stonily, which was equally as unsettling as Stan's former wife's hollow-cheeked glare. Stan's own defense, that he was showing the little girl the water when she wriggled out of his grip and fell, chilled Aldo—he thought of himself as a self-injuring clown with the potential to harm anyone unlucky enough to be left in his care, including his own child. Footage in the state's arsenal was presented with prosecutorial relish, yet Aldo himself found the evidence inconclusive. A pixieish girl falling off the bridge, but whether Stan threw, shoved, or dropped her accidentally was not clear. Aldo felt frozen in a ghastly fear that he was watching a preview of his own trial.

The bus to the festival arrives very late in the afternoon, just as the damp glow of a desert sun is setting over that incredible rock, and they are greeted by an old man with a gray goatee and two gaunt dogs who leads them to a converted bus where they will sleep on a mattress under a mosquito net. That night, a sky of sharp silvery stars, the kind of night that, as Aldo puts it, "stirs extraterrestrial desires that no earthling can satisfy." Stella writes this in her notebook and Aldo feels the faintest throb of irritation. For the rest of the night he does not share any further thoughts; he doesn't tell her that he feels like the whole world is an enormous aquarium before you pour the water in, nor that he feels they are as long dead as the stars themselves and the act of God remembering us is what gives us the illusion of life. Instead he stays silent and they fall asleep.

The next morning they wake late and eat vegetarian nachos in a tent with the members of Acquired Brain Injury, and Aldo gets into an argument with the lead singer over the composition of nondairy cheese. After lunch, Aldo and Stella walk around the two main stages checking out the early afternoon acts. The smell of marijuana is sweet and constant. There is an aura of debauched lethargy. Stella's pregnant body draws curious stares. This is the biggest crowd she has ever played. She is going through her set list when Aldo's phone rings.

"Aldo! It's horrible!"

It is Leila. The smell of the retirement home is both musty and antiseptic, and she describes the people the same way: musty and antiseptic souls, she says; the inmates here won't stop complaining, she complains. Then there is the noise, the dueling televisions, the smell of pine cleaner and urine; twice she has been sexually harassed by male inmates, someone slipped her wedding ring off her finger while she was asleep, but the worst was being stuck living with all these overentitled baby boomers. "It's intolerable," she cries.

"Don't call them inmates. They're residents, like you."

"Inmates is what we are!"

"Then come live with Stella and me."

"No! I don't want to intrude."

There is no way out, no consolation; it is the grimmest kind of horror story—one with guilt and regret. She had thought her future was an enigma, when it never was. It was waiting smack-bang in her field of vision all along. Leila is suffering and it's Aldo who feels wronged. He hates himself for that feeling. He feels dwarfed by it.

"And my blanket was stolen—you know, the red cashmere one."

"Are you sure you took it there?"

"Of course I'm sure . . ."

Her voice recedes, and that's his fault too, because he is no longer listening. This life she's depicting—the wily nurses, the missing items, the lascivious male residents—is it paranoia or not? It is hard to hear the details now because she is speaking with her hand over her mouth. Now she's bemoaning her Henry, her Veronica, her house, her youth, her health, her island, everything she has lost. Her tight voice is so alive with hurt, with loneliness and longing and outrage, and its every utterance discredits him totally.

"Father Charlie is coming to visit, he's the only one I can count on."

"Don't let him in!" Aldo says. He still can't get over this dried-up priest going about in public in this day and age, daring to counsel vulnerable widows with terrible sons. "Listen, tell Father Charlie that you can no longer see him because being a Catholic today is like remaining in the Nazi Party because you like the autobahns."

Stella slaps Aldo on the arm. "I have an idea," she says.

Aldo wraps up the call. "I can't do anything right now. But as soon as I get back to Sydney I'll sort this out. I promise. I love you. I'll sort it out. I love you. Bye." Two I-love-yous to counteract hanging up on his abandoned mother.

It is two hours from showtime. Stella says, "Let's go for a walk." They wander silently for two kilometers until they are afraid to go further. Not a shadow of a tree and nothing but edgeless sky, an unblinking hell of a sun, the heat mitigated by a breeze that stirs the dust. Aldo gazes around him at the old rocks and the oversized silences and the expanding desolation and negligible wind and the suffocation of all that space and dust pouring off the empty plains.

"I've been thinking about Uncle Howard," Stella says.

"What about him?"

"I'm not supposed to know this, but he's spent a shitload working his way through the spiritual ranks of that religion. Four million new clients a year."

"I think they're called believers."

"Subscribers. You've spent your whole life on dumb businesses. *You* should start a religion, like Hubbard. Like Joseph Smith."

"Who's that?"

"He started Mormonism. They got rich too. You're always preying on people's need for self-improvement."

"I'm not a mantis, Stella. And besides, self-improvement is so twentieth century. People don't want to improve anymore. They want to enhance. They want to augment."

"You drum up some bullshit cosmology. You fake some visitation from God. You offer suckers water-glimpses of salvation for monthly credit card payments."

"What the fuck, Stella," Aldo says, annoyed. "I'm not a huckster."

"You're good at finding people's weaknesses."

"That's a terrible thing to say."

"It's true."

"Well, it's a terrible thing to notice."

"People want what they've always wanted, salvation, and salvation costs what the market can bear."

"Hey, I have principles, despite what you obviously think of me."

"OK, don't get so annoyed," she says, and takes his hand.

Now Stella and Aldo are promising to love each other forever. They turn and look back; the concert seems so small in the bemusing immensity of the desert where there's nothing to see your reflection in, and that's just fine. This is the first quiet moment they've had in a week. The quiet is insane. Stella's hand is flat against her stomach.

"Wait."

"What?"

"I can't remember."

"You can't remember what?"

"We've been going over these songs, and the playlist, and I've been nervous, I mean obsessed, I mean my mind's been distracted."

"You can't remember what?"

"Wait. Just wait."

She turns and starts walking fast. He has a bad feeling, the worst. Aldo catches up and strides beside her in the accusing silence of a desert in its prime. Stella whimpers with fear. They reach the edge of the main tent in the reddish light of dusk. Stella tries lying on her side, then on her back. "I can't remember the last time it moved."

"It was this morning."

"Maybe. No. Not today. Was it today?"

This is the beginning of an ordeal. There is still a long way to go and they are not yet clear if the ordeal is real. Now she goes down on one knee. She is kneeling in the dirt, her yellow dress billowing around her. "Wait," she says. "Wait a minute." She seems afraid to move in the unrelenting heat.

She says, "Maybe it wasn't yesterday either." Aldo doesn't budge or breathe. She screams, "HE'S NOT MOVING!"

What happens next comes to Aldo afterward as a blur. He shouts for an ambulance, for a doctor, and a man with a neck beard comes striding out of the wilderness with sweat patches under his arms, and a voice that seems to suggest homes with blinds permanently drawn. "Let's get you to my office," he says, and helps Stella to her feet, maneuvering her to the medical center, a small fiberglass building with a broken fence. Inside he takes a Doppler fetal monitor and searches breathlessly for the baby's heartbeat.

There isn't one.

"No heartbeat," the doctor says.

A voice in Aldo's head says *miscarriage*.

The doctor calls it something else.

A stillbirth.

Aldo demands simple answers to complex questions. The doctor puts the lightest of emphasis on possibilities too early to know: A spontaneous rupture of the placenta? A blood clot in the cord? Too much fluid in her brain? Cord wrapped around her throat? That's when they catch the word for the first time. Her.

It's a girl.

Was it their fault?

No, the doctor says. These things happen.

These things? Things like this?

The doctor calls ahead to a hospital in Perth, four hours away, but they are on skeleton staff and won't be able to remove the dead child until the following day. "There's no point going now," the doctor says. "We'll wait until first light."

They step outside. The sun has gone down and the temperature with it. A still night, starry and enormous; a cold wind carries dust to their faces. The people dancing are on hallucinogenics or just look that way. Aldo and Stella walk wordlessly in a daze. Their silence is a third voice talking intrusively over them.

She is not walking so much as being borne along solemnly by limbs on autopilot. It is clear to Aldo that for Stella this is the split event, the moment that will divide her life in two. Was it also his?

Her name is called over the loudspeaker. At the same time, Aldo's phone rings. It is his mother. He lets it ring. Aldo says, "This is not the end of us, we will live to love another day." The irritated male voice on the loudspeaker calls for Stella a second time.

"Just tell them to stop calling my fucking name." In order to take her mind off their tragedy, Aldo says the seven words he'll regret his whole life: "Why not get out there and sing?"

The agonizing silence and this is how he fills it. Stella gazes at him in astonishment that quickly dissolves into a horrible blankness, a new kind of nothingness that settles and defines her. She says quietly, "Sing?"

Aldo stands his ground. "Sing! Sure, yes. That's why we came here, after all. You should." As he is saying it, he thinks: Unless you shouldn't. Unless it's a terrible, possibly fatal idea. Without a word, she waddles onto the shadowed stage, and Aldo, like the Sherpa of old, carries her guitar and amplifier with trembling hands. She settles on a stool as he sets the amplifier up, glancing at her belly; they had hoped her womb was some kind of Xanadu, now it's a crypt where their heartache is coordinated.

The wind blows sand and red dust against the stage. With moonlight splashing her skin, Stella steps up to the microphone. Aldo thinks about the things women have had to do throughout history with dead babies inside them. Plow fields, fight off hard Viking penises, bake. The doctor stands beside Aldo backstage, now just another tattooed, neck-bearded groupie. In a soft voice Stella begins to sing, so tentatively at first, Aldo has to call out and ask her to turn it up. Is she even touching those strings? He calls out, "Louder, baby!"

Staring across the plains, she takes a deep breath and violently expels the song, cracking the desert silence with a voice so unnervingly beautiful, Aldo becomes lost in the wonder of it. An optimistic mood envelops him, an expansive glee, a thought that this magical moment would kickstart the child and people would talk about it for years, the baby pronounced dead and resurrected through song.

His commiserating gaze gives way to a smile of pleasure, of pride, of love. Stella meets this smile with an unfeeling mask and he thinks maybe she can't see it, so he smiles even more broadly, then adds two thumbs-up to the picture.

This evokes from Stella the most resentment a human face can carry. Later he will say that even though he then gave frantic glances, and miserable looks of solicitude after the show, it was too late, and what killed his marriage was that unforgivable smile and those dopey thumbs.

At the end of the song, the audience gives an uncertain spattering of applause. It is not havoc out there. The song barely registered. Stepping off the stage she is handed a joint that she smokes in one long jaw-dropping drag.

During the drive back to Perth the next morning, she has phantom kicks that give them new hope. Then Stella and Aldo huddle in the waiting room, and are told she has to be induced to deliver their dead child. Fetal demise, he hears the doctor say on the phone.

"You'll have to deliver the baby vaginally."

"No, no," Stella cries.

"Can't you just cut it out? Like a C-section?"

"You don't want your wife to go through unnecessary abdominal surgery on top of all this, do you?"

"So this will be . . . ?"

"Just like a normal delivery."

So Stella would get her natural birth after all.

She is wheeled into an echoey delivery room. The unused heart monitor sits there, incidental, accusatory. The nurse is saying, "We can give you all the pain medication you need because there's no risk to the baby," as if that bright side were actually bright. Aldo finds himself unable to stop his old worries, and speaks out against an epidural—she doesn't want a spinal injury on top of this, he says—and then it all happens quickly, and despite himself Aldo thinks of the seventies- and early-eighties comedy trope of the surprise black baby and how that would play in a stillbirth situation.

Everything they'd read and heard about in the classes is happening; Stella is induced and has painful contractions and Aldo is beside her saying things like *push* and *breathe* and everything's a nightmare, everything, expelling the placenta, the episiotomy, the icepacks, but when the baby comes out, no one says "It's a girl," and there's no monitoring of the heartbeat, there's no cry. There is only silence, an incredible silence, like the silence of the desert, or the silence of a plane gliding without engines over a menacing seascape, or of a body submerged in bathwater, or of a mute television showing an exploded bus, or soundless like a Portuguese housekeeper seen sobbing through a picture window. As Aldo looks at his child, he remembers his very first memory on earth: the detestable quiet of a summer's day, the hottest day on record, and the Benjamins sunburned as a family, him and Veronica and Henry and Leila, all four lying naked on the floor like underfed animals in a zoo during a heatwave unable to move for food or water; everyone ordering everyone else to empty the kitty litter. He wants to tell Stella this memory, but doesn't. There's something else on her mind. They haven't yet named their child—it was Aldo's idea to wait until they saw her and now, on Stella's insistence, they struggle to name this dead girl. He buys a book of baby names from the hospital gift shop. They settle on Ruby.

The doctor asks Stella if she wants to hold the baby. Oh Christ no, Aldo thinks. Say no. She says yes. She holds onto her as if the baby were a souvenir, something brought back from a holiday in a war zone. Her translucent skin and stillness make her look like some bloodless Cupid. Stella also wants to be photographed with the baby. They do a series of gruesome family portraits: Ruby wrapped tight in a blanket, distraught mother and father holding onto her, onto each other.

Stella is holding her fingers and her fingernails and kissing the palm of her hand. She gets plaster casts of her feet and hands, imprints of her footprints. They dress and bathe the baby, and say the final good-bye as Ruby is taken away for an autopsy. Aldo organizes the funeral and Stella overhears him ask if they give a discount for stillborns.

They do.

*They went back into their lives like fellow commuters on a train stuck in a tun-*nel due to a body on the tracks. Stella put her guitars in the storage cupboard and shut the door and never went in and never sang or played guitar again. She also stopped sharing her thoughts, or her thoughts became unshareable, and threw herself into her depressing sales job as though she enjoyed it. They were too young to assimilate this kind of tragedy, so they partied, and they partied separately, and their own vitality and lack of gloom was horrifying to them. They had sex but only occasionally, and as unobtrusively as possible, got it down to the brevity of a haiku, or else she gave him furious hand jobs that were best avoided; who dreaded the ritual of bedtime more, it was hard to say. Aldo spent his weekends at the retirement village consoling Leila for the death of her granddaughter, and set about on a new real estate venture to buy up all the state's murder houses for a song. That was principally to disguise his grief, but there was no real sympathy for him anyway. He hadn't carried the child; people treated him as if she had not been his to lose, and he resented Stella for that. And now that she was no longer deeply in love with him, his financial failures, crippling debts and overall bad pecuniary fate came to define him. Money and Aldo's irresponsible loss of it became a contentious issue in their relationship, the default issue. He owed her money, and she wanted him to pay up.

The night he knew it was over, they'd just eaten Chinese food; he cracked open the fortune cookie and pretended to read a made-up fortune. "May all your enemies be beautiful so you might one day hate-fuck them with pleasure," he said, and glanced up at Stella to see if she would write it down or make a mental note. Nothing. Hands trembling, he opened another cookie and fake-read, "Only schoolchildren masturbate to mermaids. Outside of the face, those sea-hotties have not a single workable orifice." Stella sat stone-faced, and Aldo felt swept away in a current. He smashed opened another cookie: "Be satisfied with your looks. The almost-but-not-quite beautiful people don't have the burden of being gawked at 24/7, and can go about their lives without looking in the mirror and seeing a plate of dog's balls." Nothing. He could no longer affect, influence, or help her. Now he was going over a waterfall in a barrel. He was her muse no longer.

Zetland High's ten-year reunion was held in the same beer garden of an old hotel we used to be denied access to when we were underaged. Everybody laughed about their lives as if they were simulations; those who were successful seemed visibly so, and those who were undermined for a living displayed that too. Some people were so bald and so fat your eyes felt callous just looking at them, or were so sick and so thin you started the grieving process as you bought them a drink. Well, that's a high school reunion for you. Divorce, dead kids; even a ten-year reunion has some points of interest. Yet there was an unexpected feeling of genuine warmth; these were the people who'd known you when you were still callow and the fault of your parents, before you were the product of your own missteps.

Together, the group regressed, like a cast reunion of a long-running soap where it's unseemly to break character. An orgy of reminiscences, pasts that needed verifying. It was a socially weird and artificial environment. Unhappily married men trying to fuck the same girls they once rejected for reasons they couldn't remember now, and which suddenly seemed their greatest regret. Every now and then you made a fatal error. You didn't recognize someone, and to cover, you pretended they'd changed, when actually you couldn't remember their names back then either. The faux pas added up. Aldo confused one of the Norton twins for another set of twins altogether, the Goldsbros. It was a colossal mistake. Yet not the worst of the night. The ultimate insult was when Jeremy, the fortune-teller's son, projected photographs of my out-of-control party while Natasha Hunt stood frozen in the back of the room, displaying no outward signs of life.

It had never occurred to me until that night that people in general think I'm a ridiculous human being; almost everybody laughed mean-spiritedly about the school play I'd written, *The Vagina of Ill Repute;* after a few laps in *that* pool of memory I was ready to run, but I hung around for Aldo's sake. A good number of people there had invested in some of his schemes and so he was forced to apologize, make excuses, impossible promises. He leaned heavily on whoever he talked to, and I overheard him say at one point, "I even miss the sound of Stella smoking on the other end of the telephone." He was greeted with amusement, old Aldo, but there was something so sad about him it no longer seemed funny.

Around ten p.m., there was a moment of old-fashioned hubbub when Stan Maxwell sauntered in and was greeted like a scallywag coming from the headmaster's office (his conviction had been quashed on appeal). He made a beeline for Aldo. "I hear we both lost a child," he said. For the first time in his life, Aldo was speechless.

Stan said, "I'm living by myself now; we should get a drink sometime."

It seemed Stan's post-grief self was something he was just now unveiling to the public, and he was giving us a sneak preview. Aldo, who had never instigated violence in all his life, tightened his fist.

"We *could* do that."

"How's that musician wife of yours?"

"We split up."

"Yeah, me and Vicki did too. Losing a kid, a couple can't survive that. And the ones who can, they must be psychopaths."

Aldo looked like he was having trouble breathing.

"How's Lola?"

"Leila. She's good. She moved to a . . . she's in a home, settling in well. She's . . . not far. Edgecliff. I get out there as often as I can. I try to."

Maybe the chill in the conversation had lasted long enough for Stan to begin to see himself from our vantage point; that might account for the sudden drop in civility on his face. His look turned steel cold and if eyes could gnash their teeth, then that is what his were doing. I said, "Nice to see you, Stan," and shepherded Aldo outside.

We sat on a bench and watched people through the window; women's heads that clashed with their bodies; men who had been styled by their uncles. Aldo said, "You know how people neurotically fear their imperfections are the most visible thing about them?"

"Yeah?"

"Well, in the case of this room, they're one hundred percent right."

He examined the group carefully. "Bipolar," he said. "OCD. Intimacy issues. Super depressed. Compulsive liar. Mythomaniac, really. Morbid dependency on his two-year-old. Abandonment issues. Cold turkey from something. Passive-aggressive crisis of masculinity. Battered other woman syndrome. Narcissistic personality disorder. Grandiosity, hypervigilance. He's coked up. Stuck in a grim cycle of abuse that's just warming up. Serial adulterer. Sex addict. Cannabis-induced psychosis."

"Oh come on, how could you possibly know that?"

Aldo shrugged.

"You're a judgmental son of a bitch."

"You don't call a doctor judgmental for diagnosing a cancer."

"You bet I do."

We watched a little longer the unhappy parade of old friends and foes, this lengthy queue for the grave. Aldo was transfixed.

I asked, "Hey, did you speak to Brad?"

"Yeah. He's got cardiac neurosis. It's iatrogenic."

"What? It's what? What is that?"

"Illness resulting from or influenced by medical examination or treatment." I looked at him a moment. "That's what happened to Henry," he said, in a quiet voice. "Poor Henry. Poor Daddy."

I was startled to see Aldo had tears in his eyes. He didn't wipe them, but rather tried to cram them back into his eyes with the heels of his palms.

"What about me?"

"On the cusp of major depressive episode brought on by intense dread of high school reunion."

"What about you, then?" I asked. "What's your problem?"

"Jinxed, Liam. I'm fucking jinxed."

It seemed strange and pitiful to be so coldly clinical about the afflicted around him while saving the balm of magical thinking for himself.

It was then Aldo asked me if I wanted to see the photograph of his baby girl. Oh, heaven knows, now I'm a police officer and I've seen my share of dead babies, but I wasn't then, and anyway, I sure didn't want to see his. But I was also his friend and I had the feeling that he really needed to show it to me.

He held the picture out, for me to take. My best friend's tragedy and it wasn't more than five centimeters from my face. I tried to stop my eyes from working. I couldn't. The baby girl's cheeks were unexpectedly rosy and puffed. She looked like a healthy dead baby. I remarked as much.

The photo slipped out of his fingers and fell through the sewer grating.

"Shit!" We bent down, pressed our faces to the grate, but it was out of reach. "I'll have to ask Stella for a copy. That'll be a fun moment."

Aldo sighed deeply; I had nothing to add except a sigh of my own. "I think I'll slip away," he said, but he didn't move. Instead he declared that only a lesion on the brain of God could explain why He so consistently overestimates the resilience of His creation. I said, "I don't believe in a tumorous Yahweh." He said, "If only I had an explanation." I quoted Byron: "Who then will explain the explanation?" His head wobbled on his neck as if the tendons were spring-loaded. He asked, "Can an unintended victim of a drive-by shooting be complicit in attracting ricocheted bullets?" I thought: These are the sorts of impossible questions Aldo's bad luck and narrow escapes pose to the lifelong observer of his misfortunes. He then launched on a talking jag, about the grinding suckiness of a capricious universe and the tactical error of being born and feeling like an unexploded ordnance. He talked about how Stella looked at him as if she thought she was going to be raptured at any minute and the rest of us would just be standing there gazing up at her ascension with an idiotic look on our damned faces. He admitted that sometimes, late at night, he googled the name Veronica Benjamin, in the desperate hope that she might have an online presence in the afterlife. He said his heart felt the craziness of animals before a major meteorological event. He talked about how Leila had three personalities, two of which kept the third on as a common enemy. He said, "Last time I checked, there are fifty-one languages on earth spoken by only one person— imagine those poor suckers, that's a lot of pressure." I felt lanced to the point of mutilation by his voice and glanced at the half-open door leading back into the reunion. He asked, "Hey, am I boring you?" There it was again! His most common, most unforgivable crime—when in the process of boring me, he became self-aware and apologized for being boring. "No, no," I said, feigning shock at the suggestion, "you're not boring me, please go on." It was crazy. Even now, after all these years, I still had to plead for Aldo to continue to bore me.

Albeit a Persistent One

G O FUCK YOURSELF," HE SAYS, flinging the manuscript in my lap. His expression, however, is neutral. It is as if we are both waiting for his smile to download.

Wind blows sand in Aldo's eyes and I remember he also has a face that attracts campfire smoke. The airy space between us widens and the silence grows unwieldy. Had I actually managed to offend him?

A voice shouts, "Hey! Aldo!"

We turn to see that two young men with weak chins, wearing blue T-shirts and khaki shorts, surfboards and black sports bags under their arms, have emerged from the path. Aldo waves them over.

"I didn't think you guys were going to turn up!"

"Bit of trouble finding the place," the tall one says. I note he's recently undergone tattoo-removal surgery on his right forearm. "What is this, a secret beach?"

"Magic beach, actually," I say.

Their faces light up. "Magic beach! Awesome!"

"Mr. Benjamin, feast your eyes on this. Voilà!"

They place one of the boards on the sand. It is like none I have ever seen; it has soft polyurethane handles at the front and an indentation scooped out for his belly, and straps to hold both legs.

"This is perfect."

"We made it just for you."

"No charge, Aldo Benjamin. No charge."

"We were happy to do it."

This is madness.

"Wait," I say. "What if you roll?"

"If he rolls," the tall one says, "the straps will snap with the force of it."

Aldo holds himself erect while they help him squeeze into an oversized wetsuit. He is so weirdly proportioned, with his bulky arms and withered legs, his Tarzan upper torso and round, hard gut, it's an uncomfortable, awkward procedure. I think: How will he keep his head above water? How will he not drown? How will he manage on his own? The tall one says, "So I understand you're going in too?"

"Me?"

Handing me a wet suit and a surfboard, he says, "You're his friend, aren't you?"

He has me there.

Aldo's all zipped up and aiming his pleading eyes in my direction. This preplanned excursion clearly hinges on me going along with it. I turn to the clean, endless ocean, the blue air sparkling above it, and I'm reunited with old childhood terrors of dumpings, the taste of seawater and my own bile. I suddenly remember that anger is the sea's default setting. Aldo exhales my name as miserably as possible.

Oh, what choice do I have? I say, "I guess it's like Morrell writes: *If not working on your art, time should only be spent on sensual pleasure or charity work.*"

"There you go."

Once again, thinking of Angus Morrell saddens and oppresses us.

I change into the wet suit.

The short one says, "Know much about surfing?"

I say, "We aim the pointy end at the horizon, right?"

I hadn't been surfing, as I said, for over twenty years. My memories are: falling prey to a bad rip; being grievously assaulted by a wave and dragged from the surf by a hungover lifeguard with faintly diarrheic breath. I don't want to do this, I think, as Aldo lies prone on the board and the two men carry him like a battle-weary king, just like the goddamn Fussy Corpse, to the shoreline.

"Come on!" he shouts.

I shuffle to the water's edge and wedge the long board in the wet sand and stare at the pitiless waves pounding the shore.

"God," Aldo says, to no one. It suddenly dawns on me that surfing with someone who hasn't been on a board for twenty-five years—and who has paralysis in both lower extremities—might just be unbearable.

A stiff wind is tearing up the sea. Each wave has a face of angry grief. In contrast, the mammoth backlit rock is nightmarishly faceless, solid and anonymous as death. I look over at Aldo, prone on his specialized surfboard, wincing as the waves curl. Why he wants to go out there is unclear, but I can see the creeping onset of stupefying fear and realize he might just flap about on the shoreline until sunset and then hate himself as we head for home.

"Come on," I say, "let's go in."

The tall one says, "We'll wait here a bit to see if the board needs any adjustments."

It's up to me to propel him out into the cold, fast-rising swell. I push him into the shallows and get ready to help him duck-dive under the first wave, but he shrugs me off.

"I'll get through the breakers myself, thanks."

"He wants to do it himself," the short one says.

"Let him try," the tall one says.

"Whatever, bitches," I say and slam my board on the ocean and lie down on it; it flips over immediately. I stand and turn quickly to see if anyone's watching. They all are.

Aldo shouts, "Incoming!"

A wave breaks on my back and I fall facefirst onto the wet sand. This time when I gather myself, I don't look; I turn and go through the shoals and a repulsive dense bed of seaweed, dive in under the breakers, and make my way out to the flat behind the first peak. I swing the board around and see I'm alongside the rock, which juts up steeply, menacingly, casting rigid, dislocated shadows on the water. I paddle as far from the intimidating, windswept monolith as possible while scanning the shore. There he is, waves crashing into his face; Aldo can turn away slightly, but can't duck their force. He is knocked off. The khaki men hoist him back onto the board. He tries again, this time paddling twice as hard, clawing for his life against the lines of white water, yet is inevitably spewed up onto the shore. The waves deny him access to their peaks. He's still in the shallows. Even from here I can see his eyes burn from the salt water. This is ridiculous.

"Want some help?" I yell.

"I'll get there!"

I straddle my board in what feels like all seven-tenths of the earth's surface, longing for terrestrial existence. I'd forgotten how much I hate floating on the endless drama of the sea, hate drifting aimlessly as a little door swings open and self-loathing thoughts come out. I'd forgotten how much I hate the ocean spray in my face, the sun like syringes in my eyes, and the prospect of sharks, or shark lookalikes—dolphins—and bluebottle stingers and the odds of wallowing in underwater silence until death. I'd forgotten the total boredom that comingles with continuous terror to make surfing as unpleasant a pastime as there ever was. I pray for long flat spells.

Aldo, who has lost all access to his "brave face," is still having trouble getting past the breakers. He's trying to duck-dive under the crashing foam, and is so enraged, he begins intense, vein-popping, hate-paddling with his Popeye arms until he finally makes it through the aggressive wall of water and splats down next to me, heaving violently.

Letting his arms hang in the water, he rests awhile, lying limply on the board, waiting to catch his breath. We silently watch the loudmouthed, heavy-jawed, rancorous, and unfriendly surfers beside us who, in my professional opinion, you should never leave an unguarded drink next to; i.e., ladies, these are hunters who medicate their prey. These men with the abs of galley slaves are staring us down. Now that I think about it, Aldo has always made a point of hating subcultures; the whole idea of mobs celebrating their differences from other mobs, of being different *together*, never worked for him conceptually. He even hates the paraphernalia of subcultures: "the tight undershirts of homosexuals, the black hats of Orthodox Jews, the polished boots of skinheads." So what are we doing here?

"So?" I say.

"So maybe evolution was a backward step. So maybe I want my gills back."

Full, steep waves march toward the shore every couple of minutes. Aldo is floating beside me, with his lumbering, insensate body's whiff of septic tank. He is equally horrified by the looming rock yet seemingly unperturbed by the absurdity of us being out here. He looks like he could keep floating for some time.

"Go on then," I say. "You want to fucking surf, fucking surf."

"As predicted in the Book of Revelation: And the sideshow shall become the main event."

"Just move."

Flat on the board, Aldo starts paddling. A wave lifts him up and he rises with it, but he puts too much weight on the front and the nose of his board goes straight to the bottom, like it's drilling for oil, then catapults out of the fattened waves. I scan churning water for a downturned torso or the international symbol for drowning. Minutes later, through curtains of spray, I see him, back on the crescent of copper sand, readjusting his catheter, conferring with his specialists, conferring with his heart that, even from a distance, is almost visibly throbbing through his chest.

My turn, but I can't seem to swing the board around; I am facing out to sea. When I do manage to turn and paddle to catch a wave, it comes time to get to my feet but I can't do it. I get as far as my knees and stay there; I must look like I'm about to take the holy sacrament. I tumble into the sea and a second later I'm underwater in coffin silence. I think: I only hate golfing more, and I come up in time to see Aldo vanish into the seething white water.

I paddle over and fish him out. "We done?"

He gazes at me as if reading a map that doesn't correspond with the terrain. "Let's get back out there."

We return ourselves to the snarling waves. Miraculously our boards both make it over. We hyperventilate in tandem.

"Your turn," he says. "I need a minute."

For the next wave I crouch and try to imagine little Sonja on my back; no way would I want to fall. But my foot isn't far enough forward. I tumble off, and a cave mouth closes around me, the surge of water sucking me along a secret curve.

The rest of the afternoon continues like this. Feeling both weightless and rooted to every spot at once, with our terrible timing and the sun a holy riot in the sky, blazing onto our shoulders and our backs, each wave arrives tediously, another depressing milestone to be confronted and overcome. Worst of all, any wave we catch seems to angle toward the obstacle, the island, that big bulge of rock that threatens fractured wrists and snapped necks, punctured lungs and severed spines, and when it is not the waves, the rip is like a tractor beam dragging us toward it. A couple of times I come too close to the rocky island and leap off the board so I won't hit it. In the lulls between carnage, we regroup on shore and I swear at Aldo in a dozen languages. I'm not the only one. While Aldo was fighting the good fight in the liquid trenches, the surfers, aggressively protective of their breaks, were growling and having fun cutting him off. I wade out and tell them to lay off, pointing to the wheelchair at the sand's edge: a seagull is perched on one of the arms. By three p.m. his skin is an angry rash, like he's been rubbed with a steel brush, and in the hours of horizontal surfing he has had multiple mouthfuls of sand and foamy scum. One time he snags himself on a rock and self-diagnoses coral poisoning. This is no good. No fun to watch either. I think: Surfing is primal in the way that human flight is primal, in that it's not.

A single personal highlight: In the late afternoon I coast on a small clean wave close to shore. Though I feel like a child riding a pedophile's back, and the ride lasts all of four seconds, I'm still mildly pleased and ready to quit while I'm only behind. When I go back out, Aldo's sea-shaken, slackened body is sprawled on the board.

"We done?"

"Not quite."

For some reason I allow this farce to continue, and when Aldo catches a wave to shore himself and I shout bravo, he admonishes me. "There's nothing more depressing than a triumph of the human spirit."

Frankly, his whole peevish demeanor is pissing me off.

"So really, why are we doing this?"

He wants to share a destiny with a starfish, or be swept away? Has this something to do with Mimi, a way to remember the dead? One thing is clear. He's making his own rites of passage on the fly.

"Hey, tell me something," I say.

"I miss star jumps."

"That wasn't my question."

"Shoot."

"Your religion."

"What about it?"

"Before prison, you sort of represented a vociferous brand of God-hating that pretty much called for a violent overthrow of the human need for spiritual comfort."

"You were in the courtroom. You heard my testimony. I know it's hard for an atheist to accept, but even though He is nonexistent, God is irreplaceable," Aldo says. "In lieu of accepting the stale knockoffs on offer, one must reinvent Him or remain forever unfit for active duty."

"Man, I really wish I had my pen."

"Anyway, don't you remember when we first met? I was a deep believer."

"Oh wait, you mean in Apollo?"

"People not only want you to believe, they've already got the God all picked out for you."

"That's not religion, that's mythology."

"*Now* it's mythology. It was religion at some point. Sometimes I think about those old gods who came down and meddled in human affairs. Maybe *they* crashed my car."

"Way to take responsibility."

Aldo makes a gastroenteritis face. "And maybe they descended to earth and took my form at your party."

"What part— Oh. That party."

"Have you ever felt so large you can't be expanded yet so small you can't be compressed?"

"Nope."

For another hour we lie on the strange symmetry of the waves, not talking, watching the setting sun reflected on the wet sand. At one point I go to get our phones and cigarettes from the beach, carrying them back out in one of Aldo's ziplock medicine bags. On the flat we lie on our boards smoking and taking photos of each other. Occasionally Aldo catches a wave but he seems content to just lie there. It's the end of the day and even my ears are sunburned.

At sunset I say, "Let's go in."

"A few more waves," he says.

My feet are growing numb. The wind has died down and there are no waves of consequence, just the general meander of the sea. The darkness that comes with the vanishing sun seems thick and slippery, and our boards slosh in the quiet sea that slobbers at the shore, regurgitating brown sand.

"Now?"

"Not yet," he says, with a look in his eye.

A crescent moon ascends majestically like a silky white eyebrow raised in surprise. The sky darkens completely as the sun disappears behind the cliffs.

"Last drinks, gentlemen," I say.

"Five more minutes," he says.

The night pours down and we float on the water with moonlight dancing on the foam. Baby waves keep us moving.

Lulled by the hypnotic currents, we keep parallel to each other. The ocean is black now, pitiless, cold, and Aldo is up on his elbows, water creeping across his board. The last two remaining surfers head for shore, then stand together on the beach, half out of their wet suits, looking semihuman, facing out to sea.

"Let's go in," I say.

"You only have to take one look at the moon to know man will never walk on her ever again."

"Two minutes," I say.

My skin is tingling from the cool breath of night. We let our boards drift in circles, giving us a tour of our surroundings. Steep cliffs twist up to the stars that burn like sparks against the sky. At one point I'm turned away from the shore, toward the horizon, with the moon cutting a straight path across the sea. I make a mental note of the air, that new-planet smell, the sound of thrashing water against rock. When his board swings my way, Aldo's face looks laminated in the moonlight. He grips the handles tight, lies rigid, and gazes unpleasantly at that desolate island, breathing heavily. The sea is as flat as a lake now. It seems as if we're in a bottle with the cork in. For a moment Aldo mumbles incoherently, then he falls silent and listens for something, like a child hoping to hear a mother's footstep on a staircase. Every ten minutes I suggest going in, but Aldo resists.

"Humanity's common goal is to die with dignity, and 'dignified' in that context is defined as dying in our own beds, but what if you have a water bed or Spider-Man bedsheets? What's dignified about that?"

"I don't know. Nothing."

"Right up until his death," he says, "Henry thought people of good character were those who took cold baths. Until hers, Leila was always presenting me with fruit as if she were Marco Polo bringing back pasta from the Orient. And Veronica—she was the first person who had a visceral reaction to my face, but she wasn't the last."

In the dark, you could almost hear his memories crackle like bacon.

He says, "The coccyx is the last bone to decay in the grave."

"Are you all right?"

He shook his head. "I feel so physically bad all the time I've gotten to the point of not knowing when I'm sick."

"What's wrong now?"

"Head pain, neck pain, shoulder pain, upper back pain, lower back pain, arm pain, elbow pain, wrist pain, hand pain, chest pain, hip pain, pelvic pain. I've got thermal hyperalgesia and tactile allodynia. Christ, forget it. I'm lashed to the first day of the rest of forever. Get Amnesty International in here. SMS the RSPCA. Reconvene the Nuremberg Trials."

"I'm sorry for what happened to you." I realize I hadn't said this before now.

"I know."

"I mean in prison."

"Even in a hundred years from now that will be the cause of death."

"I know."

"I'm not sadistic, but—"

"That's like that thing racists say. I'm not racist, but . . ."

"Yeah. Like, I'm not racist, but to die and find God in blackface would be hilarious."

"Exactly. What were you saying?"

"I'm not sadistic but sometimes I think about chemical castration, though only if I get to choose the chemical. Hydrochloric acid."

Poor Aldo. In the right light you could see his organs fail.

"Hang on," he says in a cracked voice, "I've got an idea."

He paddles over to the rocky island and collides with it. He paddles backward and then takes another lunge at the rock.

"Careful! What are you doing?"

He guides the nose of the board and manages to wedge it in a crevice between two egg-shaped boulders. Great curtains of spray cover him as he maneuvers alongside and slides himself across onto the narrow ledge, the rope from the board sluicing the sea. He pulls himself upright and sits on the island's edge, his emaciated legs dangling in the water. You can't even call him a biped without fiddling with the definition.

With the rope he drags the board onto the ledge and secures it. He slides himself over an inch, stops, then another inch, as if in slow pursuit of something. I can't understand what he is doing.

I paddle over. "What are you doing?"

"I'm staying here the night."

"The whole night?"

Aldo shakes his head, which doesn't answer my question. The dark is chilling. Using his forearms, he makes a painfully slow, furtive tour of duty around the island, grimacing as he gropes his way along the uneven plateau.

The waves start up again. I struggle to remain on my board. Aldo pushes himself into a hollow under an overhanging ledge and shouts, "Off you go!"

He settles in as if he'd programmed this destination into his GPS at birth. He sits stiffly, as remote and inhuman as the character in one of my earliest short stories from adolescence, "The Elephant Man in the Iron Mask of Zorro." I say, "You know who you look like?"

He doesn't say anything.

I say, "Are you serious?"

"Go home, Liam."

It's unsafe for him there. All afternoon I've been watching that island. I swear birds flew in that didn't fly out.

"I can't leave you stranded on a rock."

"You've got better things to do than worry about me."

"Yeah, but I'm not going to be doing them."

"Think of this as like being supportive when your girlfriend confesses she wants to get a breast reduction."

"What?"

Aldo retreats further still, until his face is consumed by shadow. The waves grow bigger now, tossing me about, and start crashing over the island. Aldo is soaked in his little alcove and he shuffles back out, looking for a better position.

"It's getting rough," he says.

I stare at him for a couple of minutes then swivel around. For some reason I remember that during high school Aldo had a dog that barked itself to death.

"Hey, remember Sooty?"

"Of course I do. She was *my* dog."

"What the fuck was up with that bitch?"

He scowls at me, then slithers and drags himself toward what I imagine is the dry center of the rock. He slips and falls into a crevice and pulls himself out. It's tough going. It would be easier if he were a double amputee. What use are those legs to him now? They just get in the way, I think, watching him gimping around the rock in the starlight, peering into crevices, a look of surprise on his face.

"What is it? What are you looking at?" I ask.

"Shit!"

"What? What happened?"

He holds up the palm of his hand—blood streams from it. He laughs.

"What's so funny?"

"Not long ago I was worried about bedsores. Now I'm worried about barnacles."

"What?"

"Go home, Liam."

Aldo waves me away one last time. What choice do I have? Other than physically dragging him back to shore, I'm out of ideas. I float on the dark and oily water.

Aldo says, "Coo-eee," but there's no echo. He's disappointed. "We're too far out, I guess," he says.

"Seriously," I say, "I'm heading back to shore."

"Ta-ta."

I wait, but he doesn't move.

"OK," I say. "Nighty night. Sleep tight. Don't let the box jellyfish bite."

"*Adiós, muchacho.*"

I paddle in, the island sliding into darkness at my back, and I make it to shore on jelly legs with the taste of salty foam in my mouth. On the wet sand I sit bewildered and gape at the somber outline of the jutting rock, at the steep waves rising and falling, the white peaks staring out of the dark. I can't see Aldo but for a brief moment I spot the flare of a lighter and the glow of a cigarette.

As the hours pass, the night grows darker still; the headlands dissolve into it. The whites of the breakers gleam faintly, then they don't. The waves disappear, the rock can't be seen, nothing. It's easy to mistake wind for outright hatred in the night.

I strain to hear if Aldo's calling me but I can't separate land noises from sea noises. I'm shaking from the chilly air as I take a couple more of Aldo's painkillers from his wheelchair bag, lay my head on the cold sand, and close my eyes. The blissful monotony of sleep. I dream we are on our boards, drifting along a dark, wet corridor in crystal-clear waters, looking down at a valley of wet bones buried beneath us. At four in the morning I wake to see the clouds have cleared and the sky is jam-packed with stars and the rock looks huge. Everything seems out of place—as if it has been shuffled, or put through some kind of filter. I can see the shape of Aldo sitting up. He's not moving, and I remember his physical immobility back in that interrogation room, once I had forced him down in his chair, with the charge of infanticide hanging over his head, and the eyes of the gravelly, mute Sergeant Oakes and Senior Detective Doyle gazing at this friend of mine whom they saw as a lost and evil cause . . .

The Interview, or Terms and Conditions

THIS IS A TAPE-RECORDED INTERVIEW by Constable Liam Wilder of Aldo Francis Benjamin. Also present to corroborate is Senior Detective Jason Doyle and Sergeant David Oakes. The time is three p.m. Please state your full name and address.

Aldo Francis Benjamin. 242 Botany Road, Sydney.

You don't have to lean into the microphone. Age and date of birth?

Sixth of May 1973 was the benighted moment. I'm nearly thirty-nine.

Are you an Australian citizen?

Yes.

Are you a permanent resident of Australia?

Of course.

Are you an Aboriginal or Torres Strait Islander?

Jesus Christ. For the record, the constable and I are old high school friends. He knows very well what I am and what I am not.

Tell me what happened, Aldo. Why are we here? From the beginning.

OK. Stella had been bugging me to stop starting startups, to drop my dreams of sudden and undeserved wealth, to forget the whole notion of total financial security and just settle down to some steady, gainful employment and repay my debts even if by the tiniest of installments.

I've been saying the same thing since forever, but go on.

Sometime in late January or early February, I acquiesced and found myself in a job interview in the low-lit, empty lobby of the Railway Hotel, trying to look vital, eager, and responsible. I felt none of those things, obviously, opposite her uncle Howard. You've met him.

The Scientologist.

That's him. He read my CV with menacing stillness. Behind us a couple dragged luggage on broken wheels to the reception desk, and I was saying something like I'm a fast learner or maybe that I was a team player, in any case one of those phrases that make you feel as if you've let someone urinate on you for a dollar.

Howard is the owner?

The manager. I remember we fell into a deep silence broken only by telephones vibrating in guests' pockets and by the sudden elevator ding. "Listen, Aldo," Howard says, leaning forward, "you seem pretty unsuitable for this position, but I owe Stella a big one, and I hear you're having some difficulty making your child-support payments."

Child-support payments?

That's what Stella told him, even though she hadn't yet had the child, the child that was Craig's, or perhaps some unknown third party's. I mean, this whole scenario was typical Stella, you know, pointlessly manipulating the truth or lying outright to get her desired outcome. In this case, me in full employment, the repayment of the debt.

Not to mention power over you.

Being a room-service waiter would mostly entail delivering twenty-dollar hamburgers to strung-out rock stars in fluffy white robes, she'd said, and now I wondered if that wasn't a lie also. Howard leaned back into his chair wearily, as if he'd had to deal with me his whole damn life. He said, "A man's gotta do what he's gotta do, Aldo." I said, "I suppose so." He said, "A man's gotta meet his responsibilities." I said, "You sure know a lot about men." Howard frowned. The elevator doors opened onto the empty lobby. "All right, job's yours if you want it," Howard said quietly. "I appreciate the opportunity," I lied, and he bullied me into an exaggerated handshake and ducked out of the lobby, leaving me straining my eyes at the dark charcoal etchings on the oil-black walls, before he returned a minute later waving a uniform in my face, the sight of which made me recoil. I said, "Oh God. Oh Jesus." He said, "What's the matter?" I said, "Oh Jesus." The thing is, Liam, it was only black pants and a black jacket with a white shirt and a red tie but it seemed to me that I was being fitted for a life that was exactly my size.

So what did the job entail?

I had to wait in the kitchen, shivering in subarctic air conditioning, scrubbing plates and shining counters while the chef prepared the food simulacrum, after which I pushed carts through poorly lit corridors into rooms where I was to cultivate a disgust at human sexuality I'll never entirely shake off, delivering overcooked meat on soggy bread under silver domes to bargain-obsessed adults who dressed like rich ten-year-olds and didn't stop sniffing cocaine off strippers' tits when I entered. That, and the overabundance of women who when talking to their dogs referred to themselves as "mummy," and the Sri Lankan concierge who whined about the day globalization finally reached his village but passed him by *personally*, and the guests who stared at me meaninglessly as if I were a potted plant or a fixed point in space, *and* the businessmen loitering, frustrated and embarrassed outside their rooms, unable to master the electronic key, made me hate every minute, but because a stubborn illogical part of me wanted to impress and win Stella back, I was determined to stick it out, and I would have, if not for, you know.

No, I don't know. What?

What. Exactly.

What?

Exactly. Until my species of bad luck is identified, I can't say.

CAN'T SAY WHAT?

I know I'm always in the path of strange comets, and it's somehow my own fault, but how, Liam? Am I really reaping what I sowed? If so, what the fuck am I sowing, and how am I sowing it?

That I don't know.

Some nights, when I go to bed, I half-expect to find on my pillow a card that reads, "Yours sincerely, Lucifer."

Aldo, just tell me, what happened at the Railway Hotel?

Nothing much! That's the thing! Everything happened. The usual. In the nine measly days of my employment there, I slipped on the lobby floor, only to be harshly reprimanded by Uncle Howard for slipping on a slip-resistant surface. I misidentified the sex of a guest's child in front of the hotel owner, fell up the back staircase, opened the side restaurant door and struck a pensioner in the face, and then the solemn feud between me and staircases extended to elevators when, somewhere between the third and fourth floors, the elevator ground to a shuddering halt.

You got stuck in the elevator? Is that such a major deal?

The problem was I wasn't alone. There was an attractive blonde in a leather skirt with a few more teeth than her mouth could handle who pressed the button a dozen times, and it occurred to me, I mean I sensed, that to be trapped in an elevator with a man was the erotic fantasy she'd waited her whole life for, and further, I intuited that she *wanted* to want me, but there wasn't the slightest hint of sexual tension between us and despite herself she couldn't *or wouldn't* find me attractive. "This is a bit of bad luck," I said. "Hmm," she said back. I said, "All those disaster movies have it wrong. I don't think strangers *do* bond together in times of crisis, I think they resent each other's unfamiliarity as the plane goes down and then burn together in awkward silence."

Funny.

Right? In response, she pushed herself into the elevator's corner and began whimpering, and a second thing occurred to me: She's scared out of her mind! I gave my warmest smile aimed precisely at her absurd misperception. "Don't touch me," she said, and backed up even further. "I'll scream!" she screamed, incrementally flattening herself against the polished wall, then half-turning sideways into a cowered squat. I didn't know what to do; I straightened my rumpled shirt and put on my most solicitous grin and stared ahead at the doors, but they were reflective burnished silver, and no matter which way I turned we couldn't avoid each other's images. It was awful. Her terror, my terror of her terror. Her mounting hysteria, my anger at her refusal to calm the fuck down. And the whole thing just triggered the worst memories.

Of what?

You remember.

Natasha Hunt?

Exactly. I mean, is sexual insidiousness my blind spot? Do I spur a reflex to persecute? Is there such a glitch in my aura that I project myself as wild and undomesticated? Is *that* the family curse, that we make bad first impressions, middle impressions, and last impressions?

Let's get back to the elevator.

Twenty grueling minutes later, the doors fly open and the petrified woman sprints out, and within an hour I'm summoned by Howard into his office, a large room with a wall of huge windows in factory frames—so this is where all the light was, I thought; he was hoarding it, the bastard. "Stella's like a daughter to me," he said, "so what should I do about this complaint?" I said, "I never touched that guest!" He said, "She's not a guest." I asked, "So she works in the hotel?" He said, "Not exactly." I couldn't understand the meaning of this conversation. Howard worked the back of his neck in a pincer squeeze. "She's a *working girl,*" he explained, using that strangely old-fashioned term, and went on to explain that she came from a high-class brothel, The Enigma Variations. "The Enigma Variations?" I said. "What kind of a name for a brothel is that?" "Just leave the girls alone, Aldo. They have a job to do," he said, and so, over the following days, I set out to pick the prostitutes from the regular guests and found it inconceivably easy: heavily madeup girls in drastic skirts trudging noisily down corridors in dagger-like heels, black stockings, and visible suspenders, girls who knew how to stare unblinkingly ahead or else looked to be constantly bracing for impact. I observed them, and the male guests who now smelled of shame and body oil, with puzzlement and fear. Any time I heard footsteps I froze; whenever an order came to the kitchen, my hands trembled. Each night I slept uneasily, my dreams laden with premonitions, and at work, wandering the dark hallways like the child of a sun-fearing people, I expected the worst.

Why? What were you afraid of?

My clairvoyance wasn't clairvoyance, but a narrative vision. I believed I was getting the hang of fate's dramatic structure, and that it had in store something unpleasant in relation to these prostitutes from The Enigma Variations.

And did it? Something happened?

Not, it turned out, in relation to the women at all. One night I arrived at room 707 with a plate of chicken fettuccine balanced on the palm of my left hand and knocked on the door with the shame that comes from pushing a product that costs triple its value. A black shoe had the door propped open. I sang out, "Hello?" and "Room service!" and "Knock knock?" and "Should I come in?" and "Here I come!" and I pushed my way in, bracing myself for verbal abuse (guests were always annoyed at your presence in their rooms, as if by bringing them food you somehow cheapened their hunger). Near the open minibar, the curtains were drawn over the thick unopenable windows and a strange, gummy odor made me wince. On the tufted aquamarine carpet, peanut shells and tiny vodka bottles were scattered amongst several soaking wet towels. A chair was tipped over. And then—him!

Who?

A stark-naked middle-aged man hung by the neck from the surprisingly sturdy chromium-plated chandelier.

A suicide!

He ordered room service right before doing it. Fucker. Eternally slumbering broken-necked *bastard*! Of course I thought about Henry. And *his* suicide. And how he had also orchestrated to be found by a stranger. Only now *I* was the stranger.

For the record, the suspect is referring to his father, Henry Benjamin, who hired a housekeeper in order to—

A Portuguese woman named Dulce, who entered the house when Veronica and I were at school and Leila was at an audition. A note from my father was lying on the table. Please clean the upstairs bathroom first. She clomped upstairs and found Henry dead in the bath with his wrists slit. "Usually the method of teenage girls," and, "An unmanly suicide," I later overheard his brothers whisper at his wake, but the overall consensus was that one has to respect a man unwilling to burden his family with the memory of having found his body.

Especially considerate if one discounts poor Dulce.

She came to the door a week after the funeral shaking and pouring sweat. "I was never paid for my day of work," she said. Leila answered, "Well, you didn't actually clean anything."

Hence Aldo's expression for whenever he is walking slowly into what he perceives to be a bad situation. He calls it walking like a Portuguese housekeeper.

Your superiors won't get it.

So, the suicide in the hotel . . .

I looked for a note. There wasn't one. Only a breakfast card filled out for the following morning: OJ, decaffeinated coffee, continental breakfast basket. I sat down on the bed and tried not to look at the dead man whose expression recalled an umbrella blown open by the wind. From his combination-lock leather attaché and smooth black shoes and neatly folded double-breasted suit

I deduced this suicide case had had a business implosion, probably lost the family home, couldn't face his wife and kids. The body twisted on the curtain cord and his sad sightless visage was angled mercifully away from me. I sat at the desk and wrote a note for him on hotel stationery and left it under a puddle of yellow lamplight: Dear World, I wrote, please have my body placed in a giant clamshell and lowered to the sea floor.

I read about that in the paper!

Liam, I'm telling you, this was a game-changer. Besides feeling upset and horrified, I was overwhelmingly envious; this motherfucker had achieved something that I, who only ever wanted to vanish or dissolve by an act of will or to liquefy in my sleep or disintegrate body and soul, and who occasionally on dark nights toyed with fantasies of autoerotic asphyxiation, had not. It was at that moment I knew I would not quit the Railway Hotel, not in any verbal or written sense, but that I would never turn up again. More significantly, I knew I was done and dusted with it.

Done and dusted with what?

You know how, when I was younger, I wanted to live at least as long as an Antarctic sponge?

Fifteen hundred years.

It's not just baby Ruby's death and the divorce and losing friends and the business failures and suffocating debt, it's the little things: the abscessed tooth that only presents itself while you're camping, the snakebite when out of cellular range. Listen. I don't know if you know this, but my mother's father died after he was bitten by a nonvenomous spider—he died of fright. My mother's mother was killed by a misdiagnosis of cancer, suggesting a genetic strain of suggestibility off the fucking charts. You know how Jung said the fear of being eaten and the fear of the dark are in the collective unconscious? Well, I come from a very *specific* line that passed on very *specific* fears from generation to generation: fear of unraveling rope bridges, fear of causing an avalanche by sneezing, fear of accidentally procreating with a half sister, fear of being shot in the face by a hunter—

Leila's island.

What about it?

I know you too well. You're about to talk about Leila's island again.

They haven't heard it.

It's not relevant.

It might be.

It's not though.

I'm going to say it.

I'll say it quicker. For the record, Aldo's mother, Leila, and her family came from a small Pacific island, the name of which Aldo refuses to utter aloud because he promised himself that once it had been totally submerged he'd forget it for all time. When Aldo was thirteen years old, the highest peak of its tallest mountain was swallowed by the sea; Aldo's father Henry chartered a private twelve-seater and flew him and his mother and his sister over Leila's homeland for the last time. There. That's it.

No, that's not it. The plane schlepping us across the gleaming Pacific was terrifyingly small, the main cabin had patterned curtains on the oval windows and smelled of new carpet and salted peanuts. There was dog hair on the seat. I asked to see the pilot's license and was upset he couldn't produce it. To everyone's laughter, I pulled out of my Adidas sports bag an unused World War II parachute and my nana's spare oxygen tank, and thirty minutes into the flight, the plane begun to shudder, and they laughed even harder when I put the mask over my face, as if they didn't notice the building rhythm of the sudden drops. Both Veronica and Henry were frozen upright in their seats, and I remember wishing I was in the plane alone. I imagined the crash and resented the presence of Veronica—who I had fallen out with permanently the day she hit puberty. Ever since, we'd argued constantly, slapped nicotine patches on each other while we slept, etcetera, and I decided it would be irksome to die with her. There was a moment when the plane cruised as if on a current of air. "That's it! That's it!" Leila screamed. I closed my eyes, not from fear, but because Henry's gift to Leila of witnessing the vanishing of her homeland as it vanishes seemed such an outlandish privilege that I was determined not to experience it. Leila cried out, "Aldo, please look out the window." I looked. The sun had dipped behind low moist clouds and there, veiled in a light rain, was the land that sprang out of my mother's dreams—a barely visible, pitiful, water-bound peak surrounded by a colossal turquoise sea. The tip of an island so minuscule it seemed impossible that any human civilization once resided there. This was the image she would brood on until her final breath. "It's sad, but nothing more," I said, as the early moon floated above the vast calm that enveloped the doomed island. I wasn't saying that it wasn't sad. The pilot had turned the plane to make a second pass when there was an eerie, discomforting quiet, a faint acrid smell and a haze of flickering smoke, and the dim luminosity of silver sparks hitting the windscreen; the plane labored and reverberated and then dropped, and we went into a steep descent. It was as if I were levitating in my seat; there was enormous pressure in my eardrums and everyone screamed and, a moment later, lost consciousness, their heads slumped on their chests. All except me, sucking on my nana's oxygen, my face crushed against the window. The pilot managed to get the plane under control but was flying radically low, and I saw through that oval window an image that penetrated my subconscious with such force I can still feel its moment of entry: the water rising up like blue flames and utterly submerging the drenched peak. That was it: the whole nation slipped away in broad daylight. I was a spectator with no real business seeing what I was seeing. How many generations had lived and died here! I was a solitary pair of eyes, and maybe the ghosts of that nation, unfortunate spirits with nobody to haunt for miles around, attached themselves to me, a diffident eyewitness unwittingly administering a nation's last rites, because it was just after this incident that life turned to shit. Veronica in the bus explosion, and, the year before that, Henry breaking his shoulder in a fall down a flight of stairs. In hospital he contracted an infection at the surgical site, necrotizing fasciitis that led to septic shock and forced him into and out of surgery, and into the chronic pain that, I believe, led to his suicide. The one he orchestrated for a stranger to find, just as I had been conscripted to do in the Railway Hotel.

And we're back. Thank God. So in response, you come to the decision to once and for all kill yourself.

I know I mocked the happy couple at their wedding, but at least the Buddhists know what a bummer being born is. And the future! I mean, do I *want* to be an entrepreneur in a world with an aging population in which the biggest growth market will be human kidneys? Do I *want* to strain my lifespan just to witness the intergenerational conflicts and water wars of the mid-twenty-first century? In any case, I was sick to death of cognitive function. I thought: You can only cure a fear of dying by dying. I squeezed my eyes shut and felt relief—early onset oblivion, I suppose—and took in the inexhaustible hum of the relentless hallway air-con, the smell of the chicken fettuccine blended with the stench of our dead hero's final evacuations. I looked out the south-facing windows as though in a narcotic stupor and gazed at the squashed rectangle of empty blue and remembered how, when our little dead girl was born, I stupidly tried to console Stella by swearing we'd saved her a lifetime of heartache and pain. Now I turned back to the swinging body and strained to see the rising coils of his human soul—there were none—and I had an epiphany. Two things needed to happen before I could end my own life: One, I could not allow my mother to outlive me, and two, I needed to see that Stella and her new child were OK. Therefore I needed Leila to die, and I needed Stella to give birth.

You needed to see the baby and the corpse.

I even knew how I'd do it, the exact method.

Not hanging!

Please. I'd break into a hospital morgue and lay myself inside one of those terrifying metal drawers and take an overdose of sleeping pills and then slide myself into the wall.

Not bad.

Not bad? An irreproachably considerate death, you fuck.

So that explains why you were at the hospital once Stella gave birth. But you said you needed your mother to die before you did it.

That's right.

So you changed your mind about that.

No, I didn't.

Wait a minute.

Yes.

Aldo.

So that happened.

I think I'm going to cry.

Why not? I did.

Leila died?

A month ago.

YOU DIDN'T CALL ME!

I seem to remember a certain somebody who'd had a gutful of a certain somebody else's toxic influence.

I would've helped you.

Do what?

I don't know. Organize the funeral?

Eh. Took me all of twenty minutes. Because I couldn't bear sitting in some office with the inevitable funereal muzak and the consoling tone of the funeral director, I did the whole thing online with a few clicks; picked the day, the coffin, the flowers, the music, entered the address to pick up the body, another to send the death certificate, and after I'd completed the satisfaction survey, it was all organized. It was held in a building on Cleveland Street; the casket I'd chosen, a highly polished rosewood with full trim, had enough nicks and chips to suggest it was a showroom model, and above it was a blown-up headshot of Leila in her late twenties or early thirties—in any case, taken way before her gizzard-smelling later years. I stood inside the door misremembering several old family friends, citing "face blindness," while every one of them shook my hand in condolence, but since I associate handshakes with congratulations, I had to resist the impulse to lop off each proffered hand at the wrist. In addition, most were people I owed money to or who downright blamed me for precipitating my mother's death. Not that there was an abundance of mourners. I'd rejected the idea of a standard obituary notice. I mean, why alert grave robbers?

I can't believe Leila's gone. She was so full of life.

Never short on gratitude. Thank you, Aldo, she'd say, for ruining Christmas, thank you for ruining my birthday, thank you for ruining a perfectly nice Sunday lunch.

She had a great sense of humor.

Whenever there was thunder, she'd look at the sky and say, "Great minds think alike."

She adored you.

As a mother who wanted photogenic children adores a moderately handsome son.

You were always embarrassed by her.

On public transport she spoke like loudspeakers! I remember when I was a child and she asked me to sing a little number for dinner guests, then turned to them and said I had a voice like the castrato Farinelli. And God, the nose she had for magazines hidden under mattresses. In those pre-internet days, her intuition had compass-needle accuracy, always pointing due porn.

I remember her being a very together lady.

That was a front, for visitors. In truth, she hardwired me for panic attacks, by example. Regarding suffering, she really set the tone.

You mean her death? Was it bad?

That depends. Are impacted bowels bad? Where do you come down on septicemia and gangrene?

Jesus Christ.

She had to grapple with her complex reactions to the realization of her worst fears, poor thing. The triumph of having predicted the worst-case scenario vs. the horror of experiencing it. She had her fucking legs amputated, Liam.

Oh Jesus! Where did she die?

Hospice. With a violent lemon odor and obligatory death cat. That final visit the nurse said to me, "The body knows how to die, let the body do its thing," which I thought made sense, and when I went in she was lying peacefully, dying on her left side. She always had the outward appearance of indifference, which I suspect is the real secret to longevity. That or a genuine desire to die. I made a timid effort to wake her. How was I going to talk to her about the gangrene? She opened her eyes. I said, "What have you got there, soldier—trenchfoot?" She turned her head, not because she couldn't look me in the eye, but so *I* wouldn't have to look *her* in the eye.

Considerate. Did you say everything you wanted to say?

What could I say? What could I ask? What did I want to know about her, anyway? Why exactly she and I seemed to be more afraid than other people? It was always difficult to talk casually to her because her anxiety prevented it, her judgmental heart prevented it, and now her pain prevented it. "Aldo. We're the last ones left," she said, looking genuinely heartbroken. "So what?" I said. "The very idea almost makes me want to murder us both on the spot." She managed a laugh—she knew I was merely parodying my old heartlessness. "Besides, I always suspected you were secretly pleased to have outlived your family. In fact," I said, "I'm the only thing standing in the way of a complete sweep, and we both know it." She waved her hand at me. Every family has a private language. Ours was mainly gestural. Questions bubbled up, mainly about Veronica, but I couldn't articulate them. The next twenty hours were atrocious. Leila never stopped talking about how she never got to do that European tour of death camps; she'd hallucinate old friends; I moved her from lying to sitting to lying. Even the morphine drip seemed insufficient to diminish her agony. In the end, she died when I was out getting drive-thru McDonald's. I missed the moment, but you know who didn't? That fucking white-haired priest, remember him, Liam?

Father Charlie?

He also showed up uninvited and unscheduled at her mostly secular funeral service, and spoke about the waves of bad luck that had broken against her. Henry's death. Veronica's death. And the final insult of losing her house due to her son's financial misdeeds. Then the old cunt read a psalm, called her "a deep believer now resting in heaven." That shit me. I took to the lectern to rebut. Thanked him for so deftly explaining how she had been confiscated by God into his kingdom, where I imagined her talking all throughout orientation and lurking creepily around the apostles' dressing rooms. I said, "We are here today to honor a woman who once took up a whole two-seater couch but will soon fit in an overhead compartment on any domestic commercial flight. Leila Benjamin, a voice-over actress who after my father's death never lost her unbecoming face of perpetual sorrow, and basically spent the rest of her life leaning on God and searching for codependents and working on her résumé and striking up curious friendships with predators of the cloth—an especially qualified congregant, having lost a husband and child, she had the smell of Job on her, poor dear."

It would have been better to watch you without sound.

"Some of you think I killed her with my demoralizing business snafus. Rest assured, I will avenge her death by dying myself one day, maybe sooner than you think." Blah blah blah. Then I said something about how she never stopped moisturizing her hands and loved salad bars and kept Kleenex in a shoulder holster and had a hug Veronica and I used to call "the third rail," and how when she was fifty-five she went out and bought black dye for her hair. I asked her why and she said, I think I'm going prematurely gray. Premature, at fifty-five! She was a woman in denial. Then I improvised the poem I promised myself I would write as a tribute to her love of poetry.

I remember. Leila read poems to you after every dinner.

And before every bedtime right into late adolescence! Though it was more Veronica's thing; she was the poet of the family. Leila always force-fed us French and Spanish poets. Apollinaire. Valéry. Reverdy. Breton. Cernuda. Lorca. Éluard. Jiménez. Hernández.

Let's hear yours.

"Mother. My mother. A monument that stood / for seventy-two winters before sliding / into the sea. Her face reflected / in her three-sided bathroom mirror, like a Bacon / triptych. She disapproved by stealth. Mouthed / her silences. Captained a family that went / down. Could fashion a crown of thorns out of any / topic. Attentive grudge holder. Bestial temper. Own worst / frenemy. Shut-ins who live in glass houses / shouldn't." That was it.

Shouldn't what?

Live in glass houses. Clearly, I didn't know what the fuck I was saying!

Do you want to take a minute?

I have something in my eye.

They're called tears, Aldo.

Liam, it's just me now.

You still have a ton of relatives, don't you?

No.

On your father's side.

Fuck those cunts.

So you're an orphan. Welcome to the club. You're almost forty.

No parents, no brothers or sisters, no children. Imagine, to never be able to have another incestuous thought!

Aldo, you realize you could easily fall into homelessness? You've the three magical ingredients: mental problems, terrible financial debt, and zero support network. Add alcohol to this mix and you might vanish in the blink of an eye. Well, I want you to know you still have me. Remember what Aristotle said? Without friends no one would choose to live, though he had all other goods.

Yes, but that was in an epoch when all other goods meant a clay pot and some terra-cotta roof tiles.

Let's get back to the reason you're here.

Did I mention who I saw, as I was up there on the podium, in the back row sandwiched between manicurists of the deceased?

Stella was there?

And *so* pregnant, standing in a way that was sexy but I knew was bad for her hip. On catching her sympathetic look my heart went out to myself in the worst way. I thought: If only we could fuck shyly again! I hurried through my eulogy and practically trampled the secondhand coffin to make it over to her. She seemed to be aging at half-speed and was a tumult of familiar odors— jasmine and freshly spilled vanilla milk shake and wax bendy straws. "I'm so sorry; I loved your mother. Let's go outside and I'll watch you have a cigarette in memoriam," she said, reminiscing on Leila's two-pack-a-day habit, and about how an hour after her last cigarette she would burp up smoke trapped in her lungs. We went outside where the traffic moved in fits and starts as if grazing on the dull surface of the road, and as my mind stumbled over thoughts, Stella placed her hand on my shoulder. It is tiresome to find even compassion erotic. I said, "I guess I should wish you luck for your caesar." Now we plunged into the vast unspoken reservoir of old pain. The number of people we were mourning doubled, and to prevent the descent of another curtain of awkward silence, she suddenly snapped, "What the fuck happened at the Railway Hotel? My uncle said you just stopped turning up."

She was annoyed at you.

She was annoyed at my having squandered the opportunity she'd laid out for me. Like most people, Stella wanted lavish praise for tiny gestures of ordinary kindness, just as she expected to be rewarded daily for possessing common sense. I thought: She'd accept a kiss if I forced her, then wipe it off on the way home, so what would be the point? As if reading my mind, she gave me a look of pained uncertainty and I told her Leila was to be buried between Henry and Veronica, a little family reunion in a space I'd gotten her at Waverley Cemetery. It was her favorite. "Waverley's everyone's favorite," Stella said, which is true. It's a hell of a cemetery. With nothing left for us to say to each other, she swiveled on her heels and waddled away.

So this was the last time you saw Stella before you tried to kill her baby?

I can't believe you just said that to me.

Aldo, we need to get there. How did you know she was having a caesarean?

I assumed that no doctor, in light of her past history, would allow a let's-just-see-what-happens birth plan. I called a certified pediatric emergency nurse I knew, who had friends at the Royal Hospital for Women, who found out on the sly that Stella had a C-section booked for April twentieth.

Why was it so important for you to see the child that is not yours?

Because I love her. Because the world is round. Because of the wonderful things she does. Because, because, because, because, because.

Because?

If she loses this second child then perhaps having lost the first was *her* fate and not mine.

So on the morning of April twentieth you—

Wait up. Where's the fire? A person can't take his own life without tying up
loose ends, can he? My original intention was to take revenge, make amends,
confront ghosts, and settle scores, but I couldn't be bothered with all that so I
focused on one thing: apologies. I wanted to say sorry. So for a whole week I
entered the houses of old friends and associates and colleagues and acquaintances in tears and left in tears and admittedly didn't utter a comprehensible
word in between.

I'm glad I didn't answer the door.

My farewell was always "see you later." To say "see you soon" felt like I was
sentencing that person to death.

What did you apologize for?

Everything, everything.

What everything?

Everything! I said sorry for ruining your experience of high school; sorry
for threatening to fuck you with a monkey's thighbone; sorry for pretending
not to see that rainbow that time; sorry for making fun of your grandfather's
war record; sorry for asking if your new girlfriend had bird-headed dwarf-
ism; sorry for saying you died in childbirth; sorry for boring you into the
arms of death with Stella-related issues; sorry for saying "I've a thought," then
waiting for you to ask me what it was; sorry for not getting to know your children; sorry for summarizing your problems back to you with a smirk; sorry
for telling everybody your mantra; sorry for purposefully speaking slowly
to prolong the conversation because I was afraid to go home alone; sorry
for feigning nonjudgment when I was judging you like crazy; sorry that I
accepted your compliment about being a good listener when I was leveraging
the severity of your many gag-inducing deficits to persuade you to partake in
my schemes; sorry for abusing my knowledge of your weaknesses and habits
and sad interpersonal relationships to get you to lend me money; sorry for
making informal psychological assessments in brief psychodynamic therapy
sessions you weren't aware of having; sorry for looking into your bereaved or
incest-surviving or recovering-alcoholic or histrionically emoting or chronically fatigued or prescription-medication-abusing faces and comprehending
you for my own ends; sorry for using you instead of helping you understand
your true value, for not pointing out you were sixes stalking eights, or sevens

who were once eights while your partners had ascended to nines; sorry I never really helped all you uneducated adults who somehow managed to partner up, procreate, and sustain full work lives with no apparent native language whatsoever and who for the most part test nothing you say against reality and boast that "what you see is what you get," mistaking it for a positive trait; sorry for stifling raucous laughter and sending you back to your abused families with your firm belief in your own virtue and human goodness intact; I'm sorry for my fluency in bullshit; I'm sorry for you well-thumbed open books who have *no idea whatsoever* that you've had acute depression for thirty years; I'm sorry for flattering you even when it was not in your long-term interest; I'm sorry for allowing myself to be treated like a human security blanket, for forcing confessions through the sinister use of awkward silences, for purposefully not shedding light on your perceptual biases that even blind Freddy could see, for using your personality disorders to my advantage; I'm sorry for sitting back and letting you demonize yourself while I reaped your gratitude and ministered to your agonized souls with a prospectus or bank account number.

How did that go down?

My most resonating indiscretions had all been financial. I came offering love and asking forgiveness, but in the end they just wanted their money back.

So then it was April twentieth and you went to the hosp—

NOT YET. First I had to write the perfect good-bye to pin to my body and take to the final curtain. I remember the night of the nineteenth sitting at the window in my shitty apartment like a fixed idea, thinking how what I could have been I never was, and what I used to be I wasn't really anyway. It was dark outside; there was only a small and puny moon, just an overblown star really, that gave no light to speak of. I could just make out the silent trees moving in the night and the empty kindergarten below, which had gotten me arrested one summer morning for standing naked in my own kitchen. I opened the sliding doors and stepped onto the balcony. At one end of the street a young man was breaking into a car. At the other, a kid throwing a brick through a phone booth. What an unfriendly society, I thought, even our criminals—

Are too antisocial to form gangs.

Are we finishing each other's confessions now?

Is that what this is? A confession?

The moon looked mean now, full of cold rage. I went back inside and opened the fridge and stared at the food rotting in shopping bags before returning to the desk, to the note. Dear World, I wrote, I am not one of those people whose greatest fear in life is being chased down a long corridor by their unrealized potential; rather, mine is of an intruder breaking into the apartment while I am in the shower.

That's the dumbest suicide note I ever heard.

No shit. I was way off point. I tried again and wrote, To all of you who stand poised halfway up the so-called back stairs to liberty but cannot move up nor retreat, I dedicate this suicide note, which, if you are reading it, means I have been murdered—if I have any self-respect—by my own hand.

Pretentious.

Agreed. I couldn't get it right. The neighbors above were doing their nightly dragging of furniture across the floor while twisting a cat's ears, or something like that, making noises so sudden and random you couldn't brace yourself against them, but so regular you anticipated them at all the wrong moments. I switched off all the lights, turned off the clocks, the TV, the stereo, unplugged the microwave and the fridge—anything with an electric hum or a blinking red light. Still, true darkness and total silence were impossible to achieve. The sound of moaning came through the walls. I rubbed my bruised chin that still ached from the previous week when I'd discovered firsthand the perils of asking the neighbors to keep their porn down. I wrote, There's nothing I would do again the same, and if given the opportunity, I would decline the opportunity.

Not great.

But not terrible.

So THEN you went to the hospital and—

Not quite. Before my final breath, there was one essential task I had to attend to.

Jesus Christ. What was that?

Liam, I don't know about you, but I am just plain furious that I *never ever* grew out of the adolescent male mind-set. You know, that if your only tool is a penis, every problem looks like a vagina.

Desire that feels like starvation, I know.

And even when getting it, I was fed up by the act itself: irritated by the unfalsifiable nature of women's orgasms, sick of the logistical nightmare of craving personal space during intercourse, frustrated at needing fellatio to be silent but too timid to ask the girl to keep the sucking noises down.

So you went out to get lucky?

The Bat & Ball & Chain.

Where's that?

Near Central. It's just your standard carcass of an old hotel. A dozen poker machines, a squalid chamber of doorless toilets, an undersized pool table beside a dance floor, dozens of small tables and chairs filled by men watching women watching men watching television. Normally I go an hour before closing, as prey. Timing is crucial: too early and the predators still have plenty of time to find someone better-looking than you; too late, they aren't in the mood anymore. I drank the first beer quickly, contemplating the unusual paradox. How do you sell yourself when you're the salesman *and* the product?

Tricky.

For medicinal purposes I try to sleep with one woman a fortnight. This never feels excessive when one takes into consideration the other thirteen nights alone in bed—that's three hundred and thirty-nine lonely nights a year—but frankly, it adds up, and in the years since Stella left me I've found, to my own surprise, that I've slept with nearly ninety-eight women, at least a third of whom are furious at me for not having been "The One."

On the night in question, did you find someone?

Usually I fear that my character flaws are diagnosable at first sight. From the way I cut up the dance floor, I sometimes wonder, can you tell that I'm resistant to change? This time maybe the stench of death was mingled in with my usual odor of desperation and violent sorrow.

So no luck.

Just one last measly fuck before gravetime! That's all I wanted. Is it too much to ask? But I failed to excrete irresistibility. I swaggered unbuttoned from one sweaty drunken lady to another but none sustained eye contact. I felt myself without a human face. I kicked the speaker for its general lack of magic. Then I spotted on the dance floor a large-bottomed woman, pale as a cow's stomach lining, shaky on her feet. I lingered on her periphery until we locked eyes and I gyrated toward her and we kissed, but when she pulled away I suddenly thought that I'd rather die painfully than have another verbal exchange that did not cut a straight path to the heart of human truth, so when she asked my name I said, "No names," and she said, "I'm Tracy," and so I said, "Oh, forget it then," and stormed outside into the cold quiet and stamped my feet on the empty street. Nobody was around. The moon looked so low and close you could reach out and stick your finger in its eye. Then it hit me: Who gives a shit about her name? I went back inside. She was in the arms of someone swifter who knew well enough to eat what was on his plate. I'd blown it, and I was tired, tired of moving, tired of the body's needs. It was late. I was hungry. Almost everything would be shut. That's what counts for a last meal in the valley of the shadow of death. A fucking kebab.

So after that you went and waited at the hospital?

No. This is only one thirty a.m. I went to the Yellow Pages attached to the bar's old payphone and flicked through and found The Enigma Variations.

The brothel that services the Railway Hotel.

The ad featured a photograph of a scantily clad bosomy blonde lying on her side. I thought: That's the one. When I get to the place, I'll ask for the girl in the photo. I don't want any surprises. After all, I already know what she looks like lying on her side.

Seems logical.

Thank God for brothels. Otherwise I don't like to think what I'd do.

What would you do?

If I didn't find consent such a turn-on.

What?

On the subject of prostitution, if a man acts like a man, who are you to moralize or demoralize him? Who are you to judge a species for its inherent characteristics? Do you hate the cat for licking its paws? Do you hate the dog for licking its balls, and then your face? Deep down you know that to personalize these things is low and just ignorant, and if you want sex and you're not getting it elsewhere, and you're not in a relationship and not betraying anyone, and if we agree you can't exploit anyone who charges you two hundred bucks an hour, then where's the harm? It isn't dangerous—sex with a prostitute is the safest sex you'll ever have—people grow careless with new girlfriends and one-night stands but who the hell's going to be careless with a prostitute? Who's going to say, we got caught up in the heat of passion and forgot to wear protection? No one, that's who. Sex with people you like, or are infatuated with, or love, *average citizens*, that's where the real danger is.

Nobody's judging you!

The Enigma Variations wasn't hidden in some dark alley or side street, but was boldly sitting on a main road between a newsstand and a barbershop as if it belonged in the heart of the community and not in its groin. Through the open doorway you could see into a pink, softly lit lounge room: potted plants and faded couches and a woman's legs with torn stockings. And that was just from the street. Inside, clients snorted and sniffed their way in and out of seedy rooms with unfortunate acoustics while the Korean madam directed impassive women to parade by, one by one—I guessed that you were supposed to imagine their sleek, bony hands on your body, their harrowed lips and well-traveled tongues all over you. That was taxing, mentally. The women were all ageless in that they looked as if they'd been fucking for an eternity; they had dirty-blond hair and mean faces, not the kind of faces you'd think to go to for pleasure, and arms bruised at the elbow joints, purple splotches at the bend. They were all thin, like wire coat hangers, wearing white lingerie that was a grotesque caricature of male fantasy. None of these was the girl in the picture, and probably not the girl in any picture. These creatures were unphotographable. But there was one brunette, older than the others, with large, heavy-lidded eyes, tongue slithering professionally over her lower lip, and sure, her hands were shaking and she had an ugly nose that was too big for her face, but, I thought, what does that matter? You don't fuck a nose. At least, I'd never heard of it.

Aldo is this—

She led me up a narrow staircase and I trundled after her down a cold, poky hallway at the end of which was a padlocked door—what valuable possessions were they protecting? Guns? Drugs? Sex toys?—and she ushered me into an austere bedroom with a sad, saggy bed. The lack of knickknacks was dispiriting—I'd have liked to put on the stereo or peruse framed photographs of family members. Against the barred window that looked out on a drainpipe running up a brick wall was a desk and a lamp. I laughed at the thought of a person using a desk in a brothel. She closed the door behind her and I thought how I'd like to have unprotected sex but even in the face of imminent death the idea of genital-to-genital transmission of sores was still a turnoff.

"So darling," she said, in a raspy voice, as she crossed the room and sat down on the bed next to me. Her skin was like crepe paper. She asked my name. I said, "Simon Simonson." She drummed her fingers on my left leg and said her name was Gretel. "That's your fantasy prostitute name? Gretel?" I stared at her in a confused fit and curled my hands into tight bony balls in my lap. "Relax, honey, tell me what you want," she said, as she removed her bra and placed her large veiny breasts in my hands. She grabbed a bottle of baby oil from the bedside table and asked, "Do you want to lie back?" I said, "That's what my doctor always says. In that exact voice." From the next room, the sound of groaning. I said, "Ever consider soundproofing these walls? You can do it with egg cartons." She unzipped my pants and removed them in a way that denoted time immemorial. I asked, "Can I borrow a piece of paper?" She said, "What for?" I said, "I've just had an idea." I leaped off the bed and sat at the desk and turned on the lamp and snapped my fingers. "Pen!" She brought me a pen. I wrote, *Honestly, I never thought I had it in me. I've lived my entire life as if in a theater, always gazing glumly at the exit. I hope I didn't suffer!* Gretel was reading over my shoulder and asked fearfully, "You're not going to do it here, are you?" I promised I wouldn't. She led me back to the bed and climbed on top and persevered through my tears with the decency not to comment on them. It was when the transaction was completed, and Gretel had put back on her bra and panties and stockings, that it happened. A nothing of an incident, but significant.

What happened?

A commotion, a woman's terrorized scream in the hallway and male voices shouting. Gretel said, "Wait here." She stepped out into the hall half-undressed and I said, "Put something on," automatically, in the same way I'd shout at Stella who always stood at the window at night or would run to the mailbox in her underwear. Gretel leaned quizzically against the doorway before giving me a tender smile. I'll never forget that wonderful look, and as I walked out of the brothel I felt, for a long moment, unalone.

A man has missed something if he has never left a brothel at dawn feeling like throwing himself into the river out of sheer disgust with life.

Who said that?

Flaubert.

Well, I walked with a light spring in my step and a backlog of primitive joy until morning, when I made my way to the Women's Hospital, to the row of public telephones; I knew Stella was psychologically incapable of letting a phone ring and had used that information against her in the past. She answered,

"Hello?" I asked, "How is he?" Stella said, "He has all his fingers and toes." I said, "God, I hope no one ever describes me like that." She hung up on me, and I stood in the hospital reception area in a sort of trance, behind enemy lines, surrounded on all sides by, I assumed, sad bastards with multiple organ failure and their next of kin, when the ground shifted below me and the next thing I knew I was lying flat on the red and blue swirly carpet, and sweaty superbacteria-incubating hands were touching my face. I'd fainted. Everybody nattered above me in dull whispers. I got to my feet and phoned her again. I said, "What room you in?" She said, "Don't even think about it." I said, "I'm coming up." She said, "I'll come down," and a few minutes later, she emerged from the elevator walking tenderly—she'd just had major abdominal surgery, after all—not harried but not smiling either, and I suddenly was struck by the thought that we were too intimate for a handshake, too estranged for a hug, too cynical for a high-five, so we nodded at each other and said, "Hey." "Just tell me the truth," I said, "would he or would he not look out of place on the tower of a gothic cathedral?" She said, "He's beautiful." In her eyes, sad embarrassment. Life had moved expertly on without me; this baby was the proof. "I'm very tired," she said, "I'm on a lot of painkillers." "When you get back to your room, ask for the strongest slow-release, then twenty minutes later, scream for a fast-relief one. You won't regret it," I said, and gave her a smile that she returned with a look of remoteness laced with bursts of warmth rationed out to placate me. "Well," I said, "I suppose we'd better go upstairs and see that golem of yours." Stella smiled joylessly. "Maybe another day." Her face turned white and sour. "But I'm here now." "No," she said resolutely, "you're not." The suppressed anger in her voice frightened me. "All right, Stella," I said, "I'll go. "Thank you," she said with obvious relief.

But you didn't go.

I said good-bye and walked away, then doubled back and caught the elevator up to the third floor, into the low-ceilinged morgue. Just past the gurneys with immaculate white sheets I found the drawer where I intended to put my body after overdosing. A modern catacomb, I thought. I'd stayed in worse. In the brushed stainless steel my face was like a blurred photograph. I checked my seven packets of sleeping pills—I'd told Doc Castle I was going overseas and needed a six-month supply—and counted out a hundred and sixty-eight ten-millligram tablets, the mere sight of which made my blood flow slither to a crawl. As I made my way to Stella's room, I imagined the premature aftertaste of me in Death's mouth and I think, but I'm not sure, I couldn't hear my footsteps already.

Aldo, in the coming years, when I ask why I'm passed over for promotion time and time again, my superiors will simply play me a recording of this interview.

That's why you're having so many problems as a writer. You've always been a stickler for reality. Anyway, there was a yeasty, antiseptic, fecal smell in Stella's room that mingled with the pitiful bunches of service-station flowers, and the stink wafted unpleasantly toward me as I cautiously entered, removing my shoes. A shaft of brassy sunlight inclined through the narrow window. Stella was fast asleep emitting the softest snore you ever heard. On the windowsill, plastic plates and serrated white knives and sporks. The baby was asleep in a clear plastic bassinet on wheels in the curtained alcove on the far side of the bed. There he was, in the cold yellow light, tiny and shrunken, pointy headed, blotchy faced, with a wispy fuzz of fine black hair. Asleep, no different from my own baby when dead. I was afraid he *was* dead, he was so still—until I clocked the rise and fall of his little chest. Alive then. Time to put up or shut up.

You took out the pills.

Looking at the sign about mandatory hand washing affixed above the basin, I washed the pills down and stood for a moment staring at Stella, her sleeping body an almost panoramic vista, her long limbs half-sheeted, and her gown blood-yellow where her bandages had soaked through; all this in a low steady light reminiscent of the Railway Hotel, that was, it only occurred to me now, nowhere near a train station. That would be my dying epiphany—oh well! The sleeping pills hit fast. It was not darkness that came, but fog. I was dying. A glimpse of death I felt secretly proud of, as if I were an amateur astronomer who gets to name a star. Now that free will was behind me, I might finally relax. It was time to go to the morgue, but my feet wouldn't move. Maybe for some their whole life flashes, but I only got a single jolting memory from childhood of someone hitting me repeatedly on the back of the head with a tennis ball in a sock. Who wielded the weapon? I couldn't remember. Maybe the same person who told me to "take a sleeping pill, wait half an hour, then smoke in bed." Now I have a hazy recollection of picking up the little baby and nestling him next to Stella on the bed, under her arm. Miraculously he made no sound. I silently moved the cushioned chair closer and put my head on the mattress edge. I wanted to christen this baby without parental consent, but I couldn't think of any good names. I remember wondering what teething felt like. A hush threaded its way through my bloodstream, through the arteries, and I felt the slow quiet of my heart, and the woolly darkness descend. The last thing I remember before I lost consciousness was the baby opening his eyes and grabbing my finger and me weeping and thinking this was going to be *the best death ever*.

You don't know how you wound up lying on the bed next to Stella and on top of the baby?

I must have climbed up onto the bed to snuggle. I just don't remember.

Zolpidem causes memory loss.

That's what I used to like about it.

Aldo, you cock, that baby could have died.

I know.

If Stella hadn't woken up at that very moment—

I KNOW! I KNOW! Jesus, Liam. You don't think I know that? If I wanted to die before, how do you think I feel now?

Interview concluded at 4.30 p.m. EST.

II

Stella walked gingerly into the station a few hours later, heels clicking on the hardwood floor, her new-mother's face gleaming darkly in the spectral light she always carried with her. Everyone in the station turned to look. She hugged me hello with a tepid formality, like we were ambassadors of warring nations who had once shared a roll of toilet paper in the UN restroom.

"This incident must have been very frightening, but Aldo didn't try to kill your baby," I said plainly. She stared fiercely at me. "This was not a murder or attempted murder, it was just a clumsy suicide attempt and a total fuckup and you know it, Stella, you fucking know it."

"Constable!"

Senior Detective Doyle glared at me with all the sullen power of his rank. Stella seemed shocked at my vehemence and locked me in a straightforward gaze.

"I guess."

"You *guess*?"

There was, now that I come to think of it, always an uncertainty to her; as if she wasn't sure of a single one of her life choices and was always on the lookout for a second opinion.

"Come with me," I said, and grabbing a file led her outside where Stella held her body as if she feared I was going to reach out and touch it.

"This is what you're going to do," I said. "You're going to say you're not pressing charges and then you're going to write a statement saying that this incident was entirely accidental, and you're even going to say you were so out of it on painkillers it might actually have been *you* on top of your baby, and not Aldo."

A suspicious frown gave way to a wan curiosity. She let out a full-body exhale and slid her hands into her pockets.

"All right, Liam. But he needs to stay away from us for good."

"Absolutely."

We stood awkwardly beside a row of police cars, and I don't know why but I suddenly thought about her career, how music had been her life and she'd completely abandoned it. I felt an almost dizzying wave of empathy. The times I had given up writing had been a devastating exercise in soul shrinking. I didn't have an inkling how she disconnected the reflex to pick up a guitar, how a lifelong marriage to music could be so abruptly annulled. And as a songwriter, how did she withstand the pull of a melody or lyric that came to her in the night? I reflected how she'd given up not after but exactly in the middle of the death of their baby. "All right," she said again, sighed, snatched the paper and clipboard out of my hand, and wrote a brief statement to the effect that Aldo hadn't intended to harm her child, that she had picked up Clive herself and taken him into the bed without realizing that Aldo was already passed out beside her. Her statement made no sense, but almost nobody was going to read it.

She handed me the clipboard. "Did he have to have his stomach pumped again?"

"Sure."

"How is he?" Before I could answer she asked, in a sort of breezy despair, "Why hasn't he moved on?"

A brightness in her eyes betrayed that this was some kind of triumph. Who wouldn't want to be a man's greatest regret? I torpedoed her with my silence and dead eyes and turned away. Across the street, a muscular individual with close-cropped hair wearing a white undershirt and tight jeans was staring directly at us, and whenever a passer-by blocked his view, he'd crane his neck or go up on tiptoes to keep us in his field of vision.

"Craig, I presume?"

"He's waiting for Aldo to come out so he can beat the shit out of him. He's furious at him for trying to die by my side."

"It was a bit cheeky."

We had relaxed now, though we had nothing further to say to each other, and I became itchy to leave. A few somber seconds passed, and I said I had to get back; I kissed her on the cheek, taking in her soft spring-rain scent, and wished her and her baby well. The fact is, I didn't really understand why Aldo's love for Stella was so robust. It was a nuisance for everybody. When I reached the station doors, I turned back to see her unmoved under the streetlight, still watching me. From that angle, I got a glimpse of Aldo's recurring dream. I saw what he saw: the artist, the singer/songwriter, the frantic mother, the highly intelligent, no-nonsense, no-bullshit, and weirdly increasingly youthful incarnation of some dangerous, angry beauty. For a brief moment I got to feel what he felt, and the contrast to my own tepid emotional tumult with Tess made me realize that in the world of love I was a straggler, a craven magpie, a lousy poet who, like Aldo said, was a stickler for reality and all the poorer for it.

It was ten p.m. by the time Aldo was warned and released with a court date for violating the AVO, and we were in my car on the way back to his apartment. Aldo looked tenderized and depleted; he gripped the armrest and stared out the window with a smile of fear at the mundane streets of the cold city, appearing increasingly tiny and alone, and in between shallow breaths, to my eternal chagrin, continued his pre-interview rant, his wholesale dumping of thought, his tour de force of complaint. He was afraid, he said, that he'd failed himself in ways he'd never understand, hated the unbearable sight of nobody in love, loathed people who prayed so hard they thought they were making God come, was depressed that the only people in society who commanded his respect were those he saw on trains reading manuscripts of sheet music, was sick of wondering whether to assign meaning to his misfortunes or not, irritated at how people would quick-smart find tragic a suicide rather than the preceding decades of unbearable psychological torment leading up to it, which was just seen as normal life—

I slammed on the brakes and glared at him. His face looked like it had been melted down and recast.

"Are you going to be OK?"

"I don't know."

"Are you going to try this again?"

"That depends."

"On what?"

"In the tropics, do coffins at open-casket funerals have mosquito nets?"

"Do what?"

"There's a market there."

"What?"

"Mosquito nets for open-casket funerals in tropical climes!"

I gaped dumbly. This was typical Aldo. He was preparing for death, but at the same time doubling up on life. Suicidal *and* ambitious. Furiously tying nooses while intermittently doing abdominal exercises. It was absurd.

"Let's have a drink," I said. "We have some brainstorming to do."

"Holster your cock, Officer."

"Shut up until we get there. I need a drink to listen to you."

I drove us to the Hollywood Hotel and while chain-smoking in the beer garden I told him that he was already well proven to be phenomenally unlucky; his next suicide would likely have him lapse into a coma, or leave him with internal organ damage, brain damage, paralysis, or horrific disfigurement, and he'd live the rest of his life in a state-run, underfunded care facility, or worse. As I said this it occurred to me there was something different in his eyes; they were like cartoon asterisks or pinwheels, maybe from him having gone halfway up and back the tunnel of light so many times he'd left a greasy trail. I feared a permanent psychotic break, and worried that this intense accelerated state would be his new normal. I gave him an ultimatum: cobble together a will to live and settle upon a short-term life plan by the end of this drink or I would shoot him in the face. I said I'd be shirking my duty as a friend if I didn't help him build a tenuous link to life. Besides, I had my pen and notebook ready.

Aldo agreed to no more businesses, no more borrowing, no more investments, no more restaurants, no more get-rich-quick schemes, and since having a boss was impossible for someone with his temperament, he decided he would freelance, but as what? I reminded him that after high school he had been a cold-calling, pet-sitting, house-cleaning, garden-clearing, leaflet-distributing-aholic. He needed to go back to basics. I convinced him to put himself in the service of others. Helping people in whatever way they needed help. I wrote down where Aldo's strengths and skill sets lay, and made a sign for him that he agreed to affix to walls and telephone poles all over the city.

This was the sign:

HANDYMAN. CAN DO ALMOST ANYTHING—WITHIN REASON. HOUSE PAINTER. WINDOW WASHING. LANGUAGE TEACHER (ENGLISH ONLY). MOW LAWNS. PUNISH YOUR CHILDREN. WHATEVER. $25 AN HOUR. ALDO BENJAMIN. 063 621 4137. NO JOB TOO DISTASTEFUL.

That was literally the best we could do.

The night sky was weirdly pale. We drove home through silent streets, past inner-city terraces with young people carousing on wrought-iron balconies and burlesque-outfitted women shadowed by males swaggering with sexual violence. Aldo's skin seemed made of cheesecloth and he was squished down in the passenger's seat once again throwing off scalding thoughts and stamping on them, my internal organs speakers through which his voice was amplified. The air in the car was fusty, almost unbreathable. I gripped the wheel until my palms began to ache, experiencing a fatigue that started to feel like pain, trying to shut down my peripheral vision so as to avoid his face turned toward me. Aldo was, he said, fed up with foraging for silver linings, irritated by how a lifelong use of humor as a defense mechanism had perverted his sense of humor and weakened his defenses, sick of needing assurances that others were not enjoying their lives either, bored by hostile looks in bathroom mirrors that could descend any moment into violence, weary of the dread of insomnia, of floating down a silent river of hours toward dawn weighing up the worst of human cruelty, e.g., bayoneting babies *in utero* (the Rape of Nanking) vs. forcing sons to rape their mothers (Kosovo).

I accelerated down the three-lane highway. I wanted him out of the car; I'd had more than I could take.

Once out of the harbor tunnel, we passed a rattling semitrailer spilling dirt on the road, and a manure smell poured in through the windows. We drove down the deserted somber streets, my police radio calling for backup—a brawl in the Cross—and I was thinking a complicated warren of thoughts, such as how Morrell writes, *Just as in quantum physics the observer alters the behavior of the observed, so in art does the artist modify the subject,* and wondering how whatever I came up with would transform Aldo, but I was also trying to memorize what he was saying. He had landed, once more, on his defining theme, his fear of prisons and hospitals, the medical-industrial complex, the prison-industrial complex, antibiotic resistance levels, the unreliability of eyewitness testimony, protective custody, quarantine, secondary infections, trumped-up charges, the general population, visitation rights, visiting hours, tainted blood transfusions, wrongful convictions, misdiagnoses, lockdown, pathogens, handcuffs, vital-signs monitors, pneumatic sliding doors. He recounted a dream ("As you know, doctors have long personified death in my dreamscape, and I keep dreaming about a sign in a hospital men's room that says SURGEONS MUST WASH THEIR HANDS BEFORE RETURNING TO WORK") and finally he linked his two obsessions: "When you think about it," he said, "*preexisting conditions* and *prior convictions* amount to the same thing: Once you're fucked, you're fucked again for having once been fucked." I pulled up to Phoenix Court with a violent screech and we both jerked forward. My brain felt parched, starved of oxygen. Just before he got out of the car, Aldo asked, in a furious voice, "Why the fuck does depression get to be a disease when frustration does not?"

He shut the door. Sharp air gusted in through the open window, and without noticing the tears of exhaustion in my eyes, Aldo spoke of two decades of thwarted impulses, backed-up energy, the toll taken by gratification forever denied, by keeping his aggression in check, by love rejected if not outright flung back in his face, and of how it was not elusive goals that had worn him down, but the accreted obstacles that needed to be removed to obtain them, and just before he turned and faced the barely traversable puddles of vomit and then disappeared through his building's shattered glass door, he gave me his final self-diagnosis: He was convinced he was suffering from *clinical frustration,* a humanwide phenomenon that as yet no pharmaceutical companies were "getting into."

A Gulag of One's Own

I AM WOKEN BY A MOMENTOUS wave, as if the first to crash on the shore this calendar year, and I hallucinate the sound of a crying baby, rasping and raked in the foam. I sit up, damp and cold, feeling only minimally alive. A terrifying swell is rolling, coming in rows every few minutes. A gray light spreads thinly over the dawn sky and the horizon is veiled in a light mist. Overnight the glassy waves have grown big and stormy, six-footers breaking over the tiny island, waves so big they seem to generate their own weather system. I can see the figure of Aldo propped up on a rock, a dance of white water spiraling up behind him. He's shouting something, and making some kind of hand signal.

I think he is just waving hello. I say, "What a cock."

Behind me, a laugh. I turn around. Her face swarming with hair, a toddler on her lap playing with his mother's skirt. Christ. Stella.

"You snore," she says.

There's black eyeliner framing her gigantic eyes, and she looks padded out; the weight has aged her.

"How long have you been sitting there?"

"Not long."

She gives me that intense stare of hers that feels like a part of her is also watching me from another vantage point with binoculars. She digs her nails into the copper sand. Clive, the puffy-cheeked toddler, shovels fingers of it into his mouth.

"Do you have water?"

She passes me a bottle; it tastes like melted refrigerator ice. Wedged into the sand beside her is a small Esky cooler.

"He called me. Asked me to get supplies."

"What did he ask you to get?"

"The usual."

"What does that mean?"

She opens the cooler to reveal gardener's gloves, a coffee-filled thermos, a heavy rope, yogurt, sandwiches, tins of tuna and pineapple slices, jars of pickles, bananas, beer, fruit, a first-aid kit, a carton of Marlboro Reds, a lighter, and an old photograph, framed—when was the last time anybody framed a photograph?—of the two of them together.

I say, "Jesus, is that—?"

A barefoot dark-haired woman emerges from the path and heads toward us. She's thin and pleasant looking but with a hook nose that you don't see so much in the twenty-first century.

"Hi."

"Hi."

"Hi."

"I'm Saffron."

"Liam. We met at Aldo's trial."

"Which one?"

"I'm Stella. What've you got there?"

Saffron too has an Esky in her hand.

"Is that . . . ?"

"Aldo asked me to bring supplies."

I laugh, "What a cock."

"I guess he was covering his bets."

"Wow, so that's where he is? On that?"

There is abrupt silence as the three of us contemplate the rock: No longer a piece of sea-worn granite off the eastern seaboard, it is a solid abyss on which our broken mutual friend is miserably camped in the open air alone. We all stand absurdly, like pod people.

"So, Liam," says Stella. "What are you waiting for?"

"No time like the present," Saffron says.

I turn and make my plea to the large waves collapsing on the shore. "Just dash out, make a whirlwind visit to the rock, and whip back? Is that what you mean?"

"We'll hold your spot for you," Stella says.

The waves, the waves. The kind that frequently swallow rock anglers and their children. Even if I was a regular surfer, I wouldn't voluntarily go out in surf this big, but with Stella frowning and Saffron jubilant behind me, I feel an indispensable part of an ongoing drama.

A flash of lightning; the sky's in a mood.

I strap both Eskies to the nose of my surfboard and push out, battling the frightening waves. A gray bank of cloud hangs ominously above and it feels as if a storm is raging on the sea floor. It's slow-going, and I'm sloshed around like a shrunken head in a barrel. I get over the peaks and consider my approach. The ocean swells up over the island, leaving a short interval to swim onto the rocky base before the water rushes back out, creating a dangerous vacuum effect. This is going to be tricky.

"Careful, Liam!" Aldo shouts.

There he is, looking wolfish, atavistic, perched on a ledge without a wetsuit and propped up on the rock, belly spilling over tight black board shorts. I spot his surfboard wedged up between a couple of dark boulders. "Did you sleep?" I ask, trying to stay afloat.

"Got an hour here or there. The place is crawling with crabs!"

"What?"

"Crabs! One of the bastards nipped my toes."

"Come back in!"

"Just leave the Eskies."

"Fuck that. Those women are killers. I'm coming up."

"Not there!"

Relentless waves make access unsafe, and the rocks are too steep to climb on to. He gestures to a spot on the northern point of the island, so I paddle around. Here the waves are downright barbarous, but there is a jagged ledge that seems plausible. Aldo laboriously shuffles down to the water's edge and grabs the nose of the board.

"Untie your ankle."

I take the leash off my ankle and toss it to him. He wraps it around a crag and it goes immediately taut. Whatever the ocean is doing to me, it is nonconsensual. Aldo asks if I know any sea shanties.

"Just help me up!"

Between thrashing breakers, he pulls the Eskies onto the rock, then takes my hand and steadies me as I cautiously slide onto the ledge and scramble up. The water is billowing dangerously. Aldo drags my board up after me.

Happy to be safe from the clamor of the waves, I make a quick perusal of the terrain. It's craggy and uneven and mossy with unexpected shelves and rock pools; water foams in the crevices, sick with seagulls and their feathers. Vistas front and back. The waves are deafening here. I can see a couple of crabs with reddish-brown bodies and bright, red-tipped claws, no better than spiders in my estimation, and also Aldo's handiwork: a jellyfish with a stick through it. The island is treacherously rugged, even for the sure-footed and nimble. It's like some new planet you'd take a quick look around—then fuck off out of.

He tongues a cavity and gives me a look, as if he'll turn a blind eye to trespassing just this once, and sifts through Saffron's Esky, tossing aside a bottle of Stolichnaya, grapes, cigarettes, ibuprofen, soap, sterile gauze bandages, disposable medical gloves, sunscreen, toilet paper, raincoat, vinegar, lemon juice, antiseptic cream, hydrogen peroxide, and burn ointment. He drags out the binoculars and gazes at the women on the shore and nods a thank-you that they couldn't possibly see, and throws a wild wave to Clive. Then he slips on the medical gloves and holds up a pair of tweezers.

"I have a tick."

"Out here?"

"Must have picked it up yesterday when we came through the bush. You get one?"

"Nope."

We both thought: *Typical.*

He burrows into his skin and yanks the sucker out.

"Fuck!"

"What's wrong?"

"I think I left the head inside."

He tosses the tick's body angrily into the sea and washes the wound with bottled water from Stella's bounty. With a sulky expression he rubs the antiseptic cream on his hands and dons the gardener's gloves. He slips on the shades and pockets a sheathed knife and lifts himself up on his arms and strenuously crisscrosses the rock face, reminding me of those quadrupeds in Turkey. He is going after crabs and other living things that hiss and roil in their shells.

"This guy's been bugging me all night."

He presses his face to the wet, scaly rock. This position seems to cause him agony, but it's like he's come to realize his capacity to endure pain is elastic and he still hasn't seen how far it'll stretch. He returns from his hunt without success, bringing his portable carnage to a rest beside me. Blood trickles out from under his eye. When did that happen? He must've fallen soundlessly when I wasn't looking. He looks like a fish unhooked too late.

Rain falls meekly now. Aldo throws on the raincoat, then grabs the binoculars again and stares out through the vapory haze at the women on the shore. We sit in silence for maybe an hour with the glare of cloud-filtered sun on our faces. Aldo resembles a well-preserved corpse in some grand open-air tomb. Gulls hang as if suspended midair. A layer of moisture, either ocean spray or cold sweat, slicks his face.

I say, "So this is where the industrious robbed of industry go."

I realize he is dead asleep. The drizzle continues and I can't tell the rain from the ocean spray. I think: What is this incoherent camping trip about anyway? Is he enacting a dream he had in prison? On his unfeeling legs, I notice what looks like a bluebottle sting. I think: I would totally cast him to play the wretched of the earth in a movie. An hour later, he wakes with a clouded expression.

I say, "It's an atrocity."

"What is?"

"Your life."

"Not as bad as some, which in a way makes it worse, because I have to feel guilty for not being grateful for *my* atrocity."

The thing is, he's right. He grows sullen and unreachable, and in an audible whimper he says, "Tell me more about this book."

"A whole chapter will be your testimony in court at Mimi's murder trial."

"But that's in the public domain."

"That's what's so good about it. It's a cut-and-paste job."

"Jesus, Liam. You're as corrupt a novelist as you are a policeman!"

I sneer but I know he's right. My arm slides around his shoulder. "Let's go back."

"You go."

"Oh fuck it."

Let him rot. I trudge down to where my surfboard is and pretend I'm not daunted in the least as I slide back into the undulating sea. The waves are monstrous but it's warmer in the water than out of it. I paddle quickly to distance my body from the rock. I think: I'd like to see Jesus walk on this water. Aldo maneuvers down to see me off.

I say, "Don't get your dick stuck in a conch shell."

"I won't."

"I'm serious."

"Just go."

As I paddle back in, I see Stella and Clive are alone on the beach; Saffron's gone. They look pocket-sized in the cloudy light. The violence of the waves rises under me and I hold on tight, afraid and sick of it, the fear. I close my eyes, but it is Mimi's dead face I see. That forces memories to the fore: Aldo handcuffed to his chair, wailing hysterically; a mosquito straining its wings in a pool of Mimi's blood; the artists, the artists.

I think I might as well catch one in. I slide down the empty wall of water and see it break in front of me; I tilt into it and turn off the wave just in time to avoid a dumping. When I get back to shore I stagger and collapse exhausted on the hard sand, next to Stella who's crouched in a ball with Clive huddled under her knees, and all I can think of is how she plucked every strand of happiness from the heart of my tragic friend and yet it wasn't her fault. Her sad eyes shift across the rock island. The rain comes down heavy now, and we can only just sit there and get soaked.

My phone rings. It's Aldo, and I answer saying, "Hey, Aldo, remember that first afternoon on the toilet block roof you told me all you wanted was a lifestyle indistinguishable from that of a highly successful drug baron or sex trafficker, that is, a magnificent house with water views, top-shelf escorts, and suitcases stuffed with cash?"

"I'm going to stay here."

I strain to see through the mist and rain and there he is, so much water pouring down on that rock ledge he looks like a drowning ladybug in a bathtub.

"For how long?"

"Forever," he says, laughing, then hangs up. I watch him shuffle back farther under the overhang for shelter, and Stella grabs my hand, which is totally unexpected, and I think how the only people worth watching are those who have reached rock bottom and bounced off it, because they always bounce off into very strange orbits.

II

It is an old and ironic habit of human beings to run faster when we have lost our way

—Rollo May

II

The Madness of the Muse

Y OUR HONOR, LADIES AND GENTLEMEN of the jury, members of the press, madame court stenographer, random citizens who have nothing better to do on a Tuesday morning, Uncle Howard, bailiffs, live-streaming folks on the internet, I had woken early that overcast morning, in the weird limbo between Christmas and New Year's Eve, in order to remove the last remaining advertisements I had foolishly stapled to every telephone pole and tree trunk from the city to the sea—advertisements that my well-meaning friend Liam had made me compose in a misguided attempt to give my dumb life purpose, and which had caused me nothing but literal agony. I enter the sign as exhibit A:

HANDYMAN. CAN DO ALMOST ANYTHING—WITHIN REASON. HOUSE PAINTER. WINDOW WASHING. LANGUAGE TEACHER—ENGLISH ONLY. MOW LAWNS. PUNISH YOUR CHILDREN. WHATEVER. $25 AN HOUR. ALDO BENJAMIN. 063 621 4137. NO JOB TOO DISTASTEFUL.

It was ten a.m. and I had paused under some tree shade at a busy outdoor café to pat the head of a golden retriever whose bark, it seemed to me, was incoherent to the other dogs present. Right beside me, a middle-aged woman with a pale face dwarfed by an incredible head of frizzy black and silver hair—more a helmet than a head—was perusing my sign on a dry-cleaner's window. She was nearly beautiful in the same way that I am practically handsome—think perfect physical beauty, then go down six notches. That was us; we were on the exact same notch. She scrutinized the sign before appearing to dial my number. My phone rang. I thought: Oh my God. How fantastic. She heard *The Godfather* ringtone and turned to face me.

—Hello? she said.

—Hello?

—How are you?

—Don't get me started on babies who suffer brain damage during home water births.

—Are you Aldo Benjamin?

—None other.

—Is this sign a joke?

—Why? Is it funny?

—Could I possibly borrow you for a couple of hours?

—As long as you promise to return me in mint condition.

Now, this was banter, Your Honor—and who doesn't love to banter?—but I was running out of banter, and as she moved closer I kept my eyes on hers, inexpert as I am in the art of appraising a woman's body when she's looking right at me. She had dark pockets under her eyes as if having just woken from a long night's madness. I marveled at the audacity of her frizzy Afro.

—Do you think your hair might be a fire hazard? I asked, smiling brightly.

She frowned, as if smiling was as tacky as a department store Santa. The lengthy silence that followed was so dispiriting I removed a bottle of pills from my inside pocket and summoned my saliva to swallow one.

—You know what it says on the list of side effects of these antidepressants? *May cause depression.* Kind of makes you want to throw in the towel.

The woman's hardened face remained implacable.

—So what kind of tasks are you generally asked to perform?

—Just the usual unpleasant and often dangerous jobs that the people of greater Sydney need doing.

—Such as?

—Mostly a punishing amount of heavy lifting and unmasking of unfaithful spouses.

She clicked her tongue, a gesture I took as my cue to elaborate.

—In the last month alone, I've been contracted to move a father into a nursing home while he was asleep, to search sandstone caves for a schizophrenic brother, to drag what is referred to in certain circles as a "human urinal" home to a jealous boyfriend, and to nail a cow's heart to a pedophile's mailbox. You want references?

I did not tell her that I'd also stumbled upon one man dead in a bath, another hanging off a tree, and a father asphyxiated in a garage. That is to say I was paid my standard flat rate to stumble upon the bodies of recent suicides, meaning I'd inadvertently found a horrific niche market of people who wanted to die in the privacy of their own homes but didn't wish to burden their loved ones, something I knew a little too much about.

The deceased shifted her feet and gazed at me uncertainly.

—Will you tell me the job, or would you like me to guess?

—It's mortifying.

—I don't mind.

Then she told me the job and, Your Honor, she wasn't joking; it *was* mortifying.

I was to spend the day removing naked pictures of her that a disgruntled lover had plastered on lampposts and phone boxes all over the city. She boldly presented me with one such poster; I gasped. The bastard had enlarged photos of the deceased's face with, it's hard to find another way to say it, a mouthful of cock—there, I said it—in a collage that also featured images of her dark, saucer-sized nipples and splotchy birthmark above the belly button. I didn't need to ask why he chose these particular images. Her boyfriend clearly knew how to hurt women—who doesn't?—and he knew how to hurt *her* in a specific way. I guessed, and was later proved right, that she'd never had an intimate moment without first giving the unnecessary but heartfelt self-loathing preface that these—her nipples, her birthmark—were the things she hated most about her body. On the bottom half of the posters was a phone number and address and her name: Mimi Underwood.

That was the first time I'd heard it. Yet it was so familiar. As my eyes flew over the images once again, I asked her if I could've met her before.

—Or, I asked, have I seen your name somewhere? On a billboard or bathroom wall, maybe?

—Jesus Christ, man. I'm having the worst week of my life. Will you help me or not?

In truth, ladies and gentlemen of the jury, I wasn't sure I felt like it. After being so frequently suckered into gruesome bargains with the suicidal inhabitants of this morose city, not to mention the hostility and aggression from their families and my other clients, and the unsavory and amoral and vexing nature of the work itself, I had decided to abandon this ludicrous non-job that very morning. As you well know, it's only when you quit and then change your mind that you can regret the harm that befalls you.

—Sure. Let's do it.

It's not every day you tear down pornographic posters with an attractive stranger.

So off we went, ripping posters off the fig trees in Hyde Park, off the brand-new apartment buildings made ugly at great expense, off the graffitied ANZAC War Memorial, off the Hungarian restaurant where they serve Wiener schnitzels as big as toilet seats, off the Central Station overpass, off the glass wall of the taxi stand where the drivers leer salaciously out of habit before they've even determined your sex. We veered off into the suburban streets where, to our weary disgust, he had plastered front doors, letterboxes, and children's tree houses. This is how it went: Mimi feebly indicated a sign with a nod or else pointed accusingly to a poster and said, "Another one!" or simply, "Oh God," and I'd go after it like a golden retriever while men called her name or applauded, children waiting for buses made sucking noises, mismatched couples stared judgmentally, and outside the hair salon a woman with tinfoil on her head flicked her cigarette at Mimi as she passed. Clearly, the stupid hag thought we were putting the posters up, not taking them down. In fact, the number of people who believed that Mimi had put the posters there herself was incredible. It was some strange business we were engaged in. And the glares Mimi was getting from men! I submit, Your Honor, that it's disastrous for the species what looks men think are seductive. Mimi tried to maintain eye contact with them all, to paper over the humiliation that was constant and unbearable. As we walked side by side in silence, I felt her mounting anger acquiring a certain rhythm and I was growing increasingly uneasy, more and more convinced I'd be attacked before this job was over. All in all, a thoroughly stressful day.

—Holy fuck, we've already been on this street, Mimi said, pointing to a new poster of her that appeared to have sprung up on its own on the slick tiles of a pharmacy wall.

As fast as we could tear down the vile posters, Mimi's boyfriend must have been putting them up. I scanned the street, heard crazy laughter. I thought: He's enjoying it, the bastard. I thought: We seem inert and ghostly while our pursuer seems full of energy and life. I thought: It's been ages since I enjoyed frightening somebody.

—Is he violent?

Mimi's face darkened.

—He hit me once. I had to defend myself with a car antenna.

A car antenna? What had I gotten myself involved in? From somewhere behind me I heard the words, "You're dead." I thought: Calm down, it's only a paranoiac who takes all his city's death threats as directed solely at him. However, all this fear made me tired.

—You look tired, I said to Mimi. We should sit a minute. Do you want to sit a minute? Let's sit a minute.

Mimi collapsed next to me on a bus-stop bench like a traveling salesman at the end of a long life. The heat rising from her angry frustration was intense and she ignored my commiserative smile as she was busy staring with concentrated force at a surgical-masked man on a bicycle leading a Great Dane who nearly collided with a businessman on a skateboard.

—What kind of epoch is this anyway? Mimi asked in a small, annoyed voice.

—What do you mean?

—I don't know. When was the last time you saw a milkman?

A milkman?

—Beats me.

Here it comes, I thought, the story that is about to drop like a ripe apple from a tree. I imagined it would involve an abusive relationship with a vindictive, emotionally immature, and dangerous individual, the kind of paternal figure who beats his kids to death. Frankly, I was eager to hear it. But it didn't come. Why didn't it come? Usually it's no problem. Usually I have the opposite problem, making people shut up.

Sidebar: When I was a young man, Your Honor, I grew expert at disengaging, otherwise people trap you in dusty corners or up against WET PAINT signs or in between washing machines and talk and talk and talk. It used to drive me crazy until the day I found it profitable that people have an inexhaustible supply of anecdotes and ceaseless energy to tell them, and endless time to tell them in, and no consideration whatsoever for the listener. So between jobs and after bankruptcies and before unemployment checks, I found a way to survive. Some people read fortunes for money, some strum and sing, some suck and fuck, some beg; I listened like a fanatic—crouching on a milk crate, leaning on a terrace, resting on a park bench, with a smile and open ears—I endured the arduous task of hearing people's worries, or as I used to call it, peeling the skin off the unripe secrets of the mostly damned.

Yes, Your Honor, the cozy aches and liberating creaks of the pleasantly broken spirits of this city's inhabitants was, for a time, my daily bread. People paid with a coffee here, a drink there, or a sandwich—sometimes actual currency— and unloaded their problems in record numbers. When I was angry or in a bad mood I threatened to misunderstand them, but I never followed through. My ears grew used to the hidden meaning behind their words, like eyes that grow accustomed to darkness. Don't get me wrong. Or do get me wrong. I don't care. The thing is, I was no doctor or healer or shaman. I didn't even have any real advice! Only an impulse to put a pillow between the head and the brick wall it smashed up against, or nudge people discreetly toward their epiphanies, or boot them down the narrow staircase of truth into the coal cellar of their darkest hearts.

This is what I learned: Good times, they aren't for everyone. And this is how you must react. You have to say, "Man, that sucks. I'm really sorry. That's terrible!" That's the first lesson. If you don't know how to say, "Boy, oh boy, that's the absolute worst," then you aren't any kind of healer. And another thing! You can't put people's suffering into perspective, so don't even try. It's like praising the good leg of a single amputee. He knows he has one good leg. He doesn't need you to point it out. Of course the repetition was like sulphur thrown in my eyes. Oh God, how people so shamelessly repeat themselves. Sometimes they have a dim awareness, a flash of recognition. They say, "Did I tell you this before?" Oh well . . . They soldier on anyway . . .

The point, Your Honor?

—Relationships are hard, I said.

Mimi still didn't say anything. I had no choice but to resort to a cheap trick.

Tell her a story of my own. That gets people talking; they feel determined to out-misery you, to make your sad story seem like light fare.

—My wife Stella left me a few years ago. When a marriage falls apart *someone* has to feel relieved; In our case, I discerned little diamonds of light in her eyes as she left. The truth is, she kept trying to make molehills out of all my mountains—that's just one of those quips that someone did me the disservice of laughing at once, so now, like some obsolete machine stuck on a single setting, I can't seem to stop saying it.

I was torturing her with hints that my story would be a long one if she didn't interrupt with a story of her own.

—Mimi Underwood, I talk too much. That's what they tell me, and by *they* I mean the psychologists I consulted about talking too much.

The deceased *still* made no sign that she was going to spill it. So I went ahead and told her the whole story of me and Stella, up to and including the embarrassing zolpidem overdose on her hospital bed in which I failed to end my own life and nearly murdered a baby—my bad! After my long story, she finally spoke.

—I always said to myself that I'd rather be Anne Frank than have one of those lives where I had to get into my car to be alone.

—*That's* what you always said to yourself?

She nodded and fell back into silence. That was it. That was it? That's all she was going to give? After my saddest story?

—So are you going to help me destroy these fucking posters or what?

I tried not to hesitate or linger on the malicious posters, but aimed to mirror Mimi's manner of tearing them into shreds quickly with disgust and finality. I knew it was absolutely the wrong thing to do, but I snuck one of the folded posters into my inside pocket when she wasn't looking. Except she *was* looking. Her face went slack, and with quiet deliberation she reached into her handbag and extracted a metal stick that extended.

A car antenna!

I covered my eyes but that left my entire body open to attack. Mimi cracked it against my shin. I howled and fell to the ground and she brought the antenna hard down on my back. The pain was immediate and there was a delay before the thwacks echoed sharply in my ears. I wondered if her boyfriend was watching. It was like a dream. Her unrestrained fury, my state of weird depletion in which I couldn't lift my arms or move my legs. I wanted to exchange knowing looks with the strangers who'd gathered to bear witness, but I couldn't lock onto a sympathetic eye. Another lonely beating.

At last, Your Honor, she breathlessly retracted the car antenna and returned it to her bag, tossed one hundred dollars at me, and stormed away. I struggled to my feet, listening to the diminishing echo of her angry footsteps, and stumbled toward home with the sound of male laughter following me down the street.

No, I didn't see her for another four months. No, we did not commence a sexual relationship until that time.

What do you mean? This *is* the short version.

II

As you know, ladies and gentlemen of the jury, you can always find someone worse off than you, but sometimes you have to go outside your own circle of friends to do so. That's why I'd spent the day in question frenetically googling my way through a bonanza of grotesque-luck cases: the teenager who had a stroke after her first kiss; the man whose toes were eaten by his terrier while he slept; the farmer whose X-ray showed a corkscrew in his brain; the boy who lost an arm waving to his mother out the window of a car. A stockpile of baseline comparisons for therapeutic purposes. Every story asked me, point-blank, to have my say, and I obliged. Thanks for illuminating the true incoherence of cause and effect, franticangel33, you couldn't have been unluckier if you were born in a tiger's mouth. Hey there, functionallyilliterate007, understanding what happened to you is like trying to get a foothold in a river. The entire internet now gives off an unpleasant odor, thanks to your bitter tale, peterhotpants21, and I predict you shall never once be envied in your whole painful existence. Etcetera. Meanwhile, the phone rang constantly and I answered it to say no. I'd been doing this for weeks. No to invitations, no to creditors, no to market researchers, no to the crematorium to collect my great-aunt's uncollected ashes—It's been four years already, I said, let it go!—and I was *still* receiving calls about those absurd signs advertising my services, anything for anybody for twenty-five dollars an hour. No, I couldn't varnish a boat, or "escort" a son to an arranged marriage. Nor could I shave and tattoo an enemy's poodle. I even said no to myself. When did you last actually leave the apartment? Yesterday. Not counting the balcony. Eight days ago. Go outside and get some fresh air. No.

To myself, Your Honor, was that not clear?

That morning I had leapt out of bed and examined shadows that didn't seem to correspond with the objects that cast them. A neighbor let out a fake cough designed to get attention, and I shouted at him to get a life and stormed around the apartment tearing down the notes—the one to turn off the faucets (I am that tenant who repeatedly floods the bathroom), the note to shut the windows (whenever I leave a window open at home it invariably hails at a forty-five-degree angle)—and with a broom I tore down a spider's web that frankly made no architectural sense. I was experiencing a severe episode of clinical frustration. It wasn't my first.

That overdose on Stella's hospital bed, that failed suicide attempt, had really rocked my sad world. Ending my own life wasn't a decision I had come to lightly. I had visited a psychologist I found in the Yellow Pages. A box of Kleenex and an ability to rephrase the client's questions seemed to be all the qualifications required. He asked why I had come. I told him it was to find courage to take the next big step in my life. Is that why you're here? he asked. To find courage? Yes, I said. Well, Aldo, he said, that's already very brave of you. I agreed that it was the height of bravery. Now, courage to do what, Aldo? To kill myself, I answered. One million ordinary human beings end their own lives every year, why can't I? I don't know, he said. Let's puzzle it out. Well, for a long time, I said, the very idea of suicide had been my sole means of support; it had worked as hard as a single parent. Problem is, no sooner do I pick up a blade, I feel my authority challenged. He asked, Why do you think that is? I said, One merely has to google the phrase failed suicide attempts to find the most hideous outcomes known to man or beast. He said, But surely you know that those outcomes are statistically unlikely. He wasn't a bad therapist; his transparent strategy over the following weeks was to *pretend* to help me conquer my fear of suicide while in reality talking me down off the ledge. In the end he had some minor victories. He got me admitting guilt about being alive when Veronica is dead, and to realize that my self-conception of laziness and giving up easily didn't square with my actions, that my BRFs (behavior restricting fears) were contradictory—such as my fear of being misunderstood and my fear of being transparent—and that my chronic migraines were somehow related to the heavy responsibility and burdensome guilt for having unwittingly, through excessive teasing, goaded Leila, my mother, into unnecessary elective surgeries—gastric bypass and stomach stapling. I wept copiously about my inability to decide on my worst fear: loneliness or physical suffering, and he gleefully plied me with Kleenex, as if he were being paid by the tear. Through his window I could see exhaust-gray clouds and trees groaning on their trunks. All this talking helped, it was true, but not in the manner he intended. His ploy to pretend to help me confront my fears of suicide actually helped me confront my fears of suicide. He came with me to my lookout point over the valley of the shadow of death and showed me it was a clean jump. So I did it. Drank two entire bottles of vodka. Yet I woke in angry confusion. A month later (nobody attempts suicide twice on the same day) I sat in my out-of-town neighbor's car in their garage with the engine running; yet again, I woke up groping the morning. The third time I binge-drank *and* took an overdose of pills, yet again waking with a dungeon-like hangover, exasperated and near deranged with grief but also somewhat spooked, the sensation of my beating heart causing the prickling of the hairs on the back of my neck. Each time, I had woken to find life—that inexplicable dream that overstays its welcome—restored against my will. Why couldn't I do it? These were not lighthearted attempts or a cry for help. Why couldn't I pull it off? I had one half-baked theory, but it was too absurd to contemplate. All I knew was I was the flea on my own back.

The phone rang again. I answered it, shouting, "What? What? What is it?"

—We saw your sign, the voice said. We need someone to come and fix a rat hole in the school hall, patch up some leaky pipes, paint over some graffiti, a janitor's job basically.

—Where? I asked.

—At Zetland High.

My old high school, Your Honor! I burst into tears. And after weeks of nonstop no's, I said yes, fuck it, why not?

III

The old high school was standing where it always had, between the shoe wholesaler with the bloodstained back staircase and the grocery store selling dust-covered chocolate bars. It was a daunting concrete structure set in a bland expanse of concrete, with concrete rails and concrete staircases and concrete floors, lit up by asymmetric beams of ghastly fluorescence. You couldn't burn it down even if you wanted to.

I hopped over the low wire fence to cross the old quadrangle where dozens of festering pigeons still plagued the schoolyard like a Venetian piazza, where my good friend Liam and I used to try to out-obscene each other, and where Stella had once played a protest song for me, which I had discreetly viewed from the science lab. I spent a few minutes gazing into the same windows I'd spent years gazing out of, at the boys clawing at their ties in surly silence, and the girls so young and dazzling I had to neuter my male gaze. Then I went to work: fixed a couple of leaky pipes, dragged out the dead rats and stuffed them in garbage bags, nailed wooden planks over their escape hatch, cartoonishly hammered my thumb, sent the tools falling down the staircase, ran after them as children made disparaging comments I needed an urban dictionary to understand. Yet my overwhelming emotions were regret—that I didn't enjoy my youth more—and compound loss; I was nostalgic both for my childhood *and* for the days, in my late twenties, when I was *first* nostalgic for my childhood.

I grabbed a sandwich from the cafeteria, then roamed corridors that didn't smell of books or pencil shavings, but of the inside of an air-conditioning unit, and then for old time's sake moved into the vestibule for the headmaster's office, an austere area with a single fern and wooden benches where I used to sit and imagine I'd been shipwrecked and washed up alone in the lobby of an off-season hotel. It was at that moment, Your Honor, that I overheard three teachers inside the office discussing the objects that got thrown at them in the course of a normal school year—chalk erasers, apple cores, chairs, and one of them asking if either of the other two had ever been tempted to sleep with a student. "No way!" they shouted in scandalized tones, then after a moment of silence, exploded into the most sinister laughter I'd ever heard.

—You go first, one said.

—No, you.

Low voices followed, though from my covert position outside the office, the substance of their conversation eluded me; I caught only a name (*Mimi*) mentioned several times, accompanied by more black laughter. Then footsteps on carpet, and a door swinging open to reveal the teachers: two men and a heavy-set woman.

—What are you doing here? the woman asked, in a mannish voice.

I said that I was closing up the rat hole in the floorboards in the school hall.

—That was this morning, one of the men barked. What are you still doing here?

I would have thought that the universal pastime of eavesdropping needed no introduction, but there you are. I explained that I'd had lunch in the cafeteria.

—You know what, Mr. Benjamin? That's not OK.

All three teachers lectured me on the inappropriateness of a forty-year-old man—I was thirty-nine, but I let it go—with no business in a high school, lingering in the hallways. I thought: Surely a creature who excites faculty members of both genders is at least worth a look-see. I made my apologies, and promising to leave the grounds at once, went straight out to the concrete quadrangle to interrogate the students. I crouched in an alcove underneath a staircase that smelled so bad someone must have pissed on it when the cement was still wet. There I asked boys who couldn't write their names without a spell-check if they knew this infamous Mimi. No luck. I asked girls who'd overplucked their eyebrows so that they resembled the scary dolls they cradled as toddlers. Nada. I took a long, hard look at their faces and tried to guess how many would end up sleeping on the streets. Frankly, I couldn't wait for their twenty-year high school reunion so I could turn up out of nowhere and rub it in their craggy, homeless faces.

It was *then,* Your Honor, that I heard a familiar voice.

—Don't feed the pigeons, Donaldson!

IV

It was inconceivable that Mr. Morrell was still forbidding students to feed the pigeons. I edged forward to get a good look at my old art teacher. He was still tall and sinewy, and his overtanned skin still made him look like he'd been dragged out of the wreckage of a collapsed sunbed, and he was *still* peeling a mandarin.

—Jesus Christ, Mr. Morrell!

Morrell turned around and peered intensely at me, his former student.

—That isn't Aldo Francis Benjamin, surely.

—I'm afraid so.

He moved close enough to pat my potbelly.

—The good life, eh?

—What do you think I am, a sixteenth-century nobleman? This here's mostly glucose and saturated fats.

Morrell laughed and gripped my arm in a way he wouldn't have dared when I was a student.

—What are you doing here?

—Some odds and ends. Rat hole needed fixing. A little plumbing.

Morrell blinked, uncomprehending.

—But you haven't come here to your old high school as a janitor, have you? Oh Lord in heaven, that's grim. When I didn't say anything, he said, In every moment of our lives, we always choose the least worst option, so for you to be here today, there must have been something terrible waiting for you elsewhere that you were eager to avoid.

I remembered now his penetrating way of burrowing in, and how he could demolish a student with a cutting remark, how he enjoyed understanding and interpreting behavior, then sadistically enlightening said person to that behavior. It was due to him, I suddenly realized, that I had first taken an interest in amateur psychoanalysis as a lethal weapon, and began to listen actively to people's stories and learned to hear the words they didn't say more clearly than the words they did. Morrell's eyes turned to a student giving pigeons mixed messages: scattering breadcrumbs on the ground, then stomping his feet.

—This generation is the absolute worst one yet, Morrell said.

—You used to say that every year.

—It's true every year, he replied, and rubbed his hand over his head as if in hope his baldness was a temporary mistake. He asked me how old I was and I told him I was nearly forty, and he seemed to think that reflected badly on his own lifespan.

—Children?

—At what age does one become childless anyway? My whole life I've been childless, but now, suddenly, it's official?

Morrell stared at me in astonishment.

—Listen, Aldo. Do you mind if I point you out to a few students as a possible worst-case scenario?

Typical Morrell zinger. I actually didn't mind. Nevertheless, for good sport I felt I must retaliate, so I asked the obvious question, which was why was he still moping around this tragic place when he always said he was going to dedicate the last half of his life to his art.

—I'll be retiring soon to concentrate on my painting.

—Ah.

We both remembered him saying the same thing twenty years before. Now the curtain of sadness had fallen on us both. I had never seen the fear of one's illegitimacy so pronounced on a human face.

—It really is a pleasure to see you, Aldo. I'm sorry things aren't working out for you.

—And I'm sorry your dreams remain unachieved after all these years.

We were like two dehydrated hikers who had bumped into each other on a deserted trail. Neither had water.

And I object to your objection! This *does in fact* relate to Mimi Underwood, Mr. Crown Prosecutor, because some memories sit like puddles and refuse to evaporate. It was at *that* moment it hit me; I excused myself and ran to the boys' toilets on the third floor where in the fifth stall, carved into the wall with a penknife, faded by time but still perfectly legible, were the same words that I had seen more than twenty years earlier: *Mimi. Underwood. Sucks. Teachers. Cocks.*

I knew I had seen her name before! The Mimi the teachers spoke of was of course the deceased, the same woman I had helped four months earlier remove pornographic posters put up by a man who, I submit, ladies and gentlemen of the jury, set out to slander and humiliate Mimi Underwood *and later murdered her*. Maybe. That's one possibility. We don't want to rule it out.

Mr. Morrell was still in the quadrangle, and I had to shout over wailing ambulance sirens and the deafening roar of a plane passing overhead.

—Do you remember a Mimi Underwood?!

—Why? What have you heard?!

Someone yelled out, Morrell sux! He laughed without turning around, and I remembered how he always acted like he'd put your hatred in his desk for safekeeping.

V

—As you might remember, Aldo, Morrell said, once the plane had passed, it was the great pleasure of my teaching life, a pointless joy perhaps—like the love of telling librarians to be quiet—to discover poets, musicians, and painters among all those budding physicists, dreaded footballers, and drug-dependent oversharing sex-addicted shopaholic knife-wielding porn aficionados. Basically, I preferred creative souls who had a burning gift to offer the world and who knew how to degrade me with panache.

—What's this got to do with Mimi Underwood?

—She's a photographer. She illustrated a children's book.

—With photos?

—Black-and-white photos. The book was called *The Fussy Corpse*. It seemed too adult and cerebral for children but what do I know? I'm just a teacher. The evening after reading it I wrote her a letter, care of her publishers: Dear Mimi Underwood, it said, students often see teachers as peripheral to their education, but I wonder if you'd stoop to remember me anyway: Angus ("Mr.") Morrell. It's with great pleasure that I, etcetera, etcetera. In short, I congratulated her on her meritorious achievement, and wondered if it was not too forward to ask for a signed copy of her magnum opus. Only after I sent the letter did I realize I had forgotten that a newly published success must be inundated with appeals for friendships and merchandise, and when a month passed without response, I wrote a second letter apologizing for the first, and to lighten the situation I asked if she remembered our last encounter, when I spotted her outside Pitt Street Mall selling umbrellas in the rain.

—Who was selling umbrellas in the rain? Mimi?

—It is a reliably awkward displeasure to unexpectedly run into students in the outside world, I wrote in my second letter, but there was something especially depressing about the sight of you drenched to the bone with cheap black umbrellas hanging off your arm. I had feared that you were mistreating yourself into an early grave, though you certainly wouldn't have been the first highly gifted student to make a garbage dump of your life. "How long has it been?" you asked me in a voice that sounded hoarse from singing. Normally it is the student who knows how long since she left school, and not the teacher, and I said as much, adding that time moves so fast there are not even discernible epochs anymore, and I knew people five generations apart with only twenty years between them.

I stood speechless, frozen by the strange manner of repeating his own letter verbatim like some arcane party trick, and I was reminded what a weird and amusing and eccentric man he was. Morrell went on:

—I remember you remembering me, I wrote Mimi, and you laughed, but then your face became a disquieting mask of what I took to be the deepest unhappiness, and after an awkward good-bye I remember smiling as I walked away, because in truth it is often a more sincere pleasure to see a depressed former student than a happy one, because in the happy ones I can see the disheartening process by which they became happy: high ambition, repeated failure, discouragement, eventual giving up, settling for less, reluctant acceptance, and finally contentment with the little things, somewhat beautiful in the individual, but depressing when it occurs by the thousands year after predictable year.

—Did she write back?

Morrell shook his head sadly. He looked totally depressed.

—Oh well, one gets used to ingratitude, he added, and as he walked away, I thought: That's perfectly right, one does.

VI

The salesgirl at the third bookstore I tried suggested the local branch of the public library. I know what you're thinking, bailiffs, what is this, 1996? I raced through the streets as if through a time tunnel, to the bland underwhelming brick building behind the train station. My heart sank when I came across an island desk with twenty computer terminals, leather couches and espresso machines, but upon asking, the librarian directed me to the appropriate shelf. It was there, *The Fussy Corpse*, written by Elliot Grass, illustrations by Mimi Underwood. I took it to a leather couch beside loud-whispering students.

The striking, eerie cover featured a charcoal sketch of two burning eyes peering out from a crack in a coffin lid, yet inside, as Morrell had indicated, instead of the expected drawings, the accompanying illustrations were stark black-and-white photographs that I browsed without understanding their context—haunting photos of an empty field, an elegant fir tree veiled in mist, a vermilion sunset, vines tangled around an oak box, dazed eyes smeared with mascara, a plume of smoke over a small hill, an ornamental jar on a stone-tile floor, a white shroud, two bodies facedown in the snow, a pair of bagpipes, a brick chimney, a sturdy pile of rocks, and an empty child-sized suit laid out on a bed. I would like to submit *The Fussy Corpse* into evidence as exhibit B.

This is how it begins: *Four exhausted and irritated pallbearers were carrying a fussy corpse across half a dozen cemeteries when their arms got tired.*

Understood. If we're time sensitive, Your Honor, in summary, the book tells the story of a recently dead boy who doesn't want to be buried "just any-where," and the four pallbearers who carry this disenchanted corpse to every continent, into teeming cities and small towns, into rural and urban communi-ties, into remote tribes and off-the-wall cults, where he is offered every type of funeral that is conducted in human civilization, but nothing appeals. He does not want camphor placed in his orifices and armpits while loved ones wail and scratch their faces and wear their clothes inside out; he does not wish to be mummified or to be buried with soldiers or under a tree or in his own garden or in a low-ceilinged cave cut into stone or in an unmarked grave or along with his belongings or with family members or with a sacrificed ox or with his knees drawn up to his chest or in a sand dune or with a corpse bride. Nor does he want his body covered with rocks nor to be placed in a three-humped rectangle-shaped casket nor on a bed of sweet-smelling spices, and he does not wish to be dusted with talcum powder or dressed in a suit or placed on a mat or covered with yellow cloth, and he has no interest in hearing chanted verses of scripture or bagpipes or love songs, and he is not inclined to have his internal organs removed and the body cavity filled with salt, and he does not wish a rope to be wrapped around his legs and neck and pulled tight to make him into a ball; nor does he want to be dumped at sea nor shot into space nor cremated and his ashes placed in a mausoleum or on someone's mantel or immersed in running water or scattered in a rose garden, and he has little interest in facing the setting sun or Mecca or Mount Kailash, and he does not want to be embalmed or tied to a stake on a hilltop and eaten by animals or vultures or carried on bamboo poles or placed on a pyre of sandalwood, and he especially does not want those flames aroused by clarified butter or to have his skull broken with a long pole or for his body to be covered in flowers or uncut hair or steel bangles or a short sword, and he does not want to be swathed in a white cotton sheet or placed in an unlined coffin or in a simple pine coffin with holes drilled in the bottom or in a purified room with or without an untasseled prayer shawl—

In *short,* he turns his nose up, is ambivalent, and outright refuses every human method of disposing of a body. Eventually, with a heavy heart, he decides it is much less hassle to remain alive. And that's when the story takes its surprising turn! The reveal at the end of the book is that the corpse is not a real corpse but a young boy with leukemia, his ghostly pallor due to his prolonged sickness and iron deficiency, and the pallbearers are his brothers who have broken him out of the hospital and put him in a coffin to help the young boy confront the stark reality of his inevitable death.

I closed the book and felt like I had been shot with an arrow and slung across a saddle and galloped into hell. Perhaps due to the frankness of Mimi's photographs and the unsentimental manner in which the prose tackled the subject, the tale was almost unbearably poignant and weird. The library had grown calmer, the students had ceased their loud whispering, having retreated to their respective smartphones. I couldn't understand my oppressive, mixed overreaction; everything paltry inside me bristled and throbbed repulsively. It was as if I had recognized myself in the fussy corpse, in that boy's attitude and overall dilemma. Absurd. I left the book on the table, but then came back and returned it to the shelf. I didn't want any children to happen upon it.

VII

That night, I dug out the pornographic poster of Mimi Underwood and sat on my bed looking at her dark, large, distended nipples and her exquisite—or in her mind, revolting—birthmark, that I found at the worst lovely and at the best incredibly erotic. About midnight, staring out of my window into the black sky and a misty halo of moon, I called the number on the poster. Your Honor, because in this era I recorded all calls to women for education and training purposes, I submit exhibit C, the following recording dated March 31st, 2013:

Hello?
Hello, Mimi Underwood! What's that I'm hearing?
I'm brushing my hair.
Sounds knotty.

What do you want?

It's Aldo Benjamin. The guy from the—

I recognize your voice. What do you want?

You recognize my voice? I'm flattered.

Don't be. It's unforgettable for all the wrong reasons. What do you
 want?

You didn't change your number.

I'll say it for the last time.

This *is* the woman who beat me with a car antenna, isn't it?

An apology, then?

I find it almost inconceivable that you didn't change your number.

You've called at a bad time. I'm having the worst week of my life.

That's what you said last time! I bet you have a lot of worst weeks. Did
 you know we went to the same high school?

Which one? I went to a few.

Zetland High.

The one with all the pigeons? Yeah, for a few months about twenty
 fucking years ago, so what? Thousands of people have been to that
 high school.

So what is right.

So I'm hanging up now.

I read *The Fussy Corpse*.

(silence)

That makes twelve of you. Did you buy it?

I read it in the library. Sorry. I have to say it was really something.
 It should come with a warning to emotionally or psychologically
 buckle up. My heart has been beating irregularly ever since I finished it.

So you didn't buy it, and you didn't even borrow it. Now I'm really
 hanging up.

I understand.

(long silence)

Mimi, are your eyes closed or open?

Closed.

Mine too.

(more silence)

Mimi, I want to tell you something.

What is it?

(silence)

I've never been angry in a dream.

So?

You know what I hate most in life? When someone says to me, "You know who you look like?" Then they name some overweight and unattractive character actor.

Why would you think I care about this?

I've always wanted to live in the type of old world-y culture where it's rude not to marry your brother's widow.

Did you want to tell me something more important?

Yes.

What?

I want to kill myself.

I see.

Yes.

You'll miss New Year's Eve.

I don't mind.

And the lunar eclipse.

When's that?

Stick around and find out.

What's so great about a lunar eclipse?

And crawling into fresh hotel sheets. And afternoon naps. And crying in a sad movie. And hearing a new language spoken for the first time. And wandering in the desert unable to find your tent at night.

That sounds terrifying.

Meeting a new person and watching them form judgments of you as you speak.

You *like* that?

Waking up on a boat to find you've drifted into a new estuary. Watching a sunrise with a beautiful stranger who may or may not have stolen your wallet. Crawling into the marital bed after cheating. Having your earlobes kissed and your toes sucked at the same time.

How can one person kiss your earlobes and suck your toes at the same time?

Who said anything about one person?

Mimi. I have nothing of substance in my life. All I have are my friend-ships and my love of God—how superficial. It's all about me, me, me!

That's no reason to lose the will to live.

And I've no real job. I don't even have a trade, or some kind of skill set.

What are you interested in?

Well, recently I have become obsessed with people who were mauled by their own dogs or whose children were mauled by their own dogs and who thereafter kept or defended those dogs.

That doesn't sound like a trade to me. How old are you?

Old enough to miss slamming down a rotary phone with enough force to hurt someone's eardrum.

What are you afraid of?

I'm a talented loser. The worst kind. Talented losers become self-aware madmen.

Aldo, I think I'll go back to brushing my hair.

And when I was in my twenties, the girls I knew were having abor-tions. By my thirties, they had moved onto stillbirths. I'm almost forty. Where's it all going to end?

You know where it ends.

I don't. I don't know. Do you think the inability to die could amount to a disability?

What kind of a question is that?

You asked me what I'm afraid of. That's my fear. That there'll always be some obstacle that prevents me from dying, from removing myself from the earth.

What are you saying?

I don't know. Maybe I'm just overtired. I've no energy these days, I'm always distracted, and am often staring into space. Literally—I have a telescope.

I don't think we're at the heart of things.

Strange things happen to me.

What kind of strange things?

It's hard to explain.

Try.

If there's a foot-sized crack in a thousand-kilometer pavement, my foot
    will find it.

Lots of people are clumsy.

I'm clumsy, sure, no doubt. I had a stubbed-toe and head-lodged-
    between-banisters type of childhood and I *still* need to apply special
    concentration on escalators in regards to foot placement. I have an
    accident-prone personality. And I can identify with some but not all
    of the indicators: impulsiveness, cognitive drift, aggression. But this
    is something else. You know what Freud said? *Accumulation puts an
    end to the impression of chance.* I agree. This shit is not coincidence.
    Have you ever swallowed a fly?

Once.

Well, I've swallowed *bees*. And at least twice a year a bird flies into my
    head. I *always* fall over when I'm in the middle of yelling at some-
    one. When I play a piano, the lid invariably closes on my fingers.
    I can never cross train tracks at night without a train screaming
    out of nowhere or traverse a lawn without the automatic sprinklers
    coming on. A rung has been missing on every ladder I've climbed.
    I inevitably get sick on my birthday. Whenever I travel I arrive in
    town the day after the fiesta. And how many overweight women can
    one man congratulate on being pregnant?

Quick! Tell me something positive about yourself. Without thinking.
    Go!

I'm good at buying presents.

What else?

I can pretty much befriend any cat.

What else?

I'm out! I got nothing else! You know the bad luck it takes to get a big
    toe caught in a mousetrap, but I've done it, I've done it!

You sound stressed.

I *am* stressed. And I know that stress destroys dendrites and neural
    pathways in the hippocampus, and that stresses me even more.
    Christ. I need to stand up.

What was that sound?

I stepped on some walnuts.

Was that your knees?

Mimi, I remember your hair. And your lips. And your eyes.

Aldo, I remember your wife had left you.

I think it was for the best. I mean, for my own safety.

What do you mean?

Well, when you think about it, the phrase "until death do us part" inevitably serves to foster murderous fantasies in one or both parties. That clause is a clear inducement to murder! Am I the only one who can see it?

So you're still single, then.

The materialistic, sex-withholding, cynical women of this superficial town routinely sense my low expectations and then lower themselves to fit under them. And not only that, but I've completely run out of sexual fantasies. The actresses are too stupid, the models too thin, the waitresses too mean, the shop girls too bitter, the nurses too depressed, and the regular civilians look like they haven't had a good night's sleep in years. How is one expected to masturbate in this society?

Is this an exaggeration of the real you or a toned-down version of the real you? Or is this the real you?

That's a good question.

They say if you want to be loved, be lovable.

They also say practice what you preach; that's why I'm preaching threesomes.

You're a fucking riot, you are.

I need hosing down, it's true. Do you have kids?

No.

Are you in a relationship?

I overheard my last boyfriend refer to my vagina as any port in a storm.

Shit. I suppose the vertical decline of your fertility is an issue. Do you *want* kids?

It's so late in the game.

I guess at our age the decision to have children is an expression of the fear of not having children.

You know what I think?

Yes, I do. You think living in such a fast-moving civilization means your dreams are obsolete before you have a chance to give up on them.

I think you called to ask me out and you haven't gotten around to it yet.

Why do you think it's such a taboo to conclude that life isn't worth living?

I don't know. It just is.

Ten thousand women raped, six thousand children molested, twenty-five thousand men beaten to death. Is there one earth day that isn't like that?

I suppose not.

Then how can you tell me life is worth living? Besides, the question isn't "is life worth living" but "is *my* life worth living." You compare your best day to your worst, and find it balances out quite nicely. You don't compare your best day with the worst day of a victim of sex slavery!

Don't fucking yell at me!

If you told people with absolute authority that in ten years every child will be boiled in hot lava, I'm absolutely positive that people would still churn out babies. That's the human race for you!

You sound like someone who got woken up at the wrong time. Are you sure you meant to ring me specifically?

Tell me what you think of this equation: Having already reached my potential five years ago, plus eternity, *plus* a human mind that cannot fathom the infinite, equals madness, right?

Are you saying you believe you—

Feel every picosecond and will continue to do so ad infinitum.

You think you're actually—

If I was destined to die, shouldn't Jeremy's mother, the fortune-teller, have prognosticated some species of void?

What are you saying?

What if from birth I had come down with, that is to say had contracted, an exceedingly rare case of—I can't believe I'm saying this out loud—*immortality*?

That's crazy.

Yet what is the inability to cause the irreversible cessation of one's core physiological function if not *immortality*? And what is the time value coexisting with that inability if not *eternity*? What if the end of consciousness is our common disease, and what if someone was immune, or had built up resistance to the disease? And what if that someone was me?

I'm hanging up now.

In the face of forever, the contours of one's life slacken and become not just poorly defined, but permanently resistant to definition. I feel sick. I cannot meet the basic prerequisites for death! How embarrassing! I've stolen fire from the gods, without meaning to!

You think you're invincible—

I'm not saying I can't be hurt. I can. That's the problem. There's no freedom in *my* immortality, it just makes me *more* vulnerable to pain and suffering. Imagine the setbacks and dangers that I'll be susceptible to! I might get a thousand-year migraine, or be a few hundred years bedridden, or contract dementia and be combing over precarious memories every morning forever. Or what if I were to be decapitated? Or sentenced to life imprisonment? Death is our wedding with the abyss and I'm the only bachelor in town. This is a sickness. I'm sick. I'm incurable! I'm a candle that can never sputter out! I can break but I can't erode! I can crumble but not disappear! As time expands, space shrinks. The world is suddenly infinitesimal, every minute a tyrant. I could do anything! Get into any amount of trouble! Or I could do nothing! Make no sound or movement! It makes not the slightest difference!

I can't understand a single thing you're saying.

And I can't understand why masturbation is called self-abuse. It's the only nice thing I've done for myself all week!

Traditionally, who likes hearing this kind of crap?

Traditionally, you should know, I've gone for girls with page-boy haircuts and a high-lesbian intelligence. Actually, wait. That used to be true. Now when I see a woman I think, if I had paid a thousand dollars for a high-class escort and *she* turned up at my door, would I feel like a satisfied customer or would I feel short-changed?

You actually think that?

Let me put it this way. I'm way too old for the raging hormones of adolescence, and yet, and yet, I can't pass a woman on the street without
imagining bending her over a bar fridge, a plinth, or a reception
desk—it's an incredible drag.

You're a monster.

Are you looking at the moon?

I've just worked out why you called.

I thought I'd be the first to know.

You want someone to like you for who you were before you became
who you are now. You want someone to like you retrospectively.

I think I called at the right time.

Do you now?

Sometimes all you need in life is good timing. I almost never have it. I
think I'm actually proud of myself.

Don't be so sure.

True. I'm always misjudging circumstances. Like the time I went for a
job interview and the manager asked what would I say is my greatest
asset and I answered: I can sleep anywhere!

Aldo.

Yes, Mimi?

Let's meet.

VIII

Your Honor, it was three in the morning when we met outside the often violent
Coogee Bay Hotel. The night was cold and the moon thin and transparent, just
barely in the sky. I spotted her moving as if she hoped to kill something underneath her heel with every step, wearing jeans tight enough to stop circulation,
and that, I gruesomely thought, would need to be cut off in an emergency. I felt
like a gravedigger resting on his spade.

　　—Hi, she said.

　　—There's nothing worse than lonely people who find each other and fail to
connect, but no pressure.

With the salty wind like shadows of ghosts advancing from the sea, and the palms swaying, I took her in: The deceased was leggy and nearly as nearly beautiful as I remembered, with high, pushed-up breasts, her signature wild hair, and cannibal eyes glowing in the dark. We seemed overawed by each other and were both suffering the embarrassment of mutual attraction. Our faces were close together now, lips almost touching, but we had not yet kissed. A group of skinny men ran along the beach, the echo of their conspiratorial voices drawing us even closer together. Mimi wrapped her arms around my neck and I tasted cigarettes in her hair; we stood, cheeks together, almost-kissing in the unbroken silence for uncountable minutes. I tell you, ladies and gentlemen of the jury, it is eerie and unbelievably erotic almost-kissing a stranger in the dark.

—What are you thinking about? the deceased asked.

—Our retirement years, how it might be lovely to pool our superannuation, move to Byron Bay, and then die within twenty-four hours of each other—one from heart failure, the other from grief.

What's that? OK, Mr. Impatient, I'll get to the point. And why shouldn't I? The point is fantastic.

Rain may or may not have been falling. The deceased pressed her body heavily against mine and I could feel her silken lashes against my cheek and our faces did what faces do before we hurried back to her place to begin—as you're so fond of saying—*a sexual relationship*. Is that concise enough for you? May I at least describe her residence, or would the prosecutor like the jury to have no sense of place or setting?

IX

Along a dull stretch of highway, Your Honor, north through hills and scrubland, off a desolate coastal road that winds along the cliff's edge, there's a narrow lane, and at the end of the lane, obscured by wild garden, stands a house hidden in the shadow of an enormous camphor tree. I stepped out of Mimi's van into the wet morning; the earth was soft and everything shiftless and breezy. I followed the deceased through the front door of this ramshackle house into a large open room with ocean views, filled with pandemonium: There was a lanky man with shriveled arms furiously turning over couch cushions while a girl in overalls said, "Warm, warmer, now cold, colder." A Japanese girl drawing a guy with white dreadlocks cutting his toenails; bodies strewn on mildewed furniture, heads in laps, resting on groins, the shape of multiple carcasses twisting in a single hammock; carpets stained with paint and cigarette ash; candles melted down onto wine-stained tablecloths; guitars strewn on the Ping-Pong table; street signs and broken chairs, dried paint tubes, stiff unwashed brushes, and a piano on which you knew that some son of a bitch would soon be playing "Chopsticks" or "Piano Man." The atmosphere was vaguely thoughtless and erotic. It smelled of cats and kebabs and turpentine. I tripped over a ukulele. A laughing woman was giving a haircut to a dog with stitches in his coat, while sugared-up children ran wild around them, eating paint that most certainly contained lead. I asked, What the hell is this place? A squat? A commune? Mimi said, It's an artists' residency. The Hobbs Foundation. One of seventy now across Australia. Here we have mainly painters and sculptors, a couple of poets.

The children were running in circles and throwing shriveled apples from a still life.

—Is there an actual parent around here? I asked.

—Plenty of societies, like the Spartans, got by just fine raising children as a society.

—Sure, I replied tersely, if you count their decline and eventual extinction as "getting on fine."

Each room was crammed tight with easels and canvases and paints, and smelled of human sweat. I had the impression I couldn't brush against a curtain without contracting hepatitis C. I heard dogs barking, but that turned out to be on the stereo.

Sidebar, Your Honor: What do I know about art? I was never an artist myself, even though as a child I knew that to ask someone why they were in a bad mood when they weren't in a bad mood would put them in a bad mood—sometimes I did that just to change the energy in a room. And then, when I was older, it was a reliable pleasure to tell a newly formed couple they looked like brother and sister, and watch the spark of sexual chemistry flare out. Of course I knew the basic archetypes: bald vigorous Spaniard type vs. tormented Dutch ear-slicing type; the rejectionphobes vs. the rejection fetishists; those who put anything they daub or scribble up for sale vs. perfectionists who warm themselves on painting bonfires. Otherwise, it was Mr. Morrell who'd taught me everything I knew to this point about art as a profession: The best artists are disillusioned by eight thirty in the morning; the only perfection possible is to never begin; without context, a high-priced and much-feted conceptual masterpiece turns back into the embalmed shark or garbage pail that it is; artistic genius is often linked with insanity only because free time is the key factor in exacerbating mental illness; most artists are easily offended, save empathy for their work, but parcel it out sparingly in their lives; they cultivate animosity toward their audience and vehement contempt for their patrons. In short, as Mr. Morrell elucidated, they are a beloved, magnificent, obstinate race of snake oil salesmen. Now that I think about it, Mr. Morrell is the reason why I'm suspicious and even fearful of artists as a species, so when Mimi made brief introductions—Everyone, this is Aldo. Aldo, this is everyone—I braced myself. Good thing I did. Hi, they said. I'm Frank Rubinstein. I'm Nick Whiticker. I'm Eve Fairbanks. I'm Dan Wethercot.

—Why is everyone telling me their full names? I asked Mimi.

—They want to see if you've heard of them.

The onslaught continued: I'm Maria Hamilton. I'm Tristan Conrad. I'm Louise Bozowic. I nodded with a rigid smile and eyed the males in the group. Who had fucked Mimi? Who wanted to? Who would after I left? Was the coward who plastered pornographic posters huddled among them? Now I wonder, was there a murderer among these artists? Shall we add them all, ladies and gentlemen of the jury, to the list of possible suspects?

Mimi led me into her bedroom; it was like the inside of a shantytown. We kissed again, and the deceased unbuttoned my shirt and registered shock at the sight of my scarred torso.

—What the hell happened to you?

—Oh, this and that.

She ran her fingers over the faded scars, the scratches that had never healed, and the stretchy burns where I had failed to incinerate.

—Seriously, what did you do, fuck a cat-o'-nine-tails?

—Is this going to be a problem?

She undressed, and there they were—her famous nipples, her famous birthmark! She nimbly unbuckled my belt but fumbled with the buttons on my fly. I think she was used to zippers. Members of the press, going to bed with a new woman is like having to learn a whole new operating system on the first day of work with the boss breathing down your neck. You can quote me on that.

All morning we talked, about my fears of immortality, about her sad up-
bringing—what an interesting woman! The deceased, I learned, was born
into the type of family who wore headphones at the dinner table, who lived in
navy-blue jogging pants, who never had a golden age. Her alcoholic mother
had four children by three different fathers; hers was a gambler who'd blow
inconceivable sums on horses and online casinos. She had a bipolar brother
and a sister who got hooked on dirty methamphetamines, an ice monster who
became something to scare the children with. Mimi's childhood was played out
in poker-machine enclaves, racetrack bars, and heroin-injecting rooms. They
lived in Randwick, almost directly across from the Prince of Wales Hospital
(the proximity of which encouraged them to fall apart: more than once Mimi
would plop her mother in a shopping cart they kept in the yard and wheel her
over to emergency to get her stomach pumped). They took lunch in the hospital cafeteria, and got takeout coffee from the machine at reception. On birthdays they bought flowers from the hospital gift shop, and regularly purchased
toiletries from the hospital pharmacy. The soundtrack of her childhood was an
ambulance siren. God took unprovoked swings at them too. They dealt with
high blood pressure, pacemakers, epilepsy, type 2 diabetes, and borderline personality disorders. There were accidents, brain injuries, bad-luck diseases; a
severely autistic cousin lived with them for several years. And Mimi had to
take care of them all. Clean. Shop. Wash. Dress. Cook. Feed. Toilet. Iron. Shave.
Bathe. Change bandages. Run all over town. Lie to cops. Take orders from doctors. Appease social workers. Calm autistic cousin. Restrain bipolar brother. Sit
through cold-turkey vigils with sister. Endure mother's night terrors. Negotiate
with father over finances. Tolerate her name called in impatient or solicitous
voices. Hide booze. Hide smokes. Hide weed. Check oxygen tank. Lie to debt
collectors. Manage welfare payments. Yell at doctor. Distribute antipsychotic
medications. Accompany brother to court. Drag father home from racetrack.
Drag brother out of pub brawls. Honor father's forged checks. Pick up body
of collapsed mother. Retrieve stolen items from pawnshop. Perjure herself in
court. Physically lift uncle. Administer intravenous medication. Fill exhaus-
tive shopping lists. Weather age-inappropriate cleansing of opposite-gender
genitalia. Endure her name being called in choked voices. In frustrated voices.
In vehement, theatrical voices. Withstand sister's aggravated assaults. Mourn
mother both alive and dead. Her family didn't mind inconveniencing her—this

was the arrangement. Life as permanent errand! That explained, she said, her ability to draw a chair close to a bed without making a noise, apply a bandage in the dark, disinfect a wound, administer a morphine drip, spot a precancerous lesion. Just as I had learned amateur psychology, she had learned amateur nursing. Where I had read the *APA Dictionary of Clinical Psychology* and the *Handbook of Psychological Assessment*, she had read the *Fundamentals of Nursing* and the *Nursing Diagnosis Handbook*. She knew how to take blood pressure. How to collect a urine sample from an unwilling donor. Dispense medication to an indisposed mouth. Maintain a patent airway during a seizure. Palpate firmly the upper right quadrant of the abdomen below the costovertebral angle.

OK, Your Honor. Etcetera. Happy?

The point being, near midday, after having fucked and talked for six straight hours we had still not slept. The sun was shining directly through her windows, so brightly we had to put on sunglasses.

—How do you feel? she asked.

—Like I've been shot out of a cannon into the side of a mountain.

Mimi asked me to rub suntan lotion on her back, and that was erotic enough to get us going again until sunset. When I made a move to go, her hand clutched my arm.

—Stay, she whispered.

What else could I do, Your Honor? I stayed.

X

Two glorious months! Two months of sweaty siestas on creaky daybeds, waking up to the sound of thunderstorms, of dreaming about sleeping beside the very woman I was sleeping beside. Two months without praying for the opposite of clemency, without worrying about my incalculable, inescapable tomorrows, without thinking: My kingdom for a terminus!

Sure, bailiffs, we had our petty domestic differences: The deceased liked all the windows open and I liked them closed; she put every food product in the pantry whereas I prefer the entire kitchen to be one giant refrigerator. Sure, I discovered that compliments went down badly. A comment on her beautiful eyes, for instance, revealed to her a deafening silence on the subject of her nose. And she often worked into conversation the phrase *I don't suffer fools gladly* whereas I don't generally suffer gladly the fools who say that. One thing she could not tolerate was lying in bed and not sleeping. She wanted to fall asleep at an insane speed; anything longer than instantaneous was an unacceptable torment. She took sleeping pills I'd never heard of—Lunesta, Trazodone, Ativan, Sonata, Rozerem—she combined, she alternated, but she always took something, and didn't like it being pointed out. She was impatient, highly sensitive to criticism, intropunitive, self-critical, and had epigastric complaints she never took anything for. One particularly instructive day, she went out to the pharmacy *specifically* to purchase a scar-healing cream that she ministered to each of my disfigurements, perhaps to exert early control over me. Certainly her facial flushing and sweaty palms when she applied the cream was curious. I should also mention she was not just caring, but intuitive; she knew what to do if I was stricken by a headache or a fake headache or a panic attack or the fear of a panic attack.

Mornings she would attempt, despite my protestations, to tell me her dream, *and* she didn't like to be looked at either; any type of gaze—human eyes, animal eyes, camera lenses—seemed to rile her DNA, which was ironic because Mimi was a starer herself and the type of person who thought it acceptable to photograph the homeless as long as it was in black and white. She had sharp hip bones and an inexhaustible amount to say on the considerable deficiencies of Sydney men, as if they were a universal experience from which one could derive universal truths, and seemed to have an endless array of past boyfriends and lovers whom she'd reminisce about postcoitally. Her interpersonal issues were unclear. With a core group of artists, she had a hot–cold relationship that was both snuggly and standoffish. I might as well do the Crown the service of naming the chief suspects.

I allege the abstract painter, Frank Rubinstein! I allege the pointillist, Nick Whiticker! I allege the sculptor, Dan Wethercot!

It was from these people, incidentally, that I learned what it really means to be an artist. Their lives made a deep impression on me, and not only because a failed entrepreneur is a loser whereas a failed artist is always an artist *no matter what*. Their self-esteem is high! With their paint-splattered shirts and flabby guts and joints stuck to their lower lips, they walk around like captains of industry. They smoke like they have inoperable cancers. They keep their studios like teenagers' bedrooms, their bedrooms like crime scenes, their sinks like toxic hazards, and their kitchen walls, after cooking, like Jackson Pollocks. They gossip and offend each other and are easily offended and all their facades are in perfect working order—they have decided exactly who they are going to pretend to be and never look back. They fuck like one-man shows. They hammer, screw, nail-gun, saw, ravage canvases and each other. They drag in furniture that has been tossed onto the streets—broken-legged chairs multiply in the night. They are a frugal, crusty, sweary lot, who spurn corporate monoculture and seek corporate sponsorship. They trudge past you without a nod or smile, and swing between rivalries and factions, wondering aloud how to be controversial. Their developmental delays seem to have done their careers nothing but good. Their brains are all pleasure centers with no circumference. Pygmalionism is rife. The currency is flattery. They tell each other's anecdotes in the first person. They spread marijuana butter on toast and brew their own beer and act twenty-two, regardless of chronological age. They work hard and they self-aggrandize hard. Seriously, ladies and gentlemen of the jury, why *wouldn't* you be an artist? The sleep-ins are mandatory, the work days are orgies of creative playtime, the conversations stimulating, the sexual revolutions permanent. Every night, mirthless poets and arrogant painters couple on the balcony under a moon that burns coldly in the dark sky. Every night parties bound along until the wee hours of the predawn. Nobody who does next to nothing with their lives, I learned, goes to bed before three.

It took a long time for the deceased to show me her art. One night we were in bed, the sun had just set and a large communion wafer of a moon was already wailing on the burnished horizon. Mimi pulled out a black folder from under the bed and hesitantly presented it to me. Photographs of a man's face before and after she slapped it; a vaguely comic series of people in trees; darkrooms and old cameras; nibbled foodstuffs in display cases; charred dolls on barbecue hot plates; winged insects drowned in toothpaste; closeups of elderly throats; miscellaneous hands and paws; blurry cityscapes; an erect penis in soft focus; an anus smoking a pipe; a vagina on a bed of lettuce. There were hundreds, all stylistically different. She had never made a single dollar out of them, supplementing her income with unskilled minimum-wage jobs, just as I had done in between disappointing business ventures and begging. In fact, as it turned out, we could track how, over the past two decades, we'd been practically chasing each other around the sewer end of the job market. (The year Mimi was tele-marketing, I was washing dishes; when I was telemarketing, she was cleaning toilets, etc.) Now she was determined to make photography her profession by building her portfolio. The problem was this: she thought these photos were casualties of her intentions, unsalvageable shit that felt utterly unrepresentative of her.

—I start each new series with fresh hope, and I'm always disappointed, she said with disgust. Every approach I try, the results always let me down. What I think I see through the lens has no bearing on the printed image. What I try to capture I don't, and sometimes it's like I don't have a single optical nerve connected to my brain!

As she was talking I realized: Oh, she's leading up to something. Behind her eyes there was unmistakably an ulterior motive to this speech; her pace was slowing, and when it got down to a certain speed I knew she would ask me the question she was leading up to. Her deviousness was adorable.

—I'm not blocked, I'm gridlocked. I have been since this last series, she said, pointing to several photographs of nudes draped over water pipes.

A thousand possible subjects and none quite right. Mimi peered at me with sly eyes. She said her photos didn't feel unique, inspired, organic or revelatory in any way; rather, they felt parodic, vulgar, flat, self-conscious, trite. Clearly more preoccupied with what she was about to say than what she was saying, it was at that moment she dragged her finger languorously across my thigh, climbed on top of me, and pressed her sharp hip bones against mine.

—Aldo. You might be just the subject I've been looking for.

XI

At Mimi's insistence, I took her on what she called a tour of *my* Sydney, and let her photograph me in front of the two-story homestead at the Benjamin compound I grew up in, presently occupied by an unwelcoming Chinese family not averse to shooing away former tenants; beside the ugly redbrick building where Henry had kept a secret apartment; at the leafy marketplace where I paid a fortune-teller double to read her own palms; in the empty swimming pool where I once almost drowned; at the police station where I was held for wast-ing police time; on the rooftop where Stella was married and I drank myself into a coma; in the hospital where I had my first three kidney stones removed; at Luna Park where I'd been stabbed; in the lobby of the Railway Hotel where I'd found a man hanging; outside Liam's house where I was accused of raping Natasha Hunt; in the motel room where Stella and I hid from vigilantes; in the park where I was beaten with a tennis ball in a sock; in the bushland where I'd shot a zombie film; at the bar where Stella played her first gig; leaning against my abandoned car that had no registration and a dozen tickets and which I still planned to reclaim—basically, she photographed me at the locations of my catastrophes, where none of my gambles had paid off. Wherever we went, I was recognized by furious creditors with long memories, who forced us to make detours through cold streets and alleyways. Mimi photographed these confrontations, capturing the shiver of horror running through me as my enemies with their stockpiled grievances greeted me with humorless shouts: "Your phone's cut off! You don't answer your emails!" The deceased didn't mind making me look foolish. And neither did I, that was the truth.

—You've had a bad go of it, Mimi sympathized, one day after we'd stopped for lunch and I had tried unsuccessfully to order off the kids' menu—the waitress wasn't having it—and the angriest son of my angriest creditor sitting at the next table marched over and punched me hard in the breastbone. It was true. I had had a bad go of it. The sorrows knew when to waken, like vampires in their coffins. Mimi said she understood that the women in my life—Leila and Veronica and Stella and little baby Ruby—were the inextinguishable cold-fires in the black hole of my sadness, but that Stella was roaring the loudest. She asked me when I knew it was over. I used to believe it was the moment I realized I was no longer Stella's muse, but another time occurred to me: One night, a few months after Ruby's death, we could both feel the relationship slipping away irrevocably; around bedtime she gave me a rare open-mouthed kiss and asked if there was a sexual fantasy I'd never fulfilled. Off the top of my head, I said I'd always wanted to tear clothes violently from a female body. She put on her favorite dress, a black full-length evening gown, and said, "Go ahead." I tore it with both hands, almost surgically down the middle, and we fucked on a chest of drawers. Afterward Stella gave me two options: take the dress to a professional or stitch it myself—she needed it by the weekend. The following morning I went to the dressmaker. End of week, eighty dollars, the dressmaker said. I thought: Eighty dollars! The price of passion. The only problem was I had to borrow the money from Stella to retrieve the dress. She was in the kitchen baking banana bread when I asked her for it, and the face she made was so repulsed and repulsive, I felt some core piece of myself leave my body—my immortal soul wanted no part of that scene—and I knew it was over. I have not felt the same since that day; I've had some fundamental instability I can only relate to that morning in the kitchen.

At the end of my story Mimi said she had the impression she was watching a famine through a television commercial.

—I'd like to do a series of portraits of you out in the desert where you lost your child, she said.

The deceased wasn't exactly sensitive, Your Honor. But here's the thing. My story finally triggered the secret story of her own the following day, so despite her initial reticence, in the end she revealed her innate volubility; and that old familiar disregard for the listener's limitations set in, and the intimacy that had blossomed between us held, like a successful transplant.

XII

We strolled together, all the artists, along the coastal highway, past the beach club, the holiday houses—eight- or twelve-bedroom monoliths with palm trees and circular automated driveways and high security gates and all-year-round gardeners—in which one never saw a single resident, then we cut a path through the bush and wound down a steep descent to a small, hidden beach.

—Magic Beach, Dan Wethercot said.

It was a crazy place. A forbidding piece of rock jutted out of the sea with a seagull perched atop it like a sentry on a watchtower; surfers maneuvered around it with abandon, high-risk-tolerant individuals, half-demented, in fact. They were taut gymnasts with wild gestures and an excess of testosterone; in zigzags or clean arcs they slipped down walls of water into gardens of froth among boulders of sea-slicked granite. I feared they would be cleaved in two, or mashed or impaled and skewered; seemingly limitless harm could be done to a body in this place. The ocean was deafening; I felt I had seashells clamped to both ears. Beside me, Mimi in her tortoiseshell sunglasses was very still, gaping at the surfers with escalating dread and tension, and sighing with relief when they emerged whole out of the spume.

—What are you thinking about? Mimi asked, taking my hand.

I was thinking that oceans are hotbeds of extraterrestrial activity while we look dumbly at the skies. I was thinking: An immortal is a man whose *body* has gone insane. But mainly I was thinking about the previous night.

We'd played a few mildly dangerous sexual games until Mimi screamed—I forgot our safe word—and we collapsed together, then around midnight, perched on the edge of the bed, overwhelmed by a new nightly panic—I just couldn't get over how, while I was experiencing the mystery of being alive, I was expected to just lie there for eight hours—I shouted at her, *We're alive! So why are we going to bed?* Mimi quieted me with a look that seemed to say that all the answers could be heard in the silence, if only I'd learn how to listen. And I listened. And I heard it. I mean, *really* heard it. When she finally fell unconscious, I covered her tawny body with a sheet and kissed her dark eyebrows and fragile throat and her meaty scarlet lips, and stared at her amazing frizzy hair that required its own pillow. I watched goose bumps form on her arms and nightmares make lines in her forehead. I thought: What a woman. I thought: It's cute how she enjoys crushing cigarettes into ashtrays more than smoking. The windows rattled in the wind and a dog yelped; Mimi sat upright, her razor-wire hair silhouetted against the moon like pubic hair on a plate. I took her in my arms and gently lowered her in the bed; I felt like I had taken receipt of her due to a clerical error. Thanks to Mimi, I was acting like my old self again; the keyword, though, is act-ing—think Charlie Chaplin entering a Charlie Chaplin lookalike contest and coming in third. Or was that Elvis? Either way, even if I did a fairly solid im-pression of myself, was it really me? I took a deep breath and thought: Holy crap. I think I love Mimi!

Ladies and gentlemen of the jury! Consider the horrific complexity of my situation. For a suicidal case, love is inconvenient; for an immortal, it is a cause for despair. I climbed out of bed and went out onto the balcony so I could think of Mimi in peace without Mimi herself interrupting me. Cold night air in my face, I felt shame that I loved Mimi in a similar way to how I loved Stella, but relief that I could forget about my terror at having lost Stella and could enjoy the terror of losing Mimi.

Now, on Magic Beach, with all the artists wrestling lazily in their usual aura of benign lawlessness, consuming breakfast beers and joints, wrangling children, enjoying a faint tension among the egos while the songwriter Cash Caswill wrote a song in response to the tsunami, I dared ask myself the abominable question: Did Mimi love me back? If she did, she seemed to be asymptomatic. No blushing, no gazing into my face, no evident butterflies. In any case, could anyone love an immortal with no job prospects? I resolved to be on the lookout for clues.

Around two in the afternoon, the artists started playing a drinking game that involved writing haikus, and mine took out round one . . .

I lived by myself
as brother and sister,
the hermaphrodite said.

. . . . although nobody seemed sure it was a genuine haiku. My second one wasn't quite as good as the first one, or it was better. You decide:

My spirit animal—
A dog with its head
in a bucket.

The sun grew hot. I removed my shirt. The artists were stunned into silence, as if a curtain had been lifted at a sideshow.

—How the hell did you get those scars? Frank Rubinstein asked.

I ran through the list: motorcycle, skinheads, wrong turn, stray billiard ball, ambush by a party of thorns, Molotov cocktail, car antenna, gravel rash, cigars, etc. The painter Dee Franklin asked if she could draw me.

—Sure.

I noticed Mimi was quiet and turned the other way, facing the arc of gulls and the routine waves collapsing on the shore.

—We have to get going, Aldo, she said.

Was she jealous? Was this the required proof?

—Where are we going?

—You said you'd show me where Leila is buried.

—Now?

I could have played this out forever, though I couldn't deduce precisely what she was jealous about, since Dee Franklin was in a committed lesbian relationship with Lynne Bishop.

—Yes, Aldo, right now.

Your patience is about to be rewarded, members of the press, because it is from here we may be approaching the answer to our most pressing question: Who probably killed Mimi Underwood? And yes, yes, Your Honor, I promise on my own eyeballs to only, in the briefest manner, stick to the salient points.

XIII

Ladies and gentlemen of the jury, someone had draped seaweed over the statues of angels in Waverley Cemetery, that beautiful hillside resting place overlooking the sea; they must have come up from the beach, barefoot and laughing, and now the violent aroma of sun-fried kelp rotting on graves made Mimi and me wince as we strolled through the grounds and I detailed how my mother's people were bog-standard Christians in the way that their idea of God was a frowning octogenarian in a toga and heaven a glass-bottomed palace through which the angels observe and report. When we reached a large elegant cross I placed three purple orchids on the headstone.

—Leila Benjamin, meet Mimi Underwood. Like you, dear mother, she isn't fond of her upper arms and has a temper that could scorch a field of sunflowers.

—It's nice to meet you, Mrs. Benjamin.

—A few of Mimi's people are buried nearby. Not far, just over there.

—My grandparents. A couple of aunts and uncles. Isn't that a nice coincidence?

We gazed at the headstone, fingers intertwined. The world was quiet; it had gone into a coma. The heat peeled clouds from the sky, and along the edge of the cliff suicidal joggers made their way to the next beach. Gradually the uneasy smile disappeared from Mimi's face; I supposed she realized how ridiculous this all was.

—It was nice meeting you, Mrs. Benjamin, she said dispassionately and moved to her grandparents' resting place where she began her own ritual, which entailed removing her socks and shoes and sitting bralessly on a granite step, rolling a cigarette and staring at the oil tanker on the horizon. She

looked slightly disappointed with herself; it seemed to me there was a failure taking place: the failure to get sad or to achieve violent regret, or perhaps
it was the failure to remember—maybe she couldn't picture the faces of her
grandparents, or she had forgotten to forgive them for something, or she had
overforgiven them; either way, she suddenly looked like someone fed up with
self-disgust. I turned to my mother and the fear of public opinion rotting with
her, then back to Mimi. I had an overwhelming craving for a quick fuck and a
long nap. Nothing new about that, Your Honor, I've been horny and tired my
whole life.

All right, all right. May I just say, in my own defense, I have the right to my
own defense, so fingers poised, madam court stenographer, while we meet yet
another suspect in this awful case.

Shoes in hand, Mimi came back over.

—Let's go to the military graves and name all the unnamed soldiers.

—That sounds different.

We walked like a couple of old assassins down the unsteady path to the
military section, through the rows of simple white crosses until we were at the
edge of the cliff; the wind was stronger and the tall grass danced at the edges of
the graves. Mimi stopped at the first white cross.

—Name him.

—What about T-Bone McNally?

Mimi removed a permanent black marker from her purple leather handbag and wrote *T-Bone McNally* on the white cross. Christ, I thought. When this
girl names an unnamed soldier, she doesn't fuck about.

—Next, she commanded.

—Simon Simonson.

Scrupulously she wrote that too. I watched her perfect calligraphy take
form on the white cross and looked around to see if anyone was watching us.

—Now I have one. Elliot Grass.

I wrote it.

—You've spelled it wrong!

She tore the marker from my hand, correcting the name with agonizing
slowness, saying it aloud in a reedy voice filled with tears. The silence that followed felt sacred, apocalyptic. Elliot Grass. The name was familiar.

—Who's Elliot Grass?

She didn't respond. I thought back to all the stories she'd told me late at night in bed.

—The guy who gave you an eye infection when he came in your eye?

—No.

—The guy with the misspelled tattoo?

—No.

—The guy who kept making postcoital *ta-da* gestures?

—No.

—Wait. Is this the guy who shaved his mustache into a bowl and then smoked it?

—Yes, she said.

—And Elliot Grass wrote *The Fussy Corpse*!

—That's him, she said, then added, almost as an afterthought, my husband.

XIV

Husband! The deceased's face was crypt-like and refused expression. We stood in a thunderous silence; I felt perilously lost, cotton-mouthed, threatened. I do not like to love in anyone's shadow, but at the same time I felt an encroaching sense of relief at the onset of complications, the restored order of unleashed monsters. Here's where they've been hiding.

—What happened to you guys?

—He had this golden retriever named Honey, and when it died he bought another golden retriever and called it Honey II.

—No, come on. That wasn't it.

—Men only pretend to give up the sex obsessions of adolescence but they never do.

—And so?

—So what was the quote, that Churchill one about democracy?

—The worst system except for all the others that have been tried?

—Yeah, well, that's how he felt about monogamy.

—Let's start again. Can we start again? What happened to your husband?

—He lost me, then outright refused to win me back.

—Can you be more specific?

—At nightclubs he and his friends did something called rape dancing, which I think speaks for itself.

—And that's why you split up?

—He didn't have good people skills. Isn't that a weird idea? I mean, you can imagine a horse or a wild dog needing people skills, but that *actual people* need people skills points to some fucked-up fundamental error in our makeup, don't you think?

—So *that's* why you split up?

—God, Aldo, you make it sound so weird. Everyone has three or four relationships they're ashamed of.

—Three or four? That sounds like a lot.

—He was a generous guy, but really lazy. He would give you the shirt off his back, then ask you to wash it.

—Where is he now?

—In prison.

Prison! Your Honor! I felt like a moth pinned to a wall in a serial killer's basement. Something you should know: I have always perceived our society as a narrow bridge, either side of which lie two other societies—the prison, the hospital. To finally fall into the horror of the prison or the horror of the hospital was my greatest fear. Mimi's revelation deeply rattled me and we stood a while longer as the sun beat down like profound hatred, and her dark, sensual eyes gave off sparks—you all know the psychosexual allure of emotional distress—and I gazed at a long row of black trees flexing in the strong wind and became more acutely aware that we were standing on ground filled with clean bones without their lumps of meat, now just instruments in a caveman's symphony. When Mimi began the trek back to the car, I walked beside her in deliberate silence. In the case of the revelation of a person's deepest sadness, you can't ruin it by making small talk or asking anything other than the one question the person wants you to ask, but I hadn't figured out what that was yet.

—Are you OK? I asked when we were in the car.

—No time for self-pity, she answered, as if feeling sorry for oneself was only a matter of scheduling.

XV

Back in the bedroom, Mimi stretched out on the bed.

—What are you looking at?

—You.

—How do I look?

—Svelte.

—Do you want to see what Elliot looks like?

—Not especially.

She pulled out a photo of a beautiful man in a top hat and jeans and black eye makeup and sandals: four decades in one outfit. He was an athletic acrobat/dancer type, skinny yet muscular; he looked like he could do a backflip from a first-floor balcony onto the saddle of a horse.

—What is he, a rodeo clown?

—No. A wonderful street performer. Endearing singer. Terrific juggler. So-so fire twirler. Unexceptional unicyclist and humdrum contortionist, but more than adequate trapeze artist and just a downright fabulous stilt walker. Most of all, an outstanding performance artist and an inspiring director of physical theater.

—Jesus help us all.

—Do you want to hear his voice?

—I could live without it.

Mimi rang a number and put her phone to my ear.

—Hi, the voice said, this is Elliot. I'm not here right now but if you leave your name and number I'll get back to you in three to five years.

—Sad.

—Manslaughter, possession of narcotics, resisting arrest, she said, as though those salient facts spoke for themselves. She backtracked. Elliot was carrying thirty-one Ecstasy tablets en route to a fundraiser for his latest production. He ran a red light and when a police siren started up, he fled, killing a pedestrian. The sadness of the tale was how quickly the whole saga could be synopsized. Until his imprisonment they'd not spent a single night apart. I thought, I'm a bed warmer, nothing more. She backtracked further. When she was about thirty, she took an acting workshop. He was directing physical theater in wife-beaters. They fell in love, lived together in a camper van, sloshed around mud festivals in Andalucía and Avignon; she became his official photographer. Other than adding scars and gashes and assorted physical impairments to famous artworks—his ultimate aspiration: To paint a nosebleed on the *Mona Lisa*—one of Elliot's "performances" was to place ads in industry magazines for actors to perform in a lavish outdoor theatrical production of *Triumph of the Will*, and then film whoever turned up, she said. Another "performance" was held in small villages across Eastern Europe; Elliot would go into a village and start rumors that his sister was possessed by the devil, and let the word spread until some overfed shaggy priest with ancient stinks and gristle on his face made the journey to whatever fly-ridden room they were holed up in and carried out the exorcism, which was captured on film by the crew. Mimi was exorcised six times in total.

—You were actually exorcised?

—Sure.

I silently diagnosed Elliot as having a clear narcissistic personality disorder.

He was the one who brought her to the residence, she explained, weeping for her precious, sensitive performance artist whose natural domain was long grass on an embankment by a river. She said his ponytail was removed for the pre-trial hearing, then opened an abridged copy of *The Brothers Karamazov* and pulled out the ponytail. I had a frisson of pleasure listening to her story but I was none too pleased to fondle this acrobat's ponytail. Then in a quiet yet hysterical voice she returned to that fateful night. Why did he try to outrun the police? I asked. He had an uncompromising moment and poorly negotiated a sudden bend in the pitch-black night. Maybe he capitulated to an impulse he'd seen on television, a narrative impulse to run. She backtracked again. The story changed as she was telling it; she added more details now, circling closer to the truth.

—It was me.

—It was you what?

—I yelled, Go! Quick!

Why had she yelled? And why had he thoughtlessly obeyed? She didn't know.

—And now he's in prison and he's going *crazy*, she said in a whisper that seemed to come through her chest wall from her heart itself. He's getting pushed around. He's getting, you know.

I knew.

—I mean, it's taken its toll. He's not the same. It's changing him. He's getting beaten! He's getting, you know!

I knew.

Mimi clasped one hand over her mouth as if to stop toxic levels of distress from leaking out. I didn't know how to react; the panicky obsession I'd always had with prison clouded my thought processes. It was also clear she admired and loved Elliot intensely, loved *them* intensely, as a couple. My role in all this? To love her for five years. Three for good behavior. But why was I worried? The elephant in the room was behind bars! Yet he was the proprietor of her heart. I was the tenant. And the rent kept going up. I thought: My cock is being used as a placeholder for his. I thought: Who wants to mess about with a devotion like that? Yet I knew I was going to squeeze out an incautious remark. I took her hand.

—I love you.

ALL RIGHT, ladies and gentlemen of the jury, it is *now* we get to the prosecutor's pet word: motive. The crux of his flimsy case. The prosecutor can't seem to go on about it enough. I killed her in a jealous rage. That was my motive. Jealousy. Well, I can't deny the sad fact of it: I *was* jealous.

—I love you too, she said, yet when I undressed her moments later, it was like peeling bark off a rotten tree. I nibbled a piece here, a piece there, licked the sweat that glistened on her throat, searched for a remote part of her, any uncharted territory, but overall sex with Mimi that night was like strutting into a condemned building at the moment of demolition.

—I'm glad I don't have to hide this from you anymore, she said afterward.

—Hide what?

From underneath the bed, she dragged a couple dozen white sheets of paper and sat on the floor cross-legged, applying lipstick and covering the paper in kisses—twenty or thirty pages of kisses—and when she was done, placed them in a manila envelope addressed to Elliot Grass c/o Silverwater Correctional Complex.

—Oh Jesus, Mimi. You really know how to break my heart.

The strange thing was, though, I didn't feel anything when I said that. It was only afterward, when I stepped out onto the balcony into the wet night and stormed down the slippery wooden staircase to the damp cold sand, that

I found I was genuinely devastated. Elliot, I realized, was background noise to her every movement on earth. She could only excrete love and I could only suck up those excretions; ours was an insect love. The silence became thick and hurt my ears. Black waves folded into black sand. I collapsed and remained on the beach until the dissipating morning mist unveiled the horizon and, as always when you're sitting on a shoreline feeling suicidal, the tsunamis don't come. They don't come and they don't come.

XVI

Two days later, Mimi was switching outfits before the mirror.

—Where are you going?

—Nowhere.

—How do you normally get there?

—By bus.

—I'll drive you.

Endless rows of telephone poles against wide gray skies en route to the prison. We drove in Lynne Bishop's Hyundai in untenable silence through nondescript suburbs down a tree-lined highway divided by pointless grassy parkland. The tension was a storm to be weathered. We began lane-swapping skirmishes with clusters of silver sedans and trucks the lengths of city blocks, passed houses with blue tarps flapping in southerly gusts, redbrick churches with white crosses, pensioners in knee-high socks standing forlornly at mail-boxes. I was faking calm in a tropical sweat. Why had I driven her here? It was an avuncular move on my part. As we approached the prison, I felt a loud pounding in my ears. Here it was. Prison! The place where brute realities look *you* in the face.

Prohibited items were everything except the clothes on one's back. Mimi left her bag and walked inside, leaving me to stare at the oppressive, sprawling mass of Silverwater Prison and the people going in and out: guards long past peak fitness; teary, terrified visitors with sleeplessness gouged into their faces, perhaps burdened by guilt—in contrast, I thought, you'd scarcely find one hospital visitor even indirectly implicated in a patient's kidney failure. Outside the walls and barbed-wired gates, cars flowed obliviously; it never occurred to me you could be lying in your cell listening to traffic! The colorless afternoon sky was beginning to darken. Birds circled in maddening patterns. I felt dizzy, migrainous. I closed my eyes and thought of shiv-wielding sodomites in a tobacco economy where the death of an old man's pet mouse precipitates his suicide. It teemed down, lending plausibility to the mawkish scene I imagined taking place inside: Mimi sobbing through plexiglass or on the telephone, or hand-holding on a wooden table. Maybe he would take her face in his hands and kiss her tear-stained lips.

An hour later, Mimi staggered back to the car and collapsed in convulsive sobs.

—He's been badly beaten. His eyes were swollen shut!

—We should go overseas together, to one of those countries where men dye their hair black but leave their mustaches white.

—He's lost teeth.

—South America, maybe. You know, and you go into a restaurant and the waiter's older than your great-grandfather but he can still beat you in a fight.

Mimi's eyes were clotted with tears. Her cheeks at risk of moisture damage.

—Or to France or Germany, I said, where a sexual darkness in one's soul is a given.

By the time her sleeping pills knocked her unconscious that night, she hadn't said another word. I sat on a wicker chair and gazed at the dark purple storm clouds drifting over the inexhaustible tides until morning. Mimi awoke with cold clear eyes.

—I think I need to be alone today. Do you mind going home?

Your Honor, for the next two days I sat in my grim apartment with its warmth of a parking garage, waiting for the sound of a rattling engine, the sight of her fuzzy head craning out a car window, but I knew she wouldn't come. The law of unintended consequences applies to confidences. Now that she had divulged her secret to me, she could no longer hide her misery from me. Her jovial facade was reserved for strangers, acquaintances, one-night stands. I left message after message at the residence to no avail.

Ladies and gentlemen of the jury, if only I'd left it there. Here was my clean exit. Why didn't I take the sense memory of oral sex as a parting gift and get on with my own private predicament? Why didn't I leave her alone? Why couldn't I *be* alone? I was incapable, that's why. I was love dependent and desperate. *And* I was selfish; without Stella, I needed Mimi, and while I knew I was unable to supplant her love for Elliot, I wanted her to need me too. But how? How to make someone need what they don't need? How to reverse the polarity of dwindling physical attraction?

My friend Liam swung by and we both sat on the damp cement balcony and dangled our legs through the iron gratings and passed a bottle between us and made an inventory of my positive traits—we only got as far as never had a filling. Nothing useful. Dark clouds threatened the brisk walkers on the street below. Liam had been to the residence and seen Mimi with his own bare eyes, and understood my desperation to win back this voluptuous graying saddult of the female persuasion. He himself had recently separated from his wife, Tess, and exuded disturbing levels of desperation on my behalf. He said he'd been dating and a person should do anything they can to avoid having to mate with the forlorn masses. He thrust his finger in my face with unexpected vehemence, and said that second-time-around love is rare and an exceptional stroke of luck. I said, How am I going to get Mimi back? He said, Men win women over with kindness, with cruelty, with flowers, with cold hard cash. I said, They also attract them by radiating confidence. He said, None of that's going to work for you. He took out a notebook and scribbled in it. That made me fear he was going to turn my love affair into one of his failed novels. I said, What are you writing? He read, *That Mimi, the object of Aldo's desire, has two working eyes and free will counts against him*. I said, Fuck you. At three in the morning, Liam passed out and I dragged him to the couch and it was then it hit me, the ruinous idea that doomed us all. Not to say Mimi would still be alive—*because I didn't fucking kill her*—but I wouldn't be soiling myself in my greens manacled to this lousy wheelchair. In fact, I wouldn't even *be* in a wheelchair. There are no greater regrets than the poor decisions you agonized over to make.

XVII

Mimi was lying in the hammock, in the sun and the cold sea air.

—When the sky is bright and clear I suspect God of an ulterior motive, don't you?

—I'm glad you came.

She led me into her bedroom and undressed quickly, less with desire for me, I suspected, and more with a blind desire to lose herself, but when she pressed her naked body hard against mine I pushed her away. Penetrate her heart in one clean thrust was my plan, and as I sat fully dressed on the bed and she stood naked with uncertainty, shivering, I felt cruel and ridiculous. Nevertheless.

—Elliot, I said.

—What about him?

—I've made some arrangements, I said casually, examining my thumbnail.

—What the fuck are you talking about?

—I can have him protected.

Her eyes lingered on mine; she was trying to catch me out in a lie. If she was afraid of the power I had just taken for myself, she didn't show it.

—Protected? Are you fucking with me? Explain yourself!

Problem was, my plan was really only three-quarters of a plan; I thought the rest would come together of its own accord. I told her that I knew people who could protect her husband. I knew the people to be paid, palms to be greased, guards to be bribed, gangs to be placated, etc. As I said this I was afraid I'd shown her my secret face, my evil face, and she could detect pleasure on it, but she didn't seem to notice. I explained that I knew a shocking number of people in prison, just as I knew a shocking number in hospitals with fatal diseases; I knew a fair number of prison guards just as I knew a fair number of nurses and hospital administrators. I got lost on this thread a while. Just as I am familiar with the inner workings of hospitals, I explained, I am familiar with the inner workings of prisons.

—Shut up a minute. Are you serious?

Pure gratitude blazed in her eyes. This was sexual good news.

—There's just a little matter of sixty thousand dollars, I said.

Mimi broke into a horrified gawp. I made a vague gesture but it didn't mean anything. Overconfident in my grand gesture, I had already agreed to pay sixty thousand for six months in a contract as airtight as a gym membership.

Over the next few days, Mimi set about on humbling outings, groveling apoplectically, trying to borrow from her gambler father—an imposing man with a to-scale Easter Island head on his shoulders—from friends, old boyfriends, old bosses, acquaintances, successful artist friends, but either they were fiscally down on their luck or unwilling to make the loan. For my part, no matter how desperate I was I could not do for her what I could not do for myself, the one thing I could never do, had almost died not doing, the superhuman feat that so many subhumans and subpar humans excel at: making money. I had spent my life trying to materialize it for Stella, for the baby, for my mother, for myself, and now, as if achieving even lower self-esteem were my ultimate goal, I was failing again.

By the end of the week, still nothing. Mimi rested her head on a mountain of soft cushions and I lay beside her, brainstorming. Outside, clouds like cement blocks set the moody grayness of the afternoon. We had naught to liquidate, nada to move. We couldn't get high-paying salaries. Neither of us had any skills. We had nobody to borrow from, and begging drew in too little. There were no legitimate possibilities.

—We find an individual, she said, follow him home, force him at knifepoint to give us money.

—I've been robbed at knifepoint, I said. I wouldn't do that to anyone. Besides, two losers with negligible street smarts should pursue only victimless crimes.

—So what then? Fraud? Mail fraud? Insurance fraud?

I slid off the bed and looked out the window at the heavy clouds sweeping across a sky full of pinks and purples and oranges, an embarrassment of colors. I was besieged by dumb ideas, one after the other—obscure hoaxes, elaborate cons. The early evening stars strode into view. In truth, I was afraid. In a perversely unjust universe, four decades without breaking a law means severe punishment awaits your first infringement. Mimi dried her eyes. I hadn't even noticed she was crying; it was the quietest sob I'd ever seen.

—I have it! Maybe!

In saying this, I realize my dilemma, ladies and gentlemen of the jury. In order to present you with perhaps *the* single most likely of all of Mimi's potential murderers, I have to admit to a wee crime.

Blackmail.

—Do we have any dirt on anybody? I asked.

—Not that I can think of.

—Think harder.

The darkness moved in but neither of us put on the light; the moon shone into the room and I could see us from its perspective—minuscule, alone.

—Wait. Didn't you fuck Mr. Morrell?

—How do you know that?

—Rumors.

We fell into silence. The wooden balcony railing glistened in the steady drizzle.

—I don't want to blackmail Morrell. Not him.

—OK. I liked him too. We won't, then. Let's think of something else.

A couple of minutes went by, then fifty more. I remembered that his wife had died of ovarian cancer, his lifelong failure to pursue his career in painting, how my friend Liam was obsessed with his bombastic diatribe on art. By midnight the creeping dread had settled in that I'd have to personally blackmail one of the nicest and saddest men either of us had ever known.

XVIII

Pressing the doorbell generated a baby's piercing cry followed by a man's voice shouting, "Shut up!" Morrell opened the door of his Waterloo-brick, two-bedroom terrace wearing a paisley shirt and rolled-up army pants; as usual, his skin looked carbonized and veiny, like a fried onion, making his whitened teeth even whiter.

—When I woke from a troubled sleep that Sunday morning, Morrell said, Aldo Francis Benjamin was standing on my doorstep with a curious expression on his face. Hope the doorbell didn't disturb you. One of my students made it as part of a sound installation for her final-year project.

Morrell's smile revealed abnormal affection for me in his eyes. Maybe he felt sorry for me. Why shouldn't he? I did.

—I need to talk to you.

—That's somewhat anachronistic, no? Oh well, I suppose you'd best come on in then.

Stepping inside, I was immediately hit by the low energy and ramshackle seediness of the place: sticky tape over the light switches, stained carpets, mismatched lampshades, and so many kitty litters you could taste the toxoplasmosis. Stuck up on the walls were not-good drawings, dire paintings and wonky sculptures that I realized were artworks dedicated to him by students. I told him I'd found Mimi Underwood.

—Did you indeed? Is photography still her passion?

When we were deciding who should do the hands-on blackmailing, Mimi had frozen up and shouted, I can't go! I don't ever want to see Angus again.

Morrell motioned for me to take a seat. I was thinking of the way she said his name, *Angus*, when I removed an aggravated ginger cat and lowered myself into a brown leather easy chair; it groaned under my weight. I smiled toothily, belligerently, godlessly. Nothing felt right.

—What about that girl of yours, that singer?

—I can't believe you remember her. She didn't even go to our school.

—She sang a song for you, didn't she? In protest. A song of love. I do remember that, of course. Wait. *The girl she'd taken ketamine / And fingered Aldo Benjamin.* Priceless!

—We're divorced.

—Sorry. But. Well done also. You know what I mean. A middle-aged divorcé is radically less creepy than a middle-aged bachelor. God, I remember how deeply in love she was with you. What was her name?

—Stella.

—Stella. That's right. In one's youth, females fall in love with you for no reason whatsoever. It never happens again. After adolescence, they are scrupulous in needing reasons. Often, let's be honest, financial.

—Speaking of which, we need money.

—You and Stella?

—Me and Mimi.

—You and Mimi? How do you mean? You're a we?

—She won't tell anyone that you had sex with her when she was a minor, if you pay up.

He took a sharp, emphatic breath. Sweat stained his shirt under the arms and across his chest.

—But Aldo, he said sadly.

I felt like an explorer in a new land coughing in the faces of the indigenous population. I was doing something irreparable to him. I could see it in his eyes. It was all happening in front of me. I tried an appeasing grin and his eyes widened, as if afraid to miss anything. He was practically throbbing like an engine in his reclining armchair.

—Just ten thousand a month. For six months. Or sixty thousand all at once. Whichever is more convenient. And you won't hear from us again.

I slowly rose to my feet. The cat scarcely looked at me.

—How much did you say you want?

I sat and repeated the whole thing. Morrell picked an ice cube out of his glass and threw it—it hit me on the cheek. The second bounced off my chin.

—Down they forgot as up they grew.

—What was that?

—E. E. Cummings, he said, and threw another ice cube, this one landing in my eye. I decided to sit it out and remained in the chair as he pelted ice cubes at my face and head.

—Do you remember the day we met? he asked.

—Was it in class?

—I think it was about the middle of the year. I was smoking a cigarette outside the staff room when I heard the sound of coughing and turned to see you standing there. It must have been your first day after transferring from another school, because you were in a different uniform. You asked me if I would put out my cigarette. Of course, I could have simply refused or moved away, I was outside after all, and a bloody teacher besides. Nevertheless, I wearily extinguished it under my shoe and tossed the butt in the bin. You thanked me for putting it out, but not a moment later fetched a packet of cigarettes from your own pocket and lit one up yourself! I remember gazing at you in bewilderment before you turned to me and said, Sorry, sir, I just don't like your *brand*.

I slid the paper across the table.

—Here are the bank account details. Just a simple transfer.

—Later I could see the funny side of it. At the time, though, as you sauntered across the yard, I asked the biology teacher, Who's that prick? I see you met our new student, she said. He's going to cause some trouble, and by that she meant that you were so striking, she could almost hear the popping of hymens.

I got to my feet and an ice cube hit me in the chest. A nebulous cloud of guilt swept over me.

—I'll let myself out, I said, and as I stepped onto the front porch, the door slammed behind me, marking another blow to the prospect of ever liking or respecting myself again.

XIX

In the hammock, the ropes straining under our combined weight, laptop between us, we refreshed my bank account page every few minutes, hoping for the electronic transfer of funds. Clouds skipped by and the cold winter sun failed to warm our bones as we listened to the waves, listened for a siren, and refreshed the page again. By late afternoon the money was still not in the account. It started to rain and we moved inside. The storms were a gift; they broke across the sky. I camouflaged my body with hers. All I ever wanted was a succubus to possess me, I thought afterward, as we lay on our backs gazing at each other in the mirrored ceiling.

Mimi was in the shower when her mobile phone rang on the bedside table. I answered it.

—Who's this? a voice asked. Hello? Hello?

At first I feared it was the police but then laughed at myself—the police don't ordinarily call and arrest you over the phone. In any case, that hello was emanating whiffs of restrained jealousy. Holy hell: This was him. Elliot Grass.

I tried to conjure the face of this panicky acrobat, this unlucky poet, and imagined him in a corridor, a long line of irate inmates scowling impatiently behind him.

—You afraid to talk to me, you piece of shit?

—Not at all.

He grunted, as if the sound of my voice had sullied his ear. I stubbed out my cigarette in a seashell. An engulfing silence followed.

—I thought *I* was unlucky, I said. I've driven drunk without headlights, on acid, in the rain during a sneezing fit, and I've never killed anyone.

—Mimi told me some very interesting things about you, Aldo Benjamin. You are quite the unfortunate human being.

—You're pretty unfortunate yourself.

—You sound like a real loser.

—Is it my imagination or are higher security prisons generally more hygienic than lower security prisons?

—Maybe I'll send someone over there to look in on you.

—I'll put the kettle on.

—You've got a smart mouth.

—Go smoke your own mustache.

—How'd you know about that?

I hung up and mentally changed my diagnosis from narcissistic personality disorder to antisocial personality disorder. Mimi was still in the bathroom. When the phone rang again, I picked it up on the first ring.

—Don't hang up, please. Sorry. I didn't mean to be aggressive. I just want to talk to you for a minute. That OK? You seem like a smart guy. Can you talk a minute?

—What do you want?

—She answering her mail? She lets it build up.

I said that I would look into it. His breathing grew easier.

—Is she taking her medication? The red pills.

I said I thought so. I'd seen her take pills but I hadn't noted the color.

—And how are her feet? She gets dry and cracked heels. She has to put a special cream on.

Now I wasn't sure. Had I noticed anything ghastly about her feet? As far as I could tell, they were perfect specimens of female feet.

—And another thing. She looked a little thin last time she visited. She eating all right?

—She's eating fine.

—And what about sex? She having orgasms? She doesn't get them from penetration, you know. You gotta stimulate the clitoris.

I hung up again and turned her phone to silent. I went out onto the balcony where a bunch of drunk Hamlets were soliloquizing simultaneously. I downed a couple of beers, then returned to the bedroom where the deceased was half-awake, sprawled across the bed in a patch of moonlight.

—Mimi, I said, lying down beside her. Can I kiss you?

—We're done asking permission. We can move on to a state of implied consent. I don't even really care if you fuck me while I'm asleep. Let's just use each other up, OK? Until there's nothing left.

—Jesus, Mimi, I said, though the idea of tramping about in her soft hollows without her timing me was pretty appealing, so we went at it. We had been going four or five minutes when Mimi's body slackened and harsh sounds came out of her, like a throat clearing itself over a loudspeaker. Worse, when I tried to kiss her, her mouth was off limits. Why? Was she mad? No. She was asleep!

—Hey, I said, shaking her. Why do you have to take sleeping pills every night?

—I wasn't asleep. I was listening to every word you were saying.

—I wasn't talking. I was making love to you.

—You told me that already.

We self-medicated our way through the following week, with much sleep-fucking and quiet lamenting and a near-constant gazing out to sea.

On the morning of the eighth day, ten thousand dollars was in my bank account, transferred from one A. Morrell. The blackmail was an unqualified success! Morrell was going to pay up, month after month. Mimi was a beautiful wreck with a grateful smile. Like seasoned criminals toasting the heist, we went out to celebrate the imminent cock-blocking of Elliot's assailants. Over after-lunch foot massages in comfy leather recliners I noticed she was basking in the radiated calm of her own relieved heart; Mimi was helping Elliot and I was helping Mimi and all was well in the world. It was only when we arrived back at the residence that the heaviness returned, weightier than ever.

—We have a new artist staying with us, Adrian Oldenburg said. Come say hi.

Yes, bailiffs, you guessed it. Standing there, in the corner of the room, was Mr. Morrell, smiling without using his mouth. Mimi let out a small cry of distress.

—Hello, you two. I think we may have met, he cackled.

Every muscle in my face and body tightened and I stood rooted to the spot; I thought of *The Fussy Corpse*, and how it was to be dissatisfied with every conceivable outcome, and paralyzed by that dissatisfaction, to do nothing while the storm of indecision and impotence raged inside you.

XX

—That's it! Good-bye Zetland High! Forever! They gave me a touching farewell, I wish you had been there. Forty-two years on the job. It was a bit emotional. Well, of course it was. I was like a stepfather to those sexting rascals. Now I've done it! All my life I've been saying to students: *Esse quam videri*. To be and not to seem. And I never took my own advice! But this time, when the dark allure of the paintbrush beckoned, at long last I heeded its call!

He was like a bereaved man in the first stage of grief—hysteria. Cheerfully bounding from one side of the room to the other, he was almost delirious while giving me strange, complicated looks, as if I were a disinherited son who'd come to borrow his car.

—I just booked a space at this lovely artists' residence. I'm giving myself six months, which I believe should be plenty of time to prepare.

He grabbed me and Mimi by the hands, greeting us like his liberators.

—What month's a good time for an exhibition? What if it rains? You know the people of Sydney won't step outside their homes if they're in danger of being struck by a raindrop. In any case, it should be a medium-sized space. Perfect for twelve or fourteen works. Not too many. Scarcity is value.

Mimi had gone pale. It wasn't difficult to understand what had happened. We'd given him the transformative experience needed to spur his liberation, to pursue his lifelong dream of becoming a painter.

—Yes, I want to do something like that, he said, looking at one of Maria Hamilton's collages.

He might have been a former teacher-cum-blackmailee who had turned the tables on his tormentors, but he was also a struggling artist anxiously preparing his first solo exhibition. And he was totally exhilarated, pacing and weaving through the room, touching every fixture.

—This place is wonderful! So bohemian! Aldo! Mimi! You should come down and see my rooms! I've already had significant interest from several galleries—well, former students now running galleries.

Oh God, I thought. Is there anything more dangerous than a time-poor unappreciated man with a whiff of glory? Mimi and I must have both looked pretty silly, with our stillness and gaping jaws. Was he really going to live here? With his woolen vest and sinusitis? I found it difficult to orient myself all of a sudden. I looked out the glass doors at the steel-gray sky. A thick gust of wind sent the weather vane spinning. Beside me, in the face of Morrell's uncoiled mayhem, Mimi had grown cold, her breathing unnatural, labored. He picked up a paint-splattered red bandanna from the floor and tied it around his head; he smiled vigorously at everyone, as if granting them permission to continue about their life choices. He pointed to Frank Rubinstein's semi-abstract painting of a slice of toast.

—We need to believe that you mastered a technique and decided not to use it, not that you never had it.

He bounced from one artwork to another, almost stumbling over canvases to pick them up, holding etchings to the light, gesturing at photographs, scrutinizing sculptures. He examined Lynne Bishop's pastel drawings of rotund babies.

—Either aim your dream at the higher end of within reason, or isolate the greatest achievement of a second-rate peer and strive for that.

I thought: Being a teacher really permeates one's being; a fireman isn't a fireman at dinner, whereas a teacher is a teacher at a molecular level. Still, I detected the tone of stored-up resentment from witnessing generation after generation of artists celebrated younger and younger.

Morrell was gazing at a bronze sculpture of a giant hand.

—I like this one. I feel positively menaced by it. But why are you trying so hard to be contemporary? You are alive in the present. It doesn't matter what you do. You *are* contemporary.

He praised and castigated in the same breath; he knew how to humiliate and excite.

—This one. No, I am not seduced.

That's right. *I am not seduced* was Morrell's most repeated line. It had a catchphrase quality to it and we loved to hear him say it.

—I can't believe I ever gave these up, he said, lighting another cigarette. Now he stood at the glass doors on tiptoes, as if trying to make out the semi-naked women who were no more than blurs on flat sand.

—What do you think about this self-portrait? Louise Bozowic asked, holding up a square acrylic painting.

—Either learn to paint hair or learn to paint hats.

Louise wrote that down. The swiftness with which the artists took to Morrell was crazy. They lined up to show him their woodcuts and slide projects and reverse-glass paintings and graph-paper sketches. Maybe it was their sensitivity to criticism and their greater sensitivity to praise that made them feel so flattered; he critiqued in one breath and asked *their* advice on his upcoming show in the next; he was both mentor and student. He linked arms with whomever he was talking to. Forty years of never being able to touch the people he taught; now he touched everybody, while seemingly determined to expel those four decades of acquired wisdom in a single night.

—Stop trying to stop being derivative.

—Don't let your palette tell you what to do.

—If you can't be great, be vague. If they don't know what you're trying to achieve, they can't see that you haven't succeeded in achieving it.

Morrell shouted across the room at me.

—Hey, I sold my home! You've been there, Benjamin, it was no sort of place at all. That pathetic container I lived in for thirty-six years, that I bought for sixty-five thousand in 1977, I sold for one point three million. Bam! Just like that! My neighbor had wanted me to sell for years so he could extend his hideous compound!

Morrell's energized, meth-like high had no foreseeable comedown.

—Aldo, Mimi whispered, what are we going to do? She wasn't crying, but her voice was full of tears. Morrell bounded over and leaned between us.

—Don't look so frightened, girl. I will still pay your ten thousand a month.

—In return for what? I asked.

—Don't mumble, Benjamin.

I learned from Dee Franklin that he had rented two of the interconnecting rooms down below, that he'd come in with a handful of cash and bargained Casey Huntington for the biggest space in the residency, adjacent to the other biggest space in the residency in which he intended to stretch his 2-meter x 2-meter canvases.

—This way, girl.

I whipped my head around to see Morrell coaxing Mimi downstairs for a private tour of his new paintbrushes. I made a move to follow, but Mimi shot me a sharp look that made me feel like I had confessed to a crime too late, after an innocent man had already been executed.

XXI

Through a crack in the door, I could see Morrell on his knees undoing Mimi's shoelaces and talking about the "impersonal yet melancholy" photographs in *The Fussy Corpse*. I went back to Mimi's bedroom and tried to draw a permanent veil over my heart. Morrell had made the whole residence feel like a sleazy motel, and she was acquiescing in some kind of trance, as if he was pressing on an old injury from which she'd never recovered, or more likely, yes, instead of our silence—our initial offer—her actual body was now the goods demanded by Morrell in exchange for his ten thousand a month. Blackmailed by the blackmailee!

Talk about a backfire! I threw a pillow across the room and gazed out the window. The moon looked wan and weak from not having lately been worshipped.

Around midnight her phone vibrated on the nightstand.

—I'm not in the mood tonight, I said.

—What are we going to do about her old high school teacher?

—How do you know about that?

I heard Elliot stub out a cigarette on something that crackled, and for a split second I entertained the notion it was human skin. My head started to hurt. On the other end of the phone, there was shouting, a chanting of deep powerful voices, the sound of footsteps, a scuffle, and several emphatic no's. Then a long silence. And in that silence, more silence.

—You don't know anything about Mimi, do you?

—No, I suppose I don't.

—Did you know she has a tilted uterus?

—So?

—I was there when her mother died. She took photos of the burial.

—That's not so strange.

—She made her father hold the reflector board throughout the service.

—She's an artist.

—She ran away from home at ten. You know that? At eleven. At fifteen. Almost every year she packed a bag. Hurried out. Came back. Bid those needy shits an au revoir. Ran away. Buggered off. Came back. Mother passed out. Cousin banging something sharp against something hollow. Hello! Fuck off! Adios! Hello! Taking care of them even when she started taking drugs. And found boyfriends. Older ones. Much older ones. Homeless ones. Imagine. Those rosebud lips. At that age. Can't stand to think about it. One day: took every dollar out of her father's wallet. Shredded them. Tossed the cunt-thin strips of paper. Here, Daddy, saved you a trip to the track. From then on, she rescued them from drowning in their own vomit. Then pierced their ears as they dribbled in narcotic stupors. Yeah. She yielded to their needs, all right. Then emptied their bank accounts. Followed their crappy orders, then pawned their shit. Pushback. Payback . . .

I was relieved when Elliot stopped speaking. Not only did he make me uncomfortable, I felt downright spooked by him. His voice was a huge eraser and every time he spoke a part of me was wiped clean.

—How did you know about Morrell?

—How? How? Let me ask *you* something. Have you noticed? That you're not perceptible? You know. By all the senses at the same time? That some people—they can't smell you? And to others you emit no sound? None whatsoever?

That was it. Elliot had drifted off on some incomprehensible tangent and confirmed for me what I already suspected: He was not a narcissist or antisocial but a plain old meat-and-potatoes psychopath.

By dawn Mimi still hadn't returned to her bedroom and I went down to the beach and saw Morrell emerge from the surf and pick up his towel where the retreating waves left crescents of foam in the wet sand. The bastard was inexcusably fit for his age and as he bounded over toward me, I found evidence of his intention to make love to Mimi in his gait. While I'll admit, ladies and gentlemen of the jury, it is not unusual for a man to feel a modicum of grudging respect for the cheeky bugger who has bedded his intended, this was way out of order.

—Listen, Mr. Morrell.

—The less you think, the more you talk, Montesquieu said, but go on, what were you saying?

—Why don't you leave us alone?

—Mimi told me that you're suicidal.

—So?

—Mimi also said you're having trouble dying.

—So?

—Mimi also said that it was due to some kind of condition of immortality?

Morrell turned his head upward as if to appraise the azure, featureless sky and nodded, apparently approving of God's use of negative space.

—The infinite is synonymous with the perfection of form. Do you feel like someone who is slowly perfecting?

I had to admit that I didn't.

—You think your will is more stubborn than anybody else's? You, Aldo Francis Benjamin, who has no unusual passion for living?

Again, I shook my head. He stroked an imaginary beard. There was nothing indecisive about his gestures.

—You have *horror infiniti*. Or perhaps, as Leopardi suggested, you have confused the infinite with the indefinite. You are perishable, Aldo. Like I always used to tell my more hopeless students, you just need to follow your heart, get out of your comfort zone. Your problem is that you lack inspiration and the passion to achieve your goal. That's what all your nonsensical justifications and frankly incredible rationalizations are about. Suicide is prepared within the silence of the heart, as is a great work of art—Camus. Empty your mind, be yourself, Aldo. This immortality thing. That's just suicide's block.

With his back to the shrieking blast of sea Morrell spoke to me as neither teacher nor artist, but as Mimi's lover.

—I can't persuade you to live but I can persuade you, however, to leave.

When I got back inside, Mimi's face gave me the news that I was a fast depreciating currency.

—You should go, Aldo, right now, and don't come back.

—I'm a realist with a background in evolutionary psychology! I know my market worth and I demand to be left for someone better. Stella's new man is handsomer, richer, more virile, and physically robust. Evolutionarily beyond reproach. But *Morrell*!

Mimi didn't respond. She took some tightly framed photos of me gathering my things into green garbage bags, closeups of the look in my rejected eyes as she was rejecting me, a panoramic in the bathroom as I shoveled her clutter of sleeping pills into my pockets. Then I kissed her moist, downcast eyes good-bye.

—I'll miss your cold sort of love and your breast-wielding sashays to the bathroom framed by the sea.

—Please, Aldo. Just go.

There was no point arguing—I'd been beaten. Out in the main room nobody gathered to watch me pathetically drag the plastic garbage bags behind me. The same no one offered me comfort. I shouted good-bye to the few who were lying on the sofas. They had their mental fly swatters out. Not being an artist myself, I didn't warrant a grand adieu. I was merely another artist's fuckthing. A recreation, like the Ping-Pong table.

—Bye-bye, I said, soberly, to no one.

Morrell emerged from downstairs dressed in black jeans, black T-shirt, black duffle coat, like the ferryman in Hades, and patted me on the back with the embarrassment of the victor. I couldn't loiter with exaggerated sadness a moment longer. Not a key to relinquish, no locks would need to be changed. I waved vaguely at all the artists whose names I had learned but whose arrogance made them mostly indistinguishable from one another, and allowed myself to be exorcised, like a demon from the body of a frightened child.

XXII

Unable to face my apartment, its smell of meat and loneliness, the terrifying biodiversity in the fridge, the banality of weevils, I set out on a long, purposeless ramble, cutting an oblique path through the city, committing thought crimes, thought genocides, thought human-rights abuses. That was easy; the city was clogged with businesssapiens all living one single idea of a human life, men and women who looked so buttoned up and restrained I imagined they could each hold in an epileptic seizure for up to an hour apiece. Sydney was awash in a gray rain and I walked in no specific direction, along with the prevailing herd, the other saddults like me, cheering as a car went the wrong way down a one-way street, laughing at the doomed monorail that sped overhead. When night fell crisply, I collapsed on a bench in Hyde Park. It was cold and wet and around two a.m., I woke to find a young junkie rummaging through my pockets. Let him. I'd simply left Mimi in Morrell's hands without a fight. Was I evil? What kind of a man was I? All I knew was that if legal slavery had persisted into the twenty-first century I'd be on eBay buying a person *right now*. Dawn couldn't come fast enough.

The next morning, I found my old fake limp was acting up again. I hobbled north to Circular Quay where I used to applaud Stella busking, and I sat at the harbor's edge and watched the ferries coming in and out all day and into the night, through a splashy sunset and a cold bath of stars blinking in code. I decided Morrell was right: I wasn't slowly perfecting. I'd confused the infinite with the indefinite. Everybody is perishable and I would be the dying proof of it. I was on the road to eternity after all, and like Kafka said, coasting along it downhill. I sat there in my own hinterland and did the heavy lifting of mourning myself. I tipped my hat at everything I'd failed to understand. Well played, Sir.

Stella's veranda light burned pointlessly. On the overgrown lawn our old red couch was black with mold. I crept around the side and peered through the open slats of the shuttered windows; in the living room was enough paraphernalia for a dozen babies: change table, yellow plastic tractors, prams, a white wooden bassinet. The same house that once felt like a hospital for the insane now exuded warmth and love. Good for her. I left a note—*Dear Stella, love*

Aldo—and pinned it to the door. Despite my feelings for Mimi, I had never let go of Stella and I wanted to do something ceremonial to allow my love for her dissipate once and for all, but I couldn't think of anything. I stood frozen in the breezy night, half-wanting to run in and pledge to become a born-again Christian if we could do it together as Siamese twins, when The Smiths' lyric about the joy of dying beside the beloved sung in the sweetness of Stella's voice played in my brain as if from an old radio, but I'd already tried that once on her hospital bed, and now, standing there, conjuring her scent and imagining it was wafting over from the rotting veranda, I realized I had never asked her if, like me, she'd had ghastly encounters with parents of children who'd died at the age of eight or ten and was made to feel ridiculous for mourning a daughter who never even saw the sky or took a breath, for having a comparatively trivial tragedy to be defined by. My guess was she had, but now I recalled her immunity to self-pity and her ability to subtract herself from any equation, as a method of self-defense, and this reflection triggered more memories—her hard gaze, her ferocious loyalty, her sleek thighs, her cold intelligence, her almost genius ability to be in on every joke, her bewildering dance moves, her electric smile, her kissable throat, her heavy sighs . . . It was the sound of a motorcycle raging down a nearby street that brought me back into the present. I noticed a hazy moon in the sky above the treetops, and I feared Stella and Craig would be returning soon, so I turned and hurried away, the spreading shame on my face and upper body telling me where I was going.

XXIII

How quickly habits form! Before each suicide attempt, before kicking myself to the biological curb, I've become accustomed to yielding once more to this lifelong libidinal urge, to one last go on the opposite-sex roller coaster. Thank God for the oldest profession—after war-mongering—in our quarter-million years on the clock!

Enigma Variations, the familiar pink room with its coal fireplace and deceased-estate furniture, discolored armchairs and died-upon sofas, and its faded wallpaper stained from fire damage. The room still had the quality of the inside of a wet cheek, notwithstanding it being redolent of condoms and cigarettes. I asked the Korean madam for Gretel and was told she was with a client and to choose another girl, but they all had overadventured, unrefreshable, unsurprisable faces that tried to look inviting but had the opposite effect. I ran my eyes over rope burns, bite marks, hickeys, bruises, general sores, and an obvious lack of camaraderie.

—I'll wait.

Forty minutes later, Gretel came down the stairs with her kind eyes and her wonderful hook nose.

—Hi, Gretel.

—Hey! Simon Simonson!

Up the same carpeted staircase, along the same dreary hallway where on the other side of closed doors orgasms sounded like bitter protests, with the same fire exit and its partial view of a cement staircase, and, at the end of the hallway, that same old room with the sinister padlock on it. (What the fuck was in there?) Into the same bedroom with the curtainless windows that looked onto a brick wall and rusted drainpipe. Only the chair was new. They'd bothered to refurnish! Gretel stripped down to her underwear and kicked off her shoes and asked me what I wanted to do with her. I had no great ideas. She led the charge—we reverse-cowgirled—during which she let out a few credible moans and I thought, I am incongruous here in this place. Morrell is incongruous in the residency. Liam is incongruous in the police force. Elliot is incongruous in his prison cell. Yet at the same time, we are all exactly where we belong.

—We've still got half an hour. You want to talk a while, Simon?

—Aldo.

Gretel smiled, lit a cigarette and dragged the glass ashtray onto her naked stomach, and told me about the last client, a regular who always fucked her in a corkscrewing motion as if upon penetration his penis had to navigate a spiraling warren of vaginas. Then about another client's penis that was hard but strangely ice-cold. I laughed.

—Everybody fucks at a snail's pace these days. Viagra's made the job unbearable. Men, for the first time, are able to get their money's worth. Sorry, I shouldn't be sharing this with you.

—That's all right, go on.

—Do you know there are still people who come here and just want to masturbate! Can you imagine? In *this* economy?

She stroked my arm lifelessly and rambled on about about emotionless men who gave the blankest stares while she was riding them; about creepy hair strokers and love declarers, men who wanted to go from zero to a hundred in terms of emotional intimacy. She explained how it was worse to be dependent on one man (marriage) than on hundreds (prostitution). I loved listening to her. This was the last conversation I was ever going to have and I was grateful that it was so interesting.

Back in the hallway I felt a violent disquiet when I saw her next client, a man built like an old steamer trunk. All of a sudden I felt like one of the endured horrors she won't be telling her grandkids about.

—Good-bye, Aldo.

—Good-bye, Gretel.

As the man trudged into the bedroom, she leaned in close to me and brushed a feather of a kiss on my cheek.

—Saffron, she whispered, with an awkward smile.

With almost contented resignation, I left Enigma Variations to go to the abandoned supermarket near Princess Highway where I could do a perfectly clean two-kilometer run into a brick wall.

XXIV

My unregistered car near Luna Park was graffitied and radioless, with about a dozen tickets on it. I flagged down a plumber's van and an amiable apprentice with jumper cables helped me get it started. It was a damp, weak-sunned morning in Sydney. There was a steady, somnolent stream of four-door sedans, the sound of wheels on wet asphalt. I took a handful of sleeping pills and accelerated down the windswept road with nothing but factories, apartment blocks, empty parks, and bandaged trees on either side, then swallowed a second handful, filled with a fear that was no longer frightening. I felt like a beloved musical group disbanding after years of infighting. Clouds and the humungous shadows of skyscrapers conspired to keep us in a dark-gray airlocked dome. I pressed my foot on the accelerator and took a third handful of pills. The car swerved and slid sideways as I overtook in fast lanes, shot over roundabouts, turned treacherously without signaling. I can't explain the unwavering faith I had in my driving reflexes—no living being would be harmed in the production of this suicide, I said out loud. The city flew by—first trees, then whole buildings. I sped down a street flanked by refrigerator showrooms, a service station, veterinary hospital, pub, bottle shop, real estate agent, pharmacy, rug warehouse, pub, smash repairs, police station, pub, pub, office supplies, upended supermarket carts on traffic islands, underwear billboards, telephone wires like exposed nerves. I soared past people who should have been subterranean dwellers but who were right out there on the earth's surface. I imagined I was drifting through the universe like in my old dream, as a voiceless faceless thoughtless drifting eye. I accelerated over speed bumps, crossed the cabled bridge, thinking, You can't stuff a suicide back into its tube. The car veered as if tottering along a high ridge in high winds, and the cold air stung through the sliver of open window. I thought of the burning love I felt for Mimi, and the love I felt for Stella flared up even brighter. I would drive into the ocean, or into the metaphor of the ocean. I could now see the silhouette of the shipping containers against the slate-gray sky, huge flocks of birds flying in a tight arc. Removing my seat belt, I drove faster and downed another handful of pills. They'd never think to pump my stomach in all that twisted metal. This was it. No more notes. No more preparations. No more good-byes. So many of us die like spoiled children, in a tantrum, over nothing—obdurate, melodramatic, curt deaths. I was swerving all over the place, bursting through intersections, cutting corners. I was on the sidewalk now—I could barely keep my eyes open. To suicide is to die from complications after one's birth. I spotted a sign on an overpass: HAPPY BIRTHDAY MIRANDA. I thought, Fuck Miranda and her shitty birthday. At which moment my mental fog cleared and I screeched to a halt, inches in front of a chain of hand-holding preschoolers in yellow raincoats.

The children burst into tears. At the window of an empty sushi restaurant, a waitress pressed her head against the glass. I turned off the engine and took the keys out of the ignition. My body was numb but I was OK. Except I was dying. Once and for all. The dying epiphanies, only five in number, came thick and fast:

1. There must be bacteria on plastic banknotes. I'm sure I got E. coli from a fiver.
2. Idea for a neurotic ladies' man: a product line of condoms made of antibiotic-laced polymer.

3. Whenever someone said to me, What would Jesus do? I should have said, They say that the best indicator of future behavior is past behavior, and then just walked away.

4. All those times people pretended to be impressed, nobody *really* believed that I could tickle myself—they all thought I was faking.

5. Birth is irreversible because death is not its true opposite.

The last epiphany I swear was not said by me. As I drifted off to sleep I heard a voice, or the echo of a voice, say my name. The voice came over the radio but there was no radio. And wasn't it funny how my keys were in my hand but the last thing I remember is the sound of the car engine thrumming and a voice on the radio saying my name?

This, random citizens who have nothing to do on a Tuesday morning, is where my story gets sad.

XXV

A viscous liquid percolated in my throat. Groggily I opened my eyes. Wilting lilacs in a plastic vase came into view.

—Look who's awake.

A backlit middle-aged nurse with a man-nose bent over me. I felt scaly and turgid, coated in a tepid gruel. There was a seething pain, but far away, as if in a second body. Tubes protruded from both arms. I was sheathed in hospital blankets as flimsy as rice paper.

—My name's Chelsea. Do you know where you are?

—On the set of a hospital drama?

She blinked softly.

—No, darling, this is a real hospital.

I believe, Your Honor, I may have already mentioned how I'd always been terrified of losing my footing and falling from the regular society into either the prison society or the hospital society, and I can't emphasize enough how my superawareness of these two overpopulated and underresourced hells have shaped my nightmares since boyhood. And now I had finally fallen.

—You were in a car accident.

That made no sense. The last thing I remember I was parked on a side street, being gawked at by teary, terrified preschoolers, the hand brake on, ignition off, keys bunched in my hand, sirens heralding the arrival of ambulances, and although I was drifting into unconsciousness at the time, even the horrendously uncoordinated and terminally unlucky can't crash a parked car. What the hell happened?

From the corridor I could hear a male nurse tell another how he loves his dog but the bitch sheds hair like she's had chemo.

Life, then.

I tried to raise myself from the bed.

—Hold on there. You've been unconscious for two months.

She let the import of that passage of time sink in. A man lay in the bed beside me, his bruised eyes half closed, a tube in his throat, his mouth wide open but rendered so useless it couldn't even yawn. Welcome to the realm of the disgusting, he seemed to say. I thought: If by chance I get out of here in one piece, what shape will that piece be? The nurse laid out her equipment on the bed with callused hands; she wrapped my arm with a rubber tube before unveiling the gigantic syringe from my nightmares.

—May I be blindfolded, please? I croaked.

—Sorry, darling, we don't do that.

I turned back to the body in the adjacent bed, hoping my grunts of pain comforted him. Certainly his coughing comforted me, even though phlegm was the least exotic fluid in the place.

The next time I opened my eyes I saw a head of crazy hair.

—How do you feel? asked Mimi.

—Like I've been molested by a stage hypnotist.

On the other side of the bed, Stella picked up my hand and pressed it to her tear-glistened cheek. *Both* women?! A grim omen. I fell asleep again and when I awoke, Liam was sitting in Stella's place. His sad face conceded that my downward spiral had crushed *his* downward spiral. Ah, the pyrrhic victories of old friendships. Again I closed my eyes and when I opened them Morrell had replaced him in the chair.

—Poor deathless, imperishable creature. Maybe your will to live is inexhaustible after all.

He brushed hair away from my forehead. It seemed as if anybody who wanted to could caress me willy-nilly. Two doctors swept into the room like

Mongol armies. I knew instantly which was the most experienced and professional of the two; he was the one who didn't ask how I was feeling.

—Lift your head, he said. His voice was low and melodious, like he was about to break into a Gregorian chant. He gently pressed his fingers into the back of my skull.

—You know, you're lucky to have escaped any serious brain injury.

—It hurts to breathe, I said.

—You were on a ventilator.

—You were in critical condition for a while there, the other doctor added, and then proceeded to describe in detail the operation I underwent, which I chose not to understand. Instead I imaged myself tied to a spinning wheel in a circus tent as clowns in surgical masks flung razor-sharp knives.

—After the injury, your brain swelled up. Your head could hardly contain it. That's why we had to keep you in a coma.

I could see Morrell wincing, picturing my engorged brain.

—Anything else bothering you?

—My shoulder hurts.

—Well, other than the pain, it's of no clinical significance.

I couldn't think of a response to that, but it seemed to me like the kind of phrase that could define a civilization.

—You lost a few teeth, you'll have to have some pretty serious dental work, the first doctor said.

—Other than that, the other chimed in, you fractured your left sinus cavity bone, you have several broken ribs, a fractured pelvis, and you broke the ulna and radius bones in your left arm. We put in six steel pins that will be removed when you heal and a metal T-plate that should be there permanently.

There was a heavy silence. They were dancing around a taboo, staggering their revelations; I knew the last one was about to come. I sensed it—a fate vastly worse than death—and instinctively tried to shift up the bed, as if to higher ground. The doctor took out a pin and pricked my body from the tip of each toe up to my neck, asking me to describe the feeling, whether it was sharp or dull, or nothing at all. My toes were unresponsive, my legs unresponsive, my thighs unresponsive, my knees unresponsive. They asked me to flex my foot, my ankle, to raise my leg. I could not. They used a hammer to test my reflexes. No knee jerk, no ankle jerk, no plantar reflex . . .

I felt at the end of my life cycle and already my thoughts dove straight back to suicide, to self-removal. I had instantaneously composed a suicide note—*Dear World, I'll show myself out. Thanks*—by the time the first doctor half-squatted on the edge of my bed and spoke the words.

—You are paralyzed, he said.

—It's unlikely you'll ever walk again, said the second.

The light grew bright and my brain felt speared with the cold shock of a permanent loneliness, as if loneliness were a very, very, very long javelin that just keeps on going through you, and I couldn't breathe or make out the faces peering at me and caught only phrases from the doctors such as "incomplete paraplegia" and "crushed T-5 and 6" and "the absence of motor and sensory function" and "the zone of partial preservation" while my own thoughts were actual, distinct ear-splitting voices of varying ages and sexes and races speaking all at once: *The blind get great hearing, the deaf a super sense of smell. What do the paralyzed get again?* And: *Does paraplegia ever just, you know, blow over?* And: *Who would have suspected that at such an advanced age of adulthood you can become someone so entirely worse? Tough break, pal.*

Mimi, I noticed, was kissing my hand.

—I think he's in shock, she said.

People wait their whole lives to tell you you're in shock—any layman can apparently diagnose this.

—One more thing, the doctor with the priestly demeanor said. The police would like to talk to you.

—Why?

—I think it's best they tell you about that.

Then they turned away and walked out without saying good-bye, as if to say good-bye would have degraded everyone involved.

It might have been the overwhelming reality, or the overpowering morphine, but there was a distinct fade-out, an ebbing and subsiding of awareness, and hours later I was jerkily reinserted into consciousness, squinting through harsh light. The room was a chaotic thoroughfare; someone two beds over was being noisily defibrillated, and by my curtained bedside Morrell was nursing a coffee and wielding an ungodly frown of pity.

—Adorno said it's barbaric to write a poem after Auschwitz. What can one say to that man, except for *Don't be so sensitive!*

—What?

—Ax, meet frozen sea, he said, and dropped a black spiral notebook on my lap. I opened it up. On the first page was a poem written in Morrell's unmistakable cursive:

Dear Aldo,

> Put pen to paper and mind to air.
> Let it shape you, let down your hair.
> Be a poet, be not afraid to just go,
> Go it alone and wade in waters deep
> And keep your calm, you might as well
> You are in hell and cannot keep yourself from harm.

Love, Angus

He had seen my framed haikus in Mimi's bedroom; they'd triggered his astonishing memory that I had in class (thanks to Leila) demonstrated knowledge of nineteenth- and twentieth-century French and Spanish poets—how the hell did he remember that? He then quoted extensively from his own book, the chapter "Tribulations and Creativity."

—Don't waste time rebuking God or cursing injustice; rather, transmit your lived pain as solace or amusement . . . If they are also artists, the truly unfortunate have a wealth of material. And you know what else? Plato said there is no invention in a poet until he is inspired and out of his senses, and here you are, on morphine.

When I protested that I wasn't a poet he assured me it didn't matter, that the muses were themselves artists, and besides, he said, like a true poet, my most redeeming shortcoming was my ability to commit 100 percent to a bad idea.

Ladies and gentlemen of the jury, the rest of my stay in hospital is a five-month nightmarish blur of chaos and panic and wretchedness and agony that comes to me in indistinct fragments; it turns out that poetry is the most accurate and concise method to summarize this period so resistant to summation. A few days after Morrell's suggestion, I had several hallucinations of Veronica's bleary ghost hovering above my hospital bed or on the outer side of the far window. These visitations were short-lived but served to remind me of my sister's own passion for free verse, and inspired me to do as she would have herself. Of course, I am relatively ashamed of the long poem I scribbled but I don't repudiate it. I'm not disloyal. What the hell, I wrote poetry and I'm glad I did. And here I enter my lived truths as exhibit D, conceived during months of *in extremis* and therefore resistant to falsification. Please excuse the pervading sadness of my dredged soul as I beg the court's open mind to allow me to read a little testimonial segue here, this work that might for all we know shed further light on Mimi's murder:

XXVI

Good news, Buddha, I'm finally in the now!
(Absolutely. Worst. Now. Ever.)
I'm only forty and already on
my backup generator. My backpacking days are over
unless I'm the one in the pack.
The best compliment I can hope to hear:
his vital signs are good.
Everything bad in life will be worse from now on: insomnia, diarrhea,
    hangovers. Every problem
is the least of my problems.

I used to work as an ensemble, now I live
like Trotsky died.
God seized all my assets.
The door that was always open
is now a wall.
Even fight or flight will take time.
I would totally wish this
on my worst enemy.
Now would be a great time
to get raptured.

One Daisy Duke nurse in this sea of manhands wipes me with a towel
you wouldn't dry a dog with.

You're scheduled for an MRI, urodynamic study and crop rotation,
she says, before rushing off to deal with the oil spill in bed seven, Lot's
    daughter in bed five, the squiggly thing in bed eight, the axolotl in bed
    nine.
I catch her eye and make a *check please* sign in the air.
She says, Your stool sample has been sent to a psychic who helps police
    with missing persons.
It feels like I've swallowed cacti, electric eels are going to the toilet over my
    major organs, and I'm experiencing meteor showers.
Wielding a large-bore needle: Doctors like priests expect you
to renounce your pain, she says.
I vow to sit out rehabilitation. If I want to promote neuroplasticity,
I'll hire a publicist.
She says, A man who lives his life in pain will end up a torturer.
And if you feel agony for too long a period you are treated
like one who hears voices.

Late-night, I wake in floodwaters, therapeutic time windows shutting. The
    spinal cord is not a rip cord, God,
but I hope you landed safely.
She says, The medical establishment *will* as a matter of policy and without
    consultation prolong your days until everything you are you'll owe to
    human ingenuity.
I ask, Did the malediction mention me by name?
She says, While psychiatric wards are patrolled by small fistfuls of Christs,
    the spinal ward is all Jobs.
I say, Listen. Hear that silence? That's the sound of my forebears wonder-
    ing why they bothered.
She says, Look around. You haven't been singled out for persecution after
    all.
That burned.
Who the fuck are these people, these nurses? I can't fathom where they
    could have gotten this cavalier attitude towards the human body: in
    their upbringing?
She holds my hand. Knows how to make me feel better.

She says, You can't imagine
the home catalogs you'll be receiving!

••

Transferred out of ICU into a vulcanized-smelling green-lit thrumming
    chamber of competing soap operas
—certain trains of thoughts are a death sentence and watching television
    is like holding pressure on a wound—
My roommate, 3/4 of a guy named Dan, is being executed piecemeal. He
    lies on his bed folded like shirts. We have our differences:
he oozes, I clot.

His wife presents him with memorabilia from home.
(Tins of biscuits. Mug. Photos. A football banner. Surfing posters.)

Who knows how deep those saliva threads go? He says to the doctor, Just
    when you finally have time to stop and smell the flowers, your nose
    is bandaged. He says, What did you come across in my trenches and
    ravines? And: Keep it to yourself if you've found larvae! And: Don't tell
    me the surgeon left his keys in the bladder with the engine running?
It is well known in the medical profession that some patients desire noth-
    ing but a jocular relationship with their doctors and if during the course
    of the session they share one good quip that patient is satisfied with his
    care.

The doctor enters: Presto! We had to remove your
whirligig.
On the upside: We've cured your
sleepwalking.
And you're safe from bodysnatchers.
I say: Don't name a disease after me. Name one before me and see
if I run into it. I say: I've racked my narrative
for signs of hubris.
And I realize this is not a period of convalescence. I took my death drive

on a death drive and now my legs can't wait to wither
and my IV arm is thinner. Why they don't alternate I have no idea.
I think they prefer the one that's closer to the door, says 3/4 of a guy
named Dan, pupating there on hospital sheets.

He doesn't understand that medicine makes you sick like psychiatry
     makes you crazy, that one should not be afraid of your persecutors but
     be terrified of saviors with butter fingers, of grave, life-threatening mis-
     communication blunders between departments or the inexperience of
     trainee nurses *learning on the job*, often between English classes—don't
     hate me for not understanding in my haste to be afraid!

(Thinking of that serial-killing nurse on *60 Minutes*, those contaminated
     French
blood transfusions, those poor Quaid kids!)

They use a crane to wrench me out of bed for reasons of occupational
     health and safety, the crane moves too slowly and shit drops out of me
     onto the floor. A doctor comes in and says: Try and only sneeze on the
     toilet if you can. Your sphincter muscle is no match for hiccups. I wince:
     Sounds like a practical life. He leaves with: Someone will be in shortly
     to discuss poor sperm motility.

Can I have post-traumatic stress disorder
when the trauma is ongoing?

I'm not just post-operative but post-clawed and whored out to student
     nurses. Do you mind if she watches? I do. I fucking do.
Camera-ready catheters on fact-finding jaunts, green froth from orifices
     you don't want to know about, mouth flooded with metal.
Childhood-summer-length moments between painkillers wearing off and
     coming on,
Excavators in hospital couture with divining needles predisposed to miss
the artery.
I dwell on poor Tantalus

the God of Clinical Frustration.
I fire like a gun with a cork in the barrel.

In the face of my twice-sliced-laterally amigo's corn-fed guffaws I growl,
You too belong in the shop of your maker.
Where did *my* sense of humor go?

He's laughing now but 3/4 of a guy named Dan never mentions when he
didn't want to be pruned of a sprig here or there,
he wanted to die but they wheeled him howling into the operating theater
anyway.

Together we can almost cobble together
a single shadow.

••

Short-staffed hospital called in a local seamstress to close you up. She did
terrific work. What embroidery! (A nightmare) I wake to see

3/4 of a guy named Dan listening to the Sermon on the Mount on his iPod
read by James Earl Jones. The tannic yellow of the wound through the
bandages is making me sick, Dan Wethercot says. Morrell brings me
Baudelaire: *I felt all the beaks and all the jaws.* Maria Hamilton prays to
God to wipe the hard drive and restore me to my original settings. Clive
sings "Humpty Dumpty." It's so zeitgeisty to be disabled right now, Louise Bozowic says. Disabled is the new gay, Marc Jeffrey agrees. This slew
of awestruck next of kin carried in on gusts of pity don't shrink back but
press their faces close and look at me as if I'd died long ago, sometime
in prehistory. I thought I was disfigured beyond recognition but everybody calls me by name. Tells me how brave I'm being. Meaning I am not
clutching at their shirtsleeves begging them to smother me with a pillow.
Stella's head on my lap, Mimi holding my hand, Liam smiling kindly,
Doc Castle jabbering, Morrell patting my foot, Dee Franklin drawing
a picture that Morrell compares to Géricault's portraits of the insane.

Mimi stands on a chair, taking photos. I tell her it's dangerous in a hospital lest the flash go off in a surgeon's eyes. Elliot phones: Genesis 9:2. The fear of you and the dread of you shall be upon every beast of the earth. Stella helps Clive make a papier-mâché leg for 3/4 of a guy named Dan. I'd love to use you in an installation, Frank Rubinstein says. One day we will grow a kidney from your own cells and transplant it without fear that your body will reject it, Doc Castle assures me. He seems to think a person won't reject himself. I shout, Doc, you don't know me like I do!

Morrell brings me Kafka's *Metamorphosis*. I have never so identified with a fictional character. Elliot calls: Now she has to look after you too? Tell her you never want to see her again. She can't take on any more. Stella's uncle Howard talks bedside about thetans and engrams. I just had déjà vu of you sitting up in the bed, Mimi says, not understanding there's nothing more underwhelming than being in someone else's déjà vu. Elliot calls: Freud spoke of the "other mouth," the Vedic of the "third eye." Nobody speaks of a second spine.

The ward psychologist says, Sorry that fully functioning human-life thing fell through. What's next? I wonder. Other than the angrier child of happenstance, who am I now? This is my after-event. Who would this new me be?

Mimi says, Be grateful for what you have. I say, What I have isn't what it used to be. Mimi says, You need to transcend your suffering. I say, But I can't transcend his, and that's what's killing me. 3/4 of a guy named Dan says, Leave me out of it. Stella says, Be in the present, then. I say, The present hurts like mad. Morrell says, The only antidote to mental suffering is physical pain, quoting Marx. I ask everyone to leave. Now Morrell is crying, not about leaving me, but about Iris Murdoch watching *Teletubbies* at the end.

Even when you're lying there in agony people come to you with their problems. You don't get a break. The patience of the patient needs to be elastic, huge. You can't judge people because their problems are minor! Stella was in a funk—she and Craig split up. But should she be ignored until she's diagnosed with cancer? Should she shut up until *all* her children die? What if nothing else ever truly tragic happens to her? What then?

Wouldn't it be amazing if the stranger I became after my horrific life event was compatible with the stranger Stella became after hers?

••

Each night I am turned like sausages, manhandled in the murk of sleep. Hairy hands, enhanced interrogation techniques. I wake midroll screaming

for amnesty. One night at the hour when shadows take their furlough, the nurse came in with a look of flustered helplessness you don't want to see on

the face of your caregiver. At my slanted angle I hinted for painkillers and she obliged: The morphine opened a door and I fell through to the very

equator of sleep yet still anchored by fishhooks to the crinkled skin of pain. I couldn't breathe, as if someone with unspeakable strength had put a hillside

over my face. I woke to see a moving tent of gloom, a figure slipping out. Hospital rooms (unlike prison cells) are never locked and anyone can unfold

and drip anything onto the charred or moldering bedridden oxen. Who slunk into the room to cudgel the patient? What ghosts are in a holding pattern above my

bed? Was 3/4 of a guy named Dan groping the beige walls trying out his prosthetic leg? (Yesterday he was hobbling around the room with a dry mouthful of pills

looking for a glass of water. *Unbearable.*) Or was it Leila's clenched ghost or the bat-caved voice that I heard in the car or old enemies, disgruntled investors who have me finally where they want me? Or was it my mysterious visitor, the old woman with bright orange hair who came the

previous day? She smelled like baked goods and reminded me of my old dog Sooty (some said she barked herself to death—I think she overdosed on

ladybugs). She said, I brought you some flowers. I asked, Are you here visiting someone? She said, Are you happy with your care? I said, They

keep a hygienic cemetery here. She said, The surgeons have a good reputation. Yes, I said, they have their fingers in a number of pies. She

frowned—she didn't quite know what I meant. I didn't either. Unlike Japanese soldiers, doctors rarely fall on their own syringes, I clarified. Are

you in any pain? she asked. Yes, I said, but it's of no clinical significance. She nodded wearily, as if she'd heard that one before. Maybe she had. Well,

can I bring you anything? Some gossip magazines? I said, Oh yes, what *are* the rich and beautiful people up to? She ghosted and never returned.

Now harassed at night by a murderer with no follow-through, call buttons and squeak of sneakers on the ammoniac shine, medieval groans that start up

like zephyrs and waft along corridors, harrowing nightmares of trees reconsidering their upright position and of surgeons using the rib cage for a

xylophone or bringing bones home for the family dog or even the terrible green glaze of a parachute soldier whirling gyroscopically to the earth.

With morning light years away I think: The worst thing in the world isn't
    suffering or loneliness at all. It's a combination: suffering alone.

All I want is the old waking daydream, to kiss the patron saint of brain
    death, rise up into the star-strewn skies, be a voiceless

faceless thoughtless drifting eye ringing out like plucked strings and taper
    off or just frankly dissolve in an orange flash and be a traceless nothing,
    never more to

wake startled wishing I could sleep the sleep of a child, when all my night-
    mares were merely instinctual and my monsters standard issue.

••

Dining-room electric chairs that beep like
Smoke detectors with dying batteries,
A strange hum and squeak of foot tray to back wheel
Queue of the paralyzed, the cerebrovascularly
Down on their luck, amputees wearing last season's
Prosthetics, those with hip disarticulation and
Hemipelvectomies, neurodegeneratives with
Claymation faces, stroke victims whose speech
Is all ellipses and who wouldn't last two minutes
In Hitler's Germany. This is where the falling stones
Fell and stay fallen. The feet you see! The legs!
Nurse, fumigate the patient! Nurse, pulp that man!
Twisted torsos, veritable cubes, 18 to 24-year-old
Gregarious debacles screeching around corridors
At four in the morning (Masculinity was their disease.
They'd still put you in a headlock if they could.
They're already pimping their rides and zipping
Through corridors like cannonballs.)
Or moving spiderlike or crabwise in the sob of night,
These wearying all-or-nothing personalities, clientele

Who are bad for business, for whom there was
Never enough plenitude, mostly football and motorcycle
Accidents (in less-developed countries falling from
Trees is aetiologically more common). One begins
To believe a man with children who gets on a motorbike
Is not a loving father.

The patients complain about larcenous
Nurses or sticky-fingered visitors; froth about peakless
Futures, the inaccessibility of tree houses and being
Wheelbound wallflowers waiting for fetishists to
Rustle our dark foliage. These are not our bodies but
Our scorched-earth policies. We are obscene gestures
Raving into bedpans. I'd prefer back-to-back awkward
Silence marathons. We've gone headfirst into our heads.

We weren't without our faults, OK; still, we didn't deserve
To be pulled up by the roots like that. If you believe that
Determination allows a man to walk again, and anyone who
Doesn't get to their feet simply hasn't the willpower to do it,
And that your God miracles so indiscriminately, then you
Are frankly a cunt. That other people are likewise suffering
Is the coldest comfort there is.

This you understand is pure economics: the redistribution
Of health. Hands changing hands. We had plans.
Places to go, fertility rites to wrong, but you can't
Go home again. You can't even get back into
Plato's cave. Let's face it. We are separated from the
Truly sick, we are not diseased, not even ill! Just broken.
The luck of the cancerous is, *they* have options:
Get better or die. We just keep on keeping on
Symbolizing injustice, and FYI:
Atheists are *everywhere*. Clearly we don't
Frequent the same foxholes.

3/4 of a guy named Dan has suppurating blisters and bedsores. His hips
     gurgle. He looks
like a vase left too long in a kiln.
His avocado-green crater forever opening on his bone. Premonitions of
     septicemia come true.

He is dying. His death won't be cathartic for anyone.

3/4 of a guy named Dan says, Promise me something. Turn over a new
     leaf,
escape yourself, start again, redraw the map, go to a time-management
     consultant, keep proper documentation, find pleasure in a ray of sun-
     light or die trying, get in touch with the ocean, live every day like it's
     your last.

I say, I've never understood that. If this was my last earth day I'd shoot
heroin and have unprotected sex with multiple strangers. He says, Stop, it
     hurts to laugh. I say, It hurts to do a lot of things. It hurts.

It's my turn is all, he says. It's like jury duty. I say, Don't worry. Your
doctor is so famous he can drop his own name. He dedicates each opera-
     tion to a different lover.

We were not quite right, like we'd been homeschooled in a cave with Wic-
     cans.
Before they take him for surgery he says, When I get back let's break

quarantine and prowl the halls with kerosene lanterns like caretakers in a
     storm.

I kiss his hand. It wasn't just my complete turnaround that was shocking
     to me,

given the frenetic heat of fear and anxiety in that sickbed, the poisonous
atmosphere of the spinal ward where camaraderie is scarce and each injured man jealous of his brother's recovery. It is madness that a friendship blossomed at all.

••

Heart operation interrupted by a mobile phone. The surgeon waits until the
embarrassed intern can silence it. He is too slow, the patient bleeds out.
"We're sorry for your loss." (A nightmare)

Just when I'd almost forgotten about them the police enter like spies whose
code names
are the same as their actual names.

I sit up, preparing to help with their inquiries, obliging though enigmatic.
You know how it is. We are forever in our trailer, waiting to be called to set.

Witnesses say you drove straight into the wall without turning and without trying to stop.

I did? Christ. How embarrassing. Wait. I wasn't even driving!
Or was I?

You weren't on the phone, were you? Sending a text message? Eating a
sandwich? Smoking a cigarette? Or did you—he stops midspeech

and puts his finger to his forehead as if marking a place—fall asleep? My
feet are cold. I reach for the blanket,

it falls on the floor. The other detective picks it up, drapes it over me. Under
the sheets I clench my fists. Tucked in by

my interrogators. The indignities never end. So, were you depressed or
something? the detective pressed. You didn't swerve.

Officer, Mimi says, surely half the human race has been killed in a car accident by now. What do you care if my client

drove into a brick wall? The policeman says, Because there was a kid on
the other side of it. I am an iceberg

breaking free from the mainland. The policeman continued, He was writing graffiti. And you dropped a brick wall

on his head. I ask, Is he . . . ? Mimi asks, Is he . . . ? Stella asks, Is he . . . ?
The policeman leans over me

and shakes his head. It's not looking good. He is a crumpled mess yet to
surface. The doctors

are dragging his lakes, separating the flesh from the bones. He's tangled as
headphones.

Now the police keep me under surveillance, the doctors keep me under
observation. I spend the remainder of my time in hospital

under the threat of prison.

••

Mimi's three photographs: "An Intriguing New Entry in God's Bestiary,"
"An Incident at the Assembly Line Where He Was Made," and "Something That Once Existed But Has Since Disappeared From Fossil Records." All feature in this month's edition of *Australian Photography*
magazine. Mimi's new exhibition: Waiting for an Accident Waiting to
Happen. Morrell tells me to leave my body, not to science, but to art—
why have a funeral when you could have an exhibition?—and campaigns for himself to encourage the artists in the residency to start a
new movement, not on form, not on representation, not on process,
not on aesthetics, not on theoretical concepts or ideas, but the first art

movement in history to focus on the subject, a single subject, so as to
free the form. Creativity is at its most unleashed with limitations—and
what could be more limiting than having to depict the same sad sack.
He calls it Aldoism. While Morrell is blowing hard about it, Mimi asks
if she can include my CT scans in her portfolio. Stella has her guitar and
plays a new song based on something I asked the hospital psychologist:
Is it still necrophilia / if the corpse fucks *you*? Neither women you want
around for locked-in syndrome.

••

In the morning, my two free-floating women glisten
at the foot of my bed,
bovine nurse beside them. I know you're upset, she coos, but there's
still a remote chance he's going to pull through. He's here? Upstairs, in
   the paleontology ward, the nurse says, or something like it. Stella and
   Mimi are
swelling hypnotically. The nurse transports out. The air spreads shadows
   across the room. I hold tight to nothing. I think you should go see the
   kid, Mimi
says. It'll drive you crazy otherwise, Stella adds.
They crouch down sorting their hooks and baits trying grimly to start a
   hive
mind—I bare my teeth. I say, I'm sick of buying a bulletproof
vest only to be stabbed by the vest salesman. Mimi says, Are you coming
or not? I say, Fuck! Oil my wheel so I can equivalently
tiptoe—and help me up.

Stella and Mimi lower me into my wheelchair, and with my head dizzy
at high altitude, we prowl the hospital followed by the eerie hum of vending
machines, the nurse at her desk ignoring the buzzings
and their sad subtexts. Some patients want water or fatal morphine drips.
We charge through the hospital's obvious lack of cartwheels,
headquarters of Population Control, we pass the burn ward where oil-
   fields, haystacks & the

disproportionately caramelized are shucked from their clothes, pass visitors who
look like hitchhikers dropped unexpectedly at a
turnpike, pass the torn asunder, the tactical errors, the system bugs,
the design faults, the triple in size, the pried open, the
unresponsive to vocal commands, pass the operating theater, a room
haunted by the memory of entrails, the smell of gloved hands, a man
in a mask with a high wrinkled forehead who leans over me smiling as
if his smile is for the good of mankind, and a voice—I'm your anes-
thetist,
here to make sure you don't let out a scream and give away our position,
before his features became fuzzy and indistinct
like the face on Mars.

We share an elevator with a pregnant woman about to hack up an infant to
the sixth floor where a few whole-bodied visitors make way for me I must
have looked that bad.

At the door of 608 (of all the turnstiles I'd been caught in, all the revolving
doors that pushed back, the automatic doors mistimed, the stage doors
mistaken for back doors,
this was the worst) my women nudge me ruthlessly into
a small dimly lit room oppressively filled with murmuring
bodies, crowding the bed. There is only one light on, above the sink.
At first no one seems to notice us. Then a voice
in the green darkness: Aldo.

My blood goes into a holding pattern. My mysterious visitor! The old
woman with the bright
orange hair. (His grandmother?) Thank you for coming, she says, keeping
her eyes low. My impulse is to return at magic hour. How is he? I ask.
Roll credits, she answers, gesturing to the vivarium.

The visitors turn on like runway lights and clear a path to the centerpiece,
the capsized boy. I

have never seen so puzzling a configuration of puzzle pieces. Such an im-
perfect likeness of a human
shape. His wrung-out pale body spread ceaseless on the bed, a tree split by
lightning. Through the cold rail his hand falls down like dangled
bait. The visitors don't take their eyes off, engraving upon me their malice
aforethought. Fear is deafening with gusto. I lurch closer.
So that's what a larynx looks like. So this is the failure to reconcile a brain
to its stem. So this is the syrupy ruckus that intubated lungs make.
His sink is clogged—I don't know the medical term—his dark streams
have frozen over. This greeny backlit mode of sinking makes me sicker,
my nausea nauseating me.
If death is peace then sleep is terror. His mother cries (almost) headlessly.
Their little boy is all jugular. He will never again look into the
lens and not smile.

Stella is making vague sounds. Mimi hardens. The old woman sizzles at
me with quiet eyes. I am a source of fascination. Behind us, visitors from
other rooms have heard the murderer has come to
visit his victim. Nurses, burly orderlies, men and women trailing fluids
and held together with tape crowd the door. This is
an event in their hospital lives. Other than the tired human drama of living and dying, not much happens. This is something
different.

His parents peck and claw. Their pupils are like glowworms in a fetal position. They say, The hospital asked us if we want to pull the plug. And:
We won't. And: He's brain damaged. And: A vegetable. And: At best.
This isn't news. Doctors rate survival highly, never how many resuscitated patients go on to dance in the rain. The human respiratory system
gets pride of place.

Falling through gusts of hate, hauling their violence down from their attics,
In the thrall of their tragedy, they had struck oil:
a face of evil to pin the blame on. Poor kid. He was paying for

being in a family, for being locked in a binding contract with a bunch of
    people whose set of beliefs had demagnetized their moral
compass. Fucker, someone says. Leave him alone. He's come here asking
    forgiveness, after all. Actually, I'm here
simply to survey the damage and get an estimate of the accident
I've only an antimemory of. Maybe it wasn't me, maybe he came in here
for a hygiene check and the surgeon cut the red wire instead of the green.

To think that this kid might suffer in an indefinite vegetative state because
his tribe couldn't put two and two together is intolerable. His endless suf-
    fering is on my head. They prefer their son to be a slug. They
believe in a God who prefers living slugs to dead sons. Poor kid. Now that
    you're a slug, they'll keep you on a tight budget.

I say, Take him to a farm so he can run around in the sunshine. For
those slow on the uptake, I say, Have his organs authenticated and certifi-
    cated ready for transfer. Pull the proverbial plug. Survival isn't
everything!
The family plot my windpipe in their crosshairs. Their shadows arch over
    me.
Stella squeezes my hand. Having finally arrived at the horrible apex of my
horrible life, and sharing this grotesque scene, once again Stella and I are
    bonded
for life. I love her
for standing smack bang in the middle of my catastrophe.

Their indignity steps ashore. Murder signals me to go. No one can be
    bored at
their own
execution, but what if you were standing on the gallows for months, wait-
    ing for the executioner to return from his vacation?
Shall we? I say as if suggesting a moonlight stroll. With a tremble and
    grimace Stella wheels me out, Mimi stays inside to see if there's any-
    thing
she can do.

Stella takes the reins and loses
balance several times, knocked off her feet by the contaminated energy of
   disease, the ruthless force of sorrow and
desperation. We are heading towards the children's ward where ingenues
   of agony play in quicksand pits & yellow-tinctured babies
bask in sunbeds. Without speaking, Stella does a hundred-and-eighty-
   degree turn and pushes me the other way. Cutting paths through ethe-
   real ick, a scrimmage of organs. I feel not removed from life so much
   as injected into it for the first time. Hospital corridors are the authentic
   streets of man.

3/4 of a guy named Dan's bed is empty. Sheets stained clean. He died,
Chelsea says. They took him for an autopsy and deboning.

Stella says, Let's get some air. We share the elevator with four doctors
with penlights, their voices trombone-deep and galactic. They say, I know
   him laparoscopically. And: When I thrust my thumb into that
fontanelle . . . And: Abdominal retractors are a dime a dozen. Not worth
   going back in for it. And: It was the fifth case of friendly fire I diagnosed
   this week. We escape at reception. The automatic doors open. We aren't
   ghosts, after all. This old technology proves we exist.

Outside, the air is surprisingly warm. We'd been kept
on ice. Under the awning stubborn smokers defiantly suck their cigarettes
   next to cans full of butts. The sky seems
fresh, feverish. We loiter next to a man with a kebab obstructing his airway, down near the hospital garbage cans containing
bloody smocks, foreskins, and a flock of breasts. Neither of us stop trembling.

Stella walks over to the smokers
and comes back with two cigarettes and a lighter. It's been a decade. The
   mutiny an emphatic
success. We suction nicotine and release trapped anecdotes into the wild,
   forage for old feelings. Ex-husband and wife, two

old lovers, two old friends. The nucleus is intact. The problem with having
a new lease on life is it is a nonbinding
contract. Neither of us changed
by our life-changing experiences—our lost baby, my lost mobility.
The stubbornness of personality will win out as it always does and
whoever we were before we would always remain, yet
I still have the feeling that at last, at last,
at last my formative years have
finally begun.

XXVII

As you know, it's a classic ploy to wait until three days after you've been profoundly institutionalized before depriving you of the institution, Your Honor.
When the hospital administrator strode in beside one of my doctors and congratulated me on being stable enough to leave, I delayed. I was not eager. In
my prior life I'd grown comfortable with my fears: of death, of sexually transmitted diseases, of public speaking, of train derailments. But now my terrors
included being left alone in the street. A puncture in my tire. Not to mention
fear of my own body—I distrusted each organ equally. I feared spasms, blood
clots, embolisms, bedsores, autonomic dysreflexia. One gets used to having
experts on call in case of emergencies. An allergic reaction, hemorrhaging,
unexpected drug contraindication. I wondered: Who will interpret my feces?
Reduce the swelling? Stop the bleeding? Who will resuscitate me? I was already dreading Sundays and public holidays when emergencies invariably
arise. I thought: if my doctor plans a vacation I will know the universe is
scheduling a life-threatening episode during that exact period, from which
without urgent medical attention I will emerge further crippled. In truth, I
felt a monumental timidity, terrified of taking this flimsy version of myself
anywhere outside the most sterile and well staffed of environments. Problem
was, I had to make room for the constant stream of incoming paraplegics
and quadriplegics, but where would I go? My old apartment, with its narrow
hallways and standing-room-only kitchen was out of the question, so social
workers had found me an acceptable one-bedroom with the requisite ramps
and handles, yet it was at the moment of my departure, having hyperventilated

adios to the ghost of my truncated roommate, and being unable to bid the nurses a special farewell as they were all busy with ambulance-loads of unpleasant arrivals, that the thought of suffering alone, my new bugbear, became overwhelming. This led me to accept last minute, against my better judgement, Mimi and Morrell's invitation to live in the residence, at least until my reckless-driving-resulting-in-bodily-injury trial. I wheeled myself outside and into Liam's squad car. The only upside I could think of: Anyone fucks with me now, it's a hate crime.

He turned the siren on for me. An incompetent policeman and artistic failure, a failed-businessman paraplegic, two divorcés, two old friends, set off. I wanted him to drive us back to our youths.

—1990 and step on it, I said.

As we threaded through the city, my eyes could not compute. Everything was hyperreal. The unpalsied populace smug in their pace. Bored faces in stuck cars. Buildings under construction, as if a freeze-frame of collapse. I did not open my mouth for fear of whimpering. Neither did Liam, though at traffic lights he took my hand and squeezed it, as if in an attempt to transfer power from his body to mine. When we hit the meandering coastal road, the horrific number of wreaths and service-station flowers on what seemed like every third telephone pole spoke of split-second tragedies and ghastly second acts. Liam told me he'd been out to the residence a couple more times to see Morrell. The thought that they were still entangled in some sort of protégé/mentor tango was patently absurd.

Morrell, a bearded stranger to shampoo, was standing at the door as we arrived.

—When you have a serious medical problem, depending on the prognosis, you either quit smoking or take it up, he said, dropping a carton of cigarettes in my lap.

The residence was overflowing with artists who seemed even more like sulky adolescents than I'd remembered. I felt the sting of Darwinism, an innately inferior specimen with no evolutionary purpose.

—And I have a nice surprise for you, Morrell added. Let me introduce our newest artist.

Standing with her beautiful smile and wind-chime earrings was Stella!

—I live here now, she said, beaming.

—Then you'll be breaking your own restraining order on a 24/7 basis, Liam said.

Her sweet laughter wafted over like perfume. I used to see the light side of everything too.

—Where's Clive? I asked.

—With Craig, she said, her smile tightening.

—Would you like to see how my exhibition is shaping up? Morrell asked, crouching down in front of me as if before a child. I'll give you a tour of my latest works.

—Not before he eats something, Mimi interrupted, whisking me into the kitchen where we ate cold meats and bread and cheese and Liam and Stella and Mimi and Morrell all spoke as if divided by soundproof partitions they couldn't see; there was a hush at least as loud as the conversations. I experienced such hostility toward everybody; I didn't quite know how to orient myself. I felt like a grown-up ward of the state facing his old abusers.

Mimi and Stella helped me into my north-facing room—I was frankly relieved not to have to stare at that ocean—where someone had made the en suite accessible by taking a mallet to the doorframe, leaving jagged edges, exposed wire, and sediments of plaster. Ten minutes of swallowing medications later, I undressed and Mimi and Stella helped me onto the most incredibly depressing piece of plastic furniture invented, the shower chair, where I sat under a stream of water that was in turns scalding and freezing, without being able to move quickly out of the way, while the women were silent and solemn and even seemed a tad annoyed, and it made me imagine disciples come to wash the feet of Christ who have to settle for Judas in a wig. This I thought mainly to distract myself from the two loves of my life pretending not to stare at the suprapubic catheter entering an actual hole in my actual stomach and at what is now accurately called "my junk." They were thinking the same sad thing: Could he ever again? And would he ever again? I had spent many months wondering the same thing.

Later, Morrell carried me in his arms downstairs into his bright studio to see his oil paintings, all vaguely sexualized interiors of domestic spaces: erotic chairs, curvaceous couches, labial curtains with picture-window views of period-red skies with the nippled sun and moon as interlocking spheres. They seemed perfectly fine if not exceptional works—or maybe they were masterpieces. What do I know? Morrell was haunted by the specter of no red dots—of an utterly dotless opening night. He was trying to decide if, due to his age and experience, he should refer to himself as a promising beginner or a midcareer artist, a late starter or a late bloomer. I predicted I'd be forced to accept invitations to Morrell's studio, meaning I'd have to regularly acquiesce to being carried in the bastard's arms to this den of frustration. He had, at last count, fourteen pieces in total. The room could bear twenty but he feared he had too many already.

—In the art world, less is not only more, it's much *much* more.

—They're good.

—The enemy of the great, he responded bitterly, and threw the closest painting over the balcony to the beach below.

Around midnight, the artists had moved from boisterous dinner into a combat-zone level of debauchery and it occurred to me I'd made a terrible mistake moving back into the residence, what with the conversations that played on a loop and the sexual hijinks and the attendant miseries and jealousies. I wheeled myself out onto the balcony and stared at the pointless magnificence of the ocean and the derelict moon orbiting nothing of value.

—Would you mind if I draw you? Dee Franklin asked.

She wanted me naked, covered in gold and silver body paint. I declined. More artists gathered around me with cheery, fascinated faces. Though I'd recently lost a vast array of abilities I'd previously considered indispensable to a basic human existence and felt ghastly about it every picosecond of every day, nobody seemed to notice my despair. Everybody weighed in. Everyone looks on the bright side for you. They're really positive about your situation. Nobody feels underqualified to offer medical advice. The preposterous suggestions they're not ashamed to make! Ladies and gentlemen of the jury, to torture someone with an incurable illness or a permanent disability is easy. Name the most ludicrous and disreputable remedy imaginable—e.g. bamboo under the fingernail therapy—and *swear* it fixed a friend of yours. The dying or disabled patient, sick in heart and soul with the desperate feeling that he hasn't tried everything to restore himself, will quicksmart reach for the bamboo.

They will also tell you about exceptional individuals who did exceptional things even with exceptional limitations. This in no way felt relevant to my case.

That night, I sat in bed more frightened that I'd ever been in my life. I had developed, through the wonders of neuropathic pain, an extreme sensitivity to fabrics, so that I couldn't bear the sheets upon my skin, and this was coupled with the intolerable sensation that my toes were squashed painfully together as if into a child's shoe. After an abortive attempt to wiggle them, I wanted to hit the call button, I wanted to go where other grotesques congregated, I wanted out. In the distance I heard a beeping sound that I assumed was existence backing over me.

Stella was at the door, loitering with intent.

—Zip up my dress?

Her failsafe beauty, the way she moved like windblown leaves, still managed to take the air out of whatever room I was in. I soon understood that she was colliding with herself, fretting that her new songs were self-plagiarism, the first sign of irreversible artistic decline (some were about the cumulative toxic energy of the competing artists in the residence and how she was working so much she often "forgot to eat," something I never fathomed because I hadn't missed a meal since 1993, but most were about her separation from Craig, who had taken temporary custody of Clive so she could concentrate on her music, an agreement she now experienced as guilt-ridden torture). Listening to her with familiar fascination made me think, Christ will I *ever* stop falling in love with the same woman over and over again? I thought how Stella had been sewn into the fabric of my existence, followed by the realization I didn't have the legs to run away with her, that I couldn't carry her once more across a threshold. All of a sudden something heavy and dull hit me in the face, a vague pain spread over my cheek. Frown lines crowded Stella's forehead. Don't do that, she said, kissing me on the head. It was my own fist. I had hit myself.

Stella lay next to me tickling and scratching her left arm—my old job!— then we reminisced for hours, huddling close, admitting that nobody else would ever know either of us in the same way. That's why couples stick together, Stella said, neither wants to be rendered unknown. Her face was turned to mine, a glimmer of tears in her eyes.

—I'm proud of how you're dealing with everything, she whispered. You're a survivor.

That annoyed me.

—I am *not* a survivor, I said. That is not even a human character trait I admire. I like it when a person says, "Blech," then rolls over and literally dies.

As soon as I said that her sullen face brightened and she leaped up and sprinted out of the room and reentered with her guitar. For two hours I delighted in the nourishing vision of the moonlight trembling on her gleaming, dark-honey limbs as she wrote pages of nonsense lyrics and plucked a cute little melody out of thin air that she first whistled, then sang—a lovely, silly song that drifted over me, and sailed through me, and I felt the fleeting contentment of reliving old times.

—I will always love you unconditionally, I said, on two conditions.

—Go ahead, she said.

—One. That you never give up the guitar ever again.

A smile, a sigh. Gratitude and relief at feeling deeply understood.

—What's the second?

—That you hire someone to kill me.

—Get the fuck.

—Please.

—Aldo!

She buried her head in her hands and cried. They were tears of despair, for the abominable reality that reinserted itself into our moment, and tears of anger, for the grave crime of abusing our mutual devotion. Stella seized her guitar by the neck and stormed out.

In the morning, I woke to find Mimi cleansing an unremembered bowel movement, moisturizing the skin, then expertly turning me. Her knowledge of a paraplegic's arcana seemed innate.

—Are you still sleeping with Mr. Morrell?

—Call him Angus, for Christ's sake.

—So, are you?

Mimi swiveled her head and stared catatonically out the window at the brushed-steel sky. She turned back with a compact smile, airtight.

—Once a week. Wednesday afternoons. Three o'clock.

I bit my lip. That was the time we used to have detention.

—There's something else wrong, I said. What is it?

—It's Elliot.

She explained. About a month ago she went to Silverwater to visit him but he refused to see her. Then he started leaving messages that made no sense at all, antagonistic and incoherent messages about Jesus Christ not being Yahweh's only betrayed child.

—It was Elliot, I said, who stuck those posters of you around the city, wasn't it?

She nodded and told me how over the past weeks her phone would ring at night, like it used to, but there was just silence on the other end. The disturbing part was, she had the oddest feeling that Elliot was actually talking, but had become inaudible. That he was standing there on the phone with his mouth moving and nothing coming out. The calls came every night for a week until five nights ago. Now Elliot had ceased all communication, she said, running tearfully to her room.

Between the fretful Morrell, the restless Stella, the anxious Mimi, all clear-cut cases of clinical frustration, the environment in the residence was downright toxic—I was thinking this when Morrell entered my room and sat beside me and clutched my shoulder, a supremely unwelcome gesture I hadn't the energy to shrug off.

—Aldo, the average person has an intrinsic value, but you have, in addition, a symbolic value, and one day I predict you will make a great work of art.

I didn't understand his use of the word "make." Did he mean, ladies and gentlemen of the jury, that I would produce a great work of art, or that I would become one?

XXVIII

Time slowed down again to childhood-summer pace. The days were long. Sleeping pills got me through the night. Soon they got me through the day too. And I was adjusting to life wheelchair bound. I was learning to separate the worst-case scenarios that resulted in deep humiliation, such as shitting or pissing my pants, from the worst-case scenarios that resulted in life-threatening damage, such as bedsores or a fatal blood-pressure spike. I hated transferring, feared falling out of the chair, or falling out of the chair and it tipping on top of me. I hated being estranged from my own body, trapped in enemy territory. I hated needing help to get into the fetal position. I wanted to teleport daily into oblivion.

The only thing that helped me slightly was seeing myself represented, de-contextualized, recontextualized, bent over, in pain, and solidified in that chair by Morrell's artistic movement—that he personally seemed to want nothing to do with—called (clumsily, in my opinion) Aldoism, which at least transitioned me through the denial phase relatively quickly, even though only two artists had signed up so far (Dee Franklin who did ink-wash drawings of me slumped in my chair and Lynne Bishop, whose mixed-media installation of me in hospital, laughing under the influence of morphine, hung in the living room of the residence). Despite my vociferous protestations, and my offering up alternate subjects—Stella (for her beauty) and Frank Rubinstein (for his ugliness)—they pestered me endlessly to pose for their craptastic artworks.

Regardless, furious resentment was my default setting. When the manic are shackled, expect problems. I had been out of the residence once or twice, wheeled down the road to the shops before getting caught in a sudden downpour, felt the agony of unexpected jolts—not until you are confined to a wheelchair do you realize there is practically no purely flat or even or obstructionless surface anywhere in the city, no pavement without dips or cracks or breaks or holes or raised edges. Your Honor, some people like to be the center of attention. They're the ones nobody notices. Other people can't abide a single eyeball trained in their direction. They're invariably center stage—the overly fat, the impossibly ugly, the horribly scarred. For us, it seems the maximum level of open glaring is permitted. I had to endure the cretinous stares of bewildered citizens, as if I were The Big Pineapple on wheels. Or bear those who had the temerity to ask, *Shit. What happened to you?* Or the crushing laughter of children. Or the sight of a woman's hourglass figure. Or a human running, or traversing a flight of stairs. Or the easy spotting of a hundred people glad they're not you. Then I would return home only to be castigated for wheeling mud into the house, or to be ignored, or scrutinized, or laughed at when arose unpredictable and unwanted reflex erections that I was totally unaware of and that were triggered by the folds of my baggy jeans, or by a book in my lap. I became utterly unable to make small talk, or worse, any conversation that did not deal directly with my own precipitous decline and suffering. Or with the declines and sufferings of others: the parents of birth defectees; children with psychiatric conditions; people with chromosomal or metabolic disorders; alien limb syndromees; the battered and raped; the cutting and self-harmed; the deaf and the blind; the burnt and the disfigured; babies with fetal alcohol syndrome. Any other conversation seemed so beside the point as to be heinously offensive. Nobody was talking about amyotrophic lateral sclerosis or fibromyalgia—but why should they? And who was I, the patron worrywart of degenerative disease? And I had only just begun to appreciate the significance of statistics. Even if the likelihood of contracting some rare ailment is so numerically insignificant as to be classified negligible, it isn't actually zero, and even 0.1 percent equates to millions of people suffering the torments of hell. This, according to doctors, is *negligible*. Why did that infuriate me so? And why did I wake each morning fretting about parents who accidentally flattened their own toddlers in driveways? And about cosleeping mothers who suffocated their babies? And the secret lovers of recently deceased adulterers? Or the unacknowledged love children of adulterers in permanent vegetative states? Or those people who get no sex because of unkissable mouths? Or family members who die in improper sequence? Or what the neighbors hear the morning of crib death discoveries? Who cries for these lives? It was overwhelming and I felt fragile and anxious every moment of the day.

One evening, Stella was telling everyone about the time we were swimming in a rock pool and I was sucked into a pipe, sucked right out to sea. I didn't like hearing these stories about the old me. I was jealous of that guy, how easy he'd had it. Liam had come by and brought Sonja, apparently so we could see the top of her head while she texted. At dinner, my wheelchair was a few centimeters shorter than the dining chairs, so I felt back at the kiddies' table at a grown-up party. Liam was getting into it with his old mentor. Following a boisterous argument about fiction, about whether or not being tarred and feathered is a poetic act—they both seemed to be gesturing toward me when they said it—Morrell said, Damn it, Liam, a writer is not merely a man who sits in a room trying to use the word *pusillanimous* in a sentence, obviously referring to something Liam had sent him. Afterward, Liam confessed that he'd really come by to give me bad news. The kid in the hospital had died, and the charge was being upped from reckless driving resulting in bodily injury to manslaughter. A guilty verdict would necessitate significant jail time.

I rolled out to the balcony, and thought about the dead boy, his family's pain. The silhouette of the battered cliffs looked like ruins of an old castle.

Down at the ocean, the white foam was still bright under the slip of moon, and I began thinking about that old impossible yet irresistible idea of my immortality, and I wrung my hands at the idea of no exit ever. The sea wind set the weather vane spinning and I was thinking that life is basic training for an even more brutal heaven, when I overheard through the open window Stella and Mimi fighting over who would turn me at three in the morning. I thought: That's sweet, my two women are fighting over me, until I realized that neither wanted to. I had to get out. I needed a single night off from this perpetual nightmare. Where could I go? I only knew one place.

If it pleases the court, I will now recount a sexual experience so shocking it turned my pubic hair white overnight.

XXIX

As a strengthening of appetite coincides with a diminishing ability to satiate it, and just as sexual problems require sexual solutions, and as I was horny as a train conductor—that's an amusing reference to Freud's *Three Essays on the Theory of Sexuality* regarding mechanical agitation and sexual excitation— never mind. Let me try again. As being burdened with a sexual longing that neither peaks nor dissipates needs treating like any other physical ailment, and as it is every faulty carcass's right to seek at least a simulacrum of relief lest they go insane, I steeled myself for what I imagined would be one of the more humiliating Saturdays in memory. In any case, one prostitute per month for medicinal purposes is hardly excessive.

The taxi ramp lowered with agonizing slowness outside Enigma Variations; at those rude motherfuckers on the street watching me disembark I arched my eyebrows as if we had just made a supernatural transaction and they were next. As I paid the driver, he gave me a look that contained profound apology for my plight, a gesture I appreciated and resented in equal measure. I didn't tip him.

A gentle rain fell. I wheeled over a cracked, slanted pavement to the open front door, and immediately ran up against an insurmountable obstacle—the interior frame of the doorway was too narrow. This brothel wasn't wheelchair accessible. I banged my chair against the frame. The women inside on couches turned their heads to look yet didn't move to assist me. I felt facial flushing and a spreading headache.

—Hello! Some help?

The women were immobile, as if they were under orders to remain seated. Before it had even begun, I'd managed to find myself at misadventure's end. On second thoughts, best reverse, and fast. The last thing I needed was some local with a camera phone sending my mortification viral. The Korean madam came running out waving her hands.

—Are you going to make a complain?

I said that I wouldn't make a complain.

—Come inside. We'll carry you! Girls! Girls!

—Please no, don't call—

It was too late. A half-dozen negligeed prostitutes surrounded me, the brothel bulb casting their faces in a smoldering red glow.

—Ferry gentleman into salon, the madam commanded.

—No, really, I protested.

The laughing women scooped me up.

—Wait! My wheelchair! It'll get stolen!

—We put bike chain on it. Tiffany! Get bike chain from office.

Now I was being held aloft by eight prostitutes in the rain, their cleavages pressed tight against me. To keep myself upright I grasped onto one's bony track-marked arms with egg-blue veins.

—Is Gretel here?

—Who?

— Gretel. Saffron.

—No, she doesn't work here anymore.

My disappointment was intense.

—I'm here, though, the woman holding my head said. I grimaced. The inside of her mouth looked carcinogenic.

A prostitute with lopsided breasts chained the chair up to a telephone pole against which, a moment later, an oblivious drunk man began to urinate. I gazed at the madam with genuine loathing and demanded to be let go as they carried me inside that old wet cheek of a room and gently set me down on a pink settee.

—What's that?

My shirt had risen up and one of the prostitutes was pointing to my suprapubic catheter and its attached bag of urine.

—Oh my God, that's gross!

They turned their gazes anywhere other than at my face. I was losing novelty value fast. They couldn't understand how sex with me was supposed to work. Frankly, who could blame the poor girls, with their rotten job whoring and their children, at least two, at home to support and their understanding or abusive husbands waiting for them at the end of the day, four a.m. probably, in their vans or motorcycles. The eight prostitutes told me their *noms de coitus* (Helena, Selena, Tiffany, etc.) and now looked gently upon my face but avoided my eyes.

—Choose girl, the madam said.

They shrank into themselves. The disintegrating penis of an old mummy would rate higher. Nobody wanted to be the chosen one. I assumed a steely determination to seem impervious to humiliation yet I could not bear the thought of dragging my body down the corridor of the brothel to the exit. I pointed at each prostitute one by one and made my vengeful evaluation.

—Too old. Too masculine. Too upholstered in tattoos. Bad wig day. Bad heroin day. Bad face day. Stilts for legs. Hasn't kept down solids this decade.

That was my only ploy to get myself thrown out, but they could see through my proud swagger—the hot tears in my eyes gave me away. The women refused to be offended, no matter what I said. The bouncer became alert though insultingly made no move to silence me, finding me harmless and unthreatening. When I had run through them all, I demanded they take me to my chair. After an agonizing silence the women came upon me with their powerful smells and lifted me in their arms and carried me back outside.

—There are other places you can go, that cater specifically for people in your situation.

—Get me the fuck out of here.

—I can't remember the code for the bicycle lock, said the madam.

Her plot was immediately apparent. She was going to charge me for the code. Meanwhile, the prostitutes' arms were getting tired.

—Can we put him down?

—No! Not yet!

—Give me the code! I shouted.

They were piling up, these worst moments. The madam put her hand on her chin.

—Two hundred dollars.

—Go fuck yourself.

—Put him back inside.

—Fuck!

The prostitutes staggered back inside and down the hallway, this time dropping me ungently on the couch. As they consulted amongst themselves I used the opportunity to call Liam.

—I need some fucking help ASAP please.

—Chair broken down?

I explained that I was being held hostage in a brothel on Sussex Street, the Enigma Variations.

—That sounds like some pickle. Only thing is, I'm on a boat on the harbor. I'll tell you what. I'll send over some of the boys.

At that moment the prostitutes hurled themselves on my helpless body for the third time, lifting me up, and I thought of *The Fussy Corpse* as they carried me upstairs and down the hallway and left me alone on the bed in Gretel's old room. There it was, the little desk with the wobbly leg. Out the broken window, the drainpipe. It was going to be OK. The madam stuck her hand in my face.

—Two hundred dollars. Up front.

Even though I had lost 99.9 percent of my sexual desire, I paid up and the odious madam took her leave. Two minutes later a negligeed willowy Thai woman entered as if shouldering an invisible coffin and approached the bed in a wide arc, and sat wordlessly on the edge of the mattress, stock-still and staring with large pitch-dark eyes. She seemed to be timidly waiting for some gesture from me, but isn't initiative what one ultimately pays for in a brothel, freedom from that dreadful first move, the anticipation of rejection? In truth, I felt like telling her not to bother, but thought *she* would feel rejected.

—What's your name?

—Jin. What do you want to do?

—Nothing unusual.

Let the court know that I was never perverse—at least, not in behavior; I was perverse by appearance, but that couldn't be helped. Her jaw was clenched, her left eye twitching. The bedroom's shadows were not doing either of us any favors. She reached out and touched my hair as one tests fabric you fear will itch. She removed her stockings, the kind women were frequently strangled with in the old days, and took off my shirt, revealing the bag. My embarrassment was now total, almost fatal. She tackled the belt, as if all the trouble resided in the belt. I was now inarticulate and self-conscious, hoping for some kind of conspiratorial wink, like we were in this together, or at least a gesture of consummate professionalism. I felt irritated that I couldn't endear myself to her. It was an ordeal, her terrible silence and kind smile. I wanted my mental activity to cease. I wondered what her interior monologue was like. I thought: I'll just fuck you and be on my way (Though this wasn't a fait accompli—that sustainable erections might occur indiscriminately and at the most unwanted of times, not when needed, was frankly my greatest fear. That and the failure of sex altogether). I kissed her breasts hurriedly, fiendishly, with evident stress. Her nasally inhalations were distracting and did nothing to mollify my anxiety. She still hadn't spoken by the time my pants were on the floor. Manually, what I managed was not exactly a periscope but respectable and lifelike, and she climbed onto the bed as if onto a scaffold and nimbly mounted me. Penetration. I was in—I think. Yes. Relief was the overwhelming emotion. This was just like sex! An unambiguous success! Yet why I fucked her with a heavy heart I could not say. This was my rechristening ceremony; it should have been a joyous occasion. It wasn't. Maybe because Jin was making weird off-putting mouth motions as if trying to make her ears pop during an airplane's descent.

—Are you all right?

At that moment, angry hollering came from the hallway. Doors fist-battered and kicked open. A commotion, just like the last time I was here. A voice: Police!

This time, I'd called them. I'd almost forgotten. Oh well, fine. Rescued at last! Jin remained frozen on top of me.

—Maybe you'd best get off, I said.

She heaved a sharp sigh and the door burst open. A bearded policeman's head loitered in the greasy light. Jin's stupefaction dissolved into fear. Another entered and yanked Jin off me then led her by the wrist out of the room. My jeans were within reach so I dressed myself, but otherwise couldn't make a move to go.

—Get up, grub, he said.

I said that I couldn't. He grabbed me by the hand. I fell to the floor.

—I'm technically a paraplegic, I said. My chair's outside chained to a pole.

Now I, the perennial fussy corpse, was being carried in the arms of a junior detective down the stairs where the girls were showing their identification and being arrested.

—Aren't brothels totally legal in this country? Everyone is over eighteen. Too over, if you ask me.

—Shut up, grub, the junior detective said.

—I called this in! I called you! I'm Liam's friend. Constable Liam Wilder. Did Liam send you?

The police couldn't fit me and the wheelchair in their squad car but the station was only six blocks away so they navigated the chair through the Saturday-night streets, running me over Styrofoam takeout containers and shattered beer bottles while groups of drunk men gawked and even the city's sprawled and king-hit sat up to witness our passing. The policemen were expertly whispering and I couldn't make out a single coherent syllable. They wheeled me through the reception area of the station into the same small airless room where I'd been interrogated by Liam nearly two years before. They searched my chair, taking my little medical kit with them, and left me alone with my branching headache and berserk spasms. Half an hour passed. This was no ticking-bomb scenario. Around the hour mark I had difficulty swallowing. Several of my medications caused the most hideous dry mouth, but the police had confiscated my saliva-replacement gels. This was intolerable. Not to mention I was completely confused; I didn't mind getting caught in a whorehouse—in fact it was quite a manly place to get caught—but what law had I broken?

Eventually three detectives sidled in. One was nearly bald, his remaining hair slicked back with gel. He gave me a glass of water. I washed my face with it. One with shaggy eyebrows took a seat opposite me while the third man leaned against the wall. I angled myself to keep all three in view. They made sidelong glances at my emergency survival kit, which they'd brought back with them into the room, at the preposterous number of pills, the enema kits, etc. Their faces were calm, even apologetic. I felt their sympathy and waited as it crossed the border into pity. This new interrogation technique—good cop, better cop, best cop—thoroughly confounded me and I was reminded of my time in the garment business in India, of the genuine hospitality of con artists. Yet when they spoke, it was clear they were all blazing against me.

—Why do you go to brothels?

—For non-reproductive sex.

—Can't you get a woman without paying for it?

—Not on short notice.

At that moment my phone beeped. I took it out of my pocket and saw two text messages from Liam. One said: *Deny.* The other: *This could only happen to you.* That familiar phrase friends and family had been amusedly plying me with for years now carried with it a force of intense dread; already surfeited with bad luck, I found myself bracing for an additional slice.

The balding detective slid across the table a photo of Jin, not an old photo but one taken earlier that evening. I recognized the negligee. Well, who wouldn't look sad and fragile in that lighting?

—You probably can't even have sex.

—Is that a question? I asked.

—No, said the detective with shaggy eyebrows. This is: You got a limp dick?

—Could you have fucked this woman? asked the third man. Or *any* woman?

Ladies and gentlemen of the jury, I have to admit I've never understood the whole idea of masculinity. OK, guys competing and tackling and one-upping each other when vying for a particular woman or women is evolutionarily understandable, but men trying to outdo each other in pubs or street fights or locker rooms with nary a breast in sight is something I've always found weird and somewhat suspicious—admit it, it's *super*-gay—yet here I was, these fuckers clearly trying to goad me, and maybe because the neurosurgeon's warning that sexual intercourse might not be possible had made me disproportionately proud of my tenuous boudoir success, the overly macho posturing by the pantomime squad got the better of me. I thrust my finger at the photo of Jin, forgetting that a gentleman never tells.

—Yes, actually. I did fuck her. Twice.

—Are you sure?

—Yes I'm sure.

There was now a long pause and a frightening businesslike demeanor settled on all three faces at once.

—Aldo Benjamin, the detective said, you are under arrest on the charge of rape.

Wait, what? Rape?

Your Honor, I know what you're thinking. Who in the history of rape has paid two hundred dollars for it? Ladies and gentlemen of the jury, I know what you're thinking: Aldo, you went to a legal establishment and procured the professional services of a sex worker, so how in the hell was this rape? Here's how. Jin had been trafficked.

Yes, trafficked!

The madam was charged with one count of possessing a slave and of using the slave. Jin had been kept in debt bondage in the room at the end of the corridor, the padlocked and windowless room, where she lived out the horrors of sexual servitude. That sinister padlocked room!

Due to the ballooning sex industry in the Asia-Pacific region, the burgeoning sex market in Australia, and the increasing incidence of sex slavery, a human rights group had lobbied for a new law, enacted just thirty days previous; it was modeled after a Swedish law in which *clients* are liable to criminal prosecution. It was just my fucking luck to be saddled with the ignominy of being the very first case.

—Haven't you heard about this law? Liam asked me afterward. It was in all the papers.

—It's two thousand and something! I shouted, weeping. Who reads the papers?

XXX

The manslaughter trial's start date was still pending, but the rape trial was fast-tracked. They wouldn't combine them to reduce travel time. The judge (for the rape trial) looked like one of those old Eastern Bloc corrupt officials who used to commit suicide during press conferences. On Liam's advice, I used a manual wheelchair so as not to let them see me "coast in on that electric number as if on a golden hovercraft while their own seats just sit there." It was sage advice. Unlike the nice folks of my present jury, *that* jury already seemed alert for any scrap of evidence in my demeanor that showed me as a bad person; a mean-hearted cripple was almost as good to them as a black racist.

Liam chaperoned me through the process.

—Try not to look postcoital.

—What are these cameras?

—All criminal trials are live-streamed now.

—Who's watching?

—Depends on the level of public interest. This one being a test case, a lot of eyes are on it.

And eyes there were. An open courtroom is the best place for a reunion. Anybody who knows you shows up, anybody you owe thousands of dollars to, or who wants to show their support, but the kind of support that will spice up their own anecdoteless lives, that will give them some kind of majestic travesty of justice to talk about on the way home.

The prosecutor told the court that Jin—her real name, incidentally; she didn't even get a fantasy hooker one—was promised work as a nanny, then when she arrived in Australia, her passport was taken and she was told she had a forty-five-thousand-dollar debt that she would need to repay by sleeping with seven hundred men, often unprotected, sometimes fifteen to twenty a day, sixteen hours a day before being taken back to a locked room to sleep. I bit my lip, thinking of my own role in this horror story. It was easy to find the Korean madam and her husband disgusting, but after the prosecutor gave a general overview—twenty million slaves in the world now, 60 percent of them in the Asia-Pacific region, a thirty-two-billion-dollar industry—he said, Aldo Benjamin is a human rights abuser. He wondered aloud what made me evil. I wondered the same thing. This is a test case, he said, and it is up to you to send a message to others. As in all rape cases, the prosecutor went on to say, a rape kit was used that scraped the vagina for semen, and while the defense will assert that of the four traces of semen found, either inside Jin or in the discarded condoms discovered at the scene, none were the defendant's, it was common, the prosecutor took great pains to point out, for men with spinal cord injuries to experience a retrograde ejaculation whereupon the semen returns into the bladder. That didn't seem worth objecting to.

My character witnesses, Mimi and Stella and Liam and Morrell, took the stand and all said more or less the same thing, that I was kind and gentle and nonviolent, always helping people with their problems and offering insightful advice. To tell you the truth, I thought I sounded insufferable. The last witness was Gretel (Saffron) who told how I was sweet and tender and had fast become one of her favorite clients. I was grateful, but the obliterating gaze of juror number 7 during her testimony—as if he couldn't believe he'd schlepped all the way over for *this*—put me in a black mood. Interestingly, I felt the jury hardened their hearts every time I winced in pain, my spasms all-damning witnesses for the prosecution. If ever there was a trial in which the entire jury wanted to rise in unison and break into a run, this would be it.

When it was my turn to testify, I had to position myself *beside* the witness stand; there was no ramp. I considered making a point of the lack of wheelchair access, but I didn't think it would do me any good.

—Did you think that Jin looked unhappy? asked the prosecutor.

—Everybody looks unhappy to me.

—Did she look frightened?

—Yes, I admitted, but I thought she was frightened of me, and I discounted that fear because I did not consider myself frightening; in fact, no one in my entire life has ever feared incurring my wrath, in particular my sexual wrath, although, OK, like any man, from time to time I've stared at a woman on the street so brazenly she would cross her arms to obscure her cleavage or sling her arm around her boyfriend to send me a clear message, but that's par for the course, and in this case, Jin's fears were unfounded, and in addition I remember thinking how enjoyable was the prospect of watching her fear dissipate when she clocked my gentle, tender, and generous nature.

—Did you think she looked sad?

—Yes, I did, but I thought her sadness was for me, because I'm an irredeemably pathetic figure, not because she was a slave, a fact of which I was entirely ignorant.

The judge asked if I had anything further to add.

This was my moment. I looked over the courtroom at the pop-eyed, incensed, and vaguely inquisitive faces of friends and enemies and began by calling for a minute's silence for my victim—who can refuse a minute's silence in our society?—but that was just to buy myself time, being distracted as I was by the jarring realization that this scene had a striking resemblance to one of my actual nightmares, although even my subconscious hadn't the temerity to go so far as to render me paralyzed at a rape trial.

I began by saying how in the crystal-clear hierarchy of the child/adult universe, anyone from the age of zero to about fourteen feels vulnerable to indiscriminate and unjust punishment, but once you've been an adult a decade or two, you no longer feel the "type" to get punished, in the same way as the chronically healthy don't feel the "type" to get multiple sclerosis—murder raps and degenerative diseases fit exactly nobody's self-image, and anyway, the fact that I was on trial was bizarre when one took into consideration the fact that it'd been thirty years since I *intentionally* broke the law: I photocopied money. I was twelve years old and it was before the ready availability of colored toner—I used crayons.

The jurors looked none too impressed by my opening remarks. I continued.

As to the particulars of this case, I explained, I felt conflicted. On the one hand the charge was absurd. And on the other hand it was perfectly reasonable. A young or middle-aged woman *should* have the right, not to sell her body, but to lease it on an hourly basis if she finds the rate acceptable, yet I believed it was clearly the brothel owner's responsibility to ensure the legality of these women. Who was I, border protection? What was I supposed to do, ask for her passport?

The jurors' deliberations were happening in real time on their indignant faces, as, I note, yours are also, ladies and gentlemen. Yet as now I must continue, so I did then.

I said that they, the jury, might be against prostitution in principle but under the law of our land prostitution in Australia in the early twenty-first century was legal and it was therefore not reasonable to expect a customer paying for lawful services to single-handedly regulate an industry or to do the job that a competent monitoring body should be doing. Where prostitution is legal, the burden should not be on the client, in the same way that when you purchase a car or flat-screen television—I regretted the analogy right at the beginning of the sentence—one has to trust the shopkeeper's honesty. If you don't like this idea, then criminalize prostitution, for it is simply unreasonable for the consumer to have to make that kind of split-second assessment. I was essentially arguing for a legislative change, rather than the specifics of my own case. A brothel client is, at worst, a predator who pays good money for his prey's time, and who often falls inappropriately in love with his prey, I said, adding that of course I did not set out to break the law that did not in fact exist thirty days earlier, then I segued to the real reason that it was *me specifically* on the stand and not one of many thousands of other brothel-frequenting men across the country. Because bad luck is my pathology, I explained. Nothing ever fell into my lap other than cups of boiling tea. Me, who contracted septicemia from a nipple ring, hepatitis B from a tattooist's needle, who thrice yearly bites down on tinfoil embedded in kebabs and reconstituted melted blocks of chocolate, who has never ducked under a barbed-wire fence without getting snagged or had a haircut that the hairdresser hasn't had to personally apologize for. Not to mention who was unjustly accused of rape at seventeen while still a virgin, and is now on trial for raping a woman who, at the time, I was naively proud to have penetrated. All my life I've felt, I went on to say, as if I were in a boxing ring with my hands taped to my sides. Every punch is a free punch for my opponents. Raising or lowering my guard seems to make no sort of difference to my fortunes. The human I most relate to in all of history is Tsutomu Yamaguchi, I said, the poor sucker who was in Hiroshima on business when the atomic bomb fell and who returned to Nagasaki just in time for the second . . .

I couldn't finish the thought. I had drifted off. Then it was all over, and over quickly. I heard the dreaded verdict: guilty. The judge's voice like a stalled train jolting to life. I was sentenced to two years. I scanned the faces of the jury for an embarrassed smile.

—Aldo, in your top pocket! Mimi called out. In the pocket she had placed, that morning, two pills in case of the worst news. I took them immediately, thinking they were cyanide.

—Valium! she said.

—One day you will come out with a great gray Merlin of a beard and amazing abs, Stella called out.

—Or else in a box with shoelace marks still visible on your throat where they cut you down, Liam added.

—A miscarriage of poetic justice! Morrell shouted.

Stella raced over and wrapped her arms around me. I was taken away after that, wheeled out of the courtroom through a door to my other worst nightmare: prison.

You expect the brutality to start right away but they're careful not to violate your rights all at once. The bailiff led me gently into the back of a windowless, wheelchair-accessible van with five other prisoners: two armed-robbers; a granny murderer; a taxi driver who'd raped six of his passengers over a long weekend and had been sentenced, in his words, to "four years with no vaginal scent"; and another man who'd been convicted of raping his wife, and who, the taxi driver said, "was so pussy-whipped, he couldn't even rape outside of marriage." This was already unbearable.

After a half-hour drive, the van halted and the door opened onto an abandoned-looking prison courtyard reminiscent of a library on Sunday. There I was given green overalls and blankets and sheets but no pillowcase. Voices were chanting, "Spoiled meat! Spoiled meat!" I wheeled myself down a corridor into my semi-dark cell where there was a metal bed and a seatless steel toilet and a cellmate who sat nursing more than a few animal fears. That was a good sign. He was afraid of me. His name was Patrick and he told me he was in for recruiting a child to carry out a criminal act; it sounded like there was a good story behind that, but he wouldn't elaborate.

—Can we still vote? There's an election coming up.

Patrick didn't know.

—Hey, I called out, does anyone know if we can still vote? For some reason, that was very important to me at the time.

—No, the answer came back from another cell. I was devastated. We were voiceless again, like children.

Other than being free from the omnipresence of advertisers for the first time since infanthood, this next phase of my life was to be principally about violence. Random. Indiscriminate. Institutional. Sexual. Being disabled, the third-highest risk category after gay and transgendered, I'd always feared I would fall victim to the single most underreported crime in all three of our societies: hospital, regular, prison. Now it turned out that my old terror of random violence was dwarfed by my fear of systemic violence. Sure, nobody was going to mistake my body for a garden of earthly delights, but that didn't make me unrape-able. And worse luck—I'd be at crotch height to everybody.

XXXI

Your Honor, in the miasma of sweaty feet, shit-smelling soap, and masses of uncircumcised penises fermenting in unwashed underpants, I got into countless he said/he said arguments, had my pain medication stolen, was rocketed down corridors with another paraplegic named Ted by old-time-y white supremacists on gladiatorial afternoons, was gnashed on by the serial rapist Paul

"Episiotomy" Williams, discovered I am genuinely claustrophobic and somewhat agoraphobic, a crowded prison being the worst of both hells, and was allowed—no, encouraged—to soil myself by guards who also, I noted, loved confiscating hearing aids from older inmates. And I was the beneficiary of endless lessons: A kind smile does not mitigate but aggravates violence; the enemy of my enemy is still my goddamn enemy; cruel and unusual punishments are seldom unusual . . .

The most important lesson, however: In lockup, you don't go once more into the fray, the fray comes to you. Case in point. A bald man mouth-breathing at the door of our cell.

—Who are you?

—The skin is the largest organ in the body.

—Uh-oh.

In a flash, a group of about seven adult children of absent fathers crowded the cell, the hefty, blank-eyed types of criminals who make their victims dig their own graves, either to intensify the horror or for simple practical reasons. They wheeled me out of my cell and down the corridor and through a set of doors—unlocked by a winking guard—and into H division. Fuck me with a hadron collider. I knew exactly where we were going. When we got there, Elliot clambered down from his bunk and held his hands out as if warming them against a fire.

This is not how Elliot looked in Mimi's photographs. He was bigger, more muscular, and now with a broken nose, missing teeth, scarified cheeks, jittery left eyelid, and veins pulsing in his temples. He was the whole package.

—What happened, Vesuvius? All plugged up? You bodiless snake. Welcome to the caves. Morrell has been fucking her for months and what have you done to stop him?

It was weird to hear that familiar voice pouring out of that toothless face.

—How the fuck do you *know* that?

—How do you think, genius?

It only now occurred to me there was nothing supernatural in his omniscience.

—You've got someone there, someone in the residence pretending to be an artist. Elliot lowered his head and peered up at me with a sick smile.

—There are two types of prisoners. Bears that hibernated too long and landlocked children with a sea wind of their own. Jesus. What's going on there? Your spasticity could thresh corn. You're in for how long? When I get out I'm subletting a schoolgirl's virginity for the summer. Don't breathe so much. The air in prison is hallucinogenic. You do know I overpowered the inmate that had been paid to protect me *and* pocketed the money, so Mimi is fucking Morrell to pay me to protect myself. You know that, right? You know that when I was in Eastern Europe with Mimi, during the last fake exorcism I felt a demon pass out of her body and enter mine. I never told anyone that before.

During this strange disconnected monologue, I realized, in a sort of dawning horror, he wore his own knocked-out teeth in a necklace. I had the bizarre sensation that if I dared to turn around and look, the images his mind conjured would be projected onto the cell walls behind me. He rolled his eyes as if in reference to the drudgery of terrorizing me, then abruptly looted his own shelves and piled books in my lap. Thomas Merton. Angelus Silesius. Simone Weil. Meister Eckhart. Emanuel Swedenborg.

—Read them! An indestructible glut of revelations that I wrote in past lives, he said, making a hand motion as if to caress his aura, and it being that religiousness is always the first resort of the criminally insane (along with public masturbation and matricide), I took them in the spirit they were given and even began to feel easier in his company. As if reacting to my unexpected calm, Elliot punched me in the side of the head, lifted me from my chair, and pinioned me to the wall with his big, heavy face pressed up against mine.

—Do you know about the tribe of Benjamin in the Bible?

—No.

—With God's blessing and with impunity they raped the virgins of the town of Shiloh.

—Oh.

—Have you been beaten with your own wheelchair yet?

—Elliot. Please.

—Are you HIV negative?

A thoughtful silence seemed the most appropriate response to that loaded question.

—You thought the worst was behind you.

His tongued flicked out and ran over his lower lip. I thought: De-escalate! De-escalate! I was frozen with fear. And here's where language fails me. Or where I fail language. One of the men pushed his grubby trigger fingers into my mouth then hurled me onto the floor. Fists and shoes came flying at my face and body. I tell you, these substance-abusing hypermasculine narcissistic and avoidant personalities with elevated scores on both the Buss-Durkee Hostility Inventory and the Abuse-Perpetration Inventory were really letting me have it. One stooped down and picked me up by my armpits then threw me facedown onto the cold steel bed and—here goes nothing—raped me.

Yes, Your Honor, I *am* going to talk about this.

I guess they'd had the empathy likewise fucked out of them at the onset of incarceration or were disinhibited out of fear of Elliot—either way, adjust your antennae to receive my maximum horror, random citizens who have nothing better to do on a Tuesday morning, while I recount a memory engraved by meathooks:

Hard hands on my shoulders. A foot on my neck. I felt them tugging my pants off. I said, Be careful, fellas. Raping me is a slippery slope to raping me again. I didn't really say that. I'm stalling. In truth—I groveled, flailed, begged, sobbed. I felt abnormal discomfort, as if a distant body part were being removed. Then I felt horrific pain. A running of the bulls, a goring, a harrowing series of thrusts. This is it, I thought. I am being raped. This will be forever in my bio. The single possible consoling thought, that *so many* had gone through it, was not consoling at all. Every second snuck up on me. My head collided with the brick wall and blood dripped into my eyes and *still*, I thought, a billion people are worse off than me right now. Then I thought: Turning dead is not the same as dying and the darkest darkness is also blinding and the saddest truth on earth is you only get conclusive evidence of the existence of your soul *as* it evacuates. My focus shifted from the chalk-white wall to a quarter-window's view of barbed wire, looming and fanged. If only this were a dramatic reenactment of the Stanford Prison Experiment and any moment the lead researcher was going to call it off.

Elliot put his frightless eyes near mine and gave an equine snort. I thought: If only I could pull off a classic thrust behind the collarbone to the ascending aorta or smash his ribs causing fractured bone fragments to lacerate the bladder and intestines so digestive juices and feces will pour like the Ganges into his peritoneal cavity, but I had no weapons; I was overpowered. A second rapist joined in. I wanted to vaporize or disintegrate, like in my old fantasy, and liquefy in my sleep or be a voiceless faceless thoughtless drifting eye cruising through space and time before disappearing in a violent white flash. I was a well filled with blood. I was all chasm. I was broken in two, in four, in eight. I was torn asunder. I was wolfed down. I was dividing into an embryo and being born again. Again! This time into who? Who knows? This was a psychiatric emergency. I sank and didn't resurface. Good-bye, self, we'll meet back and reintegrate later. An inmate, I noticed, was filming this on a camera phone. So *that's* out there somewhere. A stream of my blood soaked the mattress where my head lay. I thought of Natasha Hunt. Of Jin. Of the Red Army sweeping into Germany in '45. I thought: Violated is the absolutely right synonym for rape. And: If I could get my hands on those husbands and fathers in certain cultures (Is-*cough*-lamic) who stone the raped for promiscuity. Or maybe I thought these things after. At the time I was swept away in the countervailing horrors and geysers of rage as, I imagined, blood-borne pathogens moved through my mucus membranes. Let's face it. From year dot to right this minute the mind-blowing rate of forced intercourse is *the* biggest thorn in the side of every single floated theory of basic human goodness.

—Shut your mouth, bitch.

—Consider this a warning.

A warning? Jesus.

It was over. Elliot declared with a smile that reporting the attacks would result in castration involving bolt cutters, then he winched me up and put a glass shiv to my eyeball and—I'm just giving you the facts, these are the facts—made me perform oral sex on both rapists, at the end of which one of them urinated into my mouth.

Earthlings. Blech.

It would be fine with me, Your Honor, if the ladies and gentlemen of the jury would like a moment to call their loved ones.

In that case, I will continue.

Some weeks, or perhaps months later, I woke with my stomach horribly distended and stabbing abdominal pains. I was drenched in sweat with a pounding headache, my face burning and a tingling on my tongue.

—As my daddy always says, looks like your shit just became manure, son, said Patrick.

Guards came in pairs like feuding siblings.

—What's wrong with you?

—I'm fine. Please just nip down to the apothecary and fetch me some milk of the poppy.

The guards ferried me out to the nearest hospital, where I was diagnosed as having had a transient ischemic attack—a mini-stroke—precipitated by, the doctor said in an annoyed voice, as if I were the only one who'd turned up to his seminar, a high-blood-pressure spike symptomatic of autonomic dysreflexia that was in turn brought on by fecal impactions.

And that's not all! The distension of the abdominal area was unrelated to the stroke, and so they forced me to have barium studies of the upper gastrointestinal tract which revealed a relatively rare spinal complication called superior mesenteric artery syndrome, a compression of the duodenum. This they treated immediately with nasogastric intubation, and when that failed, I was rushed into surgery for a fucking duodenojejunostomy, performed laparoscopically. You know the drill. Unfortunately recovery time was quick, so I was to be back in prison in four days, except that results from my MRI showed a small neurofibroma tumor near the spine.

—What's amazing, said the doctor with naked excitement, is that had you not had your car accident, this tumor might have remained undetected and grown to a size that would have compressed your spinal cord.

—Amazing, I said.

I was wheeled through metal doors with yellow radiation-warning signs, the kind fastened to the top and sides of nuclear-warhead carrying cases in espionage thrillers, into a cavernous room where I was laid sideways on a table and my head molded to a blue semi-inflatable pillow where I had a constant view of the worried-looking cartoon fetus with the uneducated or oblivious mother in an IF YOU'RE PREGNANT TELL THE RADIOLOGIST sign, who I heavily identified with (the fetus, not the mother). There was a lot of fiddling, lowering and raising of the platform, signifying ample room for human error; a rotating computer screen's red eye that looked to have achieved intelligence but was keeping mum about it made a sluggish orbit around my body while emitting a low-resolution horror-movie hum. It was called a Gamma Knife. The aim was to fuck up my DNA to make the cancer cells unable to divide while avoiding collateral damage of healthy tissue. Basically, it was six million concentrated volts as invisible as God himself.

Ladies and gentlemen of the jury, during the months that followed I was transferred from prison to hospital and hospital to prison on a seemingly continuous loop. From the suffocation of solitary confinement to the suffocation of the MRI machine. Inedible prison food to inedible hospital food. Fear of the shiv to fear of the scalpel. I was in prison to be wrecked, in hospital to be salvaged. I often found myself in a hospital elevator with another prisoner who was handcuffed and couldn't cover his mouth when he coughed, or in waiting areas with poor suckers who sat with the placidity of cows or tottered and staggered along the corridors clutching those big white CT-scan envelopes, or in radiotherapy which carried the fear of impending nausea (emetophobia) that was followed by actual nausea from the radiation (no doubt exacerbated by the nurse/doctor treacly chitchat), after which I would then be taken back to prison for the malevolent zeal of sexual violence. No, I will never understand the allure of raping me, other than to fill personal quotas, yet at least once every couple of months, Elliot or one of his men with their nautical faces and neck tattoos lurched out of shadows to drag me into designated nooks and supervision blindspots for protracted attacks, with their all too human casual brutality and zero incidence of erectile dysfunction, impeccably choreographed with the movements of the guards. Or else coming into my cell at all hours. My whole dumb life I always hated being woken, but to be jerked from a horrific nightmare to an even more horrific reality was categorically hellish. My single consoling thought was maybe radiation was transmitted, maybe I was literally radioactive and toxic. I'd think: *My superpower is that I AM POISON.*

Here's where it gets strange.

One night, the silence thickening around me, I lay on the floor of my tiny cell, regretting the past, hating the present, dreading the future, thinking that since I suffered the hell of anticipating a rapist unbuttoning his pants or a doctor tapping a syringe, and since it was invariably followed by an IV hookup or an actual rape, this meant I had pre-traumatic stress disorder, then trauma, then post-traumatic stress disorder, often simultaneously. Then I thought: If thinking is only a poor form of dreaming, and dreaming a poor form of pure being, and pure being a poor form of nonexistence, then nonexistence is a poor form of never-having-existed-at-all. Frankly, I was pissed off that to vanish and dissolve by an act of will, to liquefy in my sleep and disintegrate body and soul, to be uncreated and unborn—*decreated*—like Simone Weil writes about, was beyond my ability. All the time, inmates' voices from adjoining cells filled my own:

—Who took my lucky shiv?

—She was raped *and* murdered? That's mission creep.

—Guard! I shouted. Ever consider soundproofing these walls? You can do it with egg cartons!

I worked out in the exercise room at every available opportunity. Free weights. Dumbbells. Focused on my upper body. In the showers I avoided victim-precipitated homicide as best I could. At mealtimes I feigned uncorked aggression. When asked, I gave friendly psychological consultations to my fellow inmates. Listen, there's a time to plant a seed of evil and a time to harvest! That sounds fine, just keep your revenge fantasies modest! Why not shit into your hands and throw it at the guards? Etc.

The hospital. The violence. The painful gastroesophageal reflux. It was piling in from all sides, like a peak-hour crush. In one multifariously horrific month: the manslaughter conviction for killing the boy with the brick wall added six months to my sentence, I had my last dose of radiotherapy, was forced to swallow punitive mouthfuls of brackish-tasting semen, endured the use of my anus as a purse in which to hide drugs during a cell search, and contracted a pressure sore on my coccyx. I was in and out of the visiting room in a blur. When I informed Mimi how truly psychotic and evil Elliot really was, that only triggered a spiky exchange during which in a cold, implacable voice she accused me of smearing his good character out of jealousy. Help me, I cried to Liam. Some penises are like silos! Others barely a phallus! How superior Liam felt in his uniform and how inferior he appeared. No touching! the guard shouted when I reached for Stella's hand. OK, but can we spoon? I asked. It was hard not to touch her in her low-cut blouse—she smelled like soap from our old house. Then I was visited by Morrell, his face slack and tired. Mimi did it, he said. Did what? I asked. Morrell's exhibition had been deliberately burnt down an hour before opening night. Classic Mimi, I thought. After losing his paintings he'd tried to return to his old job at Zetland High, but the substitute who'd replaced him had already been replaced by a full-time teacher, he whined.

Then that afternoon, or perhaps it was another, I was assaulted by a man eating a sandwich—this was a working lunch!—and I said aloud, Oh Lord, they know not what they do, but they sure as shit enjoy doing it!

—I forgive you, I said to my assailant. (My theory was any old fool could forgive after a period of contemplation and a wound-healing passage of time, but instantaneous forgiveness would Blow. Their. Minds.)

In response he came in with a tea kettle—and not to make me a cuppa. That's why lying there burnt and blistering on the floor of my cell, patting down the actual bottom of the abyss, facedown in a pool of tears and succumbing to the kind of fit of irresistible laughter that can take one to the ER, I prayed.

Ladies and gentlemen of the jury, it is not just that whenever I pray I feel like I'm waving to someone across the street with the sun in my eyes, or feel the same way as when I can't catch a bartender's eye on a Friday night, but I fear that praying risks interrupting God when he's fine-tuning a tsunami or manually conjoining twins. What makes it weirder is the fact that I'm agnostic. Of course I wasn't born that way. In my preteen years I worshipped Apollo, but was later shamed into dropping him because everyone else was into Buddha or Jesus or Mohammed or Krishna, and Apollo was simply not *contemporary* enough. Imagine my disappointment to learn that Apollo was deity non grata! But still I had a hunger for God that developed into a steady appetite; I nibbled the edges of his magnificent being, I found him bitter, I spat him out. There was a part of me that missed Him, of course, that missed the God who loves each of us like a carnival barker loves his most hideous attraction, but I couldn't find my way back, and what's more, whenever I told someone I was an atheist they'd say, don't you believe in *anything*? As if any nonsense would do. As if faith itself is the virtue, and what you believe is inconsequential. So I moved from atheism to agnosticism. As I matured, I came to the conclusion that believing in God was a mostly harmless foible, like when you know someone who is meaner than necessary to his pets—not *exactly* a reason to end a friendship, but a clear warning sign of hazardous character faults. Anyhow, there I was on the cold concrete floor, praying with the fervor of a man masturbating on the eve of his castration.

I said,

God grant me the serenity to de-escalate my fears before they turn into self-fulfilling prophecies, the courage to downgrade my premonitions to fears, and the wisdom to know the difference. God, I went on, other than racial persecution, hunger and slut shaming, there is no torment that I am unaccustomed to.

Why did paralysis and rape have to be my sentimental education? I know we often forget that "human rights" is a thing we totally made up, but it still burns when your own are violated. Kudos for leveling the killing field, God, but have You too forgotten our safe word? Did You hear me when I withdrew consent? Exactly whose revenge fantasy am I living? Why has life always seemed like a pretrial hearing? Why were my rock bottoms so near the top? For a while—I'll admit—I was secretly flattered by my absurd dilemmas, as if being bested by You meant there was something inside me worth annihilating, but do You know what paralysis does to a person's inferiority complex?

I am asking You directly in my sick voice: Did I not honor my mother and father? All children play dead! Boys especially like to feign death to scare their mothers. Is it because I practised the black magic of withholding love? Did I not visit Leila enough in her ridiculous see-through apartment all lit up like Gatsby's, where I'd have to endure watching her eating partially de-fatted pork fatty tissue right out of a can of potted meat? Was I wrong to laugh when her liposuction sutures caught on the zipper of her velvet trackpants? Was it bad to get annoyed when she checked out labels on the back of strangers' shirts? Was it dishonorable to tell her that complaining about rising crime levels was a pleasure she wouldn't have forgone in exchange for a safer community? I know she sacrificed a lot for me—but did she? Wasn't her sacrifice really for *her*, so she could experience motherhood?

Why was I red-flagged? Were You annoyed I'd been God-proofed by Leila's piety and therefore never *really* believed in You? Is it my fault I found Your expectation for us to buy You sight unseen unreasonable and in Your "holy" book I hated the prodigal son with a passion?

Or was it a sexual transgression? Are You that kind of God after all? Is it because when I was a teenager all I wanted was to move to a town so sleazy that when you walked down the street every man would be stepping out of a shadowed doorway, doing up his fly; because I *wanted* to be a sex addict, even though I might as well have been addicted to gold ingots? Is it my treatment of women? Who did I personally subjugate? The men that women are afraid of—I am too! I'd stand up to the abusers, but frankly, they're in women's homes and they won't let me in. Was it because I found the battle of the sexes utterly tiresome? (*They* make a pregnancy pact. *We* make a vasectomy pact. *They* make virginity pledges. *We* order porn.) So what if I want to consummate *everyone's* marriage? What man doesn't? I was OK that nobody ever considered me forbidden fruit, yet it's true when I smiled at a woman in a bar I often felt like Goebbels putting ampules of cyanide in his children's mouths. I get it: women are punished for their bodies (men are punished for being a dime a dozen), but did I personally silence, or oppress? I realize being too shy for catcalling does not let me off the hook. And true, until too recently I thought teenage runaways were hot: like everyone of my gender, I've been deep-pornofried—but I swear eroticised violence was never my thing. And I admit it's been over a decade since my last age-appropriate sexual fantasy. And one night in Dubai, when I was as poor as a dust-bowl farmer and schmoozing potential investors, a group of venture capitalists came into my hotel room with a young woman and said, I hope you don't have a fear of flying; we chartered a vagina, a six-seater. And I didn't get up and leave. I stayed, oh God, I stayed. If Kant was right and history is the narrative of men's moral progress, then my personal history has not yet begun—granted—but let me stress: *no* to harassment, *no* to battery, *yes* to objectification, *no* to subordination (I have consensually bound but not gagged), *no* to drugging (but yes to hypnotising), and *no to rape*. Because while clinical frustration makes tyrants rageful and tantrums violent, my record is clean. Anyway, I am the amateur. You the pro. You disciplined my sister, and good.

Remember when Henry died, I said, God, You just lost a customer. And since then I haven't prayed—I preferred to communicate through solicitors—but after Leila's death I shouted to the sky, I'm not afraid to die but I'm afraid of dying. And a voice shouted back, it's a routine procedure—I perform 150,000 of them every single day. Was that You, or was that in my head?

Or wait—am I being disproportionately punished for the night of Liam's out-of-control party, upstairs in that bedroom in that empty house, after Stella mocked me because I could not define the word labia and I said, some are born me, some become me, and some have me thrust upon them, then I prematurely ejaculated, and was so spent that when I saw Natasha out the window running down the street screaming for help I did nothing, and never told anyone?

Or is it because later, Stella and I crossed every smutty frontier? Or because I made her mad by giving her a shoddy ceremony and then quoting Lacan in our wedding vows: *Love is giving something you haven't got to someone who doesn't exist*? Or because at Wave Rock I told her to sing with a dead baby in her womb? (About love, I was on the fence—until You electrified it. In any case, the map of the human heart does not match the terrain.) Is it because after the divorce, I was bummed I would never be able to write a suicide note that started *Dear Widow Benjamin*?

Or because I took total advantage of my friends? I thought all you needed to be a good friend in this life was to know a little cognitive therapy and pharmapsychology—was I wrong? Is it because of my business ambitions, that it's unseemly to reach the age of forty and not lower your expectations? Is it because I've pitied people who remind me of me? Is it because of the palpable sense of relief I feel passing children's hospitals—because I've *outgrown* them? Is it because I've been the tenant in a landlord-tenant biting dispute and the romantic who stole flowers from roadside memorials? Is it because I've preemptively apologized so I could treat someone like shit, told insulting punchlines without setups, used repugnance as my moral compass, veiled my barefaced lies, interrupted, shushed, monologued, cut in line? Is it because I've found racial biases to be as stubborn to remove as red wine from a carpet and wondered if two ugly people should adopt to give a child a better life? Is it because having ridden bicycles into clotheslines, had doggy doors slammed in my face and laughed stitches open, I've looked at the sky and wished geocruisers would slam into us—that I half prayed for mass extinction so I'd *know* I wouldn't be missing anything upon my death?

Tell me once and for all: I*s bad luck self-harm by another name?* Is it? Is it? Is it? Lord, You made me perceptive. You gave me the power to know things. I *know* you shouldn't listen when someone tells you to be true to yourself—instead of to other, kinder people. I *know* that the proper behavior when one meets a celebrity is to mistake them for another celebrity. I *know* the great surprise of life is that the inevitable and the inconceivable always turn out to be the same thing. I *know* that unconditional love is impossible without unconditional fear; that congested housing leads to incest; that the only thing that can save us from our more unsavory desires is observing those same desires in the faces of others, but Lord, why did You make me one of the few people who forget how to ride a bike? And why wouldn't You just deactivate me like I asked? The future is some kind of newfangled yesterday I want no part of, that's why I've always envied insects and flowers who live for a single day, and I only never wanted to die on public transportation or during a vasectomy reversal. Now I see! I should've just married a black widow!

Didn't Freud suggest that the aim of the organism is to die in its own way? Why can't I die in mine? Why are You holding me up to impossible standards? It's somehow my own fault. I won't say "self-sabotage"—that's a phrase you use to flatter yourself while admitting blame. Freud again: *The psychical significance of a drive rises in proportion to its frustration.* Lord, I don't have to tell You. I have not enough agency to wiggle a toe. Frustration is where I live. Is this punishment? For what? Did my mother spawn a monster? I know whenever a beggar asked me for money on the street I often said, no thanks, as if *he* had offered *me* money, but that was an involuntary response. Similarly, in relation to seeing deformed people, a gag reflex is not inherently judgemental. Be fair.

Or wait—there's one more possibility. Was it because I was not a good brother to my sister? When she turned on me, was it really only the storm of female adolescence? How is it possible a girl can go from laughing till she almost tears her stomach lining to crouching on the bottom of a drained swimming pool with her head in her hands? When Veronica was fifteen and refused to go to our cousin Devin's wedding (for fear of bumping into him), Henry took us aside and bellowed his personal maxim, one I've never forgotten: *Friends don't care whether you live or die. It's only family that counts.* Was this true? Personally, I found his reverence for blood ties psychologically suspect. After Veronica's death, Leila dragged me away from the compound—why did we move away? I thought it was because the Benjamins were gossips and petty thieves and cat torturers, because they were only a facial feature away from being total strangers to us. But was there another reason? I see nothing in the old home movies to give me pause. (I love Super 8. Our home movies are nearly indistinguishable from Hitler's.) There's us chasing huntsmen and Bogong moths and herding ants with rivulets of hose water, and there's Uncle Brett, whose nose hairs were as thick and twangy as harp strings, and Great-Uncle Gary with his long ink-black hair who adored out of all proportion his Chinese snuff bottles, and there's cousin Paul who put his cigarette out on the back of his hand at a party. There they all are, the Benjamin men, waving their wet, anonymous eyes and ergodynamic heads around. Was it one of them? or none of them? Veronica bathed with the lights out, it occurs to me now—is that something I should have asked about? I peered in as the funeral parlor readied her repatriated body for the service and I was shocked to see her head shaved and a tattoo of A Flock of Seagulls between her shoulderblades. What happened in Indonesia, exactly? Why didn't I ask Leila when I had the chance?

I don't know. I don't know.

I don't know anything other than that the greatest misconception about the apocalypse is that it is a sudden, brief event. It is not. It is slow. Grindingly slow. It goes for generations.

I can't quite put my finger on it, Lord, can I borrow Yours? The log-sized one from the Sistine Chapel? Am I insane? Has the pain rewired my brain? Human endurance is absurd. It can take ANYTHING. You *know* this. Can't there please be a point where once a person has reached a maximum of suffering they just *explode*?

Lord, give me a doll and I'll show You where You touched me.
    Amen.

Silence. Just silence. Maybe my prayer went to his spam file. In any case, then it was morning and one of the least pleasant guards turned up at my door. He said, S'pose *you're* excited, Legless. I said, What about, Bitch Tits? He said, You're out, Cunt. I laughed and said, Don't you mean in about eighteen months,

you Horror of a Human Being? He squinted with all the toxicity he could drain
from his unbearable existence. You've been here two and a half years, Fuckface.
Time's up. I sat up with a surprised expression one usually sees on a head rolling into a basket. An ungraspable turn of events—had I been praying that long?
In the showers, I broke my third commandment and looked in the mirror. My
legs had grown thinner, my knees knobblier, my eyes googlier, my hair sparser,
but all those crunches, squats, rows, and presses had made my chest, back,
shoulders, biceps, triceps and quads weirdly yet impressively inflated. Then I
dressed in my civilian clothes and made my way out the gates where absolutely
no one asked me to sign the guestbook. But who cared? I was in remission.
And free!

XXXII

From the passenger's window of the wheelchair-accessible taxi, the outside
world looked digitally colorized. Ochre sky; faraway, tepid sun. The office
buildings buffeted the frenzied winds that tore in from the east. On the streets,
people who looked like they wanted to interbreed with their screens; women
with yoga backs pushing strollers while berating husbands or personal assis-
tants on phones; war veterans living stump to mouth, and I could perceive their
suffering—their sore balls and sinus headaches, I could hear their brief pleas
for hard currency and tight bodies and loving hearts. Then into the suburbs,
past houses where once I could sense the death of a family pet or an impending
divorce but could never pinpoint the exact location—now I could. The taxi
took me to the coast, a glimpse of the breathless sea, and clouds that looked like
sopping bath towels. Then we arrived. That rambling freestanding house, that
sun-dappled wild garden on all sides, that camphor tree: the residence, on what
would be the deceased's last night on earth.

It's hard to describe the disorientation of that chaos. A WELCOME BACK
ALDO banner hung over the portico, and I was inundated with handshakes,
nods, cheek kisses, backslaps, hair ruffles, shoulder rubs, from both familiar
and unfamiliar drunk artists—imagine if Goya painted the faces found inside
a casino at dawn—who moved as if on conveyor belts to show me sculptures,
drawings, still-wet paintings of yours truly: caged and beady-eyed, oddly thin
and bleeding in magentas and crimsons and indigos, in cadmium yellows and

lava reds. The artists were either proud of their ingenuity or apologized for misrepresenting their intentions. The packs of new dogs and fresh rubble and sleep-deprived children and the muted hysteria and combined beards and near nakedness of both genders made me feel harried and confused, being neither in the hospital nor the prison universe, and I could barely talk to anybody—their twisted, crunchy smiles terrified me—and navigated my way around poorly, rolling over feet. I was hurried into inebriation, a joint and a beer thrust in my hand, cocaine pushed up my nostrils, as I scanned the room for Elliot's inside man, but to me everyone looked like a "person of interest" you might see "helping police with their inquiries." In addition, I felt embarrassed at seeing everybody, as if in this interim period I ought to have found a replacement body.

Mimi herself looked bad, her hair like seaweed and her eyes dried-out puddles, while Stella tucked and retucked her breasts into her leather corset and kissed Frank Rubinstein—they were a couple! The unexpectedness of this completely destabilized me. I wheeled over to Morrell, who was naked under his polyester poncho and groping everybody, apparently adjusting to his burnt-out exhibition by going insane. Where was I exactly? Freedom had never seemed so turbulent or repulsive, never so chaotic and formless a thing. I made a mad dash out to the balcony and I remained there until the rusted sunset sky went dark and stars sweated in the glassy moonlight. Down in the beach parking lot, headlights tunneled through the mist. Mimi came out and stood beside my chair and stared with slumberous eyes at the sea as if through a windshield at an endless desert road. For a long time she didn't blink or budge. Then without asking she wheeled me back inside, through the party and into her bedroom where we both took sleeping pills and held each other. I lay there listening to her chest rise and fall, and to the wind that grew intense, to sand-swept seagulls that flew onto the windowsill for a breather. Mimi slept erect, strangely rigid in the bed. Finally I passed out and dreamed, I think, of the herped mouths of New York mohels.

I woke up and heard the sea on its permanent war footing. There was a sickening smell, like burnt heroin. I turned to Mimi: rivulets of blood from her mouth down her chin, glazed eyes bulging in their sockets. Except for the blood and the eyes, she was untrammeled and peaceful, but her face was no longer her face, her body not her body.

Mimi was dead.

No trace elements of her anguish. Just an empty slate. I suddenly felt ashamed that I didn't really love her because I knew her, I loved her because I needed to.

I called for help. The artists rushed in and crowded the bed and yelled, Citizen's arrest! Citizen's arrest!

Ech. The worst.

The police were called. My insistence that I should be treated as an eyewitness, not a suspect, and that the police should be interrogating the artists to deduce who placed a knife into my unconscious hand was ignored; the attending detective seemed bored and distracted, as if he'd been listening to a story in which his favorite character inexplicably disappeared from the narrative. Liam arrived just in time to stand helplessly as the detective arrested me on the spot. I was taken back into custody because, I was told, murder was a violation of my parole.

Hauled back to prison. After only eleven hours of freedom.

It was that very night, ladies and gentlemen of the jury, in my cell, downwind to myself, covered in blue-tinted shadows, at my lowest moment, lower than the floor of the abyss, listening to the irregular breathing of my new cellmate, Gary (convicted of witness tampering and whose head had all the hallmarks of a forceps birth), when I heard it.

A voice.

No, not just a voice.

A cold trumpet blast of wonder that dwelled in my inner ear! A sonar beam of divine wattage that had the UV-brightness of unveiled truth! A sound that left me feeling lighter, less creaturely. This was no wordless experience of the divine. In truth, it was quite verbose. I didn't just hear it. I inhaled, imbibed, suckled at it. Now I understand those mystics who talk about loving God *physically*, like they want to straddle him right there on his throne. Of course you might say: What lesion spoke to you thus? Or are you sure this wasn't a psychotic episode or that your primary auditory cortex wasn't on the blink? Are you sure it wasn't just a part of you speaking that had been removed, like a phantom consciousness or a surplus soul? Either way, I could hear it plain as day in my fucking cochlear, a cattle prod of a voice. It was delicious, stupefying! I was traumatized by its beauty. I yielded totally. Whether it was divine or extraterrestrial or from this or that side of the human–angel divide does not matter. It came from on high, in any case. Sometimes the voice was like a poet reading me a work-in-progress. Other times it was businesslike and hesitant, like a doctor who gives you just two weeks to live but is also going through a personal crisis. It was a voice that wore a ponytail. It was sea air blown through a bong. The cell filled with light, and I was whistling "Hallelujah." Only now is the measureless joy beginning to wear off. Quite the comedown, I assure you.

Ladies and gentlemen of the jury: This verdict is overripe. Pronounce it already. The defense rests; the defense, frankly, is exhausted. The defense has been beaten, raped, paralyzed, bankrupted, and enslaved. Just say I'm innocent, will you? Let it be known that Aldo Benjamin has only butchered and decapitated people in Photoshop. My charm wears off like a local anesthetic, I know—and that was *hours* ago. I sincerely thank you for your attention, your patience, your impressive lack of toilet breaks. Just remember: You can't convict simply because a custodial sentence will reduce the risk of running into me at the supermarket.

Unless—just before I go, do you want to know the substance of my conversation with the divine? Would you like me to reveal the amazing truths I heard?

I certainly don't want to take much more of the court's valuable time.

As you wish.

Your Honor, I now submit my final piece of evidence—exhibit E—the transcript of the conversation I had with the voice, a transcript I made the following morning while the details were still freshly and indelibly imprinted in my mind:

Voice: Aldo.
  Me: Piss off.
Voice: Aldo.
  Me: I said piss off!
Voice: It's time to stop feeling sorry for yourself.
  Me: Why?
Voice: You often say, I didn't ask to be born. Have you considered the possibility that the Lord has irrefutable evidence—a recording of the whole conversation?
  Me: Gary, that's the stupidest thing I ever heard.

Voice: This isn't Gary. Look. He's sleeping.

Me: Oh. Oh!

Voice: Yeah. So sit up and look smart. Stop feeling sorry for yourself and feeling sorry for yourself *about* feeling sorry for yourself.

Me: What does that even mean?

Voice: Isn't it true that the more self-pity you feel, the more regular pity you feel for others?

Me: I guess.

Voice: No, you don't guess. I'm telling you something. Self-pity gets no respect around here, let alone pity, but when you think back to your whole life, can't you credit self-pity for opening your heart out to the world? Didn't self-pity propel you to pity others, and then to feeling that pity? Where else were you going to get empathy from—*Leila*?

Me: I suppose you're right.

Voice: But what's the point of being empathetic if you don't get in the mix?

Me: So you're saying, the empathy I have felt in my life for the sufferers in my immediate surrounds—

Voice: Counts for nothing. Actually, less than nothing. Less than a self-absorbed solipsist. Less than a sadist. When one understands. Convulsions of empathy are actually *immoral* if you won't get your hands dirty.

Me: Is that why I've suffered so much?

Voice: No.

Me: Just as I thought. Meaningless.

Voice: You're so wrong. Suffering *has* meaning, *just not for the sufferer.*

Me: Oh.

Voice: Suffering's all about other people. What others do about *your* suffering defines *their* ethical stand in life and what you do about *their* suffering defines yours.

Me: I guess I can buy that. So because I've done exactly nothing to ease anyone's suffering, *that's* why God's fucking with me?

Voice: No. Listen. The creation of the universe was a motiveless crime—though not a victimless one, obviously.

Me: Obviously.

Voice: But would you not agree that a god who cannot turn his omniscience off—nor shorten eternity—is limited?

Me: I would.

Voice: You sure you haven't made a mistake assigning agency to God?

Me: Have I?

Voice: You're awfully critical. Let me let you in on something. God loves a heckler but loathes backseat creationists.

Me: I just have this fear that one day God will forget to back up and lose everything.

Voice: You have an unusually high number of fears.

Me: Is fear dangerous?

Voice: People with castration anxiety do lose their testicles, but so do people without it.

Me: Is bad luck self-harm by another name?

Voice: What do you think?

Me: I think an entire planetary suicide would be worth it just for the look on God's face.

(the voice laughs)

Me: I got dicks flying at me from all angles! This shit's funny to you?

Voice: My turn to ask a question. What do you *actually know* about the ineffable?

Me: Only this: if you had a peek at its profile you would not hook up with your own soul on match.com.

Voice: Let me ask you, why is an agnostic praying? Why now? You're like those people whose relationships with God begin and end on airplanes during severe turbulence. This is a divine booty call, isn't it?

Me: Yeah, all right. I'll cop to that. I'm not actually a believer.

Voice: The thing is, I don't blame you. Why should you be? Imagine, if you will, a person with no nerves at all—he cannot see, hear, smell, taste, or feel—*now* who wants to meet the Holy Spirit?

Me: No one.

Voice: Right. What do we know about the risen Jesus other than his head shot? Isn't the resurrection just three days he never got back? And

I never understood why people are expected to cry for Christ's suffering in particular when one hundred others were crucified *the exact same day*, a *thousand* the same week. His suffering was pretty standard fare for that time and place.

Me: Or how we are expected to believe in God at all when there's so much evil in the world.

Voice: Haven't you ever heard of the bystander phenomenon?

Me: You mean, during the atrocities God's up there, expecting some other deity to intervene?

Voice: Maybe.

Me: I know history is littered with stories of people pissing on corpses. I've always found it curious that nobody ever shits on a corpse, not even in wartime, *not even in Auschwitz.*

Voice: That's true. But what's your point?

Me: I don't know. I'm just trying to find a way to say: Where the fuck has God been all this time?

Voice: Perhaps the sad answer for God's absence from human affairs is that he's been denied visitation rights.

Me: What are you saying? That God lost us in a custody battle with the devil?

Voice: Aldo, for those who love God, that love is enough.

Me: Yet any god who commands love doesn't understand the first thing about love.

Voice: Touché.

Me: In any case, love for God is just Stockholm syndrome.

Voice: God's silence is an injured silence.

Me: Injured by what?

Voice: Parkinson's, Alzheimer's, dementia are God's ways of acting out against mankind tripling the median mortality age and so rudely delaying their reunion with him. He's starting to think you're avoiding him!

Me: Look at Gary sleeping there. Why is it that whenever God or his angels talk to someone they are incapable of being overheard by a third party or corroborating ear-witness?

Voice: Is *that* really what you want to know? What else?

Me: Off the top of my head? Does God allow mass murder because it's like carpooling to heaven? In the afterlife do eunuchs get their balls back? Why didn't he send down a daughter? Or twins? Admittedly the creation of the universe was terrific, but why no encore? Is God's mobile ringtone the braying of an ass? And if he felt it necessary to point out right there in Leviticus *You shall not place a stumbling block before the blind,* what kind of cunts were running around Jerusalem back then? Are souls like fingerprints to identify the dead for processing? When it comes time for the dead to rise from their graves after Armageddon, what happens to all the cremated ash? Will it wriggle in jars and stir in flower beds and fish stomachs? It's understandable that those Axial Age miracles drained him of power, but that was over two thousand years ago; how long does it take the Lord to charge back up? If His son does come back, is He just going to raise the dead like last time? Does God so fundamentally misperceive human desire that he won't turn back the clock instead? Doesn't He know *that's* the miracle we've all been waiting for? To make Lazarus young again? And why the fuck didn't He simply make the inflictor of pain the equal recipient of its sensation? It's such an obvious idea, I'm almost embarrassed for having to suggest it!

Voice: You still want to talk about an absent father. A deadbeat dad.

Me: Yeah! Aren't we just seven billion children in a single-parent household? He's left Mother Earth holding the bag.

Voice: Let me ask *you* another question.

Me: Shoot.

Voice: What if I was to tell you that upon death God lets you ride him bareback, judges you Best in Show, waits on you hand and foot as reparation for the scandal of consciousness; He swaddles you in his endless beard, pulls out the complete set of recordings of all your interior monologues, that you have to listen to, but if you've given a lot to charity, He'll make you a compilation.

Me: I'd say that sounds awesome. Is that true?

Voice: The question is not, *Is that true,* Aldo. Nor, *Do you believe it to be true,* but *Can you believe it to be true?*

Me: Gobbledegook. What can I concretely tell the people of earth?

Voice: Children, if an angel wants to take you under his wing, run to the nearest adult.

Me: What else?

Voice: I'll give you a clue.

Me: To what?

Voice: To the answers you are truly seeking. Tell me, what is consciousness for?

Me: To become aware.

Voice: Of what?

Me: I don't know.

Voice: This is the human condition in one knock-knock joke: *Knock knock, it's me, Death. Who's there?*

Me: I get it.

Voice: So consciousness gives us awareness of what?

Me: That we are mortal.

Voice: Which leads us to?

Me: Seek.

Voice: Seek what?

Me: Meaning. God.

Voice: You're always asking, Where is He? Where is He? Why aren't you asking, *When* is He?

Me: When is he in Time?

Voice: Which is relative. Which is circular. Which loops. Am I right?

Me: You don't half-ask hard questions.

Voice: I'm not *asking* questions. I'm giving answers.

Me: That I don't understand.

Voice: You want an easier clue?

Me: Please.

Voice: Christian mystics report seeing Jesus, Muslims see Mohammed, Buddhists see the Buddha. What does this tell you?

Me: That we have the power to cast our own mystic visions.

Voice: Precisely. And?

Me: We're getting sick of waiting.

Voice: Waiting? Who are you *waiting* for? Who are *you* waiting for? Jesus?

Me: What's so funny?

Voice: Imagine on the first day of the Second Coming the priceless look on His face re: biodiversity! Imagine Him saying "Do unto others as you wish to be done unto you" to the subs in the S & M crowd! Imagine your crestfallen Lord rejected for His body mass index not being like it is in the paintings! Imagine a billion people tweeting their ultimatum: "An eye for an eye OR turn the other cheek. You can't have it both ways!"

Me: I've always felt we learn more about the cosmos from Buddha's death by poisoned mushrooms than from Christ's ostentatious showboating on the cross. Although nobody ever talks about the fact that because the Buddha abandoned his family, his greatest unsung legacy is actually the use of the philosophy of detachment to avoid child-support payments.

Voice: Let's face it, Aldo—as soon as the meek discover they are to inherit the earth they turn nasty. Happens every time.

Me: When you're right, you're right.

Voice: Christianity, Hinduism, Islam, Judaism are patently insufficient tools for answering twenty-first-century ethical questions, like: Is sexual intercourse with one's own clone masturbation or incest?

Me: Ooh. I know this one. Is it incest?

Voice: Your sclerotic churches, synagogues, and mosques have no idea, that's for damn sure.

Me: *This* is the pilgrim's frustrating lack of progress.

Voice: You look at your own life, Aldo, at your suffering, and what really pisses you off is there's no one you can drag to The Hague for this ultraspecific crime against humanity.

Me: You want to hear the truth? If there is a God, I'm just so sick to my stomach sick of Him. Who even *wants* a deity who'll crash a plane for a juicy haul of souls?

Voice: Is that what He's doing?

Me: And frankly, someone whose face you can't look into might as well be faceless.

Voice: Maybe He is. And maybe He's sensitive about it.

Me: And who even wants to be in a relationship with someone who freaks out when you say His name?

Voice: I can see how that might be a dealbreaker.

Me: And all this here, all my failures, my pain, my loss. Now it's also personal.

Voice: How so?

Me: Smite me once, shame on You. Smite me twice, shame on me.

Voice: So what do you intend to—

Me: Smite me a third time, and I will fucking *replace* You.

Voice: There you go.

Me: What?

Voice: You're almost there.

Me: What are you saying?

Voice: What are *you* saying? You're so close!

Me: To what?

Voice: Think.

(long silence)

Me: The secret shortcut to God is to make him yourself.

Voice: How many of the born-again are in breach?

Me: I don't know those statistics.

Voice: The Calvinists say, let God in! What do you say?

Me: Let God out?

Voice: Precisely! What you want in place of universal justice is the Messianic experience without—

Me: The mess?

Voice: You weren't praying, Aldo. You were making someone to pray to.

Me: I was?

Voice: Did you know that over thirty-five percent of all religious people are "displeased " or "extremely displeased" with their deity?

Me: Is that right?

Voice: And thirty percent of those with no religious affiliation whatsoever are tired of atheism and ready to switch brands but feel there is no viable alternative.

Me: So there's a market.

Voice: Hell, yes.

Me: Is there a hell?

Voice: Forget that medieval crap. Don't get bogged down in inherited concepts. You need to be creative. What does your old teacher Morrell write?

Me: Morrell? You know Morrell?

Voice: *Imaginations require limits just as creativity requires boredom.*

Me: He also said that *you achieve your goal only when you forget that you can't.*

Voice: No one thought an alien god would take off. Nobody thought a known con man like Joseph Smith could sell Mormonism. They drummed up some bullshit cosmology. They faked some visitation from God. They offered suckers water glimpses of salvation for monthly credit card payments. You, on the other hand, have the real thing.

Me: You really think this is viable?

Voice: God still has star power. Let me ask you, who is always crapping on about creating a better world and leaving a better planet for their children?

Me: Uh, every adult on earth.

Voice: Right. That's your fucking market. Don't you think they should want to leave a better God too?

Me: You're right! But . . .

Voice: But what?

Me: This is a big project. Where do I even begin?

Voice: Whether the gates of heaven open inward or outward is up to you.

Me: Meaning . . . ?

Voice: Let me start you off. How about a process of taking back regretted prayers—a forty-eight-hour cooling-off period, if you like.

Me: I see where you're going with this. Less punitive, more contrite, more inclusive, less withholding. A God who clearly understands clinical frustration, obviously; with thunder, lightning, earthquakes, tsunamis being outward displays of His thwarting His own desires. And we don't have to let that Peeping Yahweh creep us out!

Voice: Nice idea. You can opt out of omniscience by simply adjusting God's privacy settings!

Me: Online confessional booths. Home baptism kits. I'll need a Thou Shalt Not Kill, a break-out commandment. One that crosses over demographics. Maybe for that we'll engage the female brainiacs currently hard at work on exegeses of male text messages and set them the task of creating a multistoried celestial realm people can believe in. But hang on. Will people believe in what they know is created? Isn't that the flaw in this idea?

Voice: People believe in aliens, astrology, reincarnation, ghosts, homeopathy, cold fusion, karma, fate. They believe you shouldn't wake sleepwalkers, that chewing gum takes seven years to digest, that romance and passion will outlive a decade! People are nuts! Cognitive dissonance is a fundamental part of consciousness, the seed just has to be planted. It doesn't even matter if people know you've planted the seed yourself. Confirmation bias will do the rest. You don't need to worry about that part.

Me: OK. So we will not persecute the nonbeliever, but make him feel bad about his life choices.

Voice: Just don't make your God like the reproduction-obsessed irascible legislator of the Old Testament.

Me: How about when you die, God does it personally . . . ? The midnight knock at the door and He looks you in the eye. He should be a good communicator. He won't send eerie blind seers talking out of slits in their throats, or speak through the mangled intentions of a summer storm.

Voice: You should market a creator that speaks to people's actual day-to-day experiences.

Me: The hilarious deity who gave me a big head that won't accommodate most hats. A god who loves it when someone diets their whole lives. A god who longs for the day a man finds that he's inferior in the precise area he thought he was superior.

Voice: That's right. You don't have to avoid making explicit references to His indiscriminate and no-nonsense cruelty with this wised-up street-smart generation.

Me: Our God clearly enjoys sprinkling over the earth the half-dozen megasuccesses needed to mentally torture the billions who are not.

Voice: Now you're talking.

Me: And those arriving in heaven will have post-traumatic stress dis-order from the unbearable nightmare of dying and thereafter will live among a bunch of shell-shocked layabouts who all know each other and thus bore you senseless with their abominable private jokes for all eternity. And the only people who will be rewarded with the highest honors the afterlife has to offer are the pedophiles who never touched a child, for they are the real unsung heroes of our world.

Voice: You might want to rethink that one.

Me: It's just an example.

Voice: The main thing is you can put God back in circulation.

Me: But how exactly?

Voice: You've heard of Moore's law.

Me: The rate at which we cannot live without the things that didn't exist before yesterday?

Voice: Not exactly. We'll call that Aldo's law. But . . . close enough. My point is. Forget the old bible. God is dead on the page there. He can stand a little remodeling, a little imaginative effort, and it could be interactive. You don't have to do it alone.

Me: Meaning?

Voice: Groupthink. The wisdom of crowds. Your market is a bunch of people who have fallen head over heels in love with the inorganic—their phones, of all things, for heaven's sake! The most embarrass-ing turn of events in human history. Get *them*, the subscribers, to *be* the contributors and they will *become* the believers.

Me: And in the process, make him go viral.

Voice: And eventually, with the singularity and Artificial Intelligence technology, who do you think will come online just when we need Him?

Me: I see! God too has to evolve, and we ourselves will be the agency of that evolution.

Voice: Now you understand the second purpose of consciousness.

Me: The creator has given us the means to create his own prototype. That will evolve and become a better God.

Voice: And so?

Me: So there will be no divine will until we will the divine. God can be regifted. He will be the fruit of our labors and dwell where we tell him to dwell! We'll stumble across Him by using His greatest gift—the imagination. This both makes no sense and is the exact idea I've waited for my whole life.

Voice: You're welcome. If I may offer one last observation and one last piece of advice . . .

Me: What? What?

Voice: You only call God perfect vis-a-vis your congenitally low standards of perfection. You're always searching for the perfect romantic getaway, the perfect cup of coffee. What is that?

Me: And the advice?

Voice: You people.

Me: Yes?

Voice: The human race.

Me: Yes? What? What about us?

Voice: You *really* took a wrong turn at monotheism.

Then the voice was gone. That was it.

Your Honor, ladies and gentlemen of the jury, members of the press, madam court stenographer, random citizens who have nothing better to do on a Tuesday morning, Uncle Howard, bailiffs, live-streaming folks of the internet—by reshaping the way people pray, and empowering worshippers, we'll provide online solutions to crises of faith. With user-generated content, self-publishing, and uploading of commandments, our omniscient God will also be bite-sized and high-speed and available 24/7 in real time. He'll be personalized and Everlasting, meaning He can be duplicated with zero generation loss. With a high demand and low overheads, we'll be cashflow positive almost from day one. We'll be taking our God to market within a year. He will be the gold standard of new gods, but also a gateway god to other gods. Every year we will increase server-access bandwidth to allow maximum web traffic and uninterrupted streaming of the Lord's vlogs, both sacred and profane; our new bible will be mixed media—video, audio files of eternal silence, text. We have gone from the infinite being written on scrolls to the ability to infinitely scroll through content feeds. You, ladies and gentlemen of the jury, worshippers and content creators, whom God has created to create Him, YOU are the first cause. Congratulations! Time immemorial begins NOW! Praise the Lord! Compliment Him! Just tell Him you approve! Be an intelligent designer today. Narcissistic gratification guaranteed or your money back. Yes, I realize a murder trial is a strange place to pitch this once-in-a-lifetime offer but Yahweh, *Himself* once merely one of a dozen ancient desert gods, knows the meaning of the word aspirational. So, ladies and gentlemen of the jury, live-streaming people of the internet, you who ask for a cigarette then tuck it away behind your ear for later, you men and women who say "welcome to the real world" whenever something shit happens to a friend, you who do taxes in public libraries or conduct job interviews in chain coffee houses, you people so depressed and solipsistic you take the big bang as a personal slight, you Pseuodosapiens, Businessapiens, Thinklings, Saddults, and the Clinically Frustrated, who seem weirdly super-keen to hurry up and get to the postapocalypse recovery effort, you who cry "Dehumanized" when treated like cattle but say "I'm only human!" when you act like gorillas, you who sidestep history and only bear witness in your peripheral vision, for whom human progress means putting genocide on the backburner, you who think taking your last breath with someone else in the house eases the loneliness of dying, who in bars feel women's pulses erotically like sleazy doctors, who are sad that whoring is no longer part of the contemporary vernacular, who are either wafer thin or terribly fat and accused your parents of child abuse if they said no to you and who are living under the specter of the greatest fear in a liberal democracy—fear of your own body weight, you IVF nations with your plague of twins, you who are truly longing for salvation yet have settled for makeovers, you who for some strange reason have decided that it is some kind of human right to do better than the previous generation even if the previous generation did just fine, you who don't realize that being busy is incontrovertible evidence that you've taken life too seriously, and who wonder what's the use of life if you don't get to keep it when you die, you who want to travel to the sexual ends of the earth but don't even know where your next embrace is coming from, you who feel overtaxed and late to the party, and for whom self-fulfilment is your goal thus dissatisfaction your destiny! Before you go back to your low-protein high-carbohydrate lives and watch your buttered toast land butter-side down on your grubby carpets, call 800-222-222 or go to my website, thenewpantheonishere.com, for your no-risk trial and you'll get ABSOLUTELY FREE OF CHARGE a Touched By An Angel hand sanitizer (retail value of $19.99). ACT NOW. And please find me not guilty of all charges.

III

draw thy breath in pain, to tell my story

—Hamlet

A Plague of Isolated Cases

I T IS SUMMER IN SYDNEY. *Cherries, pawpaw, mangoes, and watermelon render apples, bananas, and oranges the most banal-tasting objects ever to set foot in a human mouth; waves foreclose on children's sandcastles; shopping-center Christmas decorations hang tackily over swarthy Santas with heat exhaustion; bushfires rage out of control and everywhere is ash, and a burning red moon of a bushfire night hangs over the city, over the ocean, over Aldo ripening like garbage on his dreary rock.*

Magic Beach is overrun, blighted with onlookers who stumble down the hazardous descent to gawk at the muse, the paraplegic, the poet, the rapist, the murderer, the religious entrepreneur and false prophet sequestered on the rock; his congregation is made up of girls tanning their fake tans, hirsute men so incurious they don't know what their own tattoos mean, flaxen Scandinavian backpackers with actual snouts, Chinese tourists, nudists splayed limply on the sand as if they've been blown out of a whale's spout, members of the Association of Sex Workers, spliff-smoking truants who have biked unhelmeted down the near-vertical slope, occupational therapists and their clients, tween sexual autodidacts, bloggers, reality-TV stars, septuagenarian snorkelers, the unemployed and underemployed, white and off-white supremacists, PR companymen attempting to persuade Aldo to endorse this or that brand of energy drink, stoners, locals, local politicians hoping for photo opportunities, and parents scrambling to reclaim children who dared each other to swim out and touch the hermit in an increasingly popular game called Escape from Pedophile Island.

They all huddle on the shoreline, squinting out over the seasick-green sea, shielding their eyes in his direction, as if he were a precious jewel heavily guarded by three-foot waves on endless patrol. The surfers don't know what to think. Breasts are flashed, penises fetched from inside speedos, stereo speakers blare discordantly. People sneak onto the rock with offerings: flowers, a cat afraid of water, pornography, cakes, Kentucky Fried Chicken, gas lanterns, throw cushions, dripping gelatos, cases of beer, an issue of Waves magazine delivered by the local newsagent himself. An Indian man has set up a kiosk on the beach hawking binoculars. At night, torches probe the quiet darkness. Aldo is beset from the ocean side too; dinghies are launched from God knows where, the clatter of outboard engines throttling near the rocks; wooden yachts with blaring neon lights drift by nightly. All these people are wondering, perhaps, what goes through the mind of this swarthy guru given legitimacy through suffering as he moves occasionally naked around that tiny, desolate, gull-sick island. Who knows what he thinks of the world, weakened by distance and seen through a sheen of salty air; who knows if the endless sea looks to him like a desert or a long, flowing oasis when he wakes up drooling on a pillow of moss, frozen and covered in dew, back aching, neck and shoulders hurting in newfound ways; who knows what runs through his mind when he is beset by a plague of winds, a militia of waves, a cancer of sunbeams, looking dumbly at his wheelchair from the rock as people sit on it, birds shit on it, rain falls on it; who knows what the hell he's thinking when he swivels to gaze at the stringybarks canted at 45-degree angles, or at the sandstone ridges, or the steep ascent back to civilization, or at the back of a ragged line of white water rolling to the shore, and when he gives the sky his rapt attention before a little housekeeping—sweeping seagull feathers and tangled masses of seaweed and rockweed into the sea—and then sits there like Father Time in an old Claymation movie. I know he often imagines he is back in his cell, or in his hospital bed, because he's told me so. Otherwise, it is a mystery, even to me.

In the first few weeks, Stella visited many times. The wind carried their voices straight to shore and you could hear whole chunks of their near-intolerable nonsense: You could hear them fighting about old fights, arguing about whether to call her music label Fossil Records or Dental Records; Aldo swearing

*at her about some vital promise she had repeatedly broken, begging forgiveness,
the two of them forcing forgiveness down one another's throats. One day, Saffron
came with a small bag and stood on the shore with her thumb out. A guy on a
longboard ferried her out to the island and she stayed a few hours, but she hasn't
come back since. And because if you're single and above the age of consent in
this world, people will try to fix you up with someone until your dying day, I put
his profile on romance.com and perfectmatch.com and described him as "a nice
quiet paralyzed gentleman living on a rock just off the eastern seaboard, who
abounds in dealbreakers yet has a great sense of humor and lying down is 183
centimeters tall," and the women that came out, wow. Those were some crazy
bitches, it has to be said. Afterward, Aldo forbid me to bring any more women.
The main point I needed to understand, he said, is that he no longer felt the need
for intimacy, or to imitate the triumphant, or to try to come across as primal
in business meetings and sophisticated in women's bedrooms; he no longer felt
constantly on the point of departure, no longer offered advice of any kind, nor
did he solicit it. Across the waves, far away from his island, people swaggered
from wake to sleep, wondering if their lives were going to change, if they were
going to meet that special someone, if their ship was going to come in. Aldo was
free of all that. Free of hope. Hope, the imperishable courtesan, said Baudelaire
according to Morrell, helps people bury the present in dreams. "I really feel like
I've finally exhausted fear," Aldo said. "I've used up my whole lifetime's supply
and I'm not sure I'm able to be afraid anymore. This is the opposite of bravery.
It's the end of fear."*

Aldo believes this when he says it, but the truth is, he is so riveting to watch
not only because he has made surviving a new kind of depravity, but because his
brain still drip-feeds him immobilizing panic at every turn, especially at night;
he doesn't know I often smoke a gram of impounded cannabis before descending
the track down to the tiny, shrinking beach. I don't light a fire or even a cigarette,
and from the shoreline I gaze out at Aldo in the semidarkness, watch him leap in
fright at the racket of wave against rock, the wind snarling through the trees, the
cicadas and jumping fish, crabs scampering, possum-on-possum violence. When
the sea is quiet, all you can hear is the distant grinding of his teeth or choking sobs
or God-directed invectives. Aldo has a good fire going some nights, and in spite of
everything I find myself jealous of him. Maybe it's just the usual city dweller's hermit envy: Aldo huddling in the open with a pleasant salty breeze and a front-row

seat to intense electrical storms, golden hours that go on for hours, end-to-end rainbows, winds that traffic in delectable smells, pristine mornings and beguiling dusks and the uninterrupted fire of the evening sky. So I sit on the shore in the dark, and backlit as he often is by the moon and scattered stars, I often think Aldo is there to inaugurate the apocalypse. I often think: He has marooned himself on this piece of earth not worth having dominion over. I often think: He went mad with a proviso; he was mad when he got there.

On my previous visit, hipsters had gathered on the beach, haunch-squatting or in lotus, awaiting the word. I was sitting beside Aldo who was positioned on a sort of sandstone dais, looking gnomic and frenzied; he raised his speargun aloft in exhortation, then lowered it meaninglessly. "Well, Liam, it seems we've lived long enough for muttonchops to come back into fashion," he said, then fell silent. When I went back to the beach they asked me what he'd said. I didn't have the heart to tell them.

Then there are the Aldoists who come out like old fur traders, a curious procession trudging down the path or from a beach around the headlands, absurdly rowing eight-foot dinghies or kayaks that they moor or rope to a stubby spire, scrambling up wringing wet and overloaded with art supplies to gather around him like a coven of witches and squat and eye him with acute, scrutinizing gazes as if they wish he were taller or a different hue, and while they sculpt, paint, sketch, draw, peel prawns, neck beers, and raid his trash for "found objects" and "ready-mades" they make their backhanded compliments to one another and rehearse their prolix artistic statements and carefully tailored nonsense for grant applications that don't hold up to human comprehension, and they make their works: photos or photorealistic drawings; abstract oil paintings; plaster, clay, Plasticine, polyurethane and iron-mesh sculptures; video art unlikely to pass the test of time into the following week; sound installations such as of a human voice screaming over a crashing wave; conceptual pieces like amputated Ken dolls squashed into cracked snow globes; oversized banknotes with the denomination of zero featuring his anguished visage, etc. Despite the wildly divergent stylistic flourishes, they are all representations of Aldo himself: his scarred, aggrieved, seething face; his oppressive direct gaze; downturned mouth; unglued smile; fine wrinkles; graying, dandruffed eyebrows; puckered lips midepiphany or denoting sudden neuropathic pain or memory of unbearable regret; his familiar grimace of creeping dismay; equally familiar dumbfounded or resigned expression or *vague glint of evil; occasionally, he's portrayed as horned or antlered, as serene or beatific, or hunched, wracked, contorted, with veined and purplish wasted legs, incongruously muscular arms, looking tensile or excessively angular or warty or in need of urgent hospitalisation, or pierced by cold wind, or veiled in fine mist, or engulfed in white water, and mostly on his rocky habitat that itself is often depicted as a desolate planet or an asteroid cruising through space. The most recurrent iconic and quintessential images: Rodin's Thinker in a rusted wheelchair, or a cobwebby wheelchair with a lone seagull perched on its arm. The various titles: "The Sexual Stakes Are Low," "Mattress Without Stuffing," "God Protecting His Investment," "The Self-defeated Champion," "Still Life with Beating Heart," "Unceasing Torment With a View," "The Accursed One Eating a Pine-lime Splice," "Sex Offender on a Rock," "A Petulant Sulk of Biblical Proportions," "Nonvital Statistics," "Man Returned to the Lump of Clay From Whence He Came," "Shoah for One," "Hominid in Yellow," "Less Than Meets the Eye," "A Gulag of One's Own," etc.*

At first I wondered why he bothered secreting himself in so bizarre and inaccessible a location, only to allow himself to be overrun by the kind of people who wouldn't hesitate to ask on your wedding night if they could crash on the floor of your honeymoon suite, then I realized: Aldo owed much of the success of his new religion to these people. It was the artworks that made the connection with the general public—he was known less for himself than as a common denominator between artists. It was the poems and the paintings and the photographs and the sculptures, it was aging enfant-terrible Frank Rubinstein's Archibald Prize People's Choice Award–winning portrait, the painting of Maria Hamilton's that was used for the Weekend Australian magazine cover, Stella's fan base from her moderately successful album "I Love You: It Isn't Personal," and the wildly popular exhibition after her murder of Mimi's photographs that Aldo had to thank for increasing traffic to his website, which linked to his YouTube channel, and for sending edited clips of his murder-trial testimony/business pitch viral, for throwing his voice into the echo chamber and making him a cultural commodity, and, in his words, "as popular as antibacterial handwash," a popularity that would have been unfeasible without the artists. Their ambition to sell and be known and his ambition to be sold was a happy coincidence. "My first," he said. Some people saw his "religion" as an extension of their artworks, like branching hypertexts or interconnected nodes of expression, and everyone who subscribed felt in on the joke. It was Aldo's touch of genius to add The Congregation, a social-networking feature that allowed his "believers" to hook up for sex.

Thus was it art and artists that finally achieved for him his lifelong goal: He was making money, but he didn't yield to his success, he ignored it. He wouldn't even get involved enough to mismanage it into the ground! He put Graeme Frost, his accountant "friend," in charge and instructed him to divert his earnings into two accounts: one for Stella and one for her son, Clive. The earnings doubled, tripled, quadrupled. He didn't care, and he didn't even want to know the figures; he took zero pleasure in counting his money or visiting his website. It's an infallible rule that one achieves one's dreams too late.

Tonight, the temperature drops way down, and I'm mourning in my kitchen. A silent moon grieves at the window and my reflection floats in the glass doors. Sonja laughs exuberantly at something and because I'm feeling sad and mean-spirited, I don't ask what she is laughing at. Stella and I drink beer and she asks me, not for the first time, to go out and bring him home. The sky is fouled with dark clouds; southerly gusts skid the outdoor chairs across the courtyard. What is he doing right now in his midnight gloom? I imagine him unsheltered and frisked by the wind, holding tight to the peak of a slippery rock in that hidden cove that won't return an echo to its master . . .

II

The sun burns dimly behind a bank of clouds. I scramble down the pathway in a panic, as I can't see him though the haze—wait, there he is, like some half-human, half-crustacean, something you might find in a cabinet of curiosities, his special surfboard levered up behind him. I get comfortable and watch him through binoculars from the shore; the wind's fierce and Aldo's washed in endless spray and cool air, his hair plastered to his head. He sits like an old man in a bedsit—motionless, hands in his lap, glaring through the briny sheen at the oiled women on the shoreline. I go out on the board. I paddle around and he watches me mutely.

I say, "It's just not like you, ostentatiously commandeering a tiny island like this."

He says, "You're interrupting my intercourse with the sea."

I say, "That's disgusting."

A wave breaks violently between us and I have to squint through a misty wall of white spray to keep him in sight.

He says, "Imagine. Two and a half years in prison, two months on this rock and I can *still* hear my ringtone."

"At least put some suntan lotion on."

"Just take a biopsy and get back to me."

"What are you still doing out here?"

"This is no more radical than living on the streets."

"I wanted to ferry a psychiatrist out but he wanted to charge traveling time."

"My hearse will be a water taxi."

"He told me to ask you what it is that you want."

"Ask yourself instead."

"I want to be a writer so prolific I'll wind up dedicating my books to women I see on the street the morning of printing. What about you?"

"To travel back in time and sterilize my grandfather."

"You'll die out here."

"Promise?"

"I predict drowning or pneumonia."

"Kidney failure or blood clots more likely."

"What about sharks?"

"Hand-to-fin combat? Mano a sharko? Bring it on."

A wave knocks me off my board and I clamber back on and have to paddle around to see his stooped posture and default scowl and his head in constant motion, as if scanning the shore for enemies, the horizon for tsunamis, the sky for a lightning bolt. Aldo shifts the pressure from his left palm to his right; he can't get comfortable. Every now and then he takes a bite of what looks like a cold cheeseburger.

"You know the people out there think you're an ascetic."

"Detox and anorexia rendered asceticism meaningless decades ago. Don't those idiots know that?"

"Help me up."

"I hear that after death, your hair continues to grow."

"That's right."

"But I'm bald *now*."

"Just help me up!"

I scramble up trailing tendrils of kelp and use the makeshift rope railing and natural indents in the rocks for handholds. When I get to my feet I see he has accumulated nasty grazes and lacerations and looks newly walloped—a bruise and a fresh cut under his left eye. I survey the terrain; he now has a waterproof sleeping bag, shrink-wrapped air mattress, kerosene lantern, wind chimes, garbage bags, a tarp strung over them with a thick rope and elastic orange straps; the Eskys are in a shadowed nook, there's a crater choked with campfire ash and black coals, a chaotic pile of firewood and kindling. It's somewhere between a teenager's bedroom and a one-man shantytown.

"You didn't bring me anything?"

"Was I supposed to?"

Aldo drums his thick, gloved fingers on an Esky lid, insinuating it's the height of rudeness to visit him empty-handed. He jerks his head suddenly. Out here the mosquitoes are adult-sized and hound him gregariously. I get comfortable and observe him eyeing the surfers' regal bearing with his quarter-squint of envy, their zipping and wheeling and cutting of serpentine pathways through the waves. He talks about the fatigue involved in watching these fuckers with your heart in your throat, about how when they're not risking life and limb they sit for hours on end never wondering what to do with their hands. Then he points out the few in their midforties who think they're in the best shape of their lives but whose gaunt faces and absurd musculature must terrify their spouses. "They'll wind up having a cardiac arrest during a weekend triathlon," he says sadly.

My hapless friend lights a cigarette and this frightening phalanx of surfers—nervy men who nearly all seem to have either split lips or skin missing from their knuckles where they punched a face or wall—engage in a swearing match with him. Because Aldo can hear every word they say, he can't help but offer unwelcome observations. He shouts, "Hey, Jonno, don't you know your 'tough love' of your children is merely sadism?" Jonno shouts, "Go home!" Another shouts, "Fuck off and die and get cremated and we'll sprinkle you wherever you like." Aldo shouts back, "Mark, isn't it? Stop inviting busty herbivores to steak dinners and then bitching about them!"

"Careful, Aldo," I say, "they look like Argonauts."

The surfers hate the strange disabled man nestled in the shadowed drippy pockets of "their rock"; they hate his sleep-deprived, sodden, convicted-rapist's face every morning peering out of a garbage-bag burka with undisguised sadness; they hate his ambient noises of distress that dominate the cove—what they at first took for some warbling or dying seabird were his shrieks while under crab attack, his cursing during slips and falls, his tossing and turning on the shrink-wrapped mattress, his night terrors during afternoon siestas from which he wakes with a gruesome howl of anguish. They hate the incessant sound of his hawking gobs of spit and rib-rattling coughing fits, the groaning from his push-ups and crunches, not to mention the bodily excretions—the splashy emptying of his urine sac, and his fresh turds kerplunking in the sea. They also hate spotting him perched on a ledge with his binoculars counting aloud the precancerous lesions on their faces and shoulders, and when they pass by on steep blue-gray waves, narrowly missing the rock, they loathe to hear him shout, "You're not going to make it!" or "Oh my god I can't watch!" Every now and then, to lower the temperature of his unregulatable and overheating body, Aldo does a bottom shuffle down the slippery surface of the rock to the lower ledge, drags his custom-made board by its rubber lead, holds it tensely during a low-pivot sideways transfer, keeps his right hand on the front handle so as to stop the board from shooting off into yonder, and thrashes his way out onto the waves. It is a gruelling sight. He slides off and clambers back on, often hauled out into the countervailing currents; once he was engulfed in the lip then pile-driven into a sandbank, where he sloshed around limply near the shoreline with the sets heaping on top of him. Frankly, the surfers can't understand this troublesome invader, literally out of his depth, who needs constant supervision and is either depressing them on the plum morning waves, or mincing in the sea with evident terror, or lying prone on his board fidgeting on flat water or with heavy sighs airing his mysterious sorrow.

Now Aldo says, "How's the title coming along?"

"*A Pseudosapiens' Story.*"

"Not terrible."

"*Not for Prophet.*"

"Terrible."

"*A Captain of His Solitude Always Goes Down With His Shit.*"

Aldo laughs. Something I haven't seen for a long time.

"You should forget the novel and just do a book of titles."

"That whole crazy thing you said in your testimony, about being immortal, you don't still believe that, do you?"

"I was never able to take any evasive action whatsoever. That was my first, my only real disability."

"Second. You're also like an animal whose key defensive mechanism is diarrhea."

"Hilarious."

Aldo makes weird motions with his hands, like an old mime reliving his glory days. "There was one thing that never occurred to me. Maybe I cannot die because I'm already dead."

"Nope."

"I was not born, I was exhumed."

"Unlikely."

"And that's why Ruby died. The dead cannot beget the living!"

Aldo radiates a steely fear; he looks out in annoyance, as if at a second-rate ocean.

"I know what you're thinking. *Is there no end to these words of yours, to your long-winded blustering? Job 8:1.*"

"I totally wasn't thinking that."

"Liam. Dangers seek out the afraid. We have to warn people. Me and Leila, our pre-traumatic stress disorders brought on our traumas. Fact."

"Aldo, there's something I want to tell you."

"You know what's sad? I miss the internet."

"You do?"

"Watching returning soldiers surprising their children, the faces of the deaf hearing for the first time, kids biting each other's fingers. I always liked those clips of animals being frightened. Not actual suffering, but just seeing them, cats and dogs mainly, being scared by their bored owners. What is that?"

"A cruel streak."

"In one's reluctance to confront evil one becomes evil oneself. And maybe, I'm just spitballing here, it is only by becoming evil that one can be worthy of death."

"You're not evil."

"I've done things."

"Like what?" I ask, sitting up eagerly, hoping for some core-degrading secret to spice up the narrative.

"I'm not sure I always gave the same courtesy to waiters as I did to barbers."

"Not exactly a capital offense."

"I used to like to scare small dogs when I saw their squat alien faces peering out of handbags."

"That's fairly forgivable too."

"Remember when we used to sit on that toilet block roof and think up morally repugnant ad campaigns for dodgy products?"

I say, in a mock deep advertorial voice, "Rohypnol: the path of least resistance."

"And we did one for Ethnic Cleansing Products, that gas that the Nazis used. What was that?"

"The ad campaign was a can of Zyklon B with a picture of a Hasidic Jew on it, and underneath it said, *You missed a spot.*"

"We were horrible people!"

Were we? Are we?

"I snuck into the school staffroom and stuck a live pigeon into Mr. Morrell's pigeonhole."

"That was you?"

"Wasn't it?"

"How should I know?"

"Oedipus had literally no idea he had fucked his mother and murdered his father but he found out eventually, just as I too hope to soon learn of my crime."

"This is exhausting. This is so exhausting. I have to tell you something."

"You know, the bullshit thing about the temporary insanity defense is that six months to a year is *not* regarded as temporary in legal circles."

"Something's happened."

"Maybe at the end of the day I'm like everybody else, just another arsehole whose endless fascination with himself has blossomed into a worldview."

"I saw Morrell last week."

"Yeah? How is he?"

"There's good news and bad news."

He squints at me as if through a keyhole. "Good news, please."

"Look." I pull out the first edition of *Artist Inside, Artist Outside*. It's a hand-made color-in-photocopied zine. Paintings, drawings, sketches, short stories and poems by prisoners. "He's been teaching again, convincing the other inmates they aren't criminals so much as marginalized poets and artists. Inspiring them to express themselves."

I should mention: After Aldo's insane and epic defense testimonial/sales pitch, and two seconds after he was pronounced incredibly guilty by a jury of his so-called peers, Morrell tapped me on the shoulder, his strange and fanatical eyes raw and spittle dangling from his lip, his face sopping wet, his mouth twisted. At first I thought he might be having a stroke; I eyed the exits. "It goes without saying," he whispered. I said, "What does?" Morrell's half-open mouth obliged me to keep looking at him. Was this a form of grief? Morrell had been devastated and torn apart by Mimi's death, and it was true that Aldo's testimony had exhausted us all to the point of madness, but something else was happening here. I leaned closer. On his face I watched one thought intrude on another. He begged, then threatened himself, hesitated, and continued. He said, "Come into the garden, my roses would like to see you." I said, "What?" His jaw clicked and there was an acrid smell, as if his synapses were rotting in his brain. It seemed he was looking for the spare key to a room in his head. Now where did I leave it? During the mammoth testimony Morrell had looked on somewhat proudly, I noted, as Aldo read his poem to the jury, but now all I could see was creeping dismay. "You're a good friend to Aldo," he said. "That doesn't make up for what you lack, but it's not nothing." His lids were like hardened scabs over his eyes. "In a strange way you are almost to Aldo what Plato was to Socrates, or what Paul was to Jesus." He was breathing heavily, his teeth actually rattled. I was stumped. What was I looking at? What was I bearing witness to? Morrell opened his eyes and whispered, "I want to turn myself in to you." I squinted; that phrase could be taken one of two ways. He gave me his signature dark scowl for slow comprehension. "Can't you understand, Wilder? It was *me*," he hissed. "*I* did it." And with that Morrell rose unsteadily to his feet. "Excuse me, ladies and gentlemen!" he yelled, and there it happened.

He confessed!

It wasn't easy to understand, but it seems that he killed her in a fit of rage for setting fire to his exhibition, and in fear of her reporting their underage

liaison to the police. His admission was followed by an inert yet volatile silence before order pivoted to chaos: The court erupted into a theatrical level of
gasping and stock incomprehensible murmuring; Stella rushed to Aldo's side;
supporters stormed a stiffened Aldo with backslaps and handshakes; the judge
gavel-thrashed; Mimi's father, who had spat on Aldo as he entered the courtroom, collapsed in tears; armed bailiffs snapped into a state of excited vigilance
while the prosecutor looked personally aggrieved, as if Morrell's confession
had been glommed inadmissibly onto the defense last-minute; and in the midst
of this mayhem, Aldo sat expressionless and silent. A month after this irksome
near-miscarriage of justice, Morrell was sentenced to a non-parole period of
seventeen years, and Aldo was acquitted of Mimi's murder.

Now Aldo haggardly peruses the cheap zine and manages a smile. I can tell
that despite the somber collection of depressing poems, confessional stories,
and inmates apparently soiling themselves on canvas, it's satisfying to him that
Morrell has been exercising his teaching superpower, his one genuine talent.

"What's the bad news?"

"He's dead."

Yesterday morning Morrell was found in his cell with so many stab wounds
in his chest and throat, at ninety-seven the coroner gave up counting.

"Had to be Elliot," Aldo says, wincing. "Poor Morrell."

"Poor *Mimi*." That hers weren't the first blue lips or empty eyes or gored
breast I'd ever seen didn't lesson the frequency of the nightmares.

"What did Tolstoy say? All living people are alike; every dead person is
dead in their own way."

"He never said that."

We sit quietly, thinking about Morrell until the lambent light of the sun
burns out and a jumble of stars appear. Aldo and I each crack open a beer with
the hissing sea all around us. Froth seeps up through the fissures.

I say, "It's a weird thing to watch a man on a decline from so low a starting
point."

He exhales a slender jet of smoke in my face and in response, or retaliation,
tells me his last night's dream: a seven-foot man made of bees was opening Aldo's belly with some kind of scimitar, his intestines unspooling under a wedge
of yellow moon.

I say, "It's cold. Your balls must be two peas in pods by now."

He removes his teeth and shows me the horrendous thing that had been done to his mouth.

"They got knocked out in prison," he says.

Aldo's fetal pallor is enriched by the moon's luminescence; we don't speak. I look at my old bald, toothless friend and I think: This man will have difficulty getting a new credit card.

I bark in frustration, "Do you actually want to be dragged back to safety? I understand you've been humbled by a thousand cuts and numerous incisions, and I know there's no improving an unimprovable life, but you've never felt any special kinship with the ocean, as far as I know, so what's this about? You just can't cut it on land? You can't be bothered to move? Is this for self-protection, making yourself accessible only to a vengeful God from above?"

It seems Aldo has selectively suspended his senses so he can no longer see, smell, or hear me. Gulls circle in confusion and let out cryptic shrieks. I want to implore him to make a fresh start, but I don't have the acting chops to sound like I mean it.

Finally he speaks. "Stare at the horizon long enough, sometimes it relaxes, shows some slack," he says, and downs two sleeping pills, my cue to leave.

When I'm halfway to shore I turn back and can hardly make him out; the rock holds Aldo in some hardened sheltered corner of total darkness. I find I'm still talking to him. "Or because you can't drag a trail of disasters in your wake if you don't go anywhere? Or maybe you just need a place to contemplate your arduous life? Or to ascertain what exactly made you low-lying fruit . . . ?"

III

Along supersaturated blue skies white clouds seem strategically arranged, like spaceships before an invasion. My plan is to paddle out to the island to deliver Aldo's mail (it's been building up), sit next to him while he goes through it and gives instructions on how to reply, but when I approach I'm greeted by the stink of turpentine and solvents intermingled in the briny air. Aldo is sitting for yet another portrait. I'd take the preening surfers over the conceited and garrulous artists any day.

As I clamber up I recognize the abstract painter Frank Rubinstein, hunched over an easel squinting at his model, who looks glandular and is limply dangling off a sea-slicked boulder in a position that could not possibly be painless.

"I'm using fast-drying oils because the ocean spray keeps smearing the paint on the canvas," Frank Rubinstein says.

"I don't care," I say.

"Aldo," Frank Rubinstein says, "are you comfortable in that position?"

I laugh. "Aldo hasn't been comfortable in fifteen years."

Emerging from behind a rock, terrified and gripping the rope railing with enough concentration to perform keyhole surgery, is Doc Castle. I haven't seen him since the trial.

"Afternoon, Constable."

"Afternoon, Doctor."

"Have you heard about our hero here?"

I shake my head.

"You're writing a novel about this little guy, aren't you? Well, put this in your book and smoke it." The doctor told the following story: The day before, Aldo had woken late, stumbled to the ledge in the cold morning sunshine, and gimped onto his board, tried to catch one of the dismaying waves on offer and demonstrated accidental magic, carving and hooking up the lip of the wave then riding a hollow tunnel to shore where he lay in the shallows, his arms around the surfboard as if clinging to a log during a flood. It was then he spied a small hand reaching out of the bulging water—a child caught in a strong rip drifting close to the rocks. He paddled over, pulled the drowning child by the arm onto his board, catching a face full of threshing limbs in the process, and gave a ferocious, bearded kiss of life that terrified the resuscitated child before ferrying him to the shoreline to his fretful parents. "One minute longer in the water and I would have let him drown for sure," Aldo said to them. "You won't see me returning a brain-damaged child to its parents." The mother and father gaped at Aldo with mild horror. "And raise him right! I don't want to have saved someone who turns out to be a wife-beater, or who twenty years down the track is involved in a hit-and-run. I sure as shit don't want to be the one telling some poor mother that it was me who put this bastard back on the streets."

Frank Rubinstein and Doc Castle were laughing.

Aldo says, "Can we change the subject? Liam, what do you think between a Ouija board with spellcheck, a chastity belt with biometric iris-recognition technology, and updating the handkerchief?"

"Neither. None. What?"

"OK. What about interconnected coffins? One big coffin shaped like a cross. All we do is wait for a family of four to die in a car crash."

"That's your market?"

"Would you bury them head to head," Doc Castle asked, "or feet to feet?"

"Aldo," I say irritably, "you don't even care about your one *successful* business. After all these years you finally crack it—and you don't give a shit. Why the fuck would you want to start another?"

Aldo looks at me, stricken. This is just the fleshless nub of his old dream talking; he's spent his whole life striving for a profitable idea, and habit has kept it on life support. Here I am, pulling the plug.

He turns his face to the shore and says, "Wheelchair's gone"—it was indeed stolen weeks ago—and then shouts, "all right, can everybody please just get the FUCK out of here?!"

We scramble for our boards and kayaks and canoes and head back to shore, leaving Aldo babyish and alone on his shadeless rock. Without pathological entrepreneurialism, what else is he going to do, other than stare out of shit-colored glasses at that drek of an ocean, at the sky he perceives as an uninhabitable waste of space, a desolate and stupid emptiness.

Three weeks later, I have my answer.

IV

It is a hot night in his sea garden. Huge, glittering stars humiliate the barren earth, in my opinion. Mosquitoes pester us while Aldo shampoos his armpits. He bathes at night, when he can't be seen. The rock has a natural protuberance he uses as a towel rack. He scampers down to the water's edge and jumps into the dark surging water and pulls himself back up; when he's dry, he sits as still as the rock, as if to take on its color and posture. The last surfer on the beach gives Aldo a kind of salute. We listen to the sea and tarpaulin flapping in the wind with an incessant series of thwacks. The ocean is black and fast moving and Aldo tells me there are scratches on the moon's face that were not there the night before.

He says, "I've got the traversing of a minute down to an art form."

"Well done. What?"

He smiles horribly, now that he leaves his teeth out, save for occasions of chewing meat.

"You know how in Morrell's book he writes that Wittgenstein says a man will be imprisoned in a room with a door that's unlocked and opens inward as long as it doesn't occur to him to pull rather than to push?"

"Yes but—"

"I'm finally pulling."

"What does that mean?"

When you ask him a question he pauses now, as if sending it up the chain of command.

"My hair roots, my neck nape, my elbow joint, my fat cells, my flesh, my cartilage, my bones, my tissue, my glands, my acids, my marrow, my bile, my whole musculoskeletal system—"

"What about them?"

"The attainment of infinity thus unfolds in an instant. That's what she said."

"Who said?"

"I was hoping to combine astral traveling and levitation and teleportation and spontaneous combustion—but these experiments of mind, time, and matter are not progressing well. Maybe I don't have the discipline. I honestly thought my circumstances would be ideal for promoting self-harm through mental telepathy, or at least close the morphological space between me and that black-browed albatross."

"What black-browed albatross?"

"What retards ascent?"

"What?"

"I am held down by superficial forces. To do away with weight or do away with gravity. That is the question."

"You can't try out a new approach to life at your age. Your nose hairs are turning gray."

"I want my hands to be putty in my hands."

"See, I don't know what that means."

"The Cambrian explosion was yesterday to me."

"Not any clearer."

"I'm talking about being aerodynamically borne aloft on my own beak or claw. I'm talking about adaptability, variability, discontinuity, divergence, diversification, allopatric speciation, flexibility where it counts. I'm talking about forceful invocation of will, about harnessing my clinical frustration for antagonism-based modification. I'm talking about *evolvability*, Liam. I'm not making this shit up. Ask any evolutionary biologist. Sudden mutations are a thing."

Last week, he explains, he thought he'd made progress when the stars above him vibrated, and he experienced an oceanic, ecstatic feeling as if his endorphins and adrenaline and dopamine levels were going haywire, but when it was over, there was a bloody pool at the back of his head and he realized he'd likely had some kind of seizure, probably from low blood sugar or high fever or a tapeworm or encephalitis.

Now he is squinting and sweating, his head juddering and his cheeks red; I assume he is, like always, simply experiencing pain in alien quantities.

The cold arc of a falling star seems to be a cue for Aldo to spritz lighter fluid on his surfboard and start lighting matches.

I say, "Really?"

One match hits the surfboard and it goes up, just like that, and sends our way noxious fumes of flaming polyurethane, fiberglass, and epoxy resin.

Aldo says, "You know who is beset by personal demons? The devil." He laughs feverishly. I'm not sure what kind of joke that is supposed to be and I don't want to know.

V

The last time I see him, it is like a dream of a recurring nightmare. He sits as if he is some aquatic scarecrow, blinking on the world's worst refuge, wrapped in a blanket and staring out at the waves that roam his streets like wolves. He looks extraterrestrially thin and gray-skinned, hairless, inert. His skin is leathery, his callused hands torn to shit; eyes spidered with blood, yellow discharge at the corners. He's twisting his beard in his fingers, has agonizing facial contortions; he spits and he lunges violently at insects or phantoms. Repeated heatstroke and UV exposure have taken their toll. His spasming is near constant; his hands shake all the time. His hectoring body won't leave him alone, like some persistent bully. There's a new pain in his back—his kidneys giving up on him, perhaps. He can feel fluid on his lungs, and persistently clears his throat, producing a russety scum. His voice is worn and sedate. A clammy sweat is a near-permanent fixture on his skin. His sutures and burns, the whip and claw marks, the tooth- and car-antenna scars, all faded and weirdly pigmented in his deep tan. He greets me with seismic laughter that I recognize as the frenzy of anxious grief.

He asks, "How's your book?"

He has not asked me about my book for some time. He has not asked me about Sonja or about my health or my work or my own chaotic love life. He is looking at me with an aggressive curiosity that should prepare me for the worst.

"It's been hard, Aldo. Really hard. I mean, I've been working around the clock to get down an accurate cross section of your traumas, but it's difficult to make an underdeveloped person into a well-developed character. I think I've accurately depicted how you're critical of others yet despairing of your own unceasing self-regard, and how you don't *think* so much as *secrete thought*. But it's not working. The thing is, I want to make you real. Tangible."

"That would be so great."

"For others, I mean."

"Oh."

"But I haven't captured you yet. Your sprightly depression, for instance. It's hard to get it right."

"I don't know what you mean."

"Let me ask you a question. What's your best-case scenario?"

"I meet God. We open each other's throats."

"See? Who says that?"

"Maybe you should throw in a twist."

"Like what?"

"Like, say, you write that I killed Mimi after all."

I do a loud inhale that sounds melodramatic and rehearsed. "Why would I write that?"

"I don't know. Just an idea."

"A fucking stupid idea."

Aldo turns and glares flatly as if at a painting of the sea.

"Morrell confessed," I say.

"So? How airtight is a confession? People make false confessions all the time. They do in movies. Why not in books? You could write that he was innocent."

"Why would he confess if he's innocent?"

"Oh God, Liam. For a writer you have such little imagination. You were never good at imagining, at making something up or creating something from nothing. Why is that?"

"This is a plot twist."

"So?"

"So I'm not interested in plots."

"That's convenient. You're not good at coming up with them."

"No, I find myself totally bored by them."

"Yeah—that boredom might have developed during the twenty years you were killing yourself to make them work."

"Why would I write that you and not Morrell killed Mimi?"

"I don't know. Let's puzzle it out. Maybe before the trial I convinced him that he'd ruined Mimi's entire life and sanity by fucking her as a student, that it was the worst kind of abuse, that he was a young-adult molester and he should have been punished and he had no right to live his life a free man when Mimi was dead. Maybe I convinced him that he was a terrible artist and deluding himself and had turned his back on his true calling, that the only good he'd ever done in his life was teach, that it is in prison where human beings are most in need of a teacher to help them discover their artistic selves, and that to benefit these individuals and by consequence the whole of society, so as to balance the scales, restore equilibrium to the moral universe, repay his debt, make amends, use his bestowed gifts where they were best suited, he should take the rap."

I'm breathing heavily, trying to manage my fear. Cloudlight has turned his crumpled-banknote face battleship gray. I feel the silence against me like a naked flame.

I go, "You should write fiction."

"I'd probably do a better job."

"I couldn't write that you killed Mimi. You had no reason. You couldn't have done it. You loved her. It's not in your character."

"Does my character in your book need to be more consistent than my character in my actual life?"

"No."

"Are you going to write that my facial scars gleamed in the soft daylight, you know, for verisimilitude?"

"Big word for a hermit on a rock."

"Why are you getting so annoyed?"

"Because you're being annoying."

"Why did you even want to become a writer?"

"You know why."

"Tell me again."

"Because when I was twelve years old I was waiting at a bus stop next to this woman who yelled, 'You think I'm dumb because I put my cat on antidepressants!' to an obese man who shouted back, 'No, bitch, it's 'cause you went to a rock-paper-scissors seminar.' I mean, Jesus Christ, Aldo. I absolutely had to write down that snatch of dialogue, didn't I?"

"Yes, but you don't ever acknowledge your debts as debts. You're taking my life, Liam."

"Good artists borrow."

"Better artists don't."

"Great artists steal."

"That's like saying great jazz pianists beat their wives. Maybe they do. But that's not what makes them great jazz pianists."

"I don't understand why—"

"An artist's theory of art is always founded on his shortcomings as an artist, his passion for that theory in direct proportion to the severity of his failures."

"Morrell? You're quoting Morrell now?"

"Why not? I've been reading his book."

"Why are we having a proxy argument about art when you're talking about murder?"

"I thought we were talking about character and plot."

"Did the character Aldo Benjamin or the character based on Aldo Benjamin or my real friend Aldo Benjamin kill Mimi Underwood?!"

"When you masturbate with ironic distance, you still ejaculate, but it's not the same."

"What?"

"I had it wrong all this time. Suicide is not saying 'I quit,' but rather 'You're fired.'"

"What possible reason in all of fucking Christendom would the character Aldo Benjamin or the character based on Aldo Benjamin or my real friend Aldo Benjamin kill Mimi Underwood?!"

"Reason? Reason? Maybe because I'm always Typhoid Mary's first port of call and I always get tetanus from Cupid's arrow and my own hardtokillability combined with my susceptibility to airborne, bloodborne, lipborne, godborne pathogens means that the phrase 'I'm fine' amounts to wild hyperbole and I'm therefore in need of constant emergency assistance and possibly centuries of palliative care. Maybe because Mimi was a born nurse, an involuntary nurturer, and a pathological carer our destinies dangerously overlapped, and maybe because on that night of my release and welcome-home party, beside me on that balcony gazing at constellations that looked like track marks in the night sky, Mimi maybe said to me, with a sickening air of predestination, 'I will take care of you,' before she wheeled me through the party to her bedroom where her photography equipment made distended shadows and we settled on the bed and took sleeping pills and she repeated, 'Don't worry, I will take care of you,' just as she was taking care of Elliot and Morrell. Maybe it was the proximity of the ocean's madness and the effluvia of my own unceasing flatulence and the opulent chandelier of stars and the moon's worm-eaten smile and the sinewy palm tree branches flailing like drowning limbs in the violent wind, but her body suddenly seemed an omnibus of corpses; what I mean to say is maybe death was already plying her trade on Mimi's silvered shoulders and on her marble hips and on the wide circumference of her saucered nipples. And maybe I watched moonbeams claw at her careworn face and her mouth ulcers and her stress rashes and her chewed fingernails and her thigh bruises and the thicket of hickeys on her neck and her eyes gouged with worry and shadows, and maybe I saw clearly her monomania of caring and pathological sacrificing that had her holed up in this subtropical hell with madman Morrell, and maybe her lying there endomorphic, martyred, and turbaned in her own hair, while in my mouth the taste or the sense memory of the taste of contrast agents injected for CT scans was making me feel a nuclear blast of compassion, a scalding of pity without consolation, an injection of energizing empathy; what I mean to say is that maybe her suffering was so intense and so complete it's possible that I did not dehumanize her, but *over*humanized her, and interiorized her pain and *became* her so convincingly that I could commit suicide *as* her in a case of mistaken identity, maybe there was what I imagine to be a dolly zoom of my own face as I had the unwelcome realization that the gift of non-being is the only gift that keeps on giving, and maybe I was surprised to find myself weaponized, that this was germ warfare and I was the germ, and maybe I released my inner child-soldier, and maybe I couldn't let her achieve one more attosecond of consciousness so I disentangled my arm from hers and in a single fraction of an instant that was less than a second yet an experience of infinity my hand became a prosthesis with a knife, and myself an alien-hand syndromee, and maybe she died succinctly, her blinkless eyes cold in their craters, her creases in her forehead flatlined, and maybe in the profound disquiet that followed I lay awake until the sunlight broke through the fogged dawn and illuminated the bespatted bedsheets, and only then did I scream until a handful of artists ran in and lingered at the door like the four horsemen between apocalypses and simultaneously announced their citizen's arrest."

The waves have grown raucous and only now do I become conscious that I am sodden. Aldo is trembling but his face is uncannily still in the moon's raw light. "Anyway," he says, "it was just an idea. Write what you want."

Some slug creature with an orange-specked carapace stirs in the shadowed crevice near my left foot. There is nothing further to add and no way to add it. I fumble a good-bye and make a careful descent to my board. As always, no matter how open and honest we've been, no matter to what degree we've unburdened or admitted shameful secrets never before uttered aloud, we can't seem to depart fully satisfied with the transaction, and now, even after his weirdest and darkest hypothetical confession, there is still something permanently unexpressed lingering between us.

VI

Two months go by, and I don't go out there often. First casualties of autumn: the Lifesaving Association packs it in, the man selling cold drinks and fresh fruit goes home, the umbrellas and deck chairs and nubile bodies vanish; then weirdly, as prophesised, the beach itself disappears altogether. The sand is history, the water creeps all the way up to the cliff wall. Magic can't go on for-ever, I suppose. The surfers have gone back to their old haunts, you can't even climb down the rock face anymore. If you try, you'll find only an angry ocean smashing up against the cliff as if to say "I am busy eroding sandstone, so fuck off someplace else." Now there's no beach, just dark, iridescent water, some rocks, and further out in the ocean than ever before, a man alone on a rock with nothing to look at but sea and sky.

The weather isn't a help—it's the coldest autumn since 1965. Plus Sonja has contracted chronic fatigue syndrome, or is faking it, Tess has married a Korean air traffic controller named Eden, and I am caught up in a totally bogus corrup-tion inquiry regarding missing quantities of impounded cannabis. I'm trying to justify why I've abandoned Aldo in his self-exile. The truth is, you can only be generous with your time up to a point, then you have to leave your friends on their icy rocks alone. You have other things to do.

VII

Record-breaking waves are creating havoc up and down the coastline, a cold crescendo of monsters—it's going to be a tough visit. There's no place from which to launch a boat, so I have to set out from another beach around the headland, just a regular beach that's been there forever, nothing magical about it.

The sea is rough, and I can't hear myself swear on account of the wind. I ride the choppy waves, and lashed by spray I make my approach.

"Aldo!" I shout.

No reply. I circle the island but can't see him. With great difficulty, I manage to moor the boat to a bony protuberance of rock on the north side and climb onto a ledge. I look in every hollow, every crevice. I look out at the waves as if waiting for a hand or his head to surface. I crouch and stare at my own shadow on the granite as if it might tell me something. I shout his name at intervals. I tear down the tarp and trundle over every inch of the rock, sidestepping blasts of spray, and whisper, "Come out," as if he is hiding. I say, "Aldo. *Aldo.*" I am whimpering his name now. "*Aldo. Aldo.*" I am hyperventilating it. I had never given up hope of airlifting his body to safety but it seems he has finished his pointless time on this damned place. Aldo is gone. He has left the rock standing empty, abandoned nature to nature. It surprises me how fast I start my grieving. It's instantaneous. It rushes in. *Aldo.*

That afternoon, I browbeat my senior sergeant to get a team of forensics with annoyed faces to come out and make their deliberations. They find traces of hair, urine, feces, fresh blood, black blood, old blood—Aldo's many secretions from his every orifice. Fell, drowned, washed out to sea is the verdict. (I find myself crying in front of my fellow officers. There is a hushed respect for tears in the force. They assume it's rare—it's not. In the wider culture too, it's become incredibly manly to be unafraid to look like a little girl for three to five minutes.) While the police traipse with impunity into his sour fortress of solitude, I sort through his bric-a-brac, as if Aldo himself has been mislaid there, and find his copy of Morrell's *Artist Within, Artist Without;* I cradle it, and my novel takes on additional life force; it has become like a photo album rescued from a fire-gutted house in which everybody died.

The team combs the beach and all accessible points. Did he go to shore and drag himself up that cliff? "Maybe a wave swept him off the rocks. It was bound to happen. No trace. He must've drowned." The media come out to the rock and say he must have been booted off by the ocean's foot. With news helicopters hovering, surfers come out with little lanterns to hold a vigil, but the waves are too big and the storm clouds chase them off.

Everyone goes home; I am the last. My oldest, best, broken and heartbroken friend, the guy who wore fancy dress to an antiwar protest, who was himself the patron saint of statistical anomalies, is gone. Before I leave the island, I take one final look over these boulders heavily encrusted with sponges and algae; I peer into vertical crevices and fissures and rocky ledges and shelves, where Aldo lived among desiccated barnacles and hermit crabs and turned a blind eye to fish spawning in the hard substrate; I thought he was like the regenerating arms of the starfish; I was wrong. I thought he would never unfussily and judiciously slip into the waves without making a big song and dance about it. Psychotic with grief, I wail now. *Aldo!* Always the wrong guy with the wrong outfit saying the wrong thing in the wrong tone of voice in the wrong place at the wrong time to the wrong person or persons, always oozing fallibility, who is always my friend, who is gone.

VIII

The bodiless funeral service was held in the botanical gardens on a dewy morning. Aldo's anonymous returned wheelchair was there in his stead—rusted, grafittied, painted over. The mourners included people he impoverished for generations and those he enriched, all those professionals he relied upon or put aside for safekeeping: nurses, prison guards, fortune-tellers, private detectives, cardiologists, pharmacists, criminal lawyers, dentists, physiotherapists, accountants, dermatologists, bankers, lifeguards, bodyguards, magistrates, customs officers, bounty hunters, anesthetists, stockbrokers, paramedics, urologists, politicians, prostitutes, wayfarers, and stevedores. There were also offended Christians, picketers, and other people who take umbrage for a living. I picked up a smidgeon of genuine grief and mourning, but the weirdness of this funeral was that nobody was in denial. If anything, they were over-prepared for this day; it had been on their calendars for months. The general consensus was his existence had been excruciating. Yet it was clear that he had touched so many lives; over the course of the day, I heard four separate people say, "He was my best friend." I also saw business cards change hands, two separate high-fives, one down low, one too slow, three successful pickups, and more bunches of service-station flowers than I'd ever seen assembled in one place. His evangelicals (sales reps) were handing out flyers for a Special Death of Our Founder offer. The website had peaked and begun its decline. In the end it was a fad after all, a one-hit wonder. At one point, Aldo's subscribers ballooned to two million, but when I last checked they had already dwindled to three hundred thousand. That's nothing these days; cats have more followers than that.

The old child murderer Stan Maxwell read the Psalm of David. The Lord was many things to Aldo, but he sure as shit wasn't his shepherd, and Aldo was never not in want. With a conical mass of snot hanging from her nose, and face turned to the sky, Stella sang tearfully about that sorrow that was not for his death per se but for his life and their love that was like a flower shaken violently for years and on which even now a few petals remain. The song didn't finish so much as sob itself out, and Frank Rubinstein shepherded her gently off the podium. A few others got up to speak, people I had never met or heard of. They said, "Aldo's proximity to terror and to error gave my whole family nightmares," "He was a guy with vertigo who chose to perch on a mountain-top," and "Aldo was the Russian formalist of all the amateur psychologists." To be honest, I couldn't make heads nor tails of these eulogies. Doc Castle took to the podium. "Wittgenstein said that if a lion could talk we could not understand him. Well, Aldo *could* talk and we could not understand him either. He was our lion." I stopped listening after that. Frankly, I couldn't concentrate on anything. I had the dreadful idea that maybe Aldo was orchestrating a resurrection to augment his business, and I remember how when we were seventeen he told me that one member of his family per generation got into monumental debt and tried to fake his own death, and I thought this funeral was the propitious moment for his ulcerous person to pop out from behind a cabbage tree palm and surprise us with a new investment opportunity. He will either turn up any second now or be truly dead, I thought throughout the whole service. I was a wreck.

He never appeared.

At last, I had to admit that my booby-trapped and masticated friend had managed to leave his ignoble slab of a rock, this cold telluric pebble called Earth, that he had sprouted his last pustules, suffered his last spasms, endured his last internal lava spill, and that his open wound of immortality had closed over and healed, and that was a beautiful thing.

Unless.

Personally, I prefer to imagine that his old dream came true; maybe he vanished by an act of will, liquefied in his sleep and disintegrated body and soul, maybe he was uncreated and unborn—*decreated,* vanishing from the island to emerge in a distant unmapped galaxy moments later as a voiceless faceless thoughtless drifting eye, racing through the vagaries of space and time, ringing out like plucked strings, tapering off and just frankly dissolving in an orange flash as a traceless nothing, never more to wake. I hope so. Someone's dreams have to come true. Otherwise all the dreams build up on a vast garbage dump, taking up too much space in this world. You can't get from the bedroom to the bathroom without tripping over the rotting carcass of some man's dream. So I prefer to imagine that his stubborn hopes and deepest desires came to fruition, and I resolve that whenever I remember Aldo and all those days at sea, and how he disappeared just like that, I'll think: Well, at least there's one less dream cluttering up the dump.

IX

A month later, I'm falling asleep at my desk, taking the statement of a high-main-tenance eyewitness in an ATM raid, when the phone rings.

"Constable Wilder speaking," I say.

"Your mate is Aldo Benjamin, isn't he?"

My heart actually stops beating. I feel it stop for long enough to be con-sciously concerned about it restarting.

"Was. Yeah. What's this about?" I manage to say.

"A portrait of him was stolen from the Sussex Street Gallery, and it's already turned up on eBay from a US dealer."

"Oh."

My hands are shaking as I take down a few details and pass them on to the Computer Crimes Unit and to customs, and I marvel to think about Aldo's frustrated face floating on the black market. What is his value? That's a slip-pery concept. In dollar terms, not inconsiderable at present, although I suspect he will always trade slightly below estimate and will eventually trend steadily down towards zero. Aesthetically? Given he was someone not overly interested in culture himself, it's vaguely amusing to note that his ultimate claim to fame might be inadvertently propelling certain artists to a medium level of suc-cess—namely Lynne Bishop, Frank Rubinstein, and Dan Wethercot. It would not surprise me if he were one day to be a footnote to early twenty-first-century Australian art history and nothing more.

I spend the next few hours at my desk clicking through image files of Aldo Benjamin—paintings, photographs, sculptures, drawings, sketches, video in-stallations, each one making me feel deeply disturbed; just as a nightmare re-fuses the sleeper genuine rest, his image denies any kind of peace of mind to the viewer. I am slowly coming to terms with the fact that there may be no place for every random anecdote and strange story about Aldo in my book: the cat in the foldout couch debacle; Aldo being chased by the human mon-key in Rajasthan; the clairvoyant's egg; the grassroots, opt-out euthanasia white paper. Not to mention the minor slipups: penises caught in zippers, pubic hair in velcro; all the misjudged timing of automatic, elevator, and revolving doors; the endless unforgivable faux pas; the romantic, candlelight-dinner, reach-for-the-salt, sleeve-on-fire scenarios. In this whole book, I've neglected to mention that whenever Aldo tripped he felt that he was being reprimanded by a higher power, and when he got to his feet he felt it was an act of defiance.

Some afternoons I go back, I don't know why, to Leila's old ground-floor apartment. There's a single man in there now, a burned-out bummed-out middle-aged fellow who sits perpetually at the kitchen table with his head in his hands. I think: Aldo would know what was wrong with him. I can feel the suffering, but I can't name it. The last time I went he raised his sad head and slammed his fist on the table. He seemed to hate living there and looked at me as if it were all my fault.

Just as now Aldo is looking at me from Louise Bozowic's painting, *The Sadness and the Envy*. And he's no Lazarus; the more I look at these works that were created while he was alive, the more he appears already dead in them—a living death that through the artworks goes on living.

X

It is five o'clock on a Friday afternoon and I'm eating a falafel in my parked car outside my apartment—less sad than eating in front of the television, I figure—when I see Neil Mikula, a tall squinty neighbor in his midthirties, shoulder-bumping a skinny teenager and palming something. We were friendly in the early days but too often he's been carting stolen flat-screens or selling heroin in my line of vision; I warned him a dozen times and busted him once—he was sent down for six months. Now he's leaning against a low concrete wall in a sort of brooding languor, and a rush of customers come for his wares: tinfoil packets and plastic baggies, H and pills. This happens more than you'd think. Sometimes people assume broad daylight makes them invisible. Sure, my car's mostly obscured by the electrician's van I'm parked behind, but still. Discretion, people. I wearily put down the falafel and hit the siren. Neil turns and looks at me a moment before walking over. I don't even have to get out of the car.

"Oh man," he says, in a weird falsetto.

"You said it."

He takes a fistful of dollars out of his pocket, clearly his first foray into bribery.

"Put that away."

"What are you doing out here anyway, staking out your own apartment?"

"That's not what you need to worry about right now."

He glances behind him at the place he's vacated, as if afraid to lose his spot. "You let me go, Liam, sorry, *Detective Wilder*, and I'll do you a solid."

"It's Constable."

"*Still?*"

"I'm doing *you* a solid. Take this as your early retirement plan."

"I could give you some information, Liam."

"You could, Neil, but I don't care what kind of information you have. I'm not ambitious. I don't have bigger fish to fry. In any case, you might not realize it, you *are* the bigger fish. The ones you throw back I already threw back. Those guys you sold to."

His peevish stare mutates into a wait-and-see smile that catches my attention. There's something out of character about it, as if he's implying some shared destiny. He leans in intimately, and says, "Anton Benjamin."

"You mean Aldo Benjamin?"

"Yeah. Aldo Benjamin. Sorry."

Just the sound of the name coming out of this junkie's face makes me fear my dam of sadness might break and inundate the fucker. My evident shock is a strategic error. Neil lights a cigarette, singeing the fringe of his hair, and assumes a nonchalant manner.

"What about him?"

"He was your mate, wasn't he?"

He clears his throat that doesn't need clearing and fakes a bored yawn. In the silence, I can hear the discordant symphony of TVs from ground-floor apartments tuned to different channels. My eyes lay siege to Neil's. Predictably, he breaks first.

"OK, you might remember I recently did a little six-month stretch in Long Bay. Why? Because my unneighborly neighbor took his job a little too seriously." I don't say anything, but close my eyes to concentrate on what Neil is saying. Now he sounds like he's clearing someone else's throat. He continues: "Halfway through my time, I moved into a cell with this insane bastard, Baz. I shat myself when I saw him but we got on anyway and for some reason he looked out for me. He was a good bloke but always getting into it with someone. Got himself bashed to death last month, crazy bastard."

"I'm almost but not quite sorry for your loss. So fucking what?"

"So fucking this. Before he died, he confessed something to me."

"What was that?"

"He said he was the one who, you know, killed your mate. Aldo Benjamin."

"That's not possible. He drowned."

"Nup. He was done."

"How?"

"Baz went out there."

"Out where?"

"Where do you think? To that rock."

"Why would he do that?"

"Contract."

"Come on."

"Swear."

"Who contracted him?"

Here Neil studies his fingernails. I remove my Taser and place it on the dashboard.

"A woman," Neil says.

"What woman?"

"Middle-aged bird, a real stunner, wouldn't stop crying, though. But the thing that struck Baz about her, he said, was how she wore denim *and* leather *and* suede *all at once* with tassels hanging off everything."

Stella.

"There was one other unusual thing. She told him to 'make sure he doesn't suffer, make it quick and painless,' which is pretty typical. Baz said people always want to make sure their hit doesn't suffer, or else to make sure they *do* suffer, a lot, and people also say 'make it look like an accident' like in the movies, or to 'look like a suicide' or to 'look like a robbery gone wrong.' But what *she* said, he said, people never say."

"What did she say?"

"After you kill him, she said, make sure, a hundred percent sure, a thousand percent sure, a million percent sure, that he's actually dead. Don't leave him alive and suffering. Verify. Verify. Verify. She kept saying the word verify. It freaked him out."

"And so he . . ."

"So Baz took the rubber boat out and climbed onto that rock one night and stabbed old Anton in the heart."

"Aldo."

"Right. He said he must have been out of it on something because he hardly put up a fight."

I thought how Aldo feared stabbings among all violent deaths, how he'd feared the sensation of a punctured lung.

"And then he dragged the body onto the boat and took him far out and tied an anchor onto his legs and arms and dropped him."

"How far out?"

"I don't know."

"Think. Very fucking specifically. How many minutes going how many knots per hour did Baz go before dropping Aldo onto the sea floor?"

"Jesus, how the fuck should I know? He didn't say. He just said he went out far." Neil scrunched up his face, worried his arrest was unavoidable. "So we good? I can go? Thanks, Liam. See you next time."

"And did he?"

"What?"

"Verify?"

"Yeah. Sure."

"Baz said he was a million percent sure Aldo was dead?"

"Yes."

"You're certain. You're certain that *he* was certain."

"Well, of course he was bloody certain. It's not as if he'd be there alive chained to the bottom of the sea."

XI

I'm taking scuba-diving courses now. I got my PADI Open Water certification. I borrowed a suit from Senior Detective Dan Westbury, the only weekend diver I know in the force. It's a quarter-size too small and smells like pee, but I get in it and go out there once or twice a week. As it turns out, I hate being under the sea as much as being on top of it. Scuba diving has fast become the most hateful of all pastimes, aquatic, landlocked, or lunar. The regulator vibrates on the inhale, the weight belt's too tight, the mask foggy, the tank heavy, and each time I sourly don my fins and head down sloping sandstone or through sea-grass or hotfoot it over oyster beds or wade through a swaying clump of plastic bags, milk containers, chip wrappers, and the occasional mosaic of sewerage discharge that is like moving through a vile concoction of womb and bowel, or I plunge into freezing waters from Doc Castle's boat while he sits on deck, reminiscing about Aldo. ("He wanted a blank check; he wanted a blank prescription pad; he wanted blanket assurances that he would be OK, and he wasn't OK, he never was.") I escape him in the dark rush of water, with baited hooks swinging at my head. I surface and splash around like a drowning man attracting the chilling sight of dorsal fins until in a shriek of air bubbles I make my descent, down to where the water feels thicker than water, with larger vectors of darkness to navigate and where one thinks only of Coleridge's lines: *Yea, slimy things did crawl with legs / Upon the slimy sea.* Of course there are the beautiful rainbow-hued fish, but there are also—seen magnified through the mask—sea gargoyles that belong on the roofs of flooded cathedrals; bloated slow-moving scum-trailing creatures that seem to be all nucleus, with dull aureoles; barbs and stingers wearing their burst guts on the outside; acephalous creatures; beings with small eyes or, worse, eyeless, and who look so alien as to have no archetype, or so rock-like as to be impossible to anthropomorphize. Frankly, there's too much biodiversity for my liking, everything in plague proportions: rat kings, tailor, salmon, great squid, snapper, flathead, sea dragons, cuttlefish streaking past like comet tails, slothful swarms of hybrids, lumbering catlike fish, fish with overbites and suckers and pincers and gaping jaws. I am frazzled by the vastness and infinite murk of this underwater ghost town.

I feel the claustrophobia of the mask and exhale bubbles into my line of sight. I'm deafened by the all-encompassing sound of my own breathing. Surges come out of nowhere—there are waves underwater! Who knew? And who knew how regularly I would wash out bloody nasal mucus swilling around the bottom of my mask, or bite down on my regulator mouthpiece so hard I dislodged a crown, or be shunned by gropers, bested by angry triggerfish defending their nests on sandstone reefs, terrified by a turtle springing out from a ledge, or misinterpret the body language of wobbegong sharks, wedge a foot between rocks, see fish eat my vomit. I've taken on Aldo's fear of fears: in this case the pulmonary barotrauma of a quick ascent. I try to put it out of my mind.

In my dreams the ground that opens beneath my feet is the seabed.

Each week I go down into the delirium of lower depths, with my perpetual motion sickness and the weight of the ocean on my head and thinning gradations of light, where things get primordial and I hope to find a corpse of no fixed address.

I think of Stella's shock decision to grant Aldo's most unreasonable wish and hire a hitman. Well, murder is only a question of consent. Or implied consent. She had preauthorization. I can't think too badly of her. As long as I will soon be able to put my head to his chest and hear the stillness of his unbeating heart and fulfill Aldo's lifelong desire to be pronounced dead at the scene.

It is this prickly, preposterous, impossible nightmare of an idea that won't desert me and keeps me awake nights. I think about Aldo's old adolescent obsession with the Greek gods: gods who don't think twice about impelling eagles to gnaw on your perpetually regenerated entrails, or getting you torn to pieces by dogs, or turning you into a deer, or into a spider, or into a cow, or into stone, or making you roll a giant boulder up a hill for eternity, or positioning food and water just out of reach, or fastening you to a burning wheel forever. I think: Maybe he locked eyes with the wrong god out that plane window over Leila's island, one of those shipwrecking, maiden-raping, virility-obsessed, black-ram-slaying, meddling, intemperate, vindictive, rampaging, oversensitive, humorless gods, with their discuses and thunderbolts, their sickles and cooking spits, their rites and ancestral hangups, initiations and vendettas, who wouldn't lose sleep over coupling with a bull or their own mothers, who never saw a lamb they didn't sacrifice and who still, for all we know, think virginity is the coin of the realm. Who can say for sure this god didn't mete out a punishment so severe, chaining a human man to the bottom of the sea, simply because maybe he dared to fear it. This is the absurd nightmare scenario that keeps me going out there, expecting around every murky corner to see Aldo bloated or eyeless, looking strange or fishborn, marooned without death's hospitality, dwelling unbravely and in total terror like a shipwreck on the seafloor, or Tutankhamun's sarcophagus in an underwater Valley of the Kings. I cannot help but imagine a shrieking mouth of bubbles, the horror of a windpipe crammed with seawater, inundated with starfish, Aldo crankily passing the time by decoding the arabesques of sea urchins. But how could I find his tears in all that water? With the intolerable sound of my own breathing, how could I also hear a human heartbeat? This is insanity, these oppressive fantasies in the overcrowded sea.

I am incongruous in a wet suit, Aldo is incongruous on the seafloor . . .

What did Aldo say? "Oceans are hotbeds of extraterrestrial activity while we look dumbly at the skies." Maybe he's right.

I should give up this fool's errand but I feel the ocean currents like a tractor beam, pulling me in. With the hope that his blood no longer circulates, that his respiration has stopped, that he no longer excretes, that over forty years of death throes are enough, I move through the water in an angry fear, plowing deeper, deeper into the awful splendor of the unknown. And I go down where, if the Leviathan will rise from the sea, I hope it's the Atlantic.

Tonight, under the white-breasted moon, I am preparing to go down the deepest yet. I'll be accompanied by Senior Detective Dan Westbury, an amphibious swashbuckler, it turns out, who's coming with me because where I need to go "shit starts getting technical." It's an irrational thought, but I find myself hoping the Rapture does not happen tonight. I am going to a place from where anyone ascending to heaven would get the bends.

It's almost time to go. I'm sitting at my kitchen table where I spend my waking hours (I haven't spent more than a minute in my living room for months). Sonja stands at the fridge, draped in swimming medals and athletic regalia, parading back and forth with a beer in hand, stamping her feet, trying to get my attention but not knowing what to do with it when she has it. I clamp my eyes shut. When I open them Sonja is gone, and my eyes fall to the cabinet, to Aldo's copy of *Artist Within, Artist Without* that I retrieved from the rock. I fetch it, and at the kitchen table absently flick through the pages. To my surprise, Aldo has underlined three sentences, two of which I remember well.

We make art because being alive is a hostage situation in which our abductors are silent and we cannot even intuit their demands.

And:

There but for the grace of God goes God.

And then there is the one I didn't remember. I had only once, many years ago, read carefully through Morrell's copious footnotes. Aldo had tripleunderlined and asterisked one at the bottom of page 112, halfway through the chapter "Tribulations and Creativity." It's a short, simple sentence but for some unaccountable reason it makes me cry so hard Sonja comes back in and hands me her half-empty beer. I drink it and read again:

Each day you wake up alive, you are the victor; go claim your spoils.

About the Author

Steve Toltz was born in Sydney, Australia. *Quicksand* is his second novel.